PEARL OF TAO

To Paul and Mary Ellen
Enjoy the fruits of
my creativity!
Charlie 11-11-08

A NOVEL BASED ON
THE WORLD'S LARGEST PEARL

CHARLIE
DIEMER

GOLDEN GATOR
PUBLISHING

First Printing 2009

ISBN- 978-0-9821689-0-5

Cover Art by Steven Bonilla

DEDICATION

Pearl Of Tao is dedicated to my inspirational supporting cast, especially my patient, and creative wife, Judy. She made writing this book a joy and motivated me to complete the journey.

The Gulf Coast Writer's Association of Ft. Myers stimulated me. My critique group of Mary Lu Williams, Sissel Robertson and Matt Gilbert gave me encouragement, sincere criticism and guidance.

Special thanks to Illonka and Bill Mackey.

Neither man nor a book is an island. Rather, like the waves of the sea, we flow together.

PEARL OF TAO

CHAPTER ONE

"DEAD, VERY OBVIOUSLY DEAD!" Frank Johnson thought the minute he saw the body in the sand on the far edge of the roadside ditch. The corpse was so out of place on Lovers Key. The name of the island aptly described the beauty of the tiny piece of sandy, palm drenched land.

The magenta sky at daybreak gave Frank enough light to reveal the deep gouges in the flesh. The man was missing his right hand and forearm. Frank kept looking at the body as he memorized every facet of the death scene.

"Numerous bite marks cover the man's naked body, torn flesh, and a missing extremity. The man was brutally mauled by a large animal." Frank mumbled aloud about what he had observed. He made his eyes back off and take a wide angle view of the whole body. He realized there was no blood to be seen on the man with no clothes. Frank saw shoe prints in the soft sand but no animal tracks or tire tracks.

Frank quickly looked up and down the paved road, desperately hoping that a car would come by and the driver would have a cell phone. There wasn't a car in sight. Should he wait for a car to happen upon the scene; or should he sprint back home to call 911? He was out for a morning run, so he turned and ran like a gazelle back home.

A 911 call brought a swarm of Lee County Deputies to the idyllic island. They arrived over the only two bridges connecting the island to the mainland of the southwest coast of Florida. From the north the deputies came over the bridge that connected Lovers Key to Ft. Myers Beach. Squad cars from the south roared with flashing lights and sirens from Bonita Beach. They crossed two uninhabited islands not worrying about traffic or their breakneck speed.

Frank quickly came back to the corpse and as he stood there, he tried to be analytical about a gory, violent murder. Lovers Key shouldn't have such an incident. The white sand paradise was the antithesis of mayhem. His immediate conclusion was that the murder couldn't have happened here, near his cottage. He changed his focus when he realized that uniformed deputies had taken control of the murder scene.

Within minutes, investigators arrived, and one had Frank take a seat in a car that looked government issue. The investigator was in his late forties, stocky and short hair. He had a large tattoo on his forearm in the shape of a ship's anchor and the letters "U.S.N." below it. Rather than a uniform, he was wearing a short sleeve shirt. His blue jeans weren't big enough to go around his waist; so his jeans hid under his belly.

The cop got right to the point: "I'm Investigator Buck Thorton. First of all, did you see anybody or anything besides the corpse when you came upon the scene?"

"No" Frank calmly answered.

"OK, I need some personal identifying data; then I'll get to what you saw. Give me your full legal name."

"Franklin Lee Johnson. I'm usually called Frank."

"Why are you here on Lovers Key?" Buck asked.

"I was recently hired as a consultant to the owner of the estate nearby. I've lived on the island only a couple of months."

"Do you know the dead man?"

"No"

"When did you discover the body?" asked Buck.

"One minute before sunrise."

"Why did you decide to use the term one minute before sunrise as the time of discovery?" Thorton queried.

"In case my jogging watch wasn't set to the correct time; I wanted to be absolutely accurate. I looked at the body for a minute and then looked to the east. I saw the sun just float above the bay; in between the palm trees."

Buck Thorton showed no visual response, but thought that he had a witness who would be accurate, yet maybe a little weird.

Thorton calmly asked: "See any large animals around here since you've lived here?"

"The biggest animals have been dolphins. No gators, no sharks. The next biggest animals have been armadillos and raccoons."

"Anyone where you're staying see anything unusual lately?" Buck asked.

"I didn't notice anything, No one has said anything, but the subject never came up."

"How many people currently reside there?"

"Four. Myself, my boss and his wife-and his daughter. My boss isn't here now, he travels a lot. Hired help come during the day to maintain the place."

"How many?"

"Up to five people come and go to maintain the estate."

"Do you happen to know if any of them have a criminal record?"

Frank responded: "I ran criminal record checks on all of them and none had anything more serious than some old, minor misdemeanor offenses."

Buck thought it was odd that the witness had run checks on the hired help, so he asked: "What type of consulting are you doing and how did you get hired?"

"I do legal work. I was hired because I needed a job and knew his daughter."

"How did you happen to hook up with his daughter?"

"I met her at a ski area in Colorado-Steamboat"

Again Thorton showed no response, but mentally pegged the man sitting beside him as a gigolo. Buck looked him over and figured Frank was a little over six feet tall, athletic build with dark hair and eyes. Buck figured that women would find his witness attractive.

Buck pulled out a tape recorder and took a statement from Frank. As the statement ended, Frank looked out the rear window to see a couple of satellite TV trucks had pulled up to the scene.

As Frank got out of the car, he commented: "It must be rare to have a death on Lovers Key. I bet its big news."

Thorton monotoned: “Five were killed here a few years ago.” Then he checked for a reaction.

Frank’s eyebrows went up ever so slightly, but he said nothing.

“We’ll be in touch Frank, here’s my business card. Call me if you think of anything you forgot to tell me.”

With a formal farewell behind them, Frank crossed the yellow police tape and headed in the opposite direction from the reporters. He walked quickly down a sandy foot path towards the beach and a minute later was on the white sandy shore of the waters of the Gulf of Mexico.

The water was sparkling in the morning sun. The beauty of this tropic isle was in sharp contrast to the violent horror of the murder scene nearby. Frank strolled the nearly deserted beach and pondered how could a small island, not much more than a mile long and at most a half mile wide, be the scene of a murder? What about the other five deaths? What were the circumstances of those deaths? This area was more likely to be the location of a moonlight romance on the sand than what he saw beside the road. He stopped walking and looked out on the water, contemplating the attitude he would portray when he told the women of the events he set in motion.

Frank walked up from the beach, entered the main house through the servant’s entrance and was in the kitchen. He walked into the adjoining dining room and was only two feet inside the door when he was bombarded by questions.

“What were the sirens all about?”

“How many ambulances are out there?”

“Was there a serious accident?”

In a calm voice, Frank related: “I came upon a man who was murdered and his body was dumped beside the road. No ambulances arrived because the man had been dead awhile. The death was not the result of a traffic accident.”

“I sure hope that the media doesn’t get a hold of this.” complained Monique Moritz. She was in her sixties, but looked much younger. Frank guessed that she had indulged in every youth preserving potion known to womankind. Her pampered lifestyle had been kind to her features.

Frank needed to keep Monique from becoming agitated so he impassively replied: "Unfortunately, the media have police scanners and they assembled on the scene shortly after law enforcement. Mrs. Moritz, I wouldn't answer the door, because the media will probably have a camera running and will want to know your reaction to the murder."

"Mother, don't be upset." Angeline Moritz cautioned, "The whole thing will be old news by tomorrow." Angeline had the youthful beauty that her mother possessed about three decades ago. Angeline had been pampered since birth, so she believed that all bad things would be dispatched quickly and appropriately.

Mrs. Monique Moritz loved the beach because the rest of the world could be shut out very easily. She felt secure during the short time Frank Johnson had been there because he dissolved problems effectively. He instilled in her the belief that he could master any disaster. She looked to Frank for reassurance: "Is Angeline correct when she says this messy ordeal will be gone by tomorrow?"

Frank reached for Monique's hand and firmly held it. "Mrs. Moritz, the usual routine will return tomorrow. This incident won't be impacting you beyond today." Frank didn't tell her that law enforcement would have an ongoing investigation until the murderer was brought to justice. Nor did he tell her that he would be a witness if there was a trial.

Angeline was intoxicated by the potential of a major news story occurring just beyond the boundaries of her home. "Frank, how do you know the man was murdered and then dumped here?"

Mrs. Moritz gasped and her knees started to buckle now that the full impact of the murder had encompassed her brain. Frank held her up and guided her to a chair.

"I don't think your mother can handle much more of this. Let me get her a glass of water and once your mother is stable we'll discuss it outside."

As they stood outside, Frank described the condition of the body and then told Angeline: "If the man had been attacked by a wild animal, I would've seen some type of animal print near the body. It's weird; there was no blood on or near the body. This means that he was murdered elsewhere. If a wild animal killed the man and dragged the body to where I found it, there would've been animal tracks AND a distinct trail in the sand showing where the body had been dragged."

Frank continued: "It's murder because the person, or persons, stopped right on the road and dumped the body. Remember, I saw no tire tracks in the ditch. He had no clothes; he wasn't even wrapped up in anything. The autopsy will show if he was shot or stabbed. There were so many wounds I couldn't tell if the wounds inflicted from the animal attack might have been a cover up to divert the cops from the real cause of death. It's definitely a homicide."

"Spoken like a true prosecutor." declared Angeline. She thought of how she had met Frank in Steamboat Springs, Colorado shortly after he had resigned from his job as a prosecutor. She had been enthralled at his detailed descriptions of the desperadoes he had prosecuted.

Their conversation was interrupted by the sound of voices. Angeline and Frank looked up the driveway to see a man with a large video camera in hand and a well dressed young woman purposefully walking towards them. Angeline was ready to be on the local news. She greeted them as she adjusted her hair. Frank backed up and walked away as Angeline prepared for her television debut.

The reporter had sweet talked a deputy handling security to reveal that the deceased had been attacked by an animal. Once they were prepared to film, the first question posed to Angeline was whether she was fearful because a fatal animal attack occurred so close to her home. She simply replied no and the reporter gave up- figuring that because Angeline wasn't afraid, this interview would figuratively end up on the cutting room floor. It would never make it past the editors.

When Frank heard of the short interview, he was glad he wasn't present. The reporter would have turned to him for a quote which would make the news. It was luck that Angeline hadn't revealed his role.

Angeline and Frank watched the evening news. Frank was surprised at the angle of the story. The spokesperson for the Lee

County Sheriff's Office stood before the cameras to report a death had occurred on Lovers Key and classified the type of investigation being conducted as simply trying to identify the deceased. In the next few days the medical examiner would release the cause of death. The spokeswoman was asking for the public's help in identifying the victim. She described the dead man as an olive skinned, Middle Eastern looking man between twenty five and thirty five years old, six feet one inch tall and about 170 pounds. The woman then gave a number for the public to call to give information.

Mrs. Moritz didn't have the strength to watch such traumatic news coverage. She was out on the patio watching the waves roll in as she sipped her glass of French wine.

CHAPTER TWO

Frank and Angeline decided to wait until Monique Moritz went to bed before discussing the events of the day. The two sat silently on the patio as the stars glistened off the water.

Angeline lovingly looked at Frank and recalled how they had met in Steamboat Springs, Colorado just before Thanksgiving over a year ago. She was enamored by his good looks and was enchanted that he had quit his job as a prosecutor to be a ski bum for the winter. She didn't meet him on the ski slopes, but had met him in a jewelry store where he was working part time after skiing all day. She bought her mother, Monique, a birthday present and Frank was a charmer in completing the sale. She chuckled to herself as she remembered how Frank's "sometime girlfriend" caught them having fun in an après ski pub at the base of Steamboat ski area.

But things didn't click for them in Steamboat the way she had hoped. She had to convince her wealthy father to hire Frank to do legal work for his many development corporations to lure him to their spectacular home overlooking the waters of the Gulf of Mexico.

Angeline's thoughts were interrupted when a dolphin jumped out of the water and the moon made the splashing waters into a cascade of liquid stars. On the horizon, white sails shimmered in the moonlight as a large sailboat silently progressed on a nighttime passage. She realized the romantic setting was one which many people would only experience in their dreams. She appreciated the setting, but wanted more. She touched his arm, looked at him and hoped that a relationship would blossom. After all, that was the desired result from all her planning.

Frank looked at Angeline and marveled at her beauty. Her athletic build, tanned skin and long blond hair made her look a sensational thirty years old in the moonlight. As he enjoyed the setting, he knew why he agreed to take a job that was located in the guest cottage at the estate of the boss.

He knew the boss would rarely be there and the boss's daughter was very instrumental in his hiring. The pay was good, the hours flexible and the amenities exceptional. No need to commute; he worked where he lived and the lodging was free. When it came to his consulting work, all his legal needs could be resolved by the electronic age. No need to have books or go to a law library.

He finally realized that Angeline was still looking at him. As he turned to look at her, their eyes fixed on each other. She clutched his hand and softly said: "Let's take your car and go for a moonlit drive down to Vanderbilt Beach."

Frank's romantic side didn't need persuading. They headed out in his 1965 red Mustang convertible with the top down. The warm night air flowed around them lifting their emotions skyward. He loved the feeling of freedom with the wind rushing by and she felt they were together floating above the earth.

They stopped at the Turtle Club and had conch fritters on the beach. The bouncing beacons of lights from Naples left them mesmerized as they munched on their appetizer. Angeline held Frank's hand and she told him about an earlier sighting of a group of Manatees migrating past Lover's Key: "Frank, it was so exciting. There were three of them- two adults and a baby. They slowly made their way northward on the bay side of the island. They must have been heading to the Orange River where they hang out for the winter. The water there is warmer because of the power plant. I love to see their chubby noses come up for air and then their tails come up out of the water. The tails look like a giant leathery fan."

"You mean like the fan blades from a ceiling fan?" Frank asked.

"No. Like in ancient Egypt: a fan that a servant would use to fan the queen. Haven't you ever seen a manatee?"

"No."

Angeline drew closer to Frank, put her hand on his thigh and softly squeezed. "Frank we need to go out in a boat on a sunset adventure to search for manatees- just the two of us."

"We should do that when they migrate back in the spring."

"We *must* go on a romantic sunset manatee adventure within a week." Angeline declared; she wasn't going to wait for months. She wanted more of a commitment and more attention than Frank was offering. She loved his dark hair, muscular build and intense dark eyes. He was over six feet tall and he captivated her. She wasn't about to let him go. She squeezed him again. "We could go to Crystal River for the weekend. A lot of manatees hang out there. It could be a little getaway for the two of us."

Frank wasn't sure what to say. He knew that he wasn't ready for an intense relationship with Angeline. Luckily, before he answered, the waitress appeared and announced the place was about to close. They left their starlit beach side table and walked back to the valet stand to get the Mustang. The parking attendant enviously commented about what a thrill it would be to own Frank's great classic convertible. Frank graciously thanked him for the compliment and gave him a nice tip.

As they cruised back, Frank changed the mood by turning up the music and having them sing along to an old Beach Boys song. Once they arrived at the estate, Angeline waited for Frank as he put the car in the garage. As he walked her up to the main residence, her anticipation heightened. Hesitation was nonexistent for Frank as he opened the door for her, bid her adieu and disappeared into the night. She stood inside the door wondering what it would take to get him to make an advance. "Not even a peck on the cheek" she grumbled to herself.

The next morning Frank read the newspaper hoping there would be information he didn't already know about the murder. Alas, nothing new, so he called Investigator Thorton

"Investigator Thorton, this is Franklin Johnson. I'm the one that found the body yesterday."

"What can I do for you? Did you call with some new information?"

"No. I was just wondering when the autopsy will be done and who's doing it."

"Dr. Doris Delaney, the Chief Medical Examiner, did the autopsy late yesterday."

"What were the results?" Frank asked.

"I couldn't tell you if I knew. The information must be OK'd for release before I say anything."

"Did she rule it a homicide?"

"She didn't rule anything. After doing the autopsy she headed to Las Vegas."

Frank was perplexed. "Is she there for a medical examiner's meeting?"

"Not that I know of. She goes there a lot."

"Seems like it would help your investigation if she ruled it a homicide."

There was a pause and then Buck replied: "It would hurt us a lot if she rules it isn't a homicide. At this stage we can go in any direction we feel is right."

Frank figured it was time to reveal his thoughts. "Your spokeswoman publicly isn't saying this was a murder. Seems like it must be, considering there's no blood at the scene. People bleed when they loose an arm. The body was dumped there by someone-it certainly wasn't an animal attack right where I found the body."

Buck wasn't going to say much about the investigation: "There's very little physical evidence at the scene, the first goal is to establish the identity of the victim. Next, we'll attempt to determine who was the last person to see him alive."

Frank chimed in: "Did the medical examiner take fingerprints from the victim and give them to you for typing and checking?"

"Let's just say we'll get more information from Dr. Delaney when she gets back." Buck replied.

"What about getting a sample from the body, submit it for DNA typing and run the results against any data base you can."

"The medical examiner has the body and will handle her part of this case as she sees fit. It takes time to determine the DNA once a sample is submitted."

Frank replied: "The sooner the better."

Buck agreed.

After the conversation, Frank pondered Buck's comment about the medical examiner not ruling the death a homicide. How could a reasonable person think it was an accident? Was there really an issue that an animal could have attacked the man on Lovers Key?

It took only a day for Frank to find out the answer to his questions. The next morning, the front page headline in the newspaper caught Frank's attention immediately:

DEATH RULED BEAR ATTACK AT LOVERS KEY

> ***The unidentified man who was found dead beside the road on Lovers Key two days ago has been declared to have died as a result of a bear attack. Dr. Doris Delaney the Chief Medical Examiner of Lee County issued a brief press release indicating that the man had lost an arm and had a number of bite marks on his body. She asked for the public's help in identifying the man.***

The story went on to describe the man and that the sheriff's office had followed up on a number of leads, but the identity of the man remained a mystery. Unnamed, reliable sources said the medical examiner had not determined if the death was accidental, or murder. The sources said the space on the autopsy form indicating manner of death had not been completed. The reporter asked for a copy of the public record and was denied. No one from the office was available to answer questions including the Chief Medical Examiner who was in Las Vegas.

The article went on to state that Florida Fish and Wildlife Conservation Commission Officers had never heard of a bear being spotted on Lovers Key. They felt it unlikely a bear could exist on the tiny barrier island for long without being spotted. Bears are native to southern Florida and the largest on record was a six hundred pound black bear found in adjoining Collier County.

Frank put down the newspaper and wondered how the medical examiner could not rule it a homicide. There was a clear lack of evidence that the attack occurred where the body was found. That would mean a human was involved in the movement of the body. In his mind if a person either accidentally or intentionally caused a death, it was a homicide. In the medical and legal communities homicide and murder are not necessarily synonymous.

He quickly realized that his tendency to want to be an investigator was reappearing. He had to fight that yearning because he was a witness- not a major one, but a witness.

He told Monique and Angeline of the Medical Examiner's ruling without adding his opinion on the accuracy of it.

Monique gasped: "Something must be done to catch that man eating bear! We're not safe here. Frank, call someone to exterminate the bear!"

Frank saw her quivering and put his hand on her arm, trying to comfort her. He tried to reassure her: "If it was a bear attack, it didn't happen on Lovers Key. I know from the physical evidence that I observed that the death happened elsewhere and the man was dumped here."

Monique continued to tremble and Frank's reassurances had little effect on her sense of security. After fifteen minutes of discussion, she was just as agitated. Angeline decided to change the subject to get her mother's mind off of the bear.

"Mother, you had been talking with your friend about the new exhibit of Chinese antiquities at The Museum of Art in Fort Lauderdale. Why don't Frank and I get tickets so the three of us can go? You seemed especially interested in seeing The Pearl of Tao."

Angeline's tactic worked and her mother launched into a long dissertation on the intriguing history of some of the ancient art work. A call was made, and tickets were obtained for the next day. Monique had to call the members of her bridge club in Naples to inform all of them of her upcoming drink from the chalice of culture.

CHAPTER THREE

Frank went back to the privacy of his cottage and called Investigator Thorton. Frank asked Buck if fingerprints had been obtained and Buck grudgingly replied they just got the prints today from the medical examiner. When questioned by Frank, he also admitted they had just gotten a blood sample for DNA analysis.

In a startled voice, Frank said: "Three days after the medical examiner's office received the body?"

"She thought fingerprints wouldn't be much help since the right hand was missing from the corpse."

Frank couldn't believe what he was hearing. In a lecturing tone of voice he let Buck know of his displeasure: "Every time a set of fingerprints is taken, they print both hands. When I saw the body in the sand, his left hand was fine. I don't believe the ignorance of this woman!"

Buck replied: "Well, yesterday, she finally agreed fingerprints would be helpful. We're getting the prints typed today so we can run them against prints in the system."

"What about the sample for DNA?"

"We sent that off to the lab today."

Frank wondered aloud: "Did the fine doctor get her degree from Swampy Waters University?"

Buck decided to be professional and did not respond to Frank's rhetorical question. "Y'all know that the Sheriff's Office is treating this case as a big priority case and it's surely being treated as a homicide."

Frank decided he better not attack any segment of the investigation or he would risk having the spigot of information turned off. Politely he asked: "Was the newspaper accurate in saying the Chief

Medical Examiner had not decided if the death was accidental or a homicide?"

Buck answered like a good old southern boy: "She's got the fishing pole in her hand, has been told that her bobber is down, but she can't decide to set the hook or let the fish continue to take her bait."

"Did she say if there were gun shot wounds, or knife wounds, or any trauma other than an animal attack?"

Buck paused: "All trauma is consistent with an animal attack."

"How did the medical examiner determine it was a bear attack and not some other large animal?"

Buck drawled: "The bobber's under on that one and no one can see it."

Frank figured that Buck was telling him the medical examiner wasn't willing to reveal how she came to her conclusion it was a bear. "Why don't you have an expert examine the body at the morgue and give an opinion on the type of animal involved? It had to be something big."

Diplomatically Buck replied: "I don't even want to ask Dr. Delaney for permission to have an expert enter her domain."

"I saw your crime scene people taking a lot of photos, including close ups of the body. Why don't you have an expert look at the photos showing the bite marks to determine if it was a bear attack?"

"If we do that and the expert says it's another type of animal, we'll be in hot water with the Chief Medical Examiner because we obviously questioned her conclusion. Plus, we'll have two conflicting theories. Do we look for someone who has a bear or for someone who has another animal, say a squirrel?" Buck sarcastically replied.

Frank could tell Buck was getting angry about a witness meddling in the direction to take the investigation. Frank surmised Buck wasn't too happy with Dr. Delaney and now a witness was putting his nose in where it didn't belong. Frank figured he better go easy on the subject. After a long discussion, Buck came around to Frank's conclusion that no bear would be on Lovers Key and other resources needed to be used to determine the type of animal that attacked the man.

Buck concluded: "It's better to know right away what type of animal chewed up the body, than search for someone who has the wrong type of animal- in this case a bear."

Frank suggested: "Find someone from the National Park Service or the state wildlife people."

"I'll look into it.' Then Buck added: "I don't like second guessing her It just gits her riled up and she's a bear to work with." He laughed at his choice of words.

As they ended their conversation, Frank said he would call back in a few days. Buck mumbled something as he hung up.

Frank decided to do some research of his own and signed onto the internet. He had visually memorized the body and could vividly recall the bite mark on the victim's right shoulder. He did extensive searching and with what he found, he believed that a bear would not have enough teeth to cause that bite mark.

He then checked his e-mail and discovered Stephanie had replied to the one he sent last night. Before opening it, he leaned back in his chair and wondered how he ended up living next to one beautiful woman and loving another one far away.

Stephanie, the beautiful woman he left in Saint Paul, was the best thing that ever happened to him. She had been upset when he left his position as a prosecutor and moved away from her to become a ski bum in Steamboat Springs. The next summer, he returned to again fall into her good graces. Seemingly, his need to wander had been quenched, when out of nowhere, Angeline found him and said her father needed a good legal mind to handle all the legalities of his many new developments. She said he would work directly with her father and live on Lovers Key. Angeline was rich, beautiful and about his age. Frank had tightened up his body from the winter of skiing and a summer of being very physically active. He looked more like an athlete than a lawyer.

There were a number of reasons two beautiful women were attracted to him. He was handsome, articulate and very charming. Women loved his spirit of adventure. It was that spirit that again separated him from Stephanie when he was offered a life on the beach.

Finally, he shook himself out of his day dream and opened the e-mail. Stephanie, always independent, wrote that she was under a tight deadline to complete the architectural drawings for an addition to a Mississippi River mansion. As usual, the e-mail was short and to the point. He noted no proclamation that she needed to have Frank close to her. However, she invited him to return to see her.

He yearned to do just that and daydreamed about the many grand times they had together. He reminisced how they had met in the Ramsey County Courthouse in St. Paul on a cold gray day in Minnesota. She asked for directions and he convinced her to give him her phone number. She was a hard working, creative architect and he was a prosecutor who never had lost a jury trial in his five year career.

Their relationship grew slowly at first because both were into a mindset to build a strong foundation for their professional careers. Finally love blossomed and then Frank put a frost on the blossom of love by quitting his job and becoming a ski bum or as he called it "a ski vagabond." Stephanie wasn't keen on his career move and she declined to join him on his excursion.

He continued to mentally float along until there was a knock on his door. Angeline didn't wait to be invited in. She just announced her presence and came in the door- which put her right in the living room. The living room doubled as Frank's office and he quickly checked out of e-mail.

"We need to talk." Angeline declared.

"And the subject is?"

"Tao."

"Tao?"

"Yes. I reserved tickets for tomorrow at The Museum of Art and I need to know more about Taoism so I don't appear to have a nonfunctional brain at the exhibit."

Frank decided to chide her like a professor does to a student: "Do you desire a dissertation on Lao-Tzu the man who is the founder of Taoism; Taoism as a religion, as a way of life; or the history of The Pearl of Tao?"

She exhaled in frustration, gave him the raised single digit and finally said: "The Pearl is enough for now professor."

Frank explained: The whole thing started over 2,500 years ago. Taoists believe that the founder of their religion, Lao-Tzu told his followers to get a clam out of the sea and place an amulet in it. The clam created a pearl which covered the amulet. Over the years, as a clam would die, the amulet would be transferred to another larger clam. As the hour glass of time wore on, the pearl grew at an amazing rate. It was a revered part of the religion. Then tragically, the pearl went to the bottom of the sea when a ship traveling from China to the Philippines encountered a typhoon in about 1750.

"What was in the amulet?"

"Busts of Confucius, Buddha and, of course, Lao-Tzu."

"So, is Lao-Tzu comparing himself to Confucius and Buddha?"

"Most assuredly. He believed that if busts of the founders of three religions could coexist in the close confines of a shell, all their followers could live in harmony." Frank then gave Angeline a little Taoist doctrine: "He is Bright Waves of Light."

"Don't get me confused. I don't want to get side tracked. Tell me how The Pearl of Tao came out of the sea."

He explained that in 1934, after almost two centuries at sea, a giant tridacna clam was found and inside it was the fourteen pound pearl. The clam was found in the waters off of Palauan Island in the Philippines.

"Wow. It must be bigger than a bowling ball."

Frank responded: "Not exactly. It is irregular in shape and doesn't have a smooth surface. It is the world's largest pearl. The amazing part of the story is that it is rumored a tribal chief sent divers down to collect shells. One diver never came back and it was believed the shell snapped shut on his hand."

Angeline responded: "How do you know all this?"

Frank gave his most professorial look and in a British accent declared: "I *am* a gifted historian in a significant multitude of areas."

"Tell me the truth Frank."

Resigned, Frank said: "When I was in Colorado, there was a lot of news coverage about The Pearl. The litigation started when the Chief Judge of the federal court in Colorado ordered The Pearl to be held in a bank vault in Colorado Springs. A number of people had an ownership interest in The Pearl. One of them hired a hit man to murder his wife. But, the husband died before he or anyone else was prosecuted. There was plenty of media coverage when the hit man was convicted of murder. The children sued the father's estate because the father left his assets to a daughter from another marriage. The children won a verdict of over thirty two million dollars. The main asset to pay for the judgment was The Pearl."

"Wow!"

"That was the biggest verdict of its type in Colorado history. People were talking."

Angeline changed the subject: "How about a brief history on Taoism?"

"That will also have to await another day. The day might be tomorrow as we travel to see the collection of antiquities. Today, I must get some work done for your father as a deadline is rapidly approaching."

Angeline moved closer to Frank and whispered: "How about a lesson on the history of Lao-Tzu tonight on the beach with a bottle of wine? The gentle sound of the waves would make me a very submissive student."

Frank then gently put his arm around her waist and led her towards the door. Angeline intently looked into his eyes, but Frank quickly looked away as he escorted her out the door.

CHAPTER FOUR

The next morning over breakfast, Mrs. Monique Moritz was ecstatic over the prospect of being drenched in the ancient culture of China while at the Museum of Art. She also wanted to be quenched at lunch. She required Frank to be sure they ate lunch at an appropriately swank restaurant directly on the ocean at Ft. Lauderdale.

Monique sounded typically aristocratic as she elegantly intoned: "The women at the bridge club would expect to get insight from me as to *the* best place to eat. In addition, we *are* leaders in viewing this very important cultural exhibit and others need correct information so they can comprehend the significance of these antiquities."

Frank hid any emotional reaction and politely responded: "Mrs. Moritz, I have the perfect spot in mind, the dining critics are just raving over it. Last night I made reservations for one o'clock today. We can dine first and then be mesmerized by the exhibit."

"Oh, Frank you are so exceptional! You make life so civilized. What time should I be ready to go?"

Frank decided to chide her: "Do you want to go the speed limit or do you want to go fast in the Bentley?"

"Fast." Angeline interrupted.

"We'll leave at eleven." Frank declared.

Monique exclaimed: "Gracious, I have to get ready. I have less than two hours before we leave." The concern in her voice was echoed by her hasty departure from the table. Frank and Angeline smirked after Monique left the room and ascended the elegant marble stairway to the master suite.

"Frank, you didn't show up last night to give me a lesson on the beach. I need more information on Taoism so I can tell my mother that during all those years at college I did learn something useful."

"Do I look like a Professor of Divinity?" Frank replied.

"More like a handsome Professor of Philosophy; who was stripped of his professorship because too many female students concentrated on him rather than his lectures."

"Before you attack me like the imaginary students you have created, let me start my lecture. The first thing to remember about Taoism is that everything is subject to interpretation. Both scholars and devotees are in disagreement about many basic issues about the religion. There are over one thousand ancient texts dating back to before Christianity. A compellation of these texts was published as the one great official record of Taoism in the 1920's in China. The founder of Taoism is believed to be Lao-Tzu who lived long before Christ and is believed to be as spiritual a being as Christ, Confucius or Muhammad, the founder of Islam."

"That's about as much as my mom or I can comprehend in one stretch. Maybe I'll do some meditation before we go." She laughed as she left Frank.

Promptly at eleven they headed to the garage and sank into the luxurious leather cabin of the fine Bentley automobile. Frank started it up and immediately there was a terrible sound in the engine. As he quickly shut it off, he saw that the dash showed there was a problem with a lack of oil in the engine. He looked under the hood and didn't see anything wrong. He looked under the car and there was a pan with engine oil slopped around and in it.

He got back in the car and told the women that someone had apparently drained the oil out of the engine. This resulted in a gasp from Monique as she put her hand over her mouth.

"What?" Frank asked

"A couple of days ago, Juan Salvador, the gardener came in to tell me the riding lawn mower needed oil and there was none in the work shed or the garage. I told him to just take some out of a car. I didn't think he would take it all out and leave it out."

"Well, we'll just take Angeline's Jaguar." Frank looked in the other stall and saw the classic car wasn't there. "Where is it?"

"At the Jaguar dealer getting a new clutch put in." Angeline replied.

"Well that means we go in my car."

They got in the Mustang and Monique demanded that the top be put up so her hair wouldn't get mussed up. Frank started to put the top up and a loud snap occurred. The top wouldn't budge. This caused another gasp from Monique.

She demanded that they get a rental car. Frank explained that by the time they got a car out to them, they would be late for lunch and might miss the exhibit. She left in a huff and reappeared ten minutes later with a huge hat held on with an elaborate set of scarves tied under her chin.

"We'll just have to make do. I can't tell the women at the club that I didn't go because we didn't have a car that would run. I'd be too embarrassed. Just don't tell anyone how I look. I brought items in my purse to freshen up once we get to the restaurant."

Frank and Angeline loved the trip. The sky was an alluring blue, they had the music cranked up and Monique was entertaining them with her demeanor. A Las Vegas comedy act couldn't have been more humorous than Monique in her continually changing facial expressions of dismay and exasperation because of the windy ride

After about an hour of this, Frank noticed a fluffy light cloud on the horizon. As they continued to drive, the clouds blackened quickly."

In a concerned voice, Frank calmly declared: "The dark clouds ahead aren't a good sign."

Angeline tried to put a bright face on a foreboding forecast: "I think the clouds will move to the south before we get to them. It's very flat here, those clouds are miles ahead."

Frank verbally agreed so Monique wouldn't get in a huff. Unfortunately, Monique's expressions turned into something much greater than murky apprehension.

Moments later Monique shrieked: "**RAIN!!**" and melted down in her seat trying to compress her body.

Frank looked ahead and realized that she was right. There was no way to escape the rain. They were on Alligator Alley, a stretch of interstate highway 75 miles long with only two exits to nowhere. Those exits were far behind them and civilization was still miles ahead. Frank could feel a momentous disaster. He could think of no words to realistically console Mrs. Moritz.

The rain started to pelt down and it stung as it hit.

Monique screamed and then cried out: "I'm sure I'm getting welts on my face and arms from the rain pelting me. Frank do *something* IMMEDIATELY!"

"Cover up with my jacket. Try to get under the dashboard. Use it as protection. We've no alternative but to keep going. I'm sorry."

Thunder drowned out his apology as the cloudburst's fury seemed directed at Monique and the little red convertible. In contrast, in the back seat Angeline laughed and tried to sing above the sound of the rain banging on them.

The ten minutes of snarling, cracking thunder and brutal rain, seemed to be hours in duration as Monique twitched and convulsed in desperate drenching ugliness. She would have preferred being thrown into the deep end of her Olympic sized swimming pool in her newest evening dress. All of them looked like intoxicated vagrants. At times, the clanging rain drowned out the sound of thunder, but Frank was more concerned about the lightning. There were enough close calls that he figured there was imminent danger of a deadly direct hit. Monique kept her head down so she couldn't see the flashes, but her body had a spasm proportional to the nastiness of each thunder boom.

Suddenly, lightning struck beside the car. It had an explosive sound that rivaled a fighter jet's sonic boom. Indeed, the flash of light exceeded paparazzi taking flash photos of the glitterati.

Startled, Monique squealed in terror and instinctively jumped up to attempt to determine exactly where tragedy was about to happen. As she jerked upward, the back of her head hit the dash. A sound that could only be described as a combination of guttural moan and terrified scream erupted from her.

She was dazed but immediately bawled: "Get me to a spa and Sak's Fifth Ave! I need a complete make over!"

Frank and Angeline could not stop laughing. Luckily, the storm muted the volume of their amusement as Monique was too engaged in her own calamity to notice their humored reaction.

Finally the rain let up as they approached the toll booth at the end of Alligator Alley. The chuckling toll booth man gave them directions to a huge shopping mall just off the Sawgrass Expressway. He assured them the mall would be able to revitalize them.

After a couple of tranquilizers, a shopping trip and a rental car, Monique was now ready to have lunch. Three glasses of wine with lunch, on top of her tranquilizers, assured that Monique was adequately sedated.

Frank drove to the Museum and commented that time was running short to see the entire exhibit. He suggested they should head towards the Pearl of Tao. Angeline agreed. The two looked at Monique who was quietly entombed in her chemicals.

CHAPTER FIVE

As they entered The Museum of Art of Ft. Lauderdale, Frank was impressed with the high level of security. Some private security people wore blazers, others polo shirts and others windbreakers. All wore khaki colored pants and many appeared to be armed. The common thread of this group of security was that they had a stylish crest with the words *LINGBAO SECURITY* below it. In addition, there were Broward County deputy sheriffs and Ft. Lauderdale police officers.

Frank, Angeline and Monique headed towards the Pearl of Tao, passing by such great artifacts as a 2,200 year old bronze carriage pulled by four bronze horses. Monique mumbled some thing about a sign saying it came from the First Qin Emperor and was on the World Heritage List. Angeline responded that they would look at it more closely later.

As they entered the area where the Pearl of Tao was being displayed, they saw a long line of people. They were surprised by the number of women in line wearing traditional Muslim clothing. They lined up behind two such women who were with their husbands. The two couples were talking loudly and were clearly agitated. Frank could hear them saying it was a scourge on Allah, to display the Pearl as part of Chinese history.

The Muslims condemned the exhibit and complained that their prophet and founder of Islam, Muhammad, had created this Pearl in his likeness and it must be called the Pearl of Allah. It was sacrilegious to have this Pearl anywhere but in a mosque. Allah would see to it that the Pearl would be returned to a proper location; as Allah is all powerful.

The conversation continued as the line moved ever closer to The Pearl. When the two couples were directly in front of The Pearl, the four Lingbao Security men guarding The Pearl tensed up. The one Muslim man named Faroque, screamed: "This is the Pearl of Allah! We must pray that Allah condemn those responsible for the public display of his likeness."

The second Muslim man named Haquan snarled: "Those that display the Pearl of Allah and call it by another name must suffer for this insult to Him!"

All four Muslims got on their knees and bowed down, praying in a foreign language. One of the security men moved forward ready to do something, but he was restrained by another guard who said: "Ying, be patient, you know the protocol. We've been through this many times before." The security man who moved forward was Asian with a red and yellow dragon tattoo up the side of his neck. The Muslims continued to pray in loud voices.

Monique started to quiver; she knew that a confrontation was about to occur and she was within arm's length of it. She grabbed Frank's shoulder with a trembling hand. Her mouth opened, but no words came out. Frank responded by putting his arm around her waist to steady her.

Angeline felt the tension. Rather than being afraid, she was absolutely absorbed in what was about to occur.

After about a minute, Ying and another security guard looked at each other, nodded and simultaneously said the line needs to keep moving.

The Muslims kept praying.

The two guards told them they must move on.

The Muslims kept praying.

All four guards moved forward and one guard sternly demanded that they must move on.

The Muslims kept praying.

The guard loudly informed them: "We will physically move you if you do not get up and move on!"

The Muslims continued to bow down in prayer.

The tension had escalated and people in line moved away. The guard pressed a button on his walkie talkie and Frank could hear the sound of rapid footsteps behind him. He knew that the Muslims had forced security to respond with a show of force.

Ying, the security guard with the dragon tattoo, quickly stepped forward ahead of the other three guards. Ying grabbed Faroque.

Faroque's religious zeal had turned him into a highly charged rocket ready to be launched if anyone stopped his prayers to Muhammad. When Ying touched him, the launch button was pushed. Faroque reached under his shirt and inside the waistband of his pants. Out came a knife in his left hand. Ying made an attempt to spin away from the thrust of the knife, but he was too late. The knife was buried into his right thigh.

The crowd both gasped and shrieked. A crescendo of chaos rocketed out as groups of people fled. Frank stepped back as he whisked Monique from the realm of peril.

Monique slurred: "This might not be a staged performance." Her legs gave out as she fainted. Frank needed both arms to keep her from collapsing on the floor. Wine, pills and bloodshed were too much for Monique's fragile countenance. Angeline's eyes signaled her alarm as she hid behind Frank, speechless.

Before Faroque could again attack with the knife, another guard did a martial arts move. The guard flew feet first with one foot hitting Faroque in the jaw and the other foot hitting him in the hand, sending the knife spinning across the floor.

The second Muslim male, Haquan, jumped on the wounded guard and started pummeling him with his fists. Additional security guards arrived on the scene just as Faroque was back on his feet attacking them with his fists. A burly deputy sheriff arrived and administered one strong blow with a night stick to the back of the neck near the shoulder blades. The mountain of momentum brought Faroque down only long enough for him to be handcuffed. Frank was amazed that Faroque wasn't down and out.

Other guards were now doing battle with Haquan who was punching the wounded guard as others were trying to subdue him. They grabbed Haquan off of the wounded Ying as he continued to claw at the wounded man. As they were separated, Ying's shirt was torn off him by his attacker. Haquan had a lot of strength and was now attacking a Ft. Lauderdale police officer.

A security guard pulled out his gun and the deputy sheriff immediately ordered him to put it away because there were too many innocent people around. The deputy sheriff again masterfully wielded his night stick by jabbing it into Haquan's guts. The wind went out of his sails and he was subdued. As he was being handcuffed, Frank noticed that Haquan had only part of his right hand-just the thumb and forefinger. Frank was astonished how Haquan had used his disfigured hand to pummel the security guard.

While holding up Monique, Frank turned to see what happened to Ying, the wounded security guard. He was on the floor holding his thigh, trying to stop the bleeding. Quickly a police officer used the torn shirt as a compression bandage. As Ying lay on the floor, Frank noticed a second tattoo on him. It was on his chest and showed an ancient Asian man in a flowing robe riding a water buffalo. Soon paramedics were doing a deft job of emergency care on Ying.

Faroque and Haquan were not giving up. Even though they were both handcuffed, they continued to struggle to escape. Faroque yelled something in a foreign language and the two Muslim women launched an attempt to free Haquan from the two private security guards. Haquan got up and attacked Ying who screamed in pain as Haquan catapulted himself onto Ying's bloodied thigh. Two deputies used their nightsticks as pressure points on Haquan until other officers put leg restraints on him.

Haquan was only a few feet from the injured Ying who insisted upon walking to the ambulance. Two paramedics grabbed Ying under each arm as they started to guide him out. Ying took two painful steps towards Haquan and vehemently shouted "I spit on you, a coward!" Startled by this outburst, the paramedics tried to steer Ying away, but it was too late, Haquan received a present of saliva. The cops again had to struggle to control Haquan. Ying continued to look back and sneer at Haquan as he was helped to the ambulance.

Frank was still keeping Monique from crumbling to the floor. He needed to get her away from the violence and get her lucid. Besides, he didn't want to stick around to be targeted by the police as a witness. He carried Monique away and found a chair to put her in. Gently, he and Angeline revived Monique.

Frank felt responsible for the fact that Angeline was now trembling and Monique was still dazed. Frank had them both rest in order to regain their composure. They stayed silent for a few minutes.

Angeline spoke first: “Why did that man call it the Pearl of Allah?”

Frank said: “Muslims believe that the shape of The Pearl resembles the face of Allah, the Supreme Being of Islam. There is a resemblance between one side of The Pearl and the image of Allah. There is an intense conflict between Muslims and Taoists because both believe that The Pearl is a sacred, ancient artifact of their religion. The Pearl is right up there in importance with the revered Christian belief in the Shroud of Turin.”

Surprisingly, Monique spoke up: “What is the Shroud of Turin?”

Angeline said: “It is the cloth that covered Jesus’ body when he was laid in the tomb after his death. His bloody body left a self portrait on the cloth.”

Frank was impressed with Angeline’s knowledge and said so. He also joined in to say that The Pearl was so important to Muslims that one of the owners of The Pearl said that the terrorist, Osama bin Laden wanted to buy it, but the owner wouldn’t sell.”

Monique asked: “So, how much is it worth?”

“One appraisal had it worth $60 million dollars some years ago, now it may be as high as $93 million.” Frank said.

Monique’s eyes opened wider and she said: “No wonder there were so many guards around it. Well, how long have the Taoists controlled The Pearl?”

“They don’t.”

“Who does?”

“A federal judge.” Frank responded matter of factly.

Frank continued by saying that over twenty years ago, a federal judge in Colorado ordered The Pearl held in federal custody. This rare procedure was used because there had been a long legal battle between the multiple owners of it and for awhile The Pearl couldn’t be located. The owners had grown very distrustful of each other.

Monique was barely coherent when she asked: "So how did it become part of this exhibit?"

Frank replied: "I've wondered about that myself."

They headed towards the exit as Monique wondered aloud what she would dare tell the ladies at the bridge club.

Frank quipped: "Tell them the event was rained out."

CHAPTER SIX

Two days later Frank was heading out the door for his daily early morning jog and thinking he should give Buck Thorton a call to find out if the dead body had been identified. As he started down the driveway, he remembered the first thoughts he had when he found the corpse: DEAD, VERY OBVIOUSLY DEAD. As he turned onto the road, he immediately thought:

"I HOPE I'M NOT SEEING THIS AGAIN!!"

Frank jogged up the road a short distance and in the sand on the far edge of the ditch was a dead body. DEAD. VERY OBVIOUSLY DEAD. He looked to the east and the sun had just risen. He looked back at the body and memorized every feature. No clothes. Hardly a square inch of the body didn't have a bite mark or a visible bruise. The left hand was missing and one side of the mans face was buried in the sand. What little he could see of the face was grotesque-partly because the nose was missing. No blood.

Frank stood and looked at the body and thought about a murder case he had prosecuted back in St. Paul. The coroner had testified bruises only occur when the heart is still pumping. Therefore, this man was first tortured. Bruises are the body's response to injury-blood flows to the damaged tissue to revitalize it. After the beating came the bites and tearing of flesh. The man had been fed to a savage animal. This man suffered a brutal death- even worse than the last one.

Just then Frank heard a car coming and flagged it down. The man had a cell phone and Frank directed him to call 911. After the call, the man got out of the car and looked at the mutilated corpse. He held his hand over his mouth ran across the road and promptly threw up. He stayed on that side of the road until the deputies arrived.

Frank again looked intently at both the bruises and the bite marks. Some of the bite marks had the same pattern as the first murder victim. The skin was not punctured at the site of most of the bruises. Some bruises also had bite marks. He stood on the pavement and visually searched hard for tracks- tire tracks, animal tracks and footprints. Nothing. He peered in the vegetation and saw some old yellow police tape, but that was it.

Frank scanned the other side of the road-everything appeared normal; so he crossed the road and walked over to the very white skinned man. The man's complexion was the color of Michelangelo's great marble statue David. The only trouble was David was solid stone and this man's knees were buckling. Frank put his forearm under the man's arm pit and told him to take three slow deep breaths. Soon the man was able to stand on his own.

Frank's emotions were on the brutality of the murder and the barbarous mentality of the killer. He did not allow himself the luxury of nausea. His career as a prosecutor had hardened him to savage attacks which left a gruesome aftermath. Serious disfigurement was better than death; yet it was a bitter pill to swallow. Early in his career as a prosecutor, he believed that savage attacks were because the person was on drugs or alcohol. But he soon came to realize some people have an executioner's mentality.

Frank was shaken out of his thoughts when he heard the sound of sirens. Finally he saw flashing lights on the top of two marked squad cars which were roaring towards him. The squad cars skidded sideways and stopped in the road blocking traffic. The lights kept flashing, the sirens ceased and the external speakers on a squad let all hear the dispatcher direct personnel to Lovers Key.

The deputies looked at the body and quickly secured the scene. Upon getting Frank's name, the deputy immediately remembered that Frank was the person who found the last murder victim. The deputy went into his car, deactivated the speaker and quickly radioed the dispatcher: "Get Buck out here right away. His witness Johnson has another dead one to his credit."

Even though the speaker wasn't on, Frank heard the deputy and didn't like the way the deputy phrased it. But Frank said nothing.

The deputy then conferred with the other deputy and the shaken 911 caller. After a few minutes, Frank was asked to have a seat in the back of the squad car. As he did, the deputy got in and turned off the squad's two way radio. Frank looked through the cage separating him from the front seat. Looking at the rear view mirror, he could see the deputy's face and it bore the look of distrust. Frank felt something wasn't right and decided to wait for the deputy to talk.

Finally the deputy said: "Buck will be here shortly to take your statement. You can just stay in the car, out of the way, until he arrives."

Frank looked at the inside of each back door- just as he suspected- no door handles. He wasn't getting out unless the deputy let him out. More law enforcement roared upon the scene and the number of flashing lights was like Las Vegas at night. A mobile crime scene van made its way between squad cars and the technicians immediately got busy processing the death scene.

An old man arrived in an old car with a magnetic sign on the door that declared; MEDICAL EXAMINER'S OFFICE. The man got out, put on latex gloves and limped over to the murder victim. After a long look at the body, and photos taken from every angle, he rolled the man over. Frank was startled to now see, for the first time, the man's right hand and arm. The right hand consisted of just the thumb and forefinger. He could now see the entire face. The face had been mauled beyond recognition.

Frank had the eerie feeling someone was watching him. Turning around he saw Buck Thorton looking at him through the window of the side door.

Buck had a concerned look on his face but said nothing. The look he gave Frank turned into an extended stare. Frank stared back and their eyes didn't blink. A silent standoff continued for what seemed to be an eternity to the two combatants.

Frank surmised Buck was more than a bit mystified why he was the one who found two murder victims. Had he concluded he had some connection to the actual murders?

Frank wanted out. He decided to move his lips without saying anything so that Buck would open the door to attempt to hear what was being said.

Buck was puzzled. “What?”

Frank did it again.

Exasperated Buck opened the door, but quickly moved into the opening he had created. Buck now stood over Frank and inside his personal space. Frank knew Buck was using this uncomfortable closeness as a tactic. In a grumpy voice Buck wanted to know what Frank had said.

“Munchausen’s Syndrome”

Buck was too smart to reveal what he was thinking, so he just let the lack of speech flow into a vacuum of silence accompanied by his hostile stare. Even the sound of squad car engines failed to cover up the tense confrontation of silence. Frank wasn’t going to submit to Buck’s domineering stance and he muscled his way up to get out of his tiny back seat cell. Now Frank’s face was in Buck’s chest forcing Buck to back peddle or get power driven backward by Frank’s momentum.

In a testy voice Frank said: “Maybe Munchausen’s Syndrome by Proxy.” He was nose to nose with Buck and felt as if they were inside a tiny tube of tenseness

Buck was waiting for Frank, the witness, to do the talking because the witness might be a suspect. But Buck didn’t want Frank to know that.

Frank was into the same psychology as Buck and let the silence envelop them again. Buck had patience and used it. The setting was curious- a silent standoff at a murder scene, at dawn on a beautiful island. Yet neither was about to give in. It was a test of wills- a silent, mental arm wrestling contest between two potent minds.

Finally Frank said: “That’s what you were thinking about me wasn’t it?”

Buck did not respond to the question even though Frank was right. “Them’s mighty big word’s you’re a spoutin’”

Frank wasn’t sure that Buck knew what he was talking about so he explained: “Munchausen’s Syndrome is an accepted psychological trait. Its main feature is that a person secretly does something very dramatic to put himself in the spot light because the person wants to draw attention to himself."

Buck responded with a noncommittal "Oh?"

Frank continued the lecture: "An example would be a mother suffocates her baby to within an inch of its life, calls 911 and reports that the baby suddenly stopped breathing for no apparent reason. The child would be rushed to the hospital and many people would feel sympathetic towards the mother for all she was going through."

After this explanation, Buck was still noncommittal in his reaction.

Frank asked: "So you were thinking it was more than a mere coincidence that I've discovered two corpses in a short period of time."

"You said it, I didn't." was Buck's third response, which still didn't directly reveal his conclusion.

Frank knew he was no longer being treated as a witness who came upon a crime scene. He anticipated he was going to the sheriff's office for questioning, but he decided it was time for Buck to be put on the spot.

"Well Buck, the facts are *ALMOST* identical to the last time. Last time I didn't get my morning jog in and I get grumpy when I miss it. So why don't you get a statement from the ashen faced 911 caller, I'll do my run and when I get back, you can take my statement."

Frank didn't wait for a response and turned to leave. Changing tactics, Buck was quick to respond: "I'd like to talk to you first."

"Really?" Frank retorted in a mocking tone of voice.

"Yes."

"Usually an investigator first gets every available fact before talking to the suspect to determine if what the suspect says is consistent with the facts which have been gathered up to that point."

"Did someone call you a suspect?" Buck sneered.

Frank was ready for more verbal jousting: "Oh, that's right, the new nomenclature is 'a person of interest'."

Frank turned and started jogging away. Over his shoulder, he yelled to Buck: "Don't worry, I'll be back in forty five minutes and I'll be good and sweaty."

Buck took one step after him, began to open his mouth and stopped both actions. He remembered he knew where Frank lived and it was right next to where both corpses were found.

Forty five minutes later, Frank returned to greet Buck with an overly cheery "I'm back!"

Buck was standing next to a squad car and was perturbed, but it didn't show until he informed Frank: "Baron Munchausen was noted for his verbose exaggerations of his far flung exploits and expeditions back in the 1700's. What made him more notorious was at age 74 he married a 17 year old girl and on his wedding night retired early but without his new bride. She danced into the night with another man. Quickly she became pregnant and when the child was born some felt the son would not live long. Sure enough, within a year, the baby boy died under a veil of suspicious circumstances."

Frank was taken aback. He had underestimated the man. Buck wasn't some hick detective. "Buck, do you think I have some of the same attention seeking traits as the Baron?"

"Well Baron, I mean Mr. Johnson, as a disappearing witness, I think you need a ride to headquarters so we can videotape your statement."

Frank wasn't ready to let Buck call the shots: "I'll take a shower, change clothes and then I'll be back for the free ride you promised."

"It's ok if you stink; cops are used to people who perspire under stressful situations. We have just the limo for you."

Frank concluded it was no coincidence that they were standing next to the same squad car he had escaped out of, with the same deputy reseated behind the wheel. In a flash Frank was again confined to a back seat cell. As the squad left the crime scene, Frank looked out the rear window and Buck was moving his lips without saying anything. Déjà vu.

CHAPTER SEVEN

The room looked too stark for an office. Frank immediately figured out that the mirror he was facing was one way glass. He scanned the ceiling and the upper walls, but couldn't see a camera or a microphone. He sat and waited, figuring he was being watched and recorded.

Finally, Buck appeared and Frank calmly asked if the people on the other side of the mirror thought he looked like a murderer. Buck had no change of expression and didn't answer the question.

"Frank, you know that a trait of some arsonists is that they come back to the fire to watch what happens as firefighters put out the inferno they started."

Frank quickly concluded that Buck was discreetly informing him that he was a suspect. Frank was distressed that the investigation focused on him. He felt it wasn't fair, but he reminded himself of the proverb that life wasn't fair. He decided to taunt Buck: "You know that by happenstance I found two victims and neither died as a result of arson. So your analogy is inaccurate. Why not return to Munchausen's?"

Buck moved in his chair and Frank figured there would be a new plan of attack. He was right.

Buck was an experienced interrogator and understood he wasn't up against a mental midget. "So, is there a correlation between the type of arsonist I just described and a person who is like The Baron?"

"Buck why don't you just take my statement and then decide if I can walk out of here?"

"You're here as a witness. The reason you received a ride down here is that it appears you want everything your way. If you decide to be uncooperative and not show up at a trial, we may be able to use this videotaped statement. I'm concerned you might get mad and not show up at a hearing."

"Get a grip, Buck. No judge is going to allow this statement to be introduced at a trial for murder when there has been no cross examination by a lawyer for the defendant. The only way it would be admitted is if I was on trial for these murders. You're trying to dance around the problem of whether I'm a suspect or a witness."

Buck was evasive: "Why do you say that?"

"If you read me the Miranda Warning, I'm obviously a suspect. That can be trouble when you find the murderer because you would have to admit, the first suspect was me."

Buck testily replied: "You're the one who's concerned about being a suspect."

Frank was determined to continue the war of wills with Buck. "Good. I will write out a brief statement, then I'll read it to the cameras and attempt to leave."

Buck knew it was time to make the call. "You're a witness. You're not under arrest. You're free to go once you give a statement in any format you choose. Any problem with that?"

"No."

"Let's start with some background. After the first murder you gave me some information about yourself. I want to follow up on it. Why'd you leave the prosecutor's office up in St. Paul?"

"I got burned out and decided to be a ski vagabond."

"You weren't fired?"

Frank's puzzled expression was the first time during the interrogation that he changed from a poker face. "Why would you think I was fired?"

Buck got right to the point: "I called up to St. Paul, Minnesota and talked to the personnel people. They said that you had tried to resign, but were fired on your last day because of insubordination. You charged a juror with perjury because she was the jury foreperson on a trial that found the accused was innocent."

"Nonsense. Check the records and you will see she was convicted of perjury. In fact, two persons on that jury were convicted of perjury and I charged both of them."

"You're not denying that it's very newsworthy that a juror is charged with perjury?"

"It's unusual." Frank replied.

"Two jurors, in one case? How rare is that? Do you know of any other case?" Buck retorted sarcastically.

"No."

Buck was on a roll: "Ski vagabond. Most people would refer to that profession as a ski bum."

"Yes."

"My information is you lasted at that profession for one ski season."

"Yes."

"Any other murder cases where you were a witness?"

"Two."

Buck's stoic demeanor changed to high drama: "***TWO***?"

"Two." Frank replied in a monotone voice as he thought this line of questioning could look incriminating.

"Both in the same location and about the same time?"

"No. One in St. Paul where I worked and one in Steamboat."

Buck jumped on this new information. "The very first time I interviewed you, didn't you say you met the woman you are living with in Steamboat?"

"Yes."

"Was she around when the murder occurred?"

Frank didn't like where this was heading but gave no obvious sign of agitation. "She was in Steamboat, but was not a witness."

"Two jurors, two murders elsewhere, two murders here. No pattern that I see." Buck summarized mockingly.

"Coincidence."

Buck wasn't letting up. "All cases made the news and I would bet it wasn't just a couple of sentences buried in the back of the newspaper."

"Correct." Frank refused to squirm at the implication that he liked to be in the media spotlight.

"The first murder was in St. Paul and you left there."

"Yes"

"The second murder was in Steamboat and you left there."

"Yes."

"The third and fourth murders are on Lover's Key. Thank goodness, the one and out pattern has ended."

Frank was boiling on the inside, but there was no external clue to his feelings. He decided to let Buck continue.

"Serial killer Ted Bundy killed in Colorado."

No response by Frank.

"He killed in Florida"

No response.

"He killed elsewhere.'

No response

"You and Ted are both lawyers."

Frank knew Buck was targeting him for an emotional outburst, but Buck wasn't going to get it. Frank decided to take control: "The murder in Minnesota was investigated by Lt. Anderson Granderson. The dead body was found by a neighbor moments after it occurred. The Steamboat murder victim was found by the girlfriend of the deceased. Contact Sheriff Moffat about that one. Both of these law enforcement people will tell you I didn't find the bodies and I wasn't a suspect. Rather, because of my experience as a prosecutor, I was a resource each used to help solve the murders."

Buck continued: "The mark of a good con man is that the guy appears to cooperate. By the way, did your girlfriend see either of the murder victims on the road?"

Frank calmly replied: "She is not my girlfriend. She is the daughter of my boss. As far as I know, she has not seen either victim. Ask her."

"Tell me about the man on the road."

"I think I have a lead as to the identity of the victim." Frank said.

"Oh?" Buck made his response sound as if he was curious, but he was more than curious. The Mr. Munchausen was about to reveal a connection to the victim- it wasn't looking like a happenstance discovery of the body.

Frank replied: "Angeline, her mother and I went to an antiquities exhibit in Ft. Lauderdale. We were in line to view the Pearl of Tao when two men got in a nasty fight with security. The security officer was stabbed with a big knife. The victim went to the hospital. I stood by, but was never identified as a witness. But, one of the attackers had only part of his right hand- just like the dead man here. Anyhow, the man was arrested so there should be fingerprints over in Ft. Lauderdale to match up with the deceased. As long as the Chief Medical Examiner doesn't need ten fingerprints for a positive ID."

"How long ago was this? Give me the exact location."

Frank wasn't sure if Buck believed the story, but he surely wanted the information. "The Museum of Art in Ft. Lauderdale and it was just days ago."

Buck was silent and then asked: "If the man was arrested, why would he be dead on Lovers Key rather than in a jail cell in Ft. Lauderdale?"

"Bail. People get out on bail awaiting trial. Check it out. If you want me to be part of the investigation rather than a suspect, I'll check it out for you." Frank curtly replied.

Buck retained his composure, but he wasn't captivated by Frank's attitude. "Frank, tell me if you think someone at the fight would have a motive to kill the guy and dump him at your doorstep so you have more publicity."

"Buck, I'm not happy I'm a suspect, but to answer your question, in the history of mankind, more wars have been started over religion than over political issues….More background for you." Frank intentionally stopped short of answering the question and waited.

"I'm glad to learn that historical fact, but who in this Ft. Lauderdale skirmish has a motive to brutally kill over religious differences?"

Frank took ten minutes to explain the conflict over The Pearl, but declined to name any of the people present in the art museum as a possible perpetrator of murder.

Buck listened and kept looking over his shoulder at the one way mirror. Buck pondered all that Frank had told him and contemplated whether to let him go. Stalling for time, he asked Frank about his religious preference and learned Frank was a multidimensional

Christian. After a few minutes of questioning about what was a multidimensional Christian, Buck figured out that Frank didn't go to church much, but when he did, he didn't care about the denomination of the Christian church.

Buck got the interrogation back on track: "Frank, the information you gave me could be helpful in identifying the deceased, but if you're right, it makes an analytical person think it is more than mere happenstance that the body ended up at your doorstep."

Frank was done. "I've told you all I know. I'm leaving."

Before Frank could get up, Buck changed tactics and dialect: "Yer as skittish as a wild hog in the Everglades. Sit for a minute. My Captain told me to git your blood pressure shootin up liken a rocket and then tell ya, he ordered it."

"Your Captain is listening in on our conversation on the other side of the mirror so I'll tell him your change of tactics is ineffectual and insulting. Now I'm going to tell you both how to investigate these murders. First, eliminate me as a suspect. Second, don't narrow the focus only to the people involved in the stabbing in Ft Lauderdale. Third, use intelligence already gathered by law enforcement. Specifically look into whether the torture and taking of blood is consistent with actions taken by a cult. Contact other police agencies to find out if their undercover intelligence has revealed a cult that is into bloodletting and torture. They're known as vampires"

Both Buck and Frank looked at the mirror. Frank was still agitated as he headed towards the door; Buck tried to appease him by saying:" Maybe we could call Lt. Granderson. Could be he wants an invitation to Lovers Key."

Frank faked a smile and was still disconcerted. He stopped and challenged Buck: "Call Granderson right now so we can both talk to him."

Buck agreed and Frank sat back down. Granderson answered his cell phone with a gruff voice, but softened when he heard who was calling. Granderson was direct: "Frank is a good guy and there's no way he'd commit a murder for publicity or for any other reason. He was a big help in solving a high profile case I worked. If you need an expert about DNA, Frank is it."

Buck showed no reaction and remained quiet.

Granderson cheerfully continued: "If you pay to fly me down there and live on the beach for a week, I'll give you all the background you need on Frank."

Frank issued an open invitation to Granderson and his wife. As the conversation ended, Frank looked at Buck, but got no sense that Buck was impressed or was eliminating him as a suspect.

Buck showed him the way out and beyond the range of the recorders told Frank he appreciated his cooperation. Frank wondered about the psychology involved in that statement.

Buck's parting words were: "You told me you were a ski bum. Yet there's no snow skiing here in Florida."

Over his shoulder, Frank let loose with a parting salvo: "Who said I didn't water ski?"

CHAPTER EIGHT

Buck and his fellow investigators sat in the conference room discussing the interview. Buck's supervisor, Captain Merrill Mastif shook his head and wondered out loud where they were headed. He then directly addressed the group of investigators seated around him: "The media's first questions are going to be 'Are the death's related? Why haven't you identified the first victim?' Ya'll know that we don't have a decent answer to either of those questions. Get working and get me some answers!"

As the group broke up, the Captain told Buck to stay so the two could join the public information officer to decide on an official statement to release. Mastif joked that more scalp would be showing through the Sheriff's thinning hair once he was told of another corpse found on pristine Lovers Key.

Mastif grunted: "Buck, what physical evidence do we have from the scene and the bodies?"

"None."

"That tells me we're not dealing with an amateur. The killer makes it difficult to identify the victim and that slows us down."

Buck nodded: "More importantly, we have no trace evidence from the killer. In almost every case the killer leaves something-blood or hair or the murder weapon. We've got zilch. The murderer is extremely smart and calculating."

The Captain turned to the subject of a press release: "The official version of the first death was that the person was killed by a bear. If we say this is another animal attack, the media will be asking *could* it be a second bear attack? If the Sheriff's Office says it could, media interest would spring higher than an Olympic pole-vaulter."

The Captain and Buck knew that the investigation wasn't focused on hunting down a man eating bear on Lovers Key; they had to uncover who was directing an animal to ferociously attack and kill. Were both attacks committed by the same animal? What was the animal?"

Meanwhile, Frank was again in the back seat of a marked squad car heading back to Lovers Key. Much to his chagrin, he was again in a mobile prison cell. After a half hour ride, he was let out in the driveway of the estate on Lovers Key. Angeline heard the car pull up and looked out the window.

She had been worried as Frank had not appeared for breakfast and he was not working in his cottage. Now she was shocked to see him let out of the back seat by a uniformed deputy. She looked for handcuffs on his wrists, but thankfully saw none. She rushed outside as the squad car backed out.

"Frank! What's going on? I was worried when I heard sirens this morning. Then I couldn't find you. I'm upset, it's long past noon."

"Is your mother around?"

"Why?"

"I need to talk to you before I talk to her."

Angeline looked perplexed and Frank steered her back down the driveway. When they were out of sight of the main house, Frank said: "I found another dead body on the road this morning."

"OH MY! So that's what those sirens were about that woke me up this morning."

"Yes. This murder victim looked even worse than the first one. It was gruesome."

Angeline's tan face turned pale and she moved up against Frank to be enveloped by the security of his strong persona. "What's going on around here? This has always been a beautiful, tranquil place. I don't know how there can be two murders here in a matter of days."

Frank put his arms around her hoping to smooth her jagged nerves: "Calm down. The body was dumped here. The murder took place elsewhere. I think the body was dumped here because it's so remote."

Angeline trembled in Frank's arms and sputtered: "This'll have a major impact on my mother. How do we keep this from her?"

"I don't know that we can. It'll be on the news and even if we shield her from the news, her friends will ask her about it. I know the term 'dreadful' will be repeatedly used by her bridge club."

Angeline then needed to know all the details. Frank was candid with her even though she gasped for air on a couple of occasions. They went inside to gently inform Monique that the victim of a savage murder was again dumped near her idyllic retreat. They found her on the patio watching the dolphins play in the sun- flecked sapphire waters.

Monique looked at Frank and said:" Sit with me and watch the dolphins play. I've been transfixed as a baby dolphin is glued to its mother."

They all sat and watched as the dolphins gave a performance only matched by their relatives at Sea World. Finally, Frank broke the serenity: "Monique, have you recovered from our day to view the Chinese antiquities over at Ft. Lauderdale?"

"The exhibit was enchanting; but I was wet and the wine didn't agree with me."

Angeline asked: "Did the brutality at The Pearl of Tao bother you?"

"Gracious yes. Those men should have respected that they were around works of art and needed to act accordingly."

Out of Monique's view, Frank and Angeline looked at each other-sharing an anxious look. Frank decided to start: "Monique, I've got troubling news."

"Oh?"

"Yes. Someone dumped a body beside the road and I found the corpse this morning."

Monique gasped, trembled and then seemed to hold her breath. Angeline was petrified at the reaction, but finally jumped to her feet in a tardy attempt to console her mother. The sudden movement startled Monique and her exhale came out as a garbled scream.

Angeline jumped back. Immediately, Frank decided he must control the situation: "Ladies, we're all safe and this crime had nothing to do with us. Take a deep breath and remember that you're safe."

Monique's color was gray and her hands flipped around like mullets escaping a tarpon. She could barely whisper: "Someone at the estate will be the next target of these shark like savages."

She frantically tried to breathe, but she could only accomplish a series of short breaths; the terror which encompassed her body then took her breath away. When she finally caught her breath, she shrieked: "We have no security! We could all be wiped out in an instant! We are more likely to be in the crosshairs of a snipers rifle than the President of the United States! Frank, get the Secret Service here before dark! We deserve protection!"

Monique had emptied her lungs of air and her brain of thoughts as her body quivered. Angeline liked the idea of Secret Service protection until Frank told them that it didn't fall within their sphere of guardianship.

Monique's lungs reinflated: "Well get the sheriff's deputies out here instantly! We need an assemblage of armed guards 24/7. Frank you were a prosecutor. Get them to protect their star witness. Isn't this what the witness protection program is all about?"

Frank wanted to direct her thoughts to reasonable alternatives: "The deputies won't come here because the investigator thinks I'm a suspect."

Frank instantly knew he shouldn't have uttered that phrase. Monique's eyes became the size of craters and a death rattle wheezed from her lungs. Her body turned rigid as her lips moved without a sound flowing out. Her eyes closed and her gray complexion drained even lower.

Shaken, Angeline grabbed her and tried to decide if the Heimlich maneuver was appropriate or did her mother need CPR? In this time of crisis, those two things confused her.

Angeline was now trying to separate her mother from the chair. Monique was so stiff that it was as if rigor-mortis had set in. Angeline exclaimed that she had to get her mother to start breathing again. Frank took control by lifting Monique out of the chair and onto the cool tile floor. In less than a minute, Monique was breathing. Her eyes opened slowly at first, but then returned to watermelon size when she realized Frank was inches from her face, checking on her condition.

Startled, she could barely draw enough breath to excitedly whisper: “Frank, what are you doing?”

Angeline was relieved and Frank disguised a smirk. After a rest, and a glass of lemonade, Monique was as lucid as she could be. The discussion returned to dealing with the aftermath of finding the corpse beside the estate. Monique insisted on hiring armed private security for the grounds of the estate. She directed Frank to decide what she should say to her bridge club. She was determined that she would not allow a couple of corpses to bring down the solid reputation of Lovers Key

As Angeline had watched this whole episode, she recognized that she yearned for Frank to be close to her for the protection and safety he gave her. She must convince him to take more interest in her because she needed his protection. Security guards might not be ever vigilant. Through this, she hoped that somehow they would become the idyllic pair of her nightly vision.

Frank said he would contact security companies and come up with a plan. He said he would never let anything happen to the ladies of Lovers Key.

Buck and the Captain agreed that they needed quick progress on solving the two murders. They anticipated that the media would grow weary of the term bear attacks and report that investigators believed that the bear was under the control of a person who trained it to kill. Then the term serial killers would spring up with the media. Mastif reminded Buck that if they could prove the murders happened outside their jurisdiction, they could downplay the perception that a serial killer was roaming the local streets.

Captain Mastif sat by as Buck called the medical examiner’s office and talked to the old guy who came to the crime scene. Buck was upset when the old guy said that he did everything by the book and he didn’t release information. Only the Chief Medical Examiner released information. He proudly declared that he had lasted this long because he never leaked information. Buck gave up and called the deputies at the scene. No one had paid much attention to the right hand. They remembered how grotesque the body looked and that the left hand was missing.

Still, Buck felt that Frank's tip regarding the man's identity needed to be checked out. It was standard procedure that while being booked into a jail, a significant amount of data was recorded including all tattoos and deformities. He called the Broward County Jail and asked the records clerk to search their booking records to find a man who was booked with part of his right hand missing. The woman on the other end said she was busy but would get back to him.

After waiting an hour Buck called her back and again explained: "This is a priority. We have a dead man we are trying to identify. He isn't just dead; he was murdered elsewhere and dumped in our jurisdiction. This is the second body in a week. It just might be that our current victim was murdered in your county. Same for the last one. If so, then you have a serial murderer on your hands. We don't have one here- *YOU* have one! I just might tell the media that in a few minutes. So get this done fast."

There was a pause on the other end. The woman started asking Buck for the same information he gave her during the first conversation. Buck was not impressed, but didn't comment. He repeated the information. The phone call ended with a reluctant consent by the woman that she would check into this and call back within an hour.

After the allotted time, Buck was still waiting. He decided to call Gustavo Lucas, an investigator he knew in the Broward County Sheriff's Office. Gustavo offered to go to jail records to investigate. An hour later, Gustavo called back and said they checked booking sheets and could find no record of a recent arrest of a man missing fingers on his right hand. They had plenty of men arrested who had tattoos. Buck thanked Gustavo and hung up.

After discussion of this information, Buck and the Captain were dismayed over what they believed was a lie that Frank had told them- that Frank knew the victim had been arrested for a stabbing. They were perplexed- why Frank would tell a story that could be so easily disproved? Frank was now less likely to be an innocent witness; rather he was somehow linked to these savage deaths. They decided they needed to know more about Frank so they called Lieutenant Anderson Granderson.

"Granderson here"

"This is Investigator Buck Thorton again from Lee County. We'd like to talk to you some more about Franklin Johnson."

"What's Frank got you so stirred up about? He's pretty intense, but I think that's good in a prosecutor."

"Well, I've got my Captain here beside me and we're just baffled about Frank."

"He's a unique guy; he loves to teach cops about the law. He knows it well. I used to have his home number on my cell phone speed dial. I'd call him in the middle of the night if I had a legal question."

Captain Mastif and Buck exchanged quizzical looks and Buck asked: "Do you think he would try to send law enforcement in the wrong direction?"

"That question makes me think you have a problem with Frank. My experience has been that he's as honest as they come."

"Why did he get fired up there in St. Paul?"

"He didn't. I don't know where you're getting that information. He gave about a month notice and headed west. As best I can tell, he made up the term ski vagabond to sweeten up the fact that he was a ski bum. He went out in a blaze of publicity because during the last few hours of his employment, he charged two jurors with perjury. It was very newsworthy because the jurors had been on a high profile case."

Concern etched the faces of Captain Mastif and Buck as they echoed "Oh?" into the speaker phone.

Granderson continued: "Frank had a lot of high profile cases. He said he got burned out." Granderson paused and then asked: "Anything else?"

"No."

"Well, I'd gladly come down to give you more background- if you foot the bill. I'm sure it's warmer there on the beach than up here."

"Thanks Lieutenant. If we need more info we'll send an airline ticket."

After hanging up, the Captain told Buck: "I think you're going to have a luncheon buffet with Frank. You'll be serving up a helping of interrogation and the sauce on the platter can be served up either sweet or sour!"

CHAPTER NINE

Frank stood outside his cottage in the predawn light and stretched. He was just about to start down the driveway and to the road when he changed his mind. He decided to jog on the beach as he didn't want to find another dead body. He wasn't going onto the road during the early morning until Buck told him they had a suspect and it wasn't him.

The clouds over the Gulf of Mexico were a light pink and a half dozen pelicans flew by. Their extended wings were motionless as they glided just above the water. It was eerie how the pelicans kept an imperceptible space between their wing tips and the calm water. Frank relaxed as he started out jogging and soon was in a smooth running rhythm. There was no one on the beach and he contemplated his luck to be in such a beautiful place. An osprey squawked overhead then dove into the water and flew off with a small sea trout. Frank marveled at the variety of wildlife and how they let humans get so close. He ran his normal pace and tried to let his mind be worry free.

On his return run he picked up the pace. Breathing hard, Frank sprinted the last one hundred yards and stopped near the patio of the main house. He picked up the newspaper sitting on the patio table and saw the headline:

ANOTHER FATAL ANIMAL ATTACK ON LOVERS KEY

Just after dawn, another person was found dead beside the road on the tranquil island of Lovers Key. Less than a week ago, a victim of a fatal bear attack was found in the same location. The most recent victim has yet to be identified and the Lee County Sheriffs

Office stated that there was significant trauma to the deceased. When asked if this was another bear attack, they said it was too early to tell if this was another bear attack, but some type of animal was involved. They were awaiting autopsy results. The Medical Examiners Office stated they had no information to release.

A Florida Fish and Wildlife Commission spokeswoman said they continued to doubt that a bear large enough to kill an adult could be on such a small barrier island without being spotted. She said they would send staff to the island to look for signs of a bear. She also offered their assistance to law enforcement in the investigation.

A confidential source close to the investigation states that they have a person of interest who is connected to both deaths and they will be exploring that person further. Investigator Buck Thorton officially denied they had a suspect or person of interest. Thorton asked for the publics help in identifying both victims….

Frank threw down the paper without finishing the article. He was enraged and stomped off to his cottage. Still dripping sweat from his jog, he pulled out Buck's business card and called him.

"Good morning Frank." Buck said in an unusually cheery voice.

"YOU'RE A JERK!!"

"Frank, is that any way to start a conversation?"

"Why are you calling me a person of interest?"

"What are you talking about Frank?"

"Don't play dumb with me! The newspaper quotes an unnamed source saying you have a person of interest."

"So? That doesn't mean I'm the source."

"The article says you "officially" denied it. That tells me you are the source. The paper didn't need to use the word "officially" unless you were talking to them off the record about me."

"The story doesn't name you." Buck said defensively.

"I tell you how to ID the victim and you turn on me! That's a cheap shot!"

"Let's sit down and talk, so we can clear the air. Come on down to the sheriffs office, I have some information I can't give you over the phone. If you need a ride, I'll send a squad."

"Forget it. I'm sure you'll have the media there ready to film me."

"OK, I'll come to your place in my unmarked, government issue car and I promise there'll be no media."

"You think I'm that dumb?"

"Frank, you need to trust me."

"No, I don't."

"You're an important person in these two cases. We need to understand each other."

Frank was reticent to endorse Buck's charisma: "I'm skeptical. But two people have been murdered and I don't believe the Chief Medical Examiner has a clue how they were killed."

"Help us out Frank."

"OK, come over in an hour-alone. Don't even think of alerting the media. If I see anyone lurking around I won't answer the door."

Frank hung up and wondered if he was being set up. For the first time in his life, he wondered if he should have a lawyer. Then he thought how strange that would be- an experienced prosecutor needing a lawyer to handle the legal issues of being a witness. The sweat continued to roll off him and it wasn't just because of his jog. This was infuriating. They had no evidence he was involved. In fact, they probably had no physical evidence. So they would put together a case based on circumstantial evidence. He decided he'd keep his guard up.

As scheduled, Buck appeared, alone. They sat at Frank's kitchen table and Buck launched in: "Frank, I appreciate the lead you gave me to ID the victim."

"I want to help."

"I told you I had information for you. Unfortunately, it's bad news. I called over to Ft. Lauderdale to check the Broward County jail records. They couldn't find any record of a man having been booked in there recently with a deformed right hand."

"What? That's impossible. There must be a foul up somewhere. I'm sure they hauled the two men off to jail"

"I'm afraid there's no foul up. I know an investigator over there and he personally went to check the jail records. Frank, I need to know more about your involvement with all of this."

"All of this? What do you mean? The assault in Ft. Lauderdale?"

"Everything. The bodies on Lover's Key; this supposed assault-everything."

"Whoa! This sounds like I'm a suspect- just like yesterday."

Buck paused and looked out the window. The conversation stopped. His gaze returned to Frank and he encountered the steely eyed stare that Frank reserved for adverse witnesses on cross examination. Buck moved uncomfortably in his chair. He wasn't in the familiar territory of the Sheriff's interrogation room.

Frank decided to take charge: "Buck, you can spend all the time you want investigating me, but I had nothing to do with any of this. I'm a witness. Call the investigator and have him find the mug shots of the people arrested in the stabbing at The Museum of Art. One has to be the corpse I just found. Check that booking record and you've ID'd the murder victim."

"OK, let's go back to my office; I'll call over to Broward. If they can find the mug shots then I'll have them faxed over and you can identify the guy you found."

Frank smelled a trap. He wasn't going to go to the Sheriff's Office again. "I can just see the run around and grilling I'll get when I end up in the interrogation room again. No way am I going back to your Gestapo Room. I'll drive both of us to Ft. Lauderdale and we'll get to the bottom of this, together."

"I don't know if that's appropriate." Buck mumbled.

"Well I do. Remember that the murder victim's face was badly mauled. He was missing a nose. I can't say who that guy is. If we get information from the jail in Ft. Lauderdale, we'll get fingerprints to match up to the corpse."

Buck shook his head: "This isn't protocol."

"You want my help, but you keep putting me in the category of a suspect. If you want me to believe I'm not a suspect, go with me to straighten this out. I know the two were not warned and released-persons are jailed when a victim is seriously wounded."

"OK. I'll call my friend Gustavo as we drive over there."

By the time they got across Alligator Alley, Gustavo had cleared the way with the jail staff at Broward County to assemble all the mug shots taken the day of the stabbing. Frank looked at all of them and picked out the pictures of Haquan and Faroque as the two involved in the Pearl of Tao assault. He remembered Haquan as the man with three missing fingers on his right hand.

Frank asked Gustavo if they could pull the booking sheets and fingerprint cards on both of them. Gustavo gave a questioning look at Buck and Buck said: "We drove all the way over here to get this straightened out. I want to be sure of this."

In a few minutes the fingerprint cards were pulled and sure enough, Haquan's didn't have fingerprints for three fingers on the right hand; the card noted "fingers missing"

Frank felt he had been proven right and emphatically declared: "Trust me. Everything I have told you is accurate. I'm an asset to you not a person of interest."

Buck commented that they still hadn't determined that this was the deceased. When the booking sheets were brought in, the physical data matched Haquan. Gustavo pointed out that under "identifying characteristics (tattoos, deformities)" the space was blank. Someone had messed up.

Buck was about to speak, but Frank was first: "Buck, you've got to trust me, this is the deceased. Look at the height, weight, age, hair color, eye color, missing fingers. This certainly is the guy. Get a copy of the fingerprint card to bring back with us and have the medical examiner print the deceased. Your staff can then do a comparison for a positive ID. Let's go."

"Not so fast." Buck said.

"What?"

"How do we know he's not still in jail? If he's out, has he been reported missing?"

Gustavo checked jail records. Haquan had posted bailed and been released. Gustavo checked and found he had not been reported missing. Buck said he was still skeptical that this was the deceased because Haquan had not been reported missing.

Frank looked at Gustavo and asked: "What did you check?"

"Sunrise."

"You checked to see if he had been reported missing since sunrise? That's a pretty limited check."

Gustavo laughed and said: "No, the City of Sunrise. It's west of here. Haquan's home address is in Sunrise."

"Ok. Let's call his home and find out."

"No phone listed and looking at his sidekick's sheet, he has the same address and no phone." Gustavo said.

Frank was determined to be vindicated: "Let's go there and check it out. How far away is it?"

Gustavo replied: "Less than ten miles west of here and just a little off Alligator Alley"

"Get the fingerprint card and write down the address. We're heading out."

Buck had no excuse to decline the stop. It was on the way back and it could give them some useful information.

As Frank drove, he noticed Buck was quiet and appeared to be deep in thought. Frank believed Buck still had him on the "A" list of suspects. Upon further reflection-indisputably the only suspect.

"Buck, you're deep in thought. I bet you're trying to decide if my uncovering the identity of the deceased makes me more of a suspect because it confirms your thesis that I'm in this for the glory?"

"Yup."

CHAPTER TEN

Frank pulled his Mustang into the apartment complex and as usual, the classic Mustang convertible made heads swivel. The complex was lush with palms and tropical plantings. There were about six buildings that appeared only a few years old; it was more upscale than he expected. They easily found the third floor apartment and knocked on the door. A waiting game ensued- knocking, waiting. Buck commented that sometimes people would answer the door after five minutes because they surmised he wasn't leaving. Unfortunately, there was no sound coming from within. Buck and Frank exchanged a nonverbal acknowledgement of no response to their inquiry and strolled down to the lawn to look up at the windows. They discovered that every blind was closed. The next destination was the rental office located by the swimming pool.

Upon being introduced to the manager, Buck decided to take charge: "I'm Investigator Thorton of the Lee County Sheriff's Office. We're looking for Haquan and Faroque. We checked their apartment, but got no answer. Could you help us out?"

A concerned look came over the manager's face and he asked to see identification. Buck pulled out his credentials and the manger gave it a long look.

"Are they in more trouble?" the manager asked.

"Why do you say *more* trouble?" Buck queried.

"Because I read in the newspaper they were arrested for a stabbing."

The question remained unanswered as Frank joined in: "When is the last time you saw either of them?"

"The day before the stabbing."

"Who lives with them?" asked Frank.

"Their wives and a total of three young children."

In a stern voice, Buck declared he was in charge and wanted to know when was the last time any family members were seen. The manager revealed that Marvin, the maintenance man, told him yesterday morning that the two women and the three children drove off the evening before in their car. The car was packed to overflowing with suitcases and other personal items. They even had boxes tied on the roof.

Buck was told that all seven lived in one apartment and they had only one car. In a series of non intrusive questions, Buck was able to get the manager to divulge that they had a number of months left on the lease and they were paid up through the end of the month. When asked if they were U.S. citizens, he said they had valid passports from Pakistan and had green cards for work. However, the manager was not willing to let either Buck or Frank into the vacated apartment with his master key or disclose if they created problems around the apartment complex.

Frank and Buck were granted permission to walk around the grounds and they kept searching until they discovered the maintenance man. Marvin was eager to talk about Faroque and Haquan – two men that he didn't get along with.

Marvin said that after the two bailed out of jail, he did not see them around the apartment complex. However, other tenants said they saw the two men. As best he could tell, neither man had a job as they came and went whenever they wanted. He asked them about employment and they never gave a straight answer. Marvin figured them as troublemakers along with their friend Akbar who lived in the next building. Marvin believed Akbar was also from Pakistan.

Frank boldly inquired: "So Marvin, any problem with us tagging along as you recharge the faulty air conditioning in Faroque and Haquan's apartment?"

"I didn't get a repair order…" Marvin stopped in mid sentence and then figured out what the two were up to. "I'll go into the apartment to see why the air hasn't been running lately. I can't let other people in, I'd lose my job."

'The complex wouldn't want mold and mildew to form in there." Frank surmised.

"Yup. I'll keep my eyes open for mold and mildew and other things."

Frank added: "Look to see if there are personal hygiene items still there. You know, just get a feel if they have left for awhile."

Marvin told them to stay put and he disappeared for about ten minutes. Excitedly he informed them that it looked like they had pretty much cleaned out all of their stuff from the furnished apartment.

Never one to give up, Frank asked if Akbar's air conditioning might also be defective. Marvin shook his head and said once was enough. After a pause, Marvin added that Akbar lived on the first floor and anyone could quickly look in the windows when he wasn't around. Marvin then pointed out the apartment and ambled off in the opposite direction.

They stood for a minute: waiting for the neighbors to grow tired of watching them do nothing. Finally, they walked over to Akbar's apartment. The blinds were only partially closed and as they stood camouflaged by the prolific landscaping, they could see that the apartment looked vacant. They looked past the jungle like vegetation to see who was watching them, and there wasn't a person in sight.

Buck's body language indicated a certain amount of uneasiness. Frank wondered out loud if anyone around the pool might have some useful information and Buck said it was time to motor back to Lee County.

As they drove with the top down, Frank turned off the radio as the old classic song "Let it be" ended. "Well Buck, we got some useful information today. I bet that whoever murdered Haquan, threatened the families and they are in hiding or have fled the country.

Buck looked disturbed and said: "I don't think the search of the apartments was legal."

"It was perfectly legal."

"We didn't have a search warrant."

"Don't need one."

Buck looked at Frank: "Well hot shot prosecutor, I've had a lot of training and I know that if I can't conduct a search then I can't get around that by directing someone else to do the search."

"Correct. But I was the one who asked Marvin to check out the apartment. I'm not a cop- I'm a private citizen - a witness in fact. The Constitution prohibits unreasonable searches by the government. So no evidence will be tossed out because I'm the one who asked Marvin to go in."

"That was no accidental glance through Akbar's windows."

"Don't worry. In the late 1990's the U.S. Supreme Court OK'd cops looking in ground floor windows. It was a case out of Minnesota."

"Your buddy Granderson was right. You do know the law."

"Maybe you should put my phone number on your speed dial too."

"Maybe I shouldn't. Maybe you're still a suspect and I don't want to be accused of harassing you."

Frank turned red, and then put on a CD of Alan Jackson- for Buck's benefit. They both enjoyed the music and the scenery as they again cruised Alligator Alley. Music, scenery and wind made the need for conversation de minimus.

Buck departed Lovers Key and headed to the medical examiner's office, knowing it was time for a confrontation with the Chief Medical Examiner. Luckily, she was in and agreed to meet with him. Buck showed her the finger print card from Broward County and she gave him a card with the fingerprints her office had taken from the latest victim.

Buck was ready to descend into the inferno called challenging the expert- especially this expert: "Doctor, I have some concerns about the animal or animals that killed these two men."

"*KILLED?*"

"Doctor, they're obviously dead."

"I have not completed an autopsy report on the second man; do not try to usurp my authority over determining the cause of death. I make that call; you do not! Understood? I have not determined if he was beaten to death first and then the animal attacked him after he was dead."

"Reckon y'all should know that I is just in from the 'glades and ain't schooled like y'all. My mammy done switched me a few times 'cause I didn't say sir or ma'am. I mean no disrespect Doctor." Buck paused and changed dialect: "I apparently needed to differentiate between pre and post mortem injuries, which may or may not have been the primary cause of death."

Her face became instantly crimson and her tongue was sharp as saw grass: "Don't mock me Investigator Thorton! Don't mock the office that I hold! Your pseudo hillbilly or cracker talk is meant to insult me and does nothing to resolve very difficult autopsy conclusions which I will have to make. I *am* awaiting an apology."

Buck remained silent and the longer the stillness remained, the more intense the stress. Buck stared at her in silence. He had grown weary of excessive deference to a combative eccentric. His muteness lasted longer than the time it takes for a pro football instant replay decision. The Doctor's glare was as sharp as her scalpel. Finally, he turned to leave.

"Where are you going?"

"You won't talk to me. So I believe our egos have won out over rational dialogue."

"Didn't you hear me? I'm awaiting an apology."

"Didn't my silence cause you to draw a conclusion?"

"Well! Let's move on. What do you want to know?"

Buck paused for effect and to let the tension surrender to borderline normal. "I would like to talk with you about the types of animals which could have inflicted the injuries on the man missing three digits of his right hand. I would also like to know what types of animals you considered and rejected as having caused the death of the other man."

"I don't have time to educate you on all of this. Make an appointment and if I have time, I will explain it all to you." The Doctor then pompously exited.

Buck decided it was time for a cold one- or maybe more than one.

CHAPTER ELEVEN

Frank sat in his cottage cultivating a psychological strategy so he could instill a willingness in Buck to see him as a good guy-not as a person with a penchant for murder. Buck would be difficult to persuade. Luring him into such a mind set would require subtle enticement. Frank's mental meanderings ended when there was a knock on his door.

It was Angeline, accompanied by her curiosity: she wanted to know where he had been with Buck for the better part of the day. Frank gave a glamorous rendition of the events; making sure he cloaked himself in the robe of a Sherlock Holmes. Angeline was enthralled. When the saga ended, she invited him to join her and Monique for dinner on the patio for grilled salmon with a peppercorn/teriyaki marinade. Frank required no further persuasion.

They dined waterside on the patio, the salmon was done to perfection and the marinade made it taste like it came from heaven. They enjoyed a dazzling sunset as they finished off the meal with coconut cream pie. The colors of the scattered, light, fluffy clouds were resplendent and the sky upon which they were staged made their hearts move. Angeline looked at Frank's wind blown hair and proposed they walk on the beach. Monique begged off, saying she had to talk to some friends about Frank's recitation of the updated murder investigation.

Angeline grabbed his hand and pulled him towards the beach. As they walked, the waves lapped at the shore and the clouds had turned tangerine after the sun was swallowed up by the water.

"Frank, what could be more romantic than walking on the beach?"

"An excellent rhetorical question."

"Frank, just enjoy the moment and don't answer my rhetorical questions." Angeline moved closer to him and tenderly put her arm around his waist.

After a few steps, she stopped and faced him. Their eyes locked and Angeline felt the power of his presence. She didn't want to move- she had been waiting for this moment. She yearned for a more romantic result than when they had been at The Turtle Club. They embraced, neither one being sure who initiated the tenderness.

She whispered to him; their lips almost touching: "Enjoy the beauty of the beach and being with me tonight. I guarantee it will be the start of something great."

Frank continued to look into her eyes. No one would question her beauty, but his heart wasn't hers. "Angeline, you're a gorgeous woman with talent galore. If I had met you before Stephanie, I'm sure a relationship would have developed. I know there's chemistry between us. Even though Stephanie and I are over a thousand miles apart, I miss her more than ever."

Angeline's eyes revealed the hurt she felt in her soul and she sought some kindness from Frank: "You were there for me when I got injured snowboarding at Steamboat. I thought you really cared for me. Then you came down here to Lovers Key. I was sure the reason you came was to explore how great we could be together."

Frank knew her emotional attachment for him was growing and she was justified in her feelings. Yet he was not there. He needed to calm her loving spirit. "I was skiing with you when you fell and were injured. Did you think I would just leave you among the trees? I hope you think more highly of me than that."

"Frank, my recollection of that day must have changed over time. I remember you as my knight in shining armor, rescuing me from a near fatal injury."

Frank was unwilling to be the hero: "I skied down and called the ski patrol on an emergency phone to report that you probably broke your leg or injured your knee. I didn't do CPR or zap you with a defibrillator to get your heart going. The ski patrol took you off the mountain on one of their toboggans."

"I remember the mind numbing pain. What I still remember is

your chivalry. That's what I'll always recall about our last day at Steamboat."

Frank downplayed his role: "It's good to keep a positive attitude about a bad day."

She rubbed up against him; then tightened her embrace. "Frank, you've been on Lovers Key for over two months and Stephanie hasn't come down to see you yet. I'm here now. Let's talk about us. It's a warm evening, the beach is empty. Why not let the aura of romance fill your soul…? You might consider a new type of relationship with Stephanie. Does she really need to be your *only* girlfriend? You're not engaged."

Frank didn't pull away, rather he responded by putting his mouth next to hers. He needed only to whisper: "Angeline, you make it difficult to resist. I wonder why I have stayed so cool towards you….But, I talk to Stephanie regularly. She has her career in St. Paul. We'll get together soon. She's been working a lot of hours now that she is a partner in the architectural firm. When I was a workaholic prosecutor, Stephanie was there for me and understood my intensity. She helped me understand my frustrations with the criminal justice system. When we're together it's very special and I hope she and I will be together soon."

Frank tried to slowly release the embrace, but Angeline was not about to let the tender moment escape. She moved forward pressing her hips against him.

"I haven't seen you fly back to Minnesota to see her."

"I should do that. I didn't think this job would take so much time, but your dad keeps giving me assignments."

She squeezed Frank, looked up at the stars and said: "Take time to be a beach bum with me. Enjoy the early stars of the evening. Let's stay out here to wait until many more appear. If we stay here together, there will be many of them twinkling down on us. Maybe the twinkling means they're trying to tell us something."

Frank ended his resistance, looked up at the stars and responded: "Maybe they're saying we're blessed to be able to live on the beach; while others only dream of such a lifestyle."

Angeline liked where this was heading and added: "We have so much going for us; we should jump at the chance to be together on an island named for us."

"You think Lovers Key was named for us?"

"Maybe it was named for all lovers. Or maybe it was named because of the natural impact it has on two people who walk its shores in the starlight."

Frank began to be swayed by the intensity of her feelings and the warm tropical breezes.

She continued to look into his eyes and finally added her voice to the soft tumbling of the waves: "When you were thinking of ending your career as a prosecutor, being a beach bum was one of the two options you considered. There's so much more to you than other men I've known. College was just a lot of partying for me.... I guess that's why it took me so long to get a degree."

"Angeline, why don't you use the knowledge you have? You're very creative. Where's your clothing design career heading?"

"I spend a lot of time in my design studio but I become frustrated with the work I turn out. The next day, when I look at the completed design, I don't think its good enough. I really need to build a good portfolio and go to New York or Paris so I can be discovered. I just need one break to get the confidence I need to succeed."

Frank felt her frustration and lack of confidence. But his ineptitude at fashion, including his own woeful wardrobe, left him without a life raft to save her as she floundered in the waters of fashion creativity.

Frank decided it was time to turn around and head back to the estate. He slowly moved away from her embrace and she reluctantly allowed it to happen. She quickly found his hand and they slowly walked in the light surf.

Angeline believed she was making progress in getting the polar ice cap between them to retreat. She wanted to get more of it to dissolve so she moved closer to him. At this moment she wasn't thinking about global warming- she was yearning for Frank's warmth. Her nirvana continued as they approached the estate. Frank started to bid her good night and she moved up against him. She was determined to have a better ending than their last rendezvous. Angeline put her arms around his waist, looked into his eyes and tenderly kissed him. Hesitantly, he returned the kiss, but then his mind turned to Stephanie and he slowly relaxed his embrace. Angeline pulled him closer and wasn't ready to end the tender moment.

Frank couldn't look into her dazzling eyes; his emotions were bouncing back and forth between the women like a tennis ball at Wimbledon. Reluctantly he stepped back, turned and they walked together towards the mansion.

Angeline watched him disappear around the corner of the mansion. She looked toward the beach and up at the stars, puzzled over his lack of passion. Bewildered, she strolled back to the beach. Her emotions shifted as she stood alone on a romantic night at Lovers Key.

In loving relationships there can be a thin line between hurt and anger. Her mind was so muddled she wasn't able to sort out exactly how she felt. At first she wondered why for the first time in her life, she had reached out to a man to start a passionate relationship. Her beauty and her style had never required such a risky venture. Frank must be very special to make her break protocol.

Then she pondered why Frank had come to live next to her in such a tropical paradise, but wouldn't allow himself to be close to her. The evening hadn't ended the way she hoped. Her ardor for Frank suddenly made her feel empty and befuddled. As empty as the beach upon which she stood.

Frank sat in his cottage replaying the moonlight shining upon Angeline's hair and the intoxicating feel of her body. He pondered the directness of her challenge for a new type of relationship- both with her and with Stephanie. He contemplated the concept of two relationships, but he kept coming back to the same question: Can a man handle two intimate relationships without at least one of them disintegrating?

Unable to answer his own question, he called Stephanie. She sounded enraptured with his vocal presence. He avoided telling her of his walk with Angeline, rather, he told her about discovering the second corpse and all that had transpired. Stephanie was concerned about Frank's safety and questioned whether Monique would follow through with hiring security. Frank said that was actually on his agenda for tomorrow.

Stephanie continued: "Frank I wonder what kind of place you're living in when two bodies are dumped in such a short period of time. I know it's called Lovers Key but it sounds like a more appropriate name would be 'Dead Man's Isle."

"Stephanie, you should come down here and you'd see its paradise; not a high crime area. When can you come down?"

She paused: "I wish I had a good answer. I'm swimming up stream trying to get ahead of an ever increasing back log of work. Unfortunately, I don't think I'm actually going up stream. I'm almost to the point of talking to the other partners about the firm hiring another architect. I don't see any let up in the work."

"Is that a 'no' or an 'I don't know'?" Frank asked.

"I can't see myself taking any time off in the near future. Why don't you come to see me? We could be together on weekends and I promise I won't work more than ten hours a day during the week."

"So during the day I could clean house and cook." Frank replied coolly.

"You could see some friends and maybe look for a job here- close to me."

Frank decided not to be so negative: "You're right. I don't know how long I'll last here. It's a great location, but maybe the legal work will get boring or I might run out of work to do. Stephanie, I really do miss you. Let me check on some airfares and talk to the boss about a week off."

They talked for a few more minutes and Frank felt in his heart that he had endangered a great relationship by moving so far away. He brooded whether it would disintegrate if he started hanging out on the beach with Angeline. Reluctantly, they said goodbye.

Frank slowly wandered down to the water and wondered why he had let Angeline talk him into this job which had been created for him as if he was a gigolo. He pegged his decision to take the job because he loved adventure and travel- and needed a job to support himself.

Finally, his brain registered the fact that he stood on the shore of a magnificent body of water. The moon glimmered and the lights of a passing cruise ship sparkled where the water touched the stars. Frank's consciousness was not on the tranquility which surrounded him; it was on his future with Stephanie. He didn't see Angeline leaning against a palm tree less than a hundred feet down the beach. She was slightly behind him as she looked upon his handsome profile. Each was lost in love.

CHAPTER TWELVE

Buck's coffee cup was filled with his morning hit of java. After Captain Mastif had been briefed on the Ft. Lauderdale trip, he asked Buck if Frank was a suspect, or was a witness who could be an asset. Buck wasn't sure. Frank seemed to be accurate with what he said, but was obsessed with being sure that he could prove he was truthful. Buck paused to take a gulp of coffee when the phone rang.

It was Investigator Gustavo Lucas. He wanted to know if there had been a confirmation that the corpse was that of Haquan. Buck told him the fingerprint man had just called and said it was a match, but it would be awhile before the Chief Medical Examiner would divulge that the murder victim was Haquan.

Buck was curious as to Gustavo's impression of Frank: "So what's your gut feeling on our boy Frank? Is he simply a witness or is he more than that?"

"I was going to ask you the same question."

Classic cop strategy caused a prickly silence. Each one wants to hear the other's analysis before committing to a position. The Captain was a master at it and broke the silence, not with a response but another question: "Gustavo, why are you concerned about Frank's role?"

Gustavo Lucas wasn't about to reveal too much: "I know it's possible you would determine that Haquan was murdered in my jurisdiction and you would try to turn the investigation over to me."

Mastif didn't get to be Captain by taking everything at face value: "Anything else?"

"Yes, but I would prefer to hear your feelings first- that's why I called."

Buck and the Captain looked at each other with raised eyebrows. Finally, Buck decided to lay down his cards: “I’m uneasy about Frank being just a witness who finds two dead bodies. Sure, it’s a remote area and he routinely gets up to go for early morning jogs, but I learned long ago to be skeptical of coincidences.”

“That makes it tougher.” said Gustavo.

“Why?”

“Because we’ve been keeping what may be a related crime under wraps. We know word will leak out soon. We were going to go public yesterday, but you called about the fingerprints of the assailant at The Pearl of Tao exhibit. We wanted to know the results of that and get some other information. By the way, what did you find out when you went to Haquan and Faroque’s home?”

Buck related in detail the encounter at the apartment complex.

Another pause enveloped each end of the phone line. Gustavo broke the silence: “The Pearl of Tao is missing and apparently stolen. The exhibition ended two days ago and everything was boxed up. When it was unloaded at the next site, The Pearl could not be located. We have tried to determine who last saw The Pearl and that hasn’t been easy. Right now, it looks like the last person to see The Pearl was a local museum curator. She can’t say that she ever saw it put in a box. A lot of very valuable items were being prepared for transport and time lines were tight.”

Mastif broke in: “What’s it worth?”

“They claim more than sixty million dollars.”

“And this has not leaked out?”

“The museum people know that the media will ask a lot of questions and currently they have an extreme shortage of answers.” Gustavo replied.

The Captain continued: “How can something worth sixty million not have more accountability for its whereabouts?”

“Our people are still asking a lot of people that question. The common answer is that this was a mammoth exhibit with most of the pieces worth enormous sums of money.”

Buck asked the obvious question: “How much security did they have considering the value of the property?”

"Their response was that they had an enormous amount of security when the public had access. In hind sight, they now believe that they did not have sufficient security and controls during the movement of the exhibit."

"How does our dead guy fit into all this?" Buck asked.

"He and his buddy were very upset that The Pearl was being exhibited as a part of Taoism and they felt it was a valuable part of their religion-Islam. They were out of custody when The Pearl disappeared. The jail staff reports that the two didn't talk much except in a foreign language. We spoke to the bail bondsman and he says they were just concerned about getting out quickly. Their public defender isn't saying a word claiming attorney client privilege."

Buck grumbled: "Privilege! Defense attorneys never tell what their client said even if it would help their client. The concept of privilege can go too far."

The Captain had heard all he needed to hear: "So, what is your plan with our All American former prosecutor-Frank Johnson?"

Gustavo replied: "I had planned to talk to him about the assault at the museum, but now I'm not sure."

"What do you hope to find out from him?" Buck asked.

"He said he was in line behind the attackers, I just wanted to know who else the two couples spoke to; things like that. Maybe I'll just talk to the two women that were with Frank."

Buck gave him some background about Monique and Angeline Moritz and a phone number. Gustavo thanked Buck and Mastif for their help and told them to keep the theft of The Pearl confidential.

The phone rang and the maid answered it. She declined to confirm that Monique was available and per protocol required the caller to identify himself and the purpose of his call. Gustavo Lucas responded with his name and position. He decided to be vague about why he was calling and he stated he wanted to converse with Mrs. Moritz regarding security.

Monique came to the phone and was excited that the Broward County Sheriff's Office was interested in providing security. She credited Frank with being efficient in the immediate response of an agency which could provide highly trained security for their estate.

Gustavo was taken aback and stammered: "I didn't call to talk about the Broward County Sheriff's Office providing security for your home."

Monique was upset: "My maid said the purpose of your call was security. Is that what you told her?"

"Yes"

"I don't understand. We need security because of murderers nearby. Frank was working on that this morning and now you call about security. Frank is handling this. Talk to him."

"I actually want to talk to you about security at The Museum of Art in Ft. Lauderdale."

"In my opinion it's not very good. We saw a person get stabbed when we were there. Anything else you need to know?"

"I wanted to get some information about that incident."

"Frank told me he didn't want to be a witness. So that's our position. If you need anything more, talk to Frank. I'm terribly late for my bridge club. Good day."

Gustavo Lucas realized that the conversation had ended and any information would have to come from Frank. He pondered the need for security by Monique. Were they connected to the murders to a greater extent than Frank had revealed to the police? The bigger mystery was why he was reticent to be a witness in The Pearl stabbing. Yet, he had no problem with actively participating in an investigation after he discovered two murder victims?

Gustavo decided he needed to talk to Frank before it became public knowledge that The Pearl was purloined. Gustavo knew that body language and facial expressions were important in the analysis of truthfulness. That scrutiny is not available over the phone. In addition, candor goes up a notch when there is a face to face interview. Gustavo headed toward Alligator Alley as he called Buck to get directions to Frank's beachside cottage. Gustavo's drive gave him plenty of time to formulate a strategy to get the truth out of the reluctant witness. Get background first, and then ask questions on the heart of the matter.

When Frank heard the knock on the door he was annoyed at the interruption. He guessed that Angeline was at the door. "Come in" came out in an irritated voice. Gustavo appeared to an astounded Frank.

Gustavo apologized: "Sorry to butt in without an invitation, but I wanted to talk to you."

"It must be important; given the drive."

"I'm not sure how important it is. But before I get to that, I'm wondering why you are seeking a security detail here.

"Monique Moritz is frightened by the fact that two murder victims were dumped next to the estate. I can't convince her that she is not suddenly at higher risk.... Investigator, tell me why you came."

"I need some of your time now so that the investigation can move forward."

Frank was puzzled: "You've become involved in the murder investigation?"

Gustavo was succinct: "The Pearl."

"Yesterday you didn't say you were part of the investigation into the stabbing case. Is that your case?"

"No it's not."

Frank's facial expression was hard to interpret but Frank's mind was easy to read-bewilderment. "Well Investigator Lucas, you can start asking me anything you want. But I don't have a clue what you're investigating. When I tell Investigator Thorton anything, he interprets it as coming from a suspect, not a witness. I hope you're more open minded."

"Tell me what you know about The Pearl."

"You want a history lesson? ...I doubt it. Be more direct in telling me why you're here." Frank was trying to sound even handed, but he was getting the feeling Gustavo was like Buck.

"I was just trying to find out if you knew that The Pearl was missing. Do you know that it's missing?"

"No. When did it disappear?" Frank then rephrased the question. "You're here, that means The Pearl isn't misplaced; it's believed to be stolen. Am I right?"

Gustavo confirmed only that it was believed to be stolen. He then thoroughly questioned Frank about his visit to see The Pearl. Frank talked about the intense desire of both Muslims and Taoists to have control of an important artifact of their religion. Each religion wanted The Pearl.

Gustavo asked: "Do you think the men intentionally ignited a confrontation so that in the turmoil, others could take The Pearl?"

"No. It would be too easy to immediately know The Pearl was missing. There would be a high risk of capture. I think they were testing the security and they learned something from what happened. If there are security cameras, you should look at the tapes and see who is watching on the sidelines."

"That's sounds reasonable." said Gustavo.

Frank decided it was his turn to ask questions: "Do you think there is a connection between Haquan's murder and The Pearl being stolen?"

"It's a theory worth considering."

"Are you going to actively investigate the connection?"

"Yes."

Frank continued: "Where is his sidekick Faroque? Do you have an "attempt to locate" out on him to law enforcement agencies?

"We will have as soon as I leave."

"I have one last question. Why did you come to see me?"

Gustavo paused, got up, and started walking out the door. He stopped, turned and whispered: "I wanted to decide for myself."

He was gone before Frank could ask him to clarify his answer. Frank considered the context and decided that the cops only had a few pieces of the jigsaw puzzle in place. They were all trying to figure out what pieces of the puzzle he was holding.

As Investigator Lucas drove away, he was bewildered. He wasn't into art but he had just as much trouble discerning Frank's role as people have had in interpreting Mona Lisa's smile.

CHAPTER THIRTEEN

Frank finally completed his work for the day for Mr. Moritz and was taking a jog at sunset rather than sunrise. He watched as an osprey soared on the wind. The beautiful bird patiently x-rayed the water just off the shoreline. The keen eyes were searching for a fish for supper. Silently the hawk like bird rocketed down at the silky smooth surface with it's talons out stretched. The claws whacked the water, the wings flapped twice and the osprey appeared with a sea trout dinner. Frank kept jogging and within a few minutes, a squadron of pelicans intersected the rays of the setting sun. He marveled at the bounty of wild happenings on this tropical island.

After he turned and headed back down the beach, he could see two men in uniform on the sand heading towards the estate. It looked like their destination was Monique who was sitting on a chaise lounge at the waters edge. Frank quickened his pace and he got to her just ahead of the uniforms.

Monique was sipping her third glass of wine, transfixed on the magenta streaked sunset as Frank spoke. She was instantly startled which sent her wine glass flying into the water.

"OH MY… OH….It's you Frank! The voice scared me. All these murders around here have me in a state of pure panic. The bridge club assured me that we need armed security guards immediately and continuously. Did you hire the man who called from the Broward County Sheriff's Office?"

Just then one of the uniforms cleared his throat to announce his presence. Monique reacted with trepidation until she saw who it was. She then relaxed: "Frank, thank goodness you got us security. You're so good at protecting us."

The two uniforms were smiling and introduced themselves as Cole Clancy and Billy Trickle, officers with the Florida Fish and

Wildlife Commission. Cole then explained they had come to search the island for bears.

Monique reacted with a quivering voice: "Frank, they believe we're in danger of a bear attack. I'm so confused. Were the men murdered or were they attacked by bears? Can you two officers protect us from both?"

Cole Clancy suppressed a smile: "Ma'am, we're not here to provide you with security. The medical examiner has determined that one person was killed by a bear and as you know, a second corpse was found near here. We've been assigned to check for a bear or signs of a bear. So far, we've not determined that a bear is in the vicinity."

Monique responded: "Frank tells me there are bears in south Florida. I thought they were only in the north where there is snow. Is that true?"

"There are bears in south Florida; I just don't think they would be on a small island like this one." Cole replied.

Billy, the other officer, joined in: "The biggest bear ever found around these parts was about six hundred pounds. That's big enough to kill a man. But such a big bear would be quickly discovered if it were on this little island."

Monique again reacted with a start. Her hands started trembling and she looked at Frank with trepidation in her eyes. "Frank I need assurance that I'm safe here. If I'm not you better get me a room down the beach at the Ritz-Carlton until its safe. My wine glass flew in the water: summon one of the staff to bring me another glass of merlot."

The two conservation officers looked at each other with suppressed grins and then looked to Frank. He decided to get the conversation back on track: "I'm the one who found both bodies. I believe they were murdered elsewhere because both had been savagely attacked but there was no sign of blood or tracks in the sand. I'm not convinced that a bear is responsible for the attack. There were bite marks but the wounds were from something that had a lot of teeth-like a big gator."

Billy asked: "Ever see a bear around here?"

"OH, MY! NO!" came the quaking voice of Monique.

"Would you know bear tracks if you saw them?"

Frank replied: "Probably not."

"Do you know what bear dung looks like?"

She gasped at the thought and mumbled something about her wine. Frank shook his head and resumed: "Assuming you find no evidence of a bear around here, I have two favors to ask. Could you visit the Chief Medical Examiner and tell her that no bear attack occurred here. Second, ask to inspect the corpses and give her your opinion whether a bear could have caused those bites."

Billy replied: "That's what our superiors assigned us to do."

Monique got up the courage to ask why they were starting after sunset. Billy said they had already covered most of the island and would quickly finish up. He said bears tend to roam at night and they would again check the island for signs of a bear about daybreak. They would spend the rest of the night doing random checks of night fishermen in the area and watching the shoreline. They then departed.

Monique dejectedly proclaimed: "They're not our security and no one has brought me any wine." Weak kneed she then made her way back to the mansion leaving the wine glass to be rocked by the waves. Frank picked up the glass and the lounge chair as he headed to the mansion. He decided to look up Cole and Billy in the morning.

The next morning as the sun peeked between the palms, Frank strode the sand looking for the conservation officers. He heard branches snapping and waited until they appeared out of the underbrush. They looked surprised to see him and said so.

"Find anything?"

"Raccoons, armadillos, a gopher tortoise and a lot of pretty shells." Cole replied.

Billy laughed at the last item and added that nothing indicated a bear had been around. Frank asked them if they were willing to take a strong stand that the men weren't killed by a random wild animal attack."

Cole replied: “We want people to respect wildlife and realize some animals can kill humans. We don’t want hysteria over attacks that really aren’t attacks in the wild. We will give the medical examiner our opinion after we see the bodies. If a strong statement is appropriate, we aren’t afraid to make it.”

They handed Frank their business cards and departed.

The Chief Medical Examiner wasn’t in the mood to speak with two nosey conservation officers. As she drove into the parking lot of the morgue, she couldn’t miss the pick up truck with a boat on a trailer parked in the lot. The markings on each left no doubt that the game wardens had arrived on time for their appointment. As she walked into the lobby she grumbled: “I don’t have much time. Get to the point.”

Cole Clancy said: “We’ve been up all night and would like to get to bed. We don’t want to take much of your time. Our bosses assigned us to look for bears on Lovers Key and to talk to you about it.”

“And…?”

“We checked Lovers Key and found no evidence of a bear.”

“Bears move around.” came the acidic response.

“Yes they do. But we found no bear fur in the underbrush; no dung; no bear prints-nothing. Just as importantly, our department has never seen a bear there; neither has the Coast Guard who patrols the waters there nor the Lee County Sheriff’s office – no one. It’s too small of an island for a bear to survive unnoticed.”

“I haven’t determined that the first death occurred on Lovers Key.”

“Have you ruled it a homicide?” Billy interjected.

“I haven’t released that information.”

Cole took the lead again: “Could we look at both bodies to observe the bite marks?”

“If it will get you out here so I can get some work done. I’m growing weary of people putting their noses in where they don’t belong.”

She led them into the morgue and showed them both corpses. Both men were not prepared for the brutality the victims had suffered, but they showed no reaction. After a close inspection, Cole nodded to Billy and Billy nodded back.

"Doctor, Billy and I have handled attacks on humans by sharks and gators. We need to confer with each other about the details of our conclusion, but it's clear to us that this attack was not by a bear. It was a gator."

"How can you so quickly make such a judgment?"

"There are less than two thousand bears in Florida and there are way over a million gators'

"I don't deal with statistics, I deal with the reality of this death" came the terse reply of the doctor.

Billy chimed in: "Plus, there has never been a documented attack by a bear on a human in the history of Florida."

"Well, history has been made and I'll be at the center of it."

Cole's lack of sleep and the disbelieving doctor had gotten him angry. In a raised voice, he snapped: "Gators have between 74 and 80 teeth. We looked closely at the pattern of teeth marks. There is no way those teeth marks could have come from a bear. We'll be at odds on this one doctor and it'll become public."

"I've taken on some abrasive defense attorneys and put them in their place, so a public battle doesn't scare me."

Billy wasn't afraid of a confrontation and joined in: "It might be wise to revise your determination so we can be in agreement before our report becomes public. Back off or we'll report that it is an outlandish conclusion that either of these men had been killed by a bear on Lovers Key. If you want the notoriety for declaring this is the first bear attack on a human in Florida, it will be at the expense of your credibility because we will categorically disagree."

Her face flushed and the tension in the cool room drew perspiration to her brow. She struggled within herself to regain her composure before speaking. "I'm too tired to argue with you over this now. Send me a confidential report within forty eight hours and I'll consider it. In the mean time, tell no one about this."

"We must report to our supervisor."

"Tell the supervisor to keep quiet too."

Cole and Billy left the chilly confines of the morgue and it wasn't just the air.

CHAPTER FOURTEEN

Frank stopped at the end of the driveway as an approaching cab turned in. He was startled when he recognized the sole passenger in the back seat-Lieutenant Anderson Granderson! Frank jumped out of his car to greet him and Granderson gave him a big bear hug as a hello. Granderson was taller than Frank- about six feet five and muscular. Granderson, a very handsome black man was almost forty but didn't look it.

"What are you doing in Florida?"

"I'm on vacation and looking for a scenic place to play and stay."

"If you're willing to sack out on a sleeper sofa, the rent is free."

Granderson smiled and added: "If I can use your Mustang convertible, it's a deal."

"I suppose you want free beer and food too."

"As long as you're offering, I won't turn it down."

Frank laughed: "Granderson, we had a number of cases together in the five years I was a prosecutor. Tell me about the other reason you're here. I think I know you and I'm not buying your story that you decide to come here on vacation just a couple of days after a detective talked to you about me being involved in two murders."

Their eyes met and Granderson's white smile lit up his ebony face: "Frank, I needed a break from the cool weather and my curiosity was up."

"Are you curious about solving the murders, or my involvement in them?" Frank asked.

"Frank, how could you think I would have more than one reason to come to see you?"

"No wonder you're a primo investigator. You're always able to spin a person's question into another question."

The two headed back to Frank's cottage. Granderson reiterated that he needed a break from the Minnesota cold and had plenty of overtime to cash in. He chuckled as he explained how he was able to escape to tropical Florida without his wife- he worked so much overtime, she rarely saw him. He then candidly told Frank that going to Florida without her wasn't going to increase her loneliness; just her envy.

As they sat at the kitchen table, Lt. Granderson inhaled the soothing salt air and heard the soft sound of waves dancing to create surf. Frank had gotten over his anxiety about the purpose of the visit and was anxious to get caught up on what was happening in Minnesota. Granderson was content to be massaged by the sea sounds.

As they ate some great chocolate chip ice cream, Granderson wondered aloud: "How could such a beautiful place be the scene of corpses? How could Buck Thorton's suspicions be on you, Frank?"

Frank became animated over the erroneous idea that he hadn't just coincidentally stumbled upon two murder victims. He pounded on the table for emphasis which startled Granderson.

"Calm down Frank. If I was investigating this case, I would be following the same course as Buck. Investigations occasionally go down the wrong road, but sometimes the road has to be traveled so the defense can't claim that the investigator didn't follow up on an obvious suspect."

"OBVIOUS SUSPECT! Even Buck didn't call me that! You're some friend. I'm starting to feel I should have just jogged by both bodies and just considered them dead rats."

"Your agitated reaction is what gets Buck to wonder about your participation in the killings. Don't forget you admit you identified the second guy because of prior contact when he was arrested for a violent act. Why wouldn't Buck speculate about you?"

"At least now I'm down to 'speculate' that is an extreme drop from 'obvious suspect'."

"Buddy, chill."

Frank wasn't cooling down: "It's like I must prove my innocence."

"The best way to do that is to hand Buck the killer."

"I could find the killer faster than Buck. The obvious place to start is with the guy who was stabbed by the dead Muslim I just found beside the road. Buck should be on that right now. The Asian security guard has a motive to retaliate after being stabbed by Haquan. In addition, if he is a strong believer in Taoism, he doesn't want a Muslim disrespecting a sacred artifact of his religion. "

Granderson cautiously replied: "This doesn't involve me; I'm on vacation."

"I don't need you. I know the stabbing victim worked at Lingbao Security. I'll start there and I'll get information."

"Go ahead. Fix me up with some fishing gear and bait. By the time you're back, I'll have caught dinner."

"I don't have any fishing gear." Frank replied.

He looked at Granderson and his friend stared right back with no visible reaction. Granderson was astounded: "you live on an island and you don't have fishin' poles? What's wrong with you boy?"

They repeatedly exchanged serious facial expressions. Finally they both broke out laughing. Granderson playfully punched Frank on the shoulder. "We can stop and get everything I need for fishing..., after we both check out Lingbao Security."

They headed out in the Mustang with the top down and a sky bluer than a promotional poster. As they approached the toll booth on Alligator Alley, Granderson read the highway sign announcing no gas for many miles. He was stunned to learn that they had a trip ahead of them.

They exited in Ft. Lauderdale and drove north on Highway 1.As they drove by a store front with a sign that announced: *LINGBAO SECURITY,* Frank looked briefly, but didn't stop. They drove up a couple of blocks and circled back on side streets where they parked just south of the building. The front door of Lingbao Security could be seen in the distance. Granderson said they should wait and watch. They did and nothing happened; so they crossed US 1 and walked up to the store front.

The building was as ancient as the ship of Ponce De Leon. Frank was about to enter when Granderson grumbled he was only along for moral support. The reception area, if it could be called that, was slightly bigger than a portable toilet. It had two beat up, greasy chairs which Frank had no desire to sit in. There was no desk and no receptionist. Frank surmised that the last time the room had been painted, lead based paint was still legal.

As they looked around trying to figure out how to announce their presence, an extremely muscular Asian man, about six feet tall came into the musty space through the rear door. Frank extended his hand to shake hands but the Asian just looked at him.

"Hi. My name is Frank Johnson. I'm an attorney seeking help finding The Pearl of Tao so the insurance company can pay out the million dollar reward for the return of The Pearl."

The man showed no sign of comprehension or response.

Frank tried some more: "I know that an employee of Lingbao Security was injured over at The Museum of Art defending The Pearl from two Muslims named Faroque and Haquan. An employee named Ying was stabbed in the right thigh. Can you help me?"

The man's facial expression changed less than that of Abe Lincoln at the Lincoln Memorial. Granderson decided to try: "Do you understand English?"

"Yes."

Frank started in: "I was hoping that Ying would like to get part of a million dollars if he could lead us to whoever took The Pearl."

"We have many employees named Ying."

I would like to talk to the one with the tattoo of a yellow and red dragon that goes up the side of his neck. He also has a tattoo on his chest that was the classic representation of Lao-Tzu- an ancient man with a flowing beard and robe, riding a water buffalo."

"Ying Lao doesn't work here anymore. How do you know so much about this?"

Frank solemnly replied: "I make it my business to know. Just like I know that lingbao means sacred treasure. How can we contact Ying?"

"He doesn't have a phone."

"How about an address?"

"Don't know."

Granderson joined in: "I bet you know where he lives and know how to get there, but you don't actually know the street name and number."

The Asian again used the silent tactic.

"Are you the head man here at Lingbao Security?" asked Granderson

"No."

"Can we talk to the boss?"

"He's not here."

The man turned and disappeared through the door he had entered. Frank and Granderson stood there and could hear the Asian talking excitedly in Chinese to at least two others. Frank waited as the talking continued, but no one returned. He yelled out asking for someone to come out to talk. The talking ended, but no one appeared. They patiently waited and then reluctantly walked out.

As they sat in the car, Granderson asked about the million dollar ransom. Frank admitted he made it up, but said that for expensive works of art, insurance companies frequently offer rewards. Granderson commented that it was a good story, but not verified. He added that it was his turn to conjecture. He bet that one of the men would lead them to Ying.

Less than a minute later, they saw a man leave the building in a hurry, jump in a car and zoom out of the parking lot. The small white Kia headed south. Granderson wrote down the license plate number and told Frank to let the driver get a lead on them.

Frank protested: "We'll probably lose him."

"If we follow too close he'll know we're following him and then he'll intentionally ditch us. This isn't like cops doing a planned surveillance-then we have lots of cars. It's just us; so we have to be tricky."

The Mustang roared to life and Frank headed south. Quickly Granderson put his big strong hand on Frank's shoulder and squeezed. Frank flinched. "Hold on cowboy, I said we need to give him some space. Throttle back."

Frank knew Granderson was right and slowed down as he nervously peered ahead for the Kia. The white car blended in with so many others. Between the two of them, they could catch sporadic glimpses of the car. This made Frank jittery, but didn't bother Granderson. As they snaked through traffic, conversation was light. They were focused on a target.

Soon they were in Hollywood, Florida. The Kia had slowed and was only a block ahead when it quickly turned left towards the beach. They lost sight of the car and Frank swore. He decided the Kia was gone forever. Granderson calmly replied that they were heading towards the ocean and they'd have to guess whether the Kia turned left or right once it hit the sand. At highway A1A they guessed a right hand turn because the Kia had been heading in that direction on US 1.

Frank was looking in every direction, afraid the car had pulled off onto a side street. Granderson's demeanor was a sharp contrast-he focused ahead looking for the Kia and hoping to see it if it turned. Granderson smiled and pointed when they got to Golden Beach. The Kia was pulled over to the curb and a man was leaning in the passenger window.

Frank stopped about a block away and saw that the pedestrian had a tattoo; his hopeful eyes made him believe it was a red and yellow dragon tattoo. Ying jumped in the Kia and it headed inland towards I-95.

Granderson laughed. "Are we lucky?"

With simulated bravado Frank retorted: "No. It's my intuition."

"Keep following at a distance .I don't think they know we're tailing them, but at some point they'll drive wildly to see if someone will do the same. Criminals know that some cops will get anxious and try to keep up. Unfortunately, sometimes cops reveal themselves."

The Kia headed back north on the freeway, accelerated wildly and frantically changed lanes. Tires squealed and bumpers scraped. Cell phones fell to the floor as drivers frantically put both hands on the wheel to take quick evasive action. Three lanes of traffic swerved. Granderson envisioned a chain reaction of collisions, but the paved shoulder offered an escape for some. Frank held back, determined to save his Mustang and his cover. Finally, the Kia gave up trying to make headway through the endless mass of cars. Frank was now far enough back that the Kia rarely was visible.

After a few miles, Frank knew he needed to close the gap. Frank gunned the Mustang; it responded with a deep growl and plenty of acceleration. The Mustang danced between cars and he was now close to the Kia. Granderson told him to back off a little. Granderson assured Frank they wouldn't lose the Kia. It couldn't effectively make many evasive maneuvers because of the traffic and the Kia could only get off the freeway at an exit.

Frank eased back, and got frantic when the Kia disappeared for a few miles. They followed the Kia on the freeway for over forty five minutes dodging semis and getting cut off by two different Jaguar convertibles; one driven by a teenager and the other by an Elvis impersonator.

Frank was an emotional twit as the Kia could barely be seen between big trucks and shiny wheeled SUVs. It exited to West Palm Beach. Frank shouted as he cut across two lanes of traffic and horns blared from all directions. Granderson chuckled as he braced for the inevitable impact. Tires screeched and a Porsche dodged onto the shoulder. Road rage was boiling in the mind of more than one driver. Frank accelerated to get away from the angry mass of motorists.

"I don't see the Kia. Head toward the water." Granderson yelled.

"I'm guessing he'll go that way" concurred Frank.

Soon they flew across the bridge, over the Intracoastal Waterway and into Palm Beach. Granderson gave a thumb's up when the Kia came into view. They turned off of Royal Palm Way and headed parallel with the ocean. The Mustang roared by the historic Breakers Hotel. But the Kia wasn't in sight. A couple miles up the road, Frank was ready to back track when he saw the Kia had pulled up to a gated, walled mansion right on the ocean. Frank and Granderson held back and watched as the car disappeared into the compound.

In awe, they drove by the enormous estate. Inscribed on the gates was "The Temple." The fortress like appearance of the walled perimeter let them know they would not be walking up and knocking on the front door. They were amazed that mansion after mansion along this stretch of ocean either had walls or thick impenetrable hedges ten feet tall. Yet the compound the Kia entered gave it the feeling it was a super mansion among breathtaking, over the top mansions. It left the impression that it was a bastion against the world. After a few blocks Granderson commented that the Kia was swallowed up by the compound like a minnow by a northern pike. Frank agreed and pulled off the road.

Granderson shook his head and smiled. "When I travel down Summit Avenue in St. Paul, the wide streets, huge trees and stately mansions make me feel like the rich have their own street. When we crested the bridge and entered Palm Beach it dwarfed Summit Avenue. The multiple symmetrical rows of stately royal palms must have been eighty feet tall. The parkway was lined with investment firms and banks. This is an exclusive city."

"We've got to go back to The Temple and look over the wall." Frank said.

Granderson protested: "We don't have a ladder and we don't know the level of security inside."

"I just want a quick peek and then we'll go. It's almost sunset, so we won't be seen as easily as in broad daylight."

"Ever hear of motion detectors which activate flood lights?" Granderson sarcastically queried.

Frank wasn't deterred and got out of the car. Granderson felt a need to protect Frank and hopped out. They trotted down a side street and saw a home with a roof under repair. Frank spied an extension ladder beside the house and borrowed it. When they got to the compound, he quickly put the ladder against the wall and scrambled up.

As his head cleared the wall, he heard a faint ringing sound come from the rear of the enormous mansion. He looked to his left and there was a small cement pool with a wall around it. A large golden colored reptile was beside the pool eating something. Frank looked closer and realized that it was a twelve foot gator eating a small horse. The horse's head and a couple of legs were the only remaining remnants.

TROUBLE! A man charged from around the side of the mansion. Instantly, Frank was in the sights of a high powered weapon. Instinctively he jumped off the ladder just a millisecond ahead of a spray of bullets. High velocity shells ripped the top of the wall and pierced the air above it. Granderson immediately feared this very rapid fire armament. He grabbed the ladder and was running down the street before Frank could get up off the ground.

Granderson snarled: "I knew this was a crazy idea! I'm the investigator, why am I following the lead of a prosecutor turned beach bum?"

"Keep running!" Frank yelled.

"I'm not stopping until I'm back in St. Paul."

They dumped the ladder and hid amongst the roofing materials. After a ten minute silent vigil, Frank spoke up: "I didn't get a good look at everything; there were some fancy cars, and a huge golden gator."

"And security with an automatic weapon." Granderson griped.

"It looked like the golden gator was having a horse for dinner."

"What?"

"I'm not kidding. This gator must have been twelve feet long and had to weigh a thousand pounds."

"In a mansion? How good a look did you get? Was it alive?"

"Gator yes. Horse, definitely not. There wasn't much left."

"Never heard of a gold colored alligator." Granderson remarked.

"Neither have I. It must have been the lighting. A lot of things turn a more golden hue at sunset."

Granderson replied: "Maybe it was an albino. There must be albino gators."

"It was golden colored to me."

Granderson was ready to move and said so. They headed for the Mustang, hopped in and then drove across the causeway to West Palm Beach. Over dinner at a barbeque rib joint, they talked about a plan of action. Granderson's plan was to go back to Lovers Key and go fishing in the morning. Frank was ready to talk to the local police.

Granderson wasn't ready to be Frank's sidekick at the Palm Beach Police Department: "Frank, I *know* you shouldn't go to the police. Think about it. Buck thinks of you as a suspect. You told me Gustavo is skeptical about you and now you want to get a third law enforcement agency wondering about you? What will they think when you tell them you stole a ladder to look over a wall and you see a type of animal which is probably non existent? Don't you think you're going in the wrong direction at the moment?"

"Maybe…. I'll have another iced tea and analyze the situation. But remember, smooth seas never made a skillful sailor."

Granderson gave Frank a disconcerted look as he chewed on another rib.

CHAPTER FIFTEEN

Cole Clancy answered his cell phone as he perched in a small boat on a bay of Cayo Costa Island. To his surprise it was Frank Johnson. After the preliminaries, Frank commented: "I'm impressed that a government worker answered a phone in the evening hours."

"Well, I'm on duty watching some manatees and recording their activities…What's up?"

Frank wondered aloud: "Is there such a thing as a golden gator?"

Clancy thought for a moment: "Well, no. There are albino gators; they're white not golden."

Frank said: "It sure looked golden to me. I don't think it was white."

"Ah, just a second, let me think… There are very rare yellow gators. They're not albino. An albino has no pigmentation; a yellow gator has lost some of its pigmentation. Both albinos and yellows don't last long in the wild because they stick out. When gators are small they are the hunted rather than the hunter."

"Well, in the evening light it looked more golden than yellow to me. It was big."

"Where'd you spot it? It may be worth tagging and monitoring."

Frank immediately knew this was trouble. He paused and spoke every third word to make it sound like the signal was breaking up. He punched the end button and smiled at Granderson.

Granderson's curiosity was piqued.

Frank said: "We're visiting the Palm Beach police."

Granderson shook his head as he finished his last rib. Before leaving, Granderson commented: "I think that your strategy to find the murderer should be to investigate the people who could gain financially from the theft of The Pearl."

Frank added: "Or their status in their religious community would be enhanced. Palm Beach P.D. is the next stop."

The shift supervisor for the Palm Beach Police Department sat down with Frank and Granderson. "Let me get this straight, you want to talk to me about stolen horses in Palm Beach?" He looked at Granderson. "You're an investigator from the Ramsey County Sheriff's Office up in St. Paul and you… you're a former prosecutor living on Lover's Key?"

Granderson said nothing and was ready to leave. Frank nodded.

Sergeant Mike Smith laughed. "You obviously know nothing about Palm Beach. This isn't the wild west. Maybe Minnesota is on the edge of it, but we have nothing in common with horse thieves or roaming horses. Upscale doesn't begin to describe Palm Beach. Now tell me honestly what this is all about."

Frank had prepared for this: "Well, do you have two hours for the complete story?"

"Not a chance." Sgt. Smith said icily.

"Ok. Only a limited number of people know that an insurance company is offering a large reward for the return of The Pearl of Tao. It has been stolen, but that is not publicly known at the moment. We are in effect bounty hunters, seeking a sixty million dollar, fourteen pound pearl. The trail led us to a compound, on the ocean, in your city."

Frank's tone of voice was as if he were giving a lecture at a scientific symposium: "Surveillance revealed a gator eating a dead horse on the grounds. It made no sense to us. One hypothesis is that someone stole a horse to feed to the gator. Another hypothesis is a horse owner, would contend the horse was stolen and attempt to collect insurance after the gator eats the horse."

Sgt. Smith wasn't about to reveal anything of importance: "There are thoroughbred horses on the west edge of this huge metro area and we have polo ponies that residents of our city own and ride. BUT the ponies are not kept in our city."

Granderson joined in: "We would like some background. We only want data which is available to the public, about a specific address on Ocean Blvd. in your city where my friend says he saw this dead horse. I want it made clear I wasn't in a position to see a dead horse so I can't verify his observations."

Sgt. Smith looked perplexed when given the address. He asked: "Were you in that area about two hours ago?"

"Why?" asked Frank.

"I ask the questions here. I want an answer."

"Yes." Granderson replied.

Sgt. Smith looked somberly at Granderson and said: "I'm waiting for an explanation."

Granderson turned and gave Frank a look which told Frank to start talking.

Frank looked the Sergeant in the eye: "Well, we were there and heard some shots fired from inside the walls. We were out on the street and took off."

Sgt. Smith was perceptibly irritated: "A minute ago you told me you saw a dead horse there while doing surveillance. Now you are out on the street. The mansion has a wall around it. I'm not getting a straight story. If you were an innocent shooting victim, we would have heard from you seconds after it happened."

Just then Frank's cell phone rang. Hoping for a diversion to buy time, Frank answered it.

"Frank, this is Cole Clancy. My cell phone broke up while we were talking. I'm now on dry land and have good reception. Tell me more about this big golden gator you saw."

"I'm in the middle of something I'll call you back tomorrow."

Sgt. Smith was close enough to monitor the entire conversation. He called a number, gave a code and hung up.

Granderson looked closely around the room. He couldn't see any small cameras or microphones but he believed they were there. He calmly asked: "Are we being recorded?"

"Any problem with that?" the Sergeant asked casually.

"Nope. Just wondering what Frank has gotten us into."

Sgt. Smith turned to Frank: "Well be sure to include in your explanation details about a golden gator."

Frank wasn't sure where he was headed, but he knew that the truth was the only option. Sgt. Smith received the story with a severe lack of reaction. When Frank had finished, Granderson asked about police calls to the mansion.

"Before I answer that, I want you to know that I believe you violated the privacy rights of the owners of the mansion. In addition, we take 'shots fired' calls seriously. We don't have many of those calls- this isn't Detroit."

Frank decided to launch a counter offensive to keep the Sergeant from becoming too domineering. "I disagree about the invasion of privacy. The information I've given you can be used for law enforcement purposes because we're not acting as governmental agents. We're private citizens and as such the exclusionary rule of evidence doesn't apply to us. I was on public property at the time I saw the interior of the compound." Frank intentionally raised his voice and became animated: "In addition, I was fired upon! I'm the victim here! I could have been killed and you treat me like I'm the criminal. Your perceptions are radically skewed. The crime you should be concerned about is the one with me as the victim."

Sgt. Smith wasn't retreating or sugar coating his answer. "Under Florida's Self Defense Act of 2005, a person can defend themselves or their home from an intruder. I don't think any charges would stick considering you were scaling the wall like a medieval invader."

Granderson tried being the mediator: "Let the Sergeant use the information as he sees fit. We just want to find out about incident reports at the mansion."

"There are few reports and even fewer contacts with the owners. We had a few complaints about unusual noises, but when an officer arrived, it was quiet and the occupants would not let the officers enter without a search warrant. They spoke to the officers through the intercom outside the front gate. We've not been inside the walls."

Frank wasn't satisfied. He was on a mission. He tried to convince Sgt. Smith to tell him about any intelligence gathered. That was more than a hard sell; it went nowhere. Sgt. Smith was mute when it came to information about whether the owners of the compound owned race horses or polo ponies. Smith checked their ID's again and then ushered them outside as he noted the Mustang that Frank was driving.

Once they were gone, Sgt. Smith reflected upon the information he had garnered. Frank was on the right track wondering about stolen horses and polo ponies. The Sergeant was not going to reveal the dark side of the competitive nature of a few of the wealthy polo club members in the Palm Beach area. He knew that the old money of the nearby Azure Polo Club valued privacy and didn't want it to be public knowledge that they had a number of their quality polo ponies disappear. Azure was now at a competitive disadvantage on the polo grounds because their best horses had been stolen. They confidentially revealed to law enforcement their theory as to why they were marked to be victimized: Lingbao Chang, the owner of the mansion, and the head of The Far East Polo Club, didn't like to lose at polo.

Sgt. Smith deposited his videotaped conversation with Frank and Lt. Granderson on an investigator's desk, along with a note discreetly detailing his reaction. He decided he wanted a couple of squads to patrol the area around the mansion so he drove to meet a patrolman. He didn't want any radio traffic or other record about a follow up to shots fired or half eaten horses.

As Frank and Granderson began the drive back to Lovers Key, Granderson said they needed to talk about Frank's investigation and the need for it. After today's adventure, Granderson was more interested in kicking back and fishing rather than working a murder which was not in his jurisdiction.

Frank was ready to talk about his theory. He believed that the obvious suspects were people involved in Lingbao Security. Haquan had been killed by a savage animal attack and the golden gator certainly was capable of such ferocity. Granderson wondered why they wouldn't let the gator eat Haquan and thus eliminate all evidence of a murder.

Frank was quick with an answer: "They didn't do that or dump him out in the Atlantic Ocean because they want to make a symbolic statement to someone. Yet they are smart enough to dump the body far enough away so that they are not immediately leading the cops back to themselves."

"I agree with your analysis, counselor."

Frank continued: "They took all the clothes off the victims so the clothes wouldn't retain any evidence. Like fibers from the perpetrator's clothes, or hair or blood from the attackers. The killers are very sophisticated. They don't want to get caught, but they want to make a statement."

"What is the statement and who is the recipient?"

"This all started before The Pearl was stolen. The Taoists are letting the Muslims know they shouldn't mess with an ancient Taoist artifact because if they do, death is the result."

"Well, who's making the statement?" Granderson asked.

"If I knew who it was and could prove it, I might be able to get Buck off my back."

Granderson chimed in: "Ying has information and maybe more than that."

"And so do the people behind the walls of the mansion."

"What is your next move?" Granderson wished he hadn't asked the question. He knew he should have told Frank to let the whole thing settle down.

"In the morning I'm going to call Buck and pump him for any new information."

Granderson groaned and asked if he could get some fishing gear in the morning before Buck was called. He leaned back in the seat, looked up at the moon and surmised that his free place to stay was going to cost him more than he could imagine. Automatic weapon fire from the mansion told him that these people could not be taken down easily.

He turned his head and stared at Frank who was oblivious to his piercing gaze. Granderson knew the wheels in Frank's brain were spinning faster than the wheels of the Mustang as they rocketed back to Lovers Key. Frank was as intense as a quarterback leading a game winning drive in the final two minutes of the Super Bowl. He shouldn't be underestimated.

CHAPTER SIXTEEN

Monique was charming as she conversed with Lieutenant Anderson Granderson over breakfast on the patio. She was enthralled with the prospect that she could dazzle her bridge club with conversations she had with her new found confidant. Her excitement bubbled over as she questioned the dark skinned, statuesque, strikingly handsome investigator. No detail was too small for her to create a dramatic reaction. She even asked why people called him by his last name rather than his first name. Granderson replied that there were many people working in the sheriff's office with the last name of Anderson.

Finally, Granderson excused himself to get a ride from Frank to buy some fishing gear and bait. He reflected on the personality of the vivacious matriarch as he walked to Frank's cottage. He decided Monique was free entertainment.

As Frank drove off Lovers Key, Granderson asked Frank if the excursion into golden gator land had brought him any closer to clearing his name and finding the killers. Frank was emphatic that progress had been made by tailing the Kia. But felt that he needed to pump Buck for any new information.

Granderson felt he needed to get Frank focused: "Remember what I said last night at the rib joint? You should investigate who would benefit financially from the theft of The Pearl. What I didn't say was once you see the financial picture then you look at who has any other motive to take The Pearl. But you have to remember, your interest is not to solve the heist of a religious artifact; it's to clear your name of being a suspect in two murders. You must believe and be able to prove that The Pearl is connected to the murders."

Frank listened intently and reluctantly agreed with Granderson: "You're right. I'll find out who insured The Pearl and try to find out if anyone has tried to extort money for the return of it. I want to explore another avenue about the theft. I believe two groups have a motive to steal it: Muslim zealots who want The Pearl as a religious keepsake and Taoists."

"Why Taoists? They effectively controlled it when it was on display. " Granderson looked perplexed.

"Because extreme believers of any religion can have a distorted belief about an important religious artifact and The Pearl is extremely significant; it's directly connected to the founder of Taoism-Lao-Tzu. After all, he is the one who directed his followers to create this unique artifact. Zealots want such an artifact to be irrevocably and completely controlled by true believers of their religion."

"Do you think religious zealots would kill to obtain The Pearl?"

Frank became animated: "It has been called 'The Pearl of Death" by people in the Philippines who found it in the Palawan Sea in 1934. Centuries ago a ship went down there, many people perished and The Pearl was feared lost forever. A diver died trying to recover The Pearl in 1934. I feel that death has followed The Pearl. So I believe there's a connection between The Pearl and these brutal murders. The Pearl is very important, but it's also very dangerous."

They had arrived at the marina and Granderson decided to drop the subject. After Granderson got his fishing gear, Frank brought him back to Lovers Key and Granderson set off for the bay side of the island to fish.

Frank called Buck and opened the conversation by asking what was new. Buck said Gustavo Lucas had called him. Buck paused for effect and it worked. Frank wondered: "What did Gustavo uncover?" Frank thought he might find out what Gustavo's' reaction was to meeting with him.

Buck replied: "Gustavo told me that intelligence from the Broward County Sheriff's Office showed that a small group of Satan worshippers were into drinking blood. A few months ago, a video had been viewed by an undercover cop and she reported that it showed them killing a small pony and drinking its blood."

"Are you pursuing Satan worshippers as potential murders of the two Muslims?"

"Certainly. It's a rare day that we find two corpses drained of blood."

"Well, I have a big question." Frank replied.

"What?"

"Why these two guys? Vampires would likely pick someone at random, but why Haquan and the unknown man found before him?"

"Good investigation will answer why they picked these two." Buck snorted.

"Good investigation usually starts with exploring a motive to kill the specific victims. Ying has a motive to retaliate and Haquan was killed shortly after he disrespected a sacred Taoist artifact."

Buck's blood pressure was rising over Frank's attitude. He had given Frank confidential information and all he got back was flack. "Well, we run the investigation- you don't."

Frank knew he better back off: "Sorry Buck. I don't want to get you upset or take up too much of your time. Just one quick question before I go. Any news from our Chief Medical Examiner?"

"Well she just sent me a fax that Haquan was killed by a gator and the manner of death was homicide, but that's not for me to release."

Frank was back on his soap box; "I bet Cole Clancy and Billy Trickle convinced her it was a gator attack. I have a good idea as to the gator that did it."

Buck's ears perked up and the string of coincidences with Frank was becoming as long as a fishing line. Buck wanted to get Frank agitated: "There're over a million gators in Florida and you think you know which one? I don't think so. Do you have a set of impressions from the gator's teeth, so friendly Dr. Delaney can do a comparison with the bite marks on the body?"

"No."

"Did you kill the gator and check the stomach for Haquan's left hand and nose?"

"No."

Buck's sarcastic tone was at a crescendo: "For sure you have the gator in your bathtub and you want us to kill it and cut it open."

"No."

"Are you afraid the gator isn't old enough to know how to tread water in your bathtub, so you have it on a leash?"

Frank's emotions were barely in check only because he didn't want to concede that Buck was able to taunt and manipulate him. "Buck, I didn't want to preempt the Medical Examiner and declare that both men had been killed by a gator."

"Wait a minute amateur private eye. I told you the medical examiner had declared Haquan was killed by a gator. At the moment, she hasn't reversed herself on the cause of death for the first body. So don't be shooting off your mouth on the first one." Buck snapped.

Frank wasn't deterred: "Now that I know the cause of death, I'll take steps to obtain the gator. Would you prefer I bring the gator in dead or alive?"

"I would hate to have to arrest you for killing a gator out of season. So you better bring it in alive and have a permit to transport the gator. It's a crime to transport a gator without a permit."

Frank's agitation level was escalating: "No one has ever been arrested for transporting a live gator. Who would be dumb enough to do it?"

Buck wasn't letting up: "It's a felony offense and yes people are prosecuted. A woman in the adjoining county hit a gator with her car, stunning it. She put the six foot gator in the back seat of her Honda and as she was driving, the gator came to. It started thrashing around and the woman crashed her car. She pleaded guilty to unlawful transportation of a gator. So Mr. ex-prosecutor, you're asking for trouble if you don't do everything legally. Why don't you just tell me how you know a certain gator is the assailant?"

"I don't think you would believe me. Plus, you would think I was somehow connected to the gator." Frank replied.

"We're getting nowhere Frank. Let's stop the games and tell me what you know."

"Buck I can't for two reasons. First, you think I'm a suspect so you'll think the evidence is really coming from me and I'm planting it on someone else. Second, if I cooperate with you, a judge could consider me an agent of law enforcement. If I'm acting as your agent, then I have to follow the same rules as you do. I would need a search warrant, and to get one I need a fair amount of evidence-probable cause. I don't have evidence right now; I have suspicions."

Buck snorted loudly in disbelief: "If you think you can play mind games with me, you're wrong. I gave you info and in return you give me grief. The Sheriff is more help than you are and he does nothing. I don't need to waste my time talking to you because any attempt at communication is met with distain. I don't need aggravation -I've had a buffet full of it. I'm done…"

Frank interjected into Buck's tirade: "What I want to give you is the firm belief I've nothing to do with these murders. My parting words for today are-golden gator."

Buck heard a click and realized Frank had hung up on him. He slammed down the phone in a repulsive reaction. Buck had enough of Frank and told himself he was done listening to the wannabe crime solver. He wasn't taking anymore of his calls.

Frank pondered his predicament and his next move. Just then, Granderson appeared with his fishing pole and a couple of sea trout on a stringer. As he cleaned the fish in the sink, he casually mentioned that he talked to Haquan's widow. Frank's eyes opened wide as Granderson did his best to make the encounter seem unimportant.

Granderson said he was crossing the road to fish on the bay side of the island when he noticed a woman with a couple of small children putting artificial flowers in the ditch, as if it was a memorial. There was still some yellow police tape dangling in the weeds.

He asked if a loved one died in a car accident. She choked back tears and haltingly explained that her husband was murdered and his body dumped here. She had been at the mosque when some women told her of the news reports of a man who had been found dead on Lovers Key. The women said the description matched her husband.

Granderson continued by saying that the woman then completely broke down in tears. Eventually she was able to say that her husband and his friend Faroque had been taken at gun point from outside their apartment by a bunch of Asian men. One of the Asians had a red tattoo on the side of his neck. They were forced into a white van with the word security on it and some of the Asians jumped into a small white car. Both vehicles took off at a high rate of speed.

Frank's eyes opened wide and he was ready to bombard his friend with questions. Granderson sensed this and continued: "The woman said she was deathly afraid to go to the police for two reasons. First, she feared the murderers would be told where she was hiding. Second, she feared deportation. They always lived with the dread that Immigration would come and deport them even though they were in the country legally. She feared Faroque was dead, but she prayed to Allah that he had escaped."

Granderson continued: "I told her I would pray fervently for her husband and Faroque, and gave her fifty dollars to help her out. She tried to stop crying so she could thank me, but it was difficult for her. I told her I believed God would give me a sign about Faroque. She said her name was Zahra and volunteered that she had no phone, but she wrote down an address in Hialeah where she was staying. She wanted to be told when I got a sign."

Frank asked: "What made her tell you all of this?"

"I think she felt I was just a fisherman who was compassionate and willing to listen."

Frank was as animated as a clown at a carnival. He couldn't decide which question to ask first, but he knew that Granderson would be permanently drawn into this murder investigation.

CHAPTER SEVENTEEN

On schedule, Frank walked briskly onto the patio to have lunch with his boss, Mr. Monty Moritz III. Monty was in an animated conversation on his cell phone, with his back to the water. Frank wondered why the boss was oblivious to the beauty of the sun drenched waters. Monty motioned for Frank to sit down. After five minutes, he hung up and got right to the point, ignoring standard pleasantries: "Frank, we're going to Palm Beach this afternoon to meet with some developers. On the drive over, I'll brief you. We'll stay overnight at The Breakers and be back late tomorrow."

Frank wondered if Monty cared if he had any commitments which would conflict with this business trip. He knew better than to raise the subject; rather he just nodded.

"Well Frank, I get e-mails from you at all hours of the night. It piques my interest to know whether those are your normal working hours or you also work during the day."

"Sir, I seem to have a multitude of responsibilities including Monique's requests, your assignments and some personal items. I juggle them all and get it done. As far as I know, I have been timely and thorough with all your projects."

"No problem with your performance, that's why you're graduating to the front lines. Consider it a promotion that you're going to have direct contact with the principals involved in this project. "

"Thank you, sir."

Monique appeared and Monty ended the business conversation by saying they would leave in an hour. Monique was miffed after she learned where Monty was going. She pouted that it had been too long since she had shopped along the fabulous Worth Avenue of Palm Beach. Frank quickly quenched his appetite with quiche and quietly excused himself to pack.

Granderson was finishing his lunch of pan seared garlic crusted sea trout as Frank careened through the door.

"The boss says I've been promoted and must join him on a business trip to Palm Beach. You've got the place to yourself until tomorrow night. Could you call Investigator Gustavo Lucas over in Ft. Lauderdale and ask him to interview Haquan's widow to get all the information she has?"

Granderson felt that the cloak of becoming Frank's investigator was being draped over his shoulders. He didn't like the feel of the garment: "Should I tell him about tailing the Kia and seeing the golden gator?"

"No. Just tell him we were at Lingbao Security and they stonewalled us."

"Frank is this trip over to Palm Beach legit? Or is it a scam so you can get into the mansion on the beach?"

"It's a legit trip. You should tell Gustavo that I feel that Faroque is still alive and law enforcement should be aggressively searching for him because his captors may not let him live much longer."

"I'll tell him what I think."

Frank hustled off to change and pack. He quickly stopped and turned as he comprehended what Granderson had just said.

Granderson continued: "It's somewhat in line with your thoughts."

As Frank chauffeured the Moritz' elegant Bentley, Monty informed him of the nature of the project. When polo ponies were mentioned, Frank's hands involuntarily did a vise-like grip on the leather steering wheel.

Monty explained that a group of financiers- he called them venture capitalists- had been approached by developers from Lake Worth, Florida about financing a huge development on the edge of Wellington, Florida, a place where there was an abundance of polo clubs.

Monty explained that Florida was consumed with the concept of golf course communities and had a few aviation communities which surrounded private airports. However, this project would be unique because it would be so upscale. The homes would be mansions- a minimum of 10,000 square feet. These upscale residences would be on large acreages with impressive stables. He warned Frank not to call the stable a barn- these people wouldn't keep their four hoofed treasures in a barn. The target population would be polo fanciers from around the world.

"Where's Wellington?" Frank asked.

"Just west of Palm Beach and Lake Worth on the edge of the Everglades. We're meeting with a man who owns a large tract of land outside Wellington. Other attendees will be developers and bankers."

Frank wondered out loud how far along this project was. Monty said: "This is a concept meeting and is very confidential. The land owner likes the idea, but his holdings might not be sufficient, depending on the scale of financial and concept commitment."

"Where do I fit into this project?" Frank asked.

"I envision you as doing more than legal work. Land acquisition, zoning, permitting and public hearings will be major concerns; you'll be at the forefront on those."

They discussed other projects Frank had been working on, and soon he eased the Bentley up to the elegant portico of the historic Breakers Hotel. The valet quickly took over.

Monty Moritz III was greeted warmly as he entered the elegant private meeting room within The Breakers. Introductions were made and Monty assumed the lead in the meeting. The project promoters were inquisitive concerning Monty's ability to assemble over a billion dollars of capital. He assured them that during his last visit to New York, his contacts there told him they could raise more than sufficient capital. The venture capitalists would commit sufficient liquid assets to fund the project only if it could be empirically demonstrated that there was a market for this type of enclave. Frank was awed by Monty's use of terms.

The assembled were also impressed and a discussion ensued regarding data required to prove the validity of the underlying assumption of the project. Then the land owner was introduced. Frank was intrigued that the man's name was Lingbao Chang.

Mr. Chang said he was very involved in the competitive polo community of south Florida and he believed that there were sufficient numbers. In his judgment, two types of people would buy. International polo fanciers would buy to be in the heart of the most competitive venue in the world- this would be a second or third residence. The second group would be people totally immersed in polo and it would be their primary residence. They would come from elsewhere or would upgrade from their current residence in the Wellington area. He believed these people were so committed to their horses that they would live in a gated community, on large estates, with their equestrian steeds on the estate. They would love to be able to just ride their horse to the adjacent new polo fields.

He added that polo members were becoming more concerned with the theft of their highly trained horses and having their horses on the estate would give them an added sense of security. Heads nodded and then they agreed upon tasks to be completed before the next meeting. They adjourned and hotel staff was summoned to set up a bar and appetizers in the room.

As they socialized, Frank and Monty sauntered over to the group that included Mr. Chang. Frank listened, but did not join in until Mr. Chang asked him if he was going to join him and Mr. Moritz for dinner. Frank accepted and again drifted to the background to scrutinize the participants.

After the meeting broke up, Frank had some time before dinner; so he changed clothes and walked up the beach to inspect the beach side of the golden gator compound. It was a longer walk than he thought- probably over two miles. He was amazed that the estate had an even taller wall on the ocean side. It was truly a fortress and any entry over the wall would take equipment and athletic ability. He looked for cameras and motion sensors but saw none. He concluded they were expertly hidden. He wondered what a heat sensing devise would look like; it would be effective in revealing intruders trying to scale the wall.

He only stopped a few seconds and then continued his tourist like stroll up the beach. From a distance he scrutinized the compound for a possible point of surreptitious entry. As he returned to the hotel, he realized that breaching the wall was one thing; survival once in the compound was another. He banged his knuckles to the side of his head as he told himself that he wasn't a trained commando.

As the Bentley left the hotel, Monty gave Frank the address of Mr. Chang and said the route was easy: take a right and just follow the road to the address. Frank's heart skipped a beat upon hearing the address and he could feel adrenaline start to run. The address was the golden gator compound! Lingbao Chang was undoubtedly the owner of Lingbao Security. As they motored up to the gate, the entrance sign exclaimed: THE TEMPLE.

The gate had a camera, intercom and a number of flood lights. After entering, Frank looked to his left and saw the golden gator enclosure. In his previous brief twilight view, he couldn't determine the height of the interior wall of the gator playpen. Now he could tell it was about seven feet tall.

Three very muscular Asian men wandered about stealing quick glances at the Bentley and its occupants. Frank felt uncomfortable and a look at Monty revealed not a trace of concern.

Frank let Mr. Moritz out, and then parked the car just up the circular driveway from the lavish front doors. As Frank stood gazing at the grandeur of the entry, Mr. Chang appeared. Frank haltingly moved as he memorized the layout and absorbed the enormity. Monty seemed unmoved by the extravagance, probably because his Lovers Key estate had numbed him to opulence.

Mr. Chang stood with them until Mrs. Chang made a demur entrance. She was classically petite and gracious. They strode through a winding hallway in the mansion with Frank spellbound at the multitude of built in alcoves containing Chinese antiquities. Frank tried to slow the pace to inspect them, but the others seemed impatient because he was acting like a visitor to an art museum. After a multitude of turns, they came upon a pool and patio that rivaled the famed Hearst San Simeon Mansion in California.

Frank was given a glass of wine by a butler who informed him of its origin. Frank surmised it must be a grand wine, but his brain was empty under the subject "wine connoisseur."

He needed to snoop around to see if there was any evidence. There were many avenues to probe. Could he find something to show Haquan had been murdered here? Could he find out the identity of the first murder victim? Could he find out if Faroque was being held here? Should he ask the gracious Mrs. Chang for a tour of the compound and then ask her typical, innocuous tourist questions in hopes she would reveal something helpful?

All this was swirling through Frank's head as Mr. Chang and Monty chit chatted at his elbow. He decided to enter the conversation: "Mr. Chang do you happen to own *Lingbao Security*?"

"Why, yes I do. It's a bigger venture in China than here, but we're expanding in the U.S. Why do you ask?"

"I saw an office with that name and wondered if you were connected with it." Frank changed the subject. "I'm very impressed with the works of art I have seen in your home; at some point, I would hope to get a tour explaining their importance. I need to be more conversant in Far East antiquities."

Mrs. Chang broke into a smile and offered a tour after dinner. Monty frowned and moved the conversation back to the project. So Frank joined in and asked if theft of polo ponies was a serious enough problem that people would change their residence to be near their horses.

Lingbao responded: "Yes, indeed. People who buy and train a horse to be used in polo matches are extremely wealthy and very successful. To rise to the top of the very competitive polo circuit requires a contender to be deeply involved. The horse and the rider work as a team. These people work with their horse for many hours, but also have many other commitments. Having their horse on their property would be a big advantage. They don't like to lose a match or lose their horse."

Frank followed up: "Do you compete in polo matches?"

Chang took a sip of wine, reflected a moment and replied: "The description I gave embraces many, including me."

Monty joined in: "These people feel significant satisfaction in winning a match over other successful people. The polo community has a burning desire to win, similar to the motivation that drives professional golfers to try to beat Tiger Woods."

Frank joined in: "And of course, Tiger Woods' competitive flame shines brightest of all. He played 91 holes in the 2008 U.S. Open with two stress fractures in his leg. He's a man that wants to win."

The butler returned to summon them to dinner. The ornate dining room seemed cavernous for the four people dining. Frank ate what was put before him, sometimes not having a clue what it was. The butler would serve it and give him a look daring him to ask.

After dinner and more tea, Mrs. Chang invited Frank to join her for a tour. She showed him elaborate vases, over two thousand years old from the Qin Dynasty and a terra cotta chariot which was life size. She seemed most proud of a solid gold Great Wall of China sitting on a gold mountain. The art work was five feet tall and ten feet long. She spoke glowingly of China's prominence and achievements during the Qin Dynasty.

Frank was intrigued, but his mind stayed focused on his investigative agenda. She was only showing him the main floor. He needed to get to other areas where their guests normally didn't venture. Finally, she led him through a sun room filled with bonsai trees and then out into a meticulously maintained garden.

"*OUCH!*" Frank feigned pain as he swatted; as if something had bit his neck. "I think I was just stung by a bee and I'm allergic to bee stings. I have medicine out in the car to prevent a serious reaction. Please excuse me."

He hustled out of the garden as Mrs. Chang stood paralyzed with a horrified look on her face. He sprinted around the outside of the mansion and slowed his pace to begin his surveillance. Impressive landscaping surrounded a small, dark building attached to the gator enclosure. He went up to a door surrounded by hibiscus plants. He listened and could hear people talking in Chinese. He thought the one voice sounded like the voice he had heard coming from the back room of Lingbao Security in Ft. Lauderdale. Frank carefully tried the door handle, but it was locked.

Faintly, he heard: "Please feed me or let me go. I need to eat. Water is not enough."

Was that the voice of Faroque? Frank wasn't sure. The only time he had heard Faroque talk was in the Museum of Art at The Pearl exhibit.

An angry response in Chinese made him believe the plea would go unheeded. Silence followed and he moved on, he couldn't linger. Frank hoped he could find a window or another view into the room. He didn't.

As he jogged to the car, it was parked just a few steps from the wall of the golden gator enclosure. He looked around; no one was in sight. He took a few quick steps, a strong leap up and now he was desperately trying to scale the brick wall. A peek over the top reintroduced him to the lonely gator. Only its eyes moved to look at Frank. It looked hungry; as it had no morsels to eat. He thought: "yellow or golden, it's still a big gator. I better get down or I'll be found and be his next meal."

Frank then considered the possibility he was in the view of security cameras and staggered over to the Bentley, holding the back of his neck. As he went into his briefcase to pretend to get medication, an Asian strong man came around the corner of the mansion. Frank gave him the bee sting story and said he needed to rest until the medication took effect. Hesitantly, the man left, but stood off in the distance watching.

Frank needed to play out the story he just gave, but he could only be away from his host and hostess a few more minutes without creating a need for them to look for him. He faked a slight stagger as he headed in the front door. He was just about to head down a side passageway when Mrs. Chang appeared. This diversion had run its course, Frank needed a new scheme.

"Mrs. Chang. I feel woozy. It takes awhile for the medication to work; maybe you could show me to a place where I could lie down."

"I'm so sorry you were stung. I haven't been in the U.S. very long and I worry I haven't been a good hostess. Please forgive me. My husband is very protective of his privacy and he not allow people in many rooms. Maybe you return to pool or rest in your car."

Before he could respond, they were joined by Lingbao and Monty. The later declared it was time to leave.

CHAPTER EIGHTEEN

Frank was mesmerized by the repeated sound of the crashing waves as he looked out on the ocean from his balcony at The Breakers Hotel. He pulled himself out of the trance when he realized he hadn't checked his cell phone for messages. Granderson had left a message in the afternoon that Investigator Gustavo Lucas was vacationing in the Bahamas. So Granderson decided not to wait and drove over to Hialeah to speak with Zahra, Haquan's widow.

Even though it was almost midnight, Frank called Granderson who was full of new information. Zahra and her husband Haquan were close friends with a fellow Muslim named Akbar who disappeared just a few days before Haquan was kidnapped and murdered. Frank's ears perked up at the mention of Akbar. Frank remembered that when he and Buck visited the apartment complex in Sunrise, Akbar lived in the same apartment complex as Faroque and Haquan.

Granderson expressed concern when Zahra told him that Akbar had moved out of his apartment after he was threatened by some Asians. Before Akbar moved, he told her what had happened to him. Men stormed into Akbar's apartment at night and brandished assault rifles. They got in his face and ordered him to stay away from the Museum of Art or he would be sorry. The Asian men said that there would be consequences if he or other Muslims kept coming to the museum.

Akbar had a quick temper and made the mistake of declaring he had a right to go there. He then wanted to know why he should stay away. The Asians put rifles to his head and chambered a round. Akbar wasn't afraid. The men assaulted him when he rebuked them by saying it was sacrilegious for The Pearl of Allah, a religious artifact of Islam, to be misnamed The Pearl of Tao. The Asians retaliated by hitting him with a metal baseball bat as they pointed the rifles at him. The attackers shouted that the founder of Taoism instructed his followers to create The Pearl of Tao and Muslims like him shouldn't ever believe they will ever see The Pearl again.

Zahra said that Akbar finally restrained his rhetoric because he didn't want to get shot. He didn't call the police because he feared he would be arrested and deported. In the middle of the night Akbar moved from his apartment into a rooming house. A few days later he disappeared from the rooming house. He did an idiotic act when he went to the Museum and prayed in front of The Pearl.

Zahra and her friends didn't say anything to police about his disappearance because Akbar was in the U.S. illegally. In the past he had associated with people in England who believed in jihad- the holy war against Jews and Christians. She didn't want her name associated with Akbar lest authorities believe she condoned unlimited jihad.

Granderson had her direct him to the rooming house where Akbar had stayed. As he drove, Zahra explained why The Pearl was so important to Muslims. In the Koran, which is their bible, it is written that believers will be allowed to enter the Gardens of Eternity if believers work righteous deeds. Once in the Gardens of Eternity, they will be adorned with golden bracelets of pearls. Zahra said the Koran clearly said that in Paradise there were fruit trees covered with pearls and beautiful maidens resembled hidden pearls. They felt that pearls were heavenly.

Zahra revealed that once The Pearl came to town, the Muslim men in their community sat around and could talk of nothing else. They fervently reread the Koran about the presence of pearls in the Gardens of Eternity. They became crusaders about the fact that the biggest pearl in recorded history was not dedicated to Muhammad- after all, they believed that if held correctly, it resembled his face. The men became very emotional and went to the mosque to pray to Allah for help. They conversed enough that they drove each other into an agitated emotional state. They became convinced that The Pearl must be returned to the home of Islam- the Holy City. There it would be put on display and worshiped during the holy days of Ramadan.

Granderson wondered aloud what they would be willing to do to accomplish their goal. Zahra's body shook and her voice trembled as she said they all believed that if they died attempting to get The Pearl they would be assured a high place in heaven.

Granderson told Frank that he drove her to an old commercial area with some rooming houses on the second and third floors. Zahra lead him to the room Akbar had been renting and talked to the new occupant- a disheveled man drinking out of a wine bottle in a brown paper sack. They discovered that the landlord had discarded Akbar's possessions beside the dumpster because Akbar had left and hadn't paid the rent. They found a family photo and she pointed him out. Granderson retrieved a hair brush from the box and hairs on it could be used for DNA comparison to determine if Akbar was the first dead man Frank found on Lovers Key.

Granderson revealed to her that there was an unidentified man found murdered in the same place as her husband. When she heard this she became incensed that nothing was being done to stop the murder of innocent Muslims. He assured her that police were investigating, and in addition, he and Frank were following leads. This included tailing Ying to the mansion in Palm Beach. Zahra extensively questioned him about the location and description of the mansion. He thought it was unusual that she wanted exact details of the mansion's location.

While talking with Granderson, Frank heard a lot of background noise and asked about it. Granderson said he was at a Ft. Lauderdale beach bar and was checking out the night scene. They continued to talk for awhile and suddenly Granderson excitedly interrupted to say four Asian men came into the night club and one had a red and yellow dragon tattoo going up the side of his neck. Abruptly, Granderson said he had to go.

Frank impatiently waited and was just about to call back, when over the sound of crashing waves, came the chilling sound of countless sirens. Frank couldn't tell how many. The sound echoed off the buildings and encircled his ears.

There was neither end to the sirens nor any ability to conclude a consistent direction they were headed. Suddenly, there was the classic sound of whirling helicopter blades accompanied by a brilliant search light on the beach. Frank watched the chopper head north and was taken aback by search lights shooting out onto the ocean. In the darkness, he saw two boats shoot southward through the off shore waves.

The serene night was transformed into an intense dose of law enforcement action. The boats reversed direction and Frank could make out "POLICE" on one and "SHERIFF" on the other. Now the helicopter was back, moving faster and lower. Hotel room lights clicked on as sleepy residents were startled at the ultra high energy police actions.

Frank yearned to be a part of it, but he didn't know which way to go. Reluctantly, he sat, watched and waited. After an hour, the boats and chopper cut their lights and disappeared into the night. Reluctantly, Frank climbed into bed still wondering if a boatload of drugs and drug dealers had come ashore or maybe it was illegal Cubans who had scrambled ashore on the pristine beaches of the elite.

The next morning, Frank could feel the espresso running through his veins and brain. He stretched his muscles as he viewed the marmalade sunrise as it danced over the water. He smoothly jogged north and soon saw in the far distance, a barricade of yellow tape. It almost stretched to the pounding surf. His conjecture was confirmed when he got to within two hundred feet. The tape had cordoned off the beach in front of The Temple. He was trying to decide what to do next when his eyes locked onto the grim expression of Sgt. Smith. No choice but to continue and be questioned.

Sgt. Smith spoke first, in a very firm voice: "Lovers Key Boy! What are you doing here?"

Frank knew he couldn't reveal the confidential polo development, so he casually replied: "I'm staying at The Breakers. Its work related. We're having a two day meeting on long term, global, strategic planning."

The sergeant growled: "In plain English you're golfing, partying and making it look tax deductible; while I work all night and into the day."

"What happened here?" Frank innocently asked.

"Don't you remember the rules from our encounter at the police station? I ask the questions."

"Right."

"Where were you last night?"

Frank decided to be brief: "At The Breakers. The sirens, helicopter and flood lights startled me."

"We had an incident here last night and two people are dead. You told me you saw a big gator here, but when we arrived there wasn't one."

"Did you see a place on the grounds where a gator could be kept?"

"I ask the questions… It seems that you're always on the outskirts of violent death. At a certain point, mere coincidence doesn't look too probable."

"It *is* mere coincidence that I dodged bullets here and later someone is killed. I noticed you haven't said who died or how, but anyone can figure out that the law enforcement response last night was not for a death from natural causes… Just an observation, Sergeant."

"How much longer are you going to be at the hotel, lover boy?"

"We'll probably check out today. But if the boss is willing to party one more day, then tomorrow. My next destination is back to Lovers Key. "

Frank looked beyond Sgt Smith and commented: "Doesn't look like there are any footprints in the sand going to or from the wall of the compound. Looks like all the footprints are people walking up and down the beach. No use taking photos or impressions….Just another observation, sergeant."

"Photos have already been taken. We're smart enough to do that before the rising tide washed them away. Now that its daylight and we've done a close inspection, the tape's coming down. We're thorough and that's how criminals are caught."

Frank's curiosity was up: "I'm going for a long jog so I'll circle back to the hotel and jog up the road. I'm certain media types are out front and can tell me what happened."

Reluctantly Smith responded: "OK… A number of armed intruders stormed the front gate and a gun battle erupted. Two security guards here were killed and two seriously wounded. The trails of blood lead out to the street and then south. Smith stated matter of factly that the fleeing intruders were shot. Neighbors heard the gun battle and saw a white van drive out pulling a large trailer. Officers responding saw it a mile from the crime scene, but didn't know it was part of this until later. A scouring of the area hasn't uncovered it."

"Sounds like the owners of this estate weren't injured because they had enough security to fend off the bad guys."

"The murderers never got in the mansion. A dedicated security force did its job."

"Keep in touch sergeant." Frank said as he turned and jogged down the pristine beach that now had an entirely different feel; a mood of assassination.

Sgt. Smith yelled to Frank's back: "You'll be in our thoughts and our investigation."

Frank no sooner got to his room than Granderson called him on his cell phone.

"Frank, things really started up after I talked to you. Ying, the tattoo man, was loud and drunk; he boasted to his buddies that The Pearl of Tao would never be defiled again by being put on public display. I could hear them say that letting Muslims view The Pearl of Tao was sacrilegious. They disgustingly said that Muslims didn't believe in the true creation of The Pearl. Muslims had insulted true believers of Taoism and they were spitting in the face of Lao-Tzu, their god-like founding father. Ying bragged that Muslims who believed The Pearl was the likeness of Muhammad got a taste of their own jihad."

Frank was excited about the discovery of this important evidence. Ying's statements revealed an intimate knowledge of the theft of The Pearl and that Muslims had been killed. Combine that with his motive to retaliate after being stabbed and evidence was accumulating to link Ying to it all. Before Frank could say anything, Granderson asked what room Frank was in because he was pulling up to The Breakers and needed a place to sleep- he had been up all night.

When Granderson got into the room he said that Ying had received a cell phone call that got him agitated and he spoke in Chinese. They quickly left and Granderson followed Ying and his buddies. Granderson said he lost them as they exited off Interstate 95 and they headed west on Highway 98 towards Wellington.

Frank wondered if the attack on The Temple could have been a retaliatory strike by Muslims who somehow figured out that Lingbao Chang was responsible for the deaths of Haquan and Akbar. Granderson paused and reminded Frank that Zahra had been told about the surveillance of Ying to Chang's mansion. Frank could now connect the dots, but before he could ask Granderson another question, Granderson was asleep.

Frank had no time to evaluate what to do; he had to shower and meet Monty and some developers for breakfast. At breakfast, they talked excitedly about the TV news coverage of Lingbao and his wife surviving the murderous attack. They surmised that the intent of the intruders was to kidnap the Changs and hold them for ransom.

Frank knew that they were wrong- the attackers wanted retaliation for the deaths of their compatriots. Frank's head wasn't into the breakfast conversation or development issues. He was trying to determine how to warn Monty that getting into a major development with Lingbao Chang could have many disastrous repercussions- the worst of which could be getting caught in a fatal cross fire. He wasn't ready to tell Monty that The Pearl of Death was entangled with Mr. Chang.

Just then, Monty's cell phone vibrated. It was Mr. Chang who said he was too shook up to meet at his land. After discussions about the horror of the attack, Monty commented he felt sure the police would be able to catch the intruders because of the security cameras at the compound. Monty learned from Lingbao that somehow the

DVD machine which contained the camera recordings did not have a DVD in it; so no recording was available.

Frank wondered whether Chang had the DVD and wasn't sharing it with the police, or anyone else. If so, was he planning his own revenge?

After a long morning meeting, the assembled people drove out to the development area. The huge tract of land had no paved roads so the suit and tie crowd looked from the perimeter. Frank's mind was not on conjecturing about possible locations for bridle paths or man made lakes with elaborate fountains.

Later, back at the hotel, Granderson agreed with Frank- the more they told the police, the more Frank looked like a suspect trying to play double agent. Or that Frank had a bad case of Munchausen's Syndrome. They agreed to look for Ying. First stop was Lingbao Chang's land.

Frank wondered if the van and trailer which fled the scene contained the Muslim attackers or if it was Ying's men transporting the golden gator to another location. Granderson decided that the van and trailer would have been bullet riddled and the tires shot out if it was part of the intruders attack. Frank remembered that Sgt. Smith said that the trail of blood led down the street. If the intruders had the van and trailer they would have jumped in it right away to escape the gun fire instead of running down the street. They agreed the van and trailer had the golden gator.

Frank was scheduled to join a video conference between Monty and investment bankers in New York, so Granderson was on his own.

It was late afternoon when Granderson took Frank's car and headed out to look for Ying and the trailer. He kept driving through the open expanses of land south of Wellington. Granderson wondered if this is what the Everglades looked like. He should have been tired from lack of sleep, but the adrenaline was keeping him in high gear. There weren't a lot of places in a city where Ying could keep the big golden gator without being discovered by persons fearful they would be attacked by the monster. Granderson was certain that the van and trailer were somewhere on Chang's vast expanse of vacant land. He believed that this was the most viable place to hide the golden gator. Granderson began to wonder if Chang's men fed Faroque to the golden gator and had to hide the gator until Faroque was digested and thus the evidence was destroyed.

Granderson bounced down a dirt path and knew Frank would ask if the Mustang was used as a four wheeler. How many more miles of dirt road could the Mustang handle? He drove slowly looking for anything unusual, but the classic car was not designed to handle rutted roads.

The sun had turned to russet and was setting as he bounced along a one lane road. Then he came to a faint trail that crossed his path. As he stopped to examine the other path, he saw some fresh tire tracks. He pulled into the weeds, shut off the car and slowly tracked his suspicions about a half mile. He was startled by a horrific scream and barely discerned some rude remarks in response. Granderson started running toward the shriek as he pulled his gun out. As he got close, he moved slowly along the brushy trail and came upon a clearing. There was the white Kia with Ying and his buddies next to a trailer and van.

Granderson had been shown a picture of Faroque by Zahra and he could see that the tied up man was Faroque. They were pushing Faroque's hand through an extremely thick wire grid that went across the back of the trailer. A large animal banged against the wire grid from inside the trailer. The golden gator was just a fence away from dinner.

Two more men emerged from behind the trailer. Six men in all. Granderson didn't like the odds. He remembered a saying of his grandma: a fool and his money are soon parted. He changed the word "money" for "life". He crouched down out of sight and waited.

The gator again banged against the grid work and Faroque let out a blood curdling scream. Simultaneously, Granderson saw the finger less hand and Faroque's horrified, tortured expression. This torture fit the pattern of what happened to Haquan and the other man whose bodies were dumped on Lovers Key- they were slowly mauled by the gigantic gator until murdered.

The gator kept banging and Granderson decided whatever the odds, he had to do something immediately. He lit the dry, dense underbrush with a match. Quickly moving, he lit more spots. The fire picked up momentum and Granderson sought refuge up wind.

Ying smelled smoke as the underbrush started crackling. Alarmed, he yelled to the others that the fire was blocking their only route of escape. Hidden in a fiery, loud crackle was the sound of Granderson's gun going off. The results of the shot weren't hidden. The man standing beside Ying collapsed and blood spurted out of the wound on his arm.

Pandemonium reigned yet Granderson waited lying low in the brush. Maybe they would abandon Faroque and flee to save themselves. The men frantically looked in many directions to see the marksman. They didn't know where to take cover. Then they argued over where to drag their fallen cohort to get out of the line of fire. They took him to the other side of the trailer and out of view. Faroque was left handcuffed to the trailer. Quickly doors slammed in the car and van. Faroque was jerked around the side of the trailer.

The caravan roared through the smoke and flames without a glance in the direction of the hidden Granderson. He couldn't see if Faroque was in the Kia or the van. He then realized the entourage would come upon the Mustang. They would be seeking the driver whom they assumed shot their friend. Granderson watched the flames grow in intensity and knew he must formulate a plan. Could he save himself and Faroque?

CHAPTER NINETEEN

At dinner, Frank Johnson sat picking at his salad. His mind raced as he considered a multitude of ways to warn his boss, Monty Moritz III to steer clear of Lingbao Chang. Frank knew that when huge amounts of money were at stake, intricate maneuvers are required to get high rollers to dump a partner. He needed to figure out how to convince Monty to have his venture capitalists buy Chang's land outright and thus eliminate him as a partner in the development. If he told Monty about his involvement in the murder investigations, Monty would order him to cease. Whatever information he gave, Monty would demand to know the source.

Monty broke the silence: "I spoke with Chang just before I came down for dinner. I told him I was concerned for his safety because of the attack last night. I asked if he had enough security now that two of them were killed and two injured.

"He didn't want to talk about the attack, but told me he was hosting a group of Amas. I didn't want to sound uninformed, so I didn't ask what they were. Chang was energized and taught me all about the Amas, so I learned by listening and asked a few discreet questions. He hired a group of them years ago and they had been in training in China. He said his Amas were devout Taoists. We had a long conversation about them"

Frank responded: "So fill me in."

"The Amas are female pearl divers originally from Japan. They're sometimes called sea women and are most famous for their long history at Pearl Island near Nagoya, Japan. They have existed for thousands of years in Japan and some believe that a splinter group migrated to China. Speculation is that they were somehow involved in forming The Pearl of Tao. Monique told me all about your trip to see The Pearl."

Monty continued: "They wear white flowing clothes including white head gear when they free dive down to 30 feet. They're noted for being able to stay under water for exceptionally long periods of time and they're able to do that because they start training during childhood. Their white outfits make them look unique."

"Why do they wear white?"

"Legend has it to scare off sharks."

Frank silently chewed then asked: "Are the white outfits supposed to make them look sexy?"

Monty laughed. "I don't think so. Mr. Chang said the white outfits are long and flowing and it makes them look celestial. On second thought, they sound almost angelic. Many people are enchanted by the sea women of Pearl Island and come long distances to watch them dive. The long standing traditions of the Amas make them almost religious. If you believe they were involved with Lao-Tzu and The Pearl of Tao, then they are part of the religion."

Frank was intrigued: "What do you mean the Amas helped form The Pearl of Tao?"

"Well, the founder of Taoism, Lao-Tzu had divers put an amulet in a clam and the clam formed a pearl around the amulet. Divers would pull up the aging clam with The Pearl and then put it in a new clam. Some believe the Amas were the ones that did this."

Monty continued: "Chang finally told me that he had a lot of land that bordered on the Chinese seacoast and he hosted a group of Amas involved in specialized training. He seemed unusually talkative as if he had been drinking. He let slip that these Amas were extremely fit because they were into a strict regimen of martial arts training. He spoke of regimented diets and a strict hierarchy of command....By the way, what are nun-chucks?"

Frank looked surprised.

Monty continued: "Chang mentioned that the Amas trained with nun-chucks."

Frank responded: "It's an oriental martial arts weapon. Usually, it's two extremely hard wood sticks which have been highly polished and connected by a chain. A person holds one stick, swings the other stick so it strikes a person at high velocity. In an experienced person's hands, it can be a deadly assault weapon."

Monty took a sip of wine and pondered the possibilities.

Frank asked: "Did he say how long they would be here?"

Monty wondered aloud: "Why would Chang have these women at his mansion?"

Frank asked: "What do they do there? Are they in training? Sightseeing? Learning English?"

Monty looked perplexed and didn't have an answer.

"Monty, Lingbao Chang owns major security companies both here and in China. He has employees who can repel attacks on the property his company is guarding. This means he has some tough men and women in his employ."

Monty pondered this for a few moments then said: "That makes sense. Why did he bring up this history about The Pearl of Tao?"

Frank paused: "Well, it isn't publicly known, but it is missing."

Monty considered the implication and asked: "What do you know about it?"

"All I know is that his company, Lingbao Security, was in charge of security right before The Pearl disappeared."

Monty took another taste of wine and asked: "Do you think it was an inside job?"

Frank decided to be discreet in his answer: "The Pearl may be worth between sixty and ninety three million and the Chang's love Chinese antiquities. This is a premier object in that class. In addition, it is a significant religious object for Taoists and the Chang's are Taoists."

Monty considered Frank's response for a long time, shook his head and said: "People who obsess over collecting certain objects sometimes do strange things, but Chang certainly wouldn't risk his career and fortune to become involved in pilferage."

Dinner was served. The tuna steaks, in a teriyaki pineapple marinade, were surrounded by sweet potato French fries. The conversation ended as they dove into dinner. But Monty continued to think about the expensive and historic pearl. Chinese antiquities were important to Lingbao Chang. He certainly had the motive to steal it.

Lingbao Chang anticipated another attack on The Temple by the Muslims and ordered out the Amas. They assembled in the Great Room of his mansion. An observer would immediately recognize that this was not an ordinary group of Amas. The usual quiet demeanor of the sea women was there, but much more could be discerned in the manner they interacted. Pao, a slender woman with long black hair pulled back in a bun, inspected the sea women. She had dark eyes and wonderous skin.

The women respected Pao and referred to her as their commander. A nervousness was present, but an aggressive confidence in the room set them apart from the typical group of Amas. Part of this aura was created by the way they were armed. Nun-chucks were carried by some and others had throwing knives.

After dark, twenty Amas silently surfaced offshore in the dark, moonless night. They rolled with the waves as they watched the beach.

Pao fervently believed in the many teachings of Lao-Tzu. One of his teachings was that everything exists in the form of Waves and that the Taoists will correct all Waves that deviate from the Universal Laws. As she floated in the ocean, she was firm in the belief that she had been destined by Lao-Tzu to come ashore on a wave to correct those that had deviated. She hoped the timing would be right.

A few minutes later, coming from the north were ten to twelve Muslim men dressed in black. They carried explosives and were heavily armed. Quickly the men hustled down the beach looking in every direction. The sea women disappeared underwater. Outside the Chang compound the men began to prepare the explosives for detonation at the base of the wall.

The sound of the ocean drowned what little noise the Amas made as they emerged from the water. They knew their mission and six of them attacked three of the men standing closest to the water. The men were caught off guard as they intently watched their team plant explosives at the base of the wall. One sea woman came from behind and quickly put the chain connecting the nun-chucks around the man's neck, forcefully tightening it just as another sea woman took the mans legs out from under him. No sound emerged from him as he was quietly disposed. Other martial arts moves by the sea women incapacitated the other two and a forceful snap of the neck sent them all to Allah.

The other Muslims heard something and spun around, but they were a split second to late. The sea women had the element of surprise and were as well trained as Navy SEALS. The Amas had superiority in numbers and with two women on each man, the men were forcefully disarmed. The women's sneak attack had caught the invaders off guard and their weapons were no longer an element of the struggle.

The Amas said nothing- their actions spoke for them. The Muslims swore and tried to resist, but each punch or kick was repelled by the sea women who inflicted painful martial arts blows. Using martial arts submission holds the Amas herded the men into a tight circle around the bodies of their three fallen comrades. The men viewed the fallen warriors and the survivors succumbed to the sea women.

At the direction of Pao, the sea women released their holds, a few Muslims fled; fearful they would meet the same fate. Their leader, Al-Qitar, jumped to his feet and in a loud voice commanded that his men must not flee from mere women- the fearful would never see Allah.

Pao determined that the Muslim leader was not going to rally his troops, so she gave him a wicked kick to the groin. The leader went down and his anguished cry created panic in his remaining men. They fled, fearful to look back at the three dead commandos and their incapacitated leader. The total domination by the precision trained Amas was astonishing.

Pao ordered that the dead men be dragged into the surf and the sea women using the dead mans crawl, swam them far out into the dark water. The women noticed barracuda swimming near them as they released the dead men. Pao watched through night vision binoculars as the women started to swim back to shore. She noticed some unusual ripples in the water when she turned her focus onto the men. She could see the barracuda biting the corpses. The escaping blood was a dinner bell for bull sharks in the area. The women were safely ashore when a major eruption started in the water.

The tide was quickly rising and when the Amas got back to the wall, they took everything the men had dropped. Swiftly they climbed up a rope ladder which had been dropped by a security guard. Their tracks would be the only evidence left behind and the incoming tide would erase that shortly.

The Amas stealthily moved through the compound after hoisting the handcuffed leader into his new prison. Blindfolded, he was led to the small building, which previously held Faroque. The security men were emotionally charged to exact revenge for their fallen friends from the previous night. Pao instructed them to tie up the leader but revenge was not theirs to achieve. The captured leader was a source of information and Lingbao's son, Cartier Chang would get it.

The Amas showered, changed into dry clothes and joined Mrs. Chang for hot tea, steaming rice and squid. The women were giggly with relief that their assignment had been perfectly implemented. Mrs. Chang told them she hoped The Pearl of Tao, which their ancestors had helped create, would never again be blasphemed by being referred to as The Pearl of Allah. She congratulated them for their defense of all things under Lao-Tzu.

Upon hearing this, Pao emitted a radiance, transmitted from her inner strength; born from her training and her belief in Lao-Tzu's teachings. She bowed at the waist towards Mrs. Chang: "Lao-Tzu teaches that there can be no greater peace of mind than that which stems from the knowledge that nothing can injure or in any way do one harm."

Mrs. Chang spoke reverently: "I believe you have entered the much revered state where your actions are performed in accordance with a profound wisdom directly from Lao-Tzu."

Other Amas listening nearby nodded in agreement. Lingbao stood on a balcony overlooking the women and smiled. As the women enjoyed their meal, Lingbao Chang raised another glass of wine in a silent toast to his dedicated militia.

Frank took a late night walk up the beach; he was worried there would be another attack on the compound. Maybe he could detect assailants before they got to The Temple. But, more importantly, he wanted to uncover who the people were that had made a shambles of the sense of safety held by the people of Palm Beach.

Frank walked barefoot in the high tide on what little beach was left. Frank's mind turned to Granderson. Why hadn't he called or returned to The Breakers? He was apprehensive about the safety of his friend and reached in his pocket for his cell phone. He was surprised he had left it at the hotel.

He shook off his deep concentration about Granderson and realized he was now at Chang's compound. He discovered tracks by the wall, but his head snapped towards the ocean. Sharks were frantically thrashing in the water to the point of attacking each other. The combat was over pieces of some kind of meat. The frenzy continued and he watched in fascination not knowing he would have seen so much more if he had been there just minutes sooner.

CHAPTER TWENTY

Granderson circled the wild fire and hoped he could find his way through the brush back to the car. He was extremely cautious so he could be sure that Ying and his gang wouldn't ambush him. He could barely hear voices in the distance and surreptitiously crept back towards the red Mustang. Then, through the dense underbrush and encroaching darkness, he caught sight of the top of the trailer and the van.

He stayed hidden and motionless; all his senses were on high alert. He must have an instantaneous response to any encounter. He listened for the sound of Ying's men coming for him and thankfully, he heard nothing.

Apprehensively, he assessed the situation. He looked back and saw smoke from the wild fire. The wind had momentarily died and the smoke was rising straight up. Granderson wasn't convinced that the fire would stagnate. The wind would come again. Even though a dark moonless night was almost upon them, someone would spot it or smell it, and firefighters would respond. Granderson held out hope that the fire would be quickly found and responding firefighters would help him.

His plan was to watch the bad guys for a few minutes and figure out a plan before the fire again started spreading rapidly. But what about Faroque? Did the silence mean a deadly silence? He moved a few steps, stopped and listened. He continued this pattern until he could survey the Mustang next to the van and trailer. Two men were circling the Mustang and peering in the windows. The other men must be on the other side of the vehicles. His eyes searched for the Kia but he couldn't locate it. Was Faroque here or gone in the Kia?

Granderson's concentration was intense. He could hear himself breathe. As he analyzed options, he became conscious of a sudden wind at his back. Suddenly, the snarl and crackle of the wild fire magnified and he spun around to see the smoke and flames coming towards him like a tsunami. He must escape or be enveloped by the wall of conflagration.

Just then the kidnappers were slapped with the roar of flames. Their voices became agitated and the criminals started frantic, directionless movements which accomplished nothing except to fuel their panic. Ying yelled something and they jumped in the van. The engine sputtered and hesitated. The fear increased as a second attempt to start the van met with an engine cough and feeble snort. Finally, the engine bellowed to life.

Two shots from Granderson's gun got caught up in the clamor. He couldn't be sure if he hit the trailer tires; he could only hope. If he had success, once they got on a paved road, the weight of the golden gator in the trailer would make it difficult, if not impossible, to drive in a straight line at highway speed. They would be easy to spot. He had fired only two rounds to conserve his limited ammunition. He might encounter them again when the circumstances were better.

The criminals rapidly retreated on the rugged trail they came on and a few seconds later, Granderson jumped into the Mustang. Weeds and dirt flew from the rear wheels as he careened down the other trail. He didn't want to risk tailing the bad guys and getting trapped inside the car if they stopped and surrounded him. Unfortunately, this winding trail wasn't separating him from the advancing wild fire; dangerous, but the only option. His heart raced, but the Mustang didn't- the road was too rough to go fast. He feared the roaring, advancing fire and looked ahead to the end of the flames. He dared not accelerate, lest he blow a tire. The dry brush snapped as the flames lit up the night sky. The center of the fire reminded him of a collegiate homecoming bonfire which had gotten out of control.

Finally, he was past the end of the line of flames and he exhaled loudly. He was out of danger. His hands still intensely gripped the steering wheel; they wouldn't release. His arms shook. While the danger had passed, his body was coiled tight. Reluctantly, he determined that freeing Faroque by himself would have to wait. Granderson had to contact law enforcement to get enough manpower to find the fleeing Ying. Hopefully, Faroque would survive.

Granderson needed to get to a marked intersection or a well known spot so he could accurately tell law enforcement his location. He flew onto a deserted, paved road and the Mustang gobbled up a couple of miles in seconds. He screeched to a halt as the headlights suddenly revealed an intersection. He immediately called 911 on his cell phone.

"911, what is your emergency?"

"I'm Lieutenant Anderson Granderson of the Ramsey County Sheriff's Office in Minnesota."

"What is your emergency?"

"I'm getting to that. There are two. A fire and a man being tortured by a gator."

"Are you working undercover with a local agency or are you reporting this as a private citizen?"

"It doesn't matter. I told you who I am so you don't think this is a goofy person calling."

"Which emergency is more serious?" the dispatcher asked.

Granderson was getting impatient: "The man being tortured. The perpetrators are in a white van with a white fifteen foot enclosed trailer with a big gator in the trailer. The trailer may have a flat tire. Also involved is a white Kia. I think they will head east towards Lee County and their destination is probably Lovers Key."

In a monotone voice the dispatcher requested: "Please tell me your exact location so I can send a squad to take a report."

Granderson's adrenaline was pumping: "The men in the van have kidnapped an adult male and they have tortured him by letting the gator eat off his fingers. Please do an immediate 'attempt to locate' as these men are suspects in two murders in which the bodies were dumped at Lovers Key."

"I will do an 'attempt to locate.' Please give me the license number and a better description of the van."

"A full size, white, Ford van a few years old. I didn't see the license."

"Please stay on the line. I will get back to you after I transmit to law enforcement."

Granderson exhaled and was relieved that cops would be alerted. Finally, the dispatcher was back: "What is your location?" Granderson described the intersection and the dispatcher repeated it over the law enforcement air waves.

Soon she was back: "Why are you investigating this torture and how are they using the gator to accomplish it?"

Before he could respond, he heard a siren in the distance. "I hear a siren; I'll tell the deputy when he arrives. Goodbye." A deputy sheriff roared up with lights and siren. Then another. Over the clamor of fire trucks rushing to the fire, Granderson impressed upon the deputies his fear that very swiftly, Faroque would meet the same fate as the other two Muslims who were found on Lovers Key.

The deputies had the dispatcher contact Lee County to post squads at each end of Lovers Key and all law enforcement agencies along the route were alerted. Granderson reminded them the kidnappers could head in any direction and the alert was broadened.

As Granderson sat in the squad car giving a tape recorded statement, he was startled when a brilliant flashlight beam blasted him in the eyes. He couldn't tell who was behind the massive candlepower. The metallic tap on his window resulted in the deputy lowering it.

Before Granderson's eyes adjusted, he heard the voice say: "Deputy, I'm Sergeant Mike Smith of the Palm Beach Police Department. I responded to this call because I had previously met Lt. Granderson. There is a web of intrigue which surrounds him and his associate, a former prosecutor."

Granderson groaned. He thought that Ying and his gang would escape because the Palm Beach cynic would derail the pursuit of the torturers. The deputy turned off his tape recorder to listen. Granderson was prepared to launch a verbal torpedo.

Granderson's phone rang and the torpedo's launch was derailed. It was Frank calling to check on Granderson's safety. After Granderson gave a lightning quick summary of the action he had encountered, Granderson handed his cell phone to Sgt. Smith.

"Sergeant Smith, this is Frank Johnson. You heard what Granderson just told me. TAKE SOME ACTION!"

CHAPTER TWENTY ONE

Buck Thorton was at home, putting on his tropical print bowling shirt with the wild colors and outlandish design. He loved the oversize bowling pin buttons. When he went bowling he was just one of the guys and he didn't need to worry about proper law enforcement etiquette. The late night bowling league was a relaxing evening for him. He fetched his bowling ball from the hallway closet and was about to head for the door when his cell phone rang. Buck had a lurking suspicion that his bowling was going to be way laid by work one more time. The Lee County dispatcher reported the alert from Palm Beach County. With flamboyant inflections, he instructed that the on duty officers handle it. After all, the criminals hadn't been spotted in his jurisdiction. The pattern indicated a potential destination of Lovers Key, but no one said that was the destination tonight.

Buck brooded about his decision not to go on duty and search for the criminals. He thought about Frank's whereabouts; was a scheme ripening in Frank's shrewd brain? He called Frank's cottage. Exasperation surfaced- no answer. Buck's countenance was crumbling. He called Frank's cell phone.

"*WHERE ARE YOU*?" Buck's voice was sharper than a buzz saw.

"From the pleasant tone of voice I think this maybe Investigator Buck." Frank replied sarcastically.

"It is. Now answer my question."

"No delicate flattery to get me to be truthful? Without it I may lie, deceive and betray you."

Buck wasn't going to brood over Frank's blasphemy. He didn't have time: ""I want a perfectly true response. Where are you?"

"The Breakers Hotel in Palm Beach." Frank stoically replied.

"What are you doing there?"

"I could be a smart ass and say 'talking to you' but I will say simply I'm here on business with my boss. I hope to be back in your jurisdiction tomorrow. Do you know about the alert sent out by Palm Beach County?"

"Yes. That's why I'm checking on you."

Frank surmised he needed to alleviate Buck's belief that he was involved in the latest incident, so he calmly replied: "I hope you find the men before they torture Haquan's buddy to death."

"Is anyone there who can verify your location?"

"Buck, I'm alone in my room but I can walk down to the front desk and give this cell phone to the front desk clerk to verify my location. I'm sure the clerk would be considered a sacred solemn source"

Gruffly Buck replied: "No need to."

"Buck, I have…," before Frank could finish, Buck hung up. Frank wanted to tell him that Granderson had crucial new information on the identity of the first dead man found on Lovers Key.

As Buck drove to the bowling alley, he thought about Frank's possible involvement in the latest crime. He bowled a crummy game, because his mind wasn't on bowling. Buck sat down trying to relax before he started his next game just as his cell phone rang. Buck answered, listened and swore repeatedly as he hung up. He immediately dialed Frank's number and yelled into his phone: "Where are you?"

"Same place, but Anderson Granderson just walked in. I'll put you on the speaker phone so he can hear your cheerful voice."

In an exasperated voice, Buck said: "Another mutilated body was found on Lovers Key."

Granderson asked: "Do you have Ying and his underlings in custody?"

"No."

Granderson shook his head in disgust. He couldn't believe they messed up such a simple, rudimentary assignment. He didn't contrive to hide his disbelief: "I thought Palm Beach County told you to station squads at each end of the island?"

"We did. The deputies were on stationary patrol just off the roadway and watched passing traffic. The description was a white van and a trailer. Nothing went by with that description."

Granderson broke in: "Didn't they tell you that a white Kia was also involved?"

"No, we never got that information."

Granderson instructed: "Tell your troops to look for one heading back to Palm Beach with Asian males in it. One has a tattoo on his neck of a red and yellow dragon."

"How do you know all of this?"

Frank chimed in: "Granderson knows a lot. You should ask him about his investigation into the identity of the first body I found and what he knows about Haquan's widow. Or you can talk to Sgt. Mike Smith"

Buck's voice was antagonistic: "Why's an investigator from up north putting his nose into a multiple murder investigation which is far outside his jurisdiction?"

"I'll get to the point." Granderson said. He ignored Buck's insulting tone of voice. Granderson then revealed how he met Zahra and had discovered items which could confirm that Akbar was the first murder victim. Buck became an excellent listener as Granderson unveiled the impressive new evidence- finding Zahra, Haquan's widow and the possible identity of the first murder victim.

Buck was formulating a new strategy. He forced a change of voice: "Granderson, I appreciate your work. It's above and beyond the call of duty. I guess I was a little too suspicious of you."

Granderson nodded and a smiling Frank waited for something more from Buck; he didn't hear anything. Frank surmised the reason Buck wasn't saying mea culpa to him was because Buck hadn't taken him off the list of suspects. Frank figured without him on it, Buck's list would be blank.

Frank ended the conversation: "Buck, you better get out an alert on the white Kia. Keep us updated. We get results."

Buck was ready to retort to Frank's snide remark, but hung up instead. Buck called the dispatcher to put out an attempt to locate on the Kia which Granderson had described.

Granderson told Frank about the ripening wisdom of Sgt. Smith. Frank learned that after Granderson had a long conversation with Sgt. Smith, they were now the good guys. The focus was on Lingbao Chang and the continuing murderous conflict between the Chang compound and the Muslims.

Frank asked: "How were you able to get the fine sergeant to see our position?"

"As you know from my work in Ramsey County, by using my voice, my size and invading someone's personal space, I get my point across"

Frank grinned, but did not reply. Granderson looked away and became silent. Based on experience, Frank knew it was time to end the conversation.

Granderson sat in silence thinking about what happened to Faroque. He wondered: *could* he have done something differently and escaped death, *could* he have saved Faroque? His quick decisions seemed to be right, but he pondered whether he had considered every option.

He wondered how an escape from the cold of Minnesota ensnared him in such a web of international violence. The Pearl of Tao had ignited intense passions by Taoists and Muslims. So much had happened so quickly. His advice to Frank to follow the financial trail of The Pearl was outdated. Tortures and murders now were trails that were interwoven with The Pearl. It was The Pearl of Death. He and Frank would have to keep working to insure that admissible evidence would be uncovered to prosecute the savage killers. His anguish over the ability of men to be so violent made him squirm in his chair. He knew he'd have trouble falling asleep.

Buck was incensed that another corpse had been deposited in his jurisdiction. Still wearing his bowling shoes, he hustled to his car and roared off as he called Sgt. Smith to find out what had happened in Palm Beach. Smith told Buck what happened and that Frank and Granderson were a terrific team that should be used to their advantage. Buck made no comment-he just said he had to go because he was almost at Lovers Key.

Buck knew the media would have a field day when they learned that the deputies missed arresting the murderers. After all, there were squad cars at each end of Lovers Key; a small island with no other through roads. The killers must have driven by the squad car, and dumped the body right where two had previously been inhumanely discarded.

He stood next to the lifeless remains of Faroque and swore at the killers. How could they kill a man in cold blood for an insult to a Taoist artifact? Buck imagined these thugs were callous enough that they laughed as they did it.

Buck had conceded that Granderson was a formidable ally. Now, after getting information from Sgt Smith, he had to dismiss Frank as a target of the investigation. Frank and Granderson seemed to know how to get information about this bizarre trio of Lovers Key murders.

Buck knew his department was going to take a lot of heat for this fiasco. The media would declare a serial killer was on the loose. The sound bite would include that the Sheriff's Office didn't even have a single suspect or a way to stop the slayings. Buck knew they needed to use every resource to stop the carnage.

He stood there in silence, but the momentary reflection on how to investigate the new murder was broken by the rattling of an old car as the investigator from the Medical Examiners Office rolled up and the old guy limped towards the corpse. "Buck, you've got to get these killers."

Buck didn't need the sermon: "You're telling me something I already know."

"The media would love to hear you explain why three murders happened so quickly on a tranquil, exclusive, vacation island. I'm not sure the tourist bureau wants this kind of publicity."

Buck decided to change the subject as he pointed to the body: "Well, the deceased isn't mangled like the other two, but it isn't a pretty sight. He lost his fingers on one hand and was probably done in by a gun shot to the right temple."

The old medial examiner investigator did not seem repulsed by the violence as he surveyed the man lying in the ditch next to him:

"This one was not as well planned. The victim still has clothes and has fewer mutilations. There may be some evidence on the body. Let your forensic team go over this in detail. It's late. I'll just nap in my car. Make sure they get everything. Makes my job easier."

Meticulously the Lee County Sheriffs Office forensic team processed the body and murder scene. Buck stood by as the technicians made an impression of a tire track next to the body.

He decided to talk to Captain Mastif about engaging the help of the men from Minnesota. He needed help. Buck's gaze returned to the body and then he spotted a TV truck just beyond the yellow tape. The media were not going to put a warm image of the Sheriff's Office on this latest murder.

Just then Buck's cell phone rang: "Buck here."

"This is Sergeant Mike Smith again. Are you at the crime scene?"

"Yes. Fingers gone on one hand and possible cause of death is a gun shot to the head, execution style." Buck decided to listen and learn: "Well Mike, tell me your thoughts."

"We've got a lot of related violence here in Palm Beach, including two deaths at a mansion on Ocean Blvd. After talking with Lt. Granderson, I believe that the common denominator is The Pearl of Tao."

Buck swore to himself. He knew his intuition had let him down. After all, Frank had told him that The Pearl was the connection and he brushed it off, erroneously focusing on Frank. "Sgt. Smith, I agree. It's time we got together with Gustavo Lucas down in Ft. Lauderdale and solve this together."

Now Sgt. Smith wanted to know about Gustavo. Buck stood near the forensics team as he explained to Smith about the theft of The Pearl and the assault on Ying by two of the deceased. They agreed to co-ordinate their efforts to capture the fleeing Kia.

The police were now moving rapidly and in synch. The little Kia was the subject of a concentrated search throughout south Florida. The eyes of the Florida State Troopers and city police departments in Lee, Collier and adjacent counties were scrupulously looking at every car driven in the dead of night. They wanted the screw up to be minor news because they got the murderers. Lee County Sheriffs Deputies were intense- any small white car got a passionate visual examination.

Quickly, success! Just over thirty miles away, near Corkscrew Swamp Sanctuary, a Lee County deputy found the abandoned Kia with blood in it and a shell casing. The car was off the main road to Immokalee and just a hundred yards down a sandy side road. The murderers had dumped the car just off the paved road to the Sanctuary. The deputy called in his discovery and immediately sealed off the area to preserve all evidence.

Buck listened to the radio report on his hand held and sprinted to his car. He roared off with little concern for the speed limit. Just after cresting the bridge at New Pass, his car went airborne and came down with a loud bang as the suspension bottomed out. The frame of the car sent sparks flying as it gouged the pavement. Buck pressed on the gas harder as he had a level, straight stretch of road ahead. Soon he was on Bonita Beach and he reluctantly slowed down. He got on the radio and ordered all K-9 units to the scene. He knew the Kia had been abandoned in an area where the foliage was as dense as a Brazilian jungle. He thought that the forensics team was going to have a busy night and morning.

Other deputies were already at the Kia and when he got out of his car, Buck was surprised that they weren't searching the area for the killers. He yelled at them: Get in gear and get a plan together for a coordinated search."

A gray haired sergeant pointed and said: "Look at this and then tell me what we are searching for."

Buck ran up to the edge of the taped off area looked for about five seconds and swore. He concluded that the murderer got out of the Kia and was picked up by another car. Buck shook his head as he saw a short set of footprints in the sand. They started at the drivers door to the Kia, went about forty feet and ended abruptly right next to a set of tire tracks. They concluded no suspects were hiding in the area; they were long gone in a car or truck of unknown type. Thankfully, the scene had been immediately contained and no cops had let their curiosity overcome their training. When curiosity overcomes professionalism, the forensics people have more footprints, hair, and fingerprints to compare. Cops leave their own evidence at the scene when they walk around it looking for evidence.

The first deputy on the scene summarized what was on the other side of the yellow ribbon of tape: on the floor of the back seat was a shell casing, probably a forty four caliber. Other bloody evidence was in the same area. This told Buck that Faroque went to Allah from the back of the car and his killer used a semi-automatic hand gun.

Buck called the dispatcher to cancel the search for the Kia. Law enforcement was now looking for one or more people with Faroque's blood on them. Without a vehicle to search for, the odds of an arrest tonight were slim.

The dispatcher reported that the license plate came back to a Buick reported stolen in Ft. Lauderdale and the Kia's serial number came back as a stolen from Palm Beach. Buck asked the name of the owner of the Kia and learned it was Cartier Chang. Buck had a lead and some evidence. He knew the murderers had stolen a license plate from the Buick and put it on the Kia to avoid detection because the Kia was reported as stolen. The question to be resolved was whether the Kia really was stolen. Buck formulated a plan as he watched the scene being processed; hopeful that the forensics people would find something more.

He called Granderson's cell phone as the sun peeked above the palmetto palms. "Are you coming out to Lingbao's land to help us find the exact spot where Faroque was tortured?"

"Is this Buck?"

"It ain't Barney Fife."

"I could say something about similarities, but I'll just say if I thought of you as inept, I wouldn't turn over to you the evidence I have. It's early in the morning. I didn't get much sleep last night." Granderson said wearily.

"I didn't get *any*. I'm at the intersection where Palm Beach says you made the 911 call. How soon will you get here?" Buck demanded without giving him a choice.

"An hour. While you're waiting, drive somewhere to get coffee and something for me to eat. Have you alerted emergency rooms in the area to report if they treated a gun shot wound to an Asian male? Then we would have the man who was torturing Faroque."

"Like I said this ain't Barney Fife. That's been done. Git on over here."

They met as agreed and Granderson turned over to Buck the evidence he recovered. Buck now had evidence that would identify Akbar as the first murder victim. Buck thanked him and they discussed the valuable information Granderson got from Zahra. They were convinced that it wasn't mere coincidence that immediately after Zahra found out about Lingbao Chang's compound, there had been an armed attack on it.

They bounced down the dirt roads in Buck's unmarked squad car. They drove through burned out foliage, until they came to the crossing paths where Granderson last saw the van and trailer. Stationed there were some firefighters; watching the smoldering fire to be sure it didn't rekindle. They walked to where Granderson first saw the gator and Faroque. The area had been charred and the demands of firefighting had obliterated any possible evidence. Even so, they searched closely, but to no avail.

They returned to the car and slowly drove on, hoping for a lucky break. Maybe the criminals had carelessly left some evidence. They came upon a small pond with a very sturdy, tall, chain link fence around it. They couldn't figure out why there was a fence around a pond in the middle of nowhere. Inside the fence at the edge of the pond, they discovered large splintered bones that they believed were big enough to come from a horse. They also found small pieces of what looked like horse hide.

Granderson surmised: "I think the golden gator was placed here when it was time for polo pony portions for dinner. Maybe we'll find some leftover trace evidence of the murder victims."

They moved slowly and inspected the weeds for evidence. They looked closely, pondering everything they observed. Finally, when they reached the far side of the pond, they saw two small pieces of cloth in the weeds. Dried blood was on one and the other had some type of substance on it. Buck went back to his car, put on latex gloves and returned with evidence bags to retrieve the evidence. Granderson then pointed out an area of dirt with what appeared to be dried blood. Buck looked at Granderson and they each produced the investigators smile; knowing that they were making a case. He photographed, measured and then collected the bloody dirt. He took pictures of the animal remains as they left.

Buck called Sgt. Smith and told him of their find.

"You went on a suspect's property without his consent! You went into a fenced area. Did you get a search warrant to search the property?" Sgt. Smith said dramatically.

"Don't need one." Buck said.

Granderson joined in: "Sergeant, you were concerned with Frank violating Lingbao Chang's privacy rights when he was doing surveillance outside his mansion. Now this! Why are you so protective of Lingbao Chang?"

"I want the investigation done properly so all the evidence is admissible."

In astonishment, Buck rolled his eyes as Granderson responded. "*IF* I was in doubt about the legality, I would've called my legal expert, former prosecutor, Frank Johnson. I was never in doubt. A search of open fields, even if fenced in, does not require a search warrant."

Buck added: "If you want to recover the horse evidence you better git out here. It could be the remains of a stolen polo pony. Get some DNA off the remains and compare it to the blood lines of polo ponies that have disappeared."

Buck hung up and grinned at Granderson. Buck conceded to himself that he had been wrong about the duo from the Twin Cities. He had mentally reviewed what happened in the last few hours. Frank was no longer a suspect. The suspect was a very wealthy man. Buck's steady aim was being jostled by Sgt. Smith as Buck attempted to put the suspect in his cross hairs. Why?

CHAPTER TWENTY TWO

Pao smiled as Cartier Chang climbed out of the swimming pool. It was a beautiful warm afternoon and they enjoyed each other in the palatial splendor of his parents' estate. They were both Chinese, in their late twenties and would look perfect on the cover of a fitness magazine. Pao and Cartier had been seeing a lot of each other ever since she came to the compound with her Amas troops. Pao had never experienced such regal magnificence.

"What are you doing with the Muslim terrorist I captured last night?" Pao asked.

"He needs to sit awhile. I interrogated him for a long time this morning, but he wasn't willing to tell me anything. Each day I'll ask him questions. After awhile, he'll be ready to talk. We'll get information from him. When our golden gator is hungry again, we'll be certain we have *all* the information. I think of the golden gator as a medieval truth serum- I can depend on the accuracy of statements when a terrorist is facing the jaws of death."

Pao shuddered at the tactic and asked: "Is that the most effective method of interrogation?"

"Effective means different things to different people. The golden gator loosens tongues. Unfortunately, in the past, I was a little too brutal, too quickly. I need to be more patient."

Pao felt a shiver run through her entire body. She didn't like the idea of torture to get information. She and her fellow Amas were defending against an attack on their temporary home. When the Amas eliminated the three Muslims, she knew that the Muslims were intent on gaining access into the compound to again mount a murderous attack on the innocent people inside. The attack by the sea women was self defense. Clearly, the Muslims were there to violently invade them.

She hoped Cartier could use methods other than the golden gator to reveal more information about the Muslim extremists. She believed that Lao-Tzu was assisting her in the divinely inspired defense of an abhorrent Muslim crusade.

She basked in the grandeur of the mansion as Cartier's cell phone rang. It was his father calling from The Breakers. "Son, an associate of Monty Moritz told me that the police found an abandoned white Kia which had been reported stolen. He says it's licensed in your name. I told him I didn't think you owned such a car. Please clear this up."

Cartier boldly responded: "Put him on the phone. I do own such a car."

"This is Frank Johnson. Could you tell me about the Kia?"

Cartier wanted to know why questions were being directed at him. "How did you find out about the car? Why do you want to know?"

Frank considered the response as defensive and not cooperative. "I've a friend in law enforcement and he joked about a little stolen Kia being recovered in a rural area and the owners address came back as Ocean Blvd., Palm Beach. He thought that with such an exclusive address, and the owner's first name was Cartier, the car would more likely be a Rolls Royce, Jaguar or a Mercedes. In a curious moment, I asked your father if he knew Cartier Chang and now we're talking."

Cartier's response was guarded: "I got a good deal on it and was going to transfer title to Lingbao Security; before I could, it was stolen. Tell my father that I'll explain it to him later."

"I hope you had insurance."

Cartier was flippant: "No. It was a cheap car. No big deal. Is that all?"

Frank knew that he had surprised Cartier and he continued: "Your father said you know about the fence around the pond on your father's land in Wellington. Do you keep the golden gator inside the fence?"

"Yes."

"Do you keep polo ponies inside the fenced area?"

Cartier paused before answering: “Not while the gator is there.”

Frank was trying to exclude all explanations about the bones: “Ever feed the golden gator a portion of, or a whole horse or pony?”

“Maybe a dead one. I’m busy at the moment can I call you back?”

Frank figured he had all the information he was going to get. “Thanks for the help. Goodbye.”

Cartier already knew about the murder of Faroque and the dumping of the Kia. He had called Ying to get updated on the location of the golden gator. Ying cautiously told Cartier that they were running out of options of where to hide the gator, but they were currently well hidden. Ying ended the conversation by joking that the gator was getting hungry and it might be time for a polo pony.

Shortly, Lingbao appeared poolside, then he and Cartier adjourned to his office to have a discussion. Lingbao’s voice was stern; “I’ve told you repeatedly that we must limit any actions which will bring attention to us. You shouldn’t have registered the Kia in your name. We have plenty of corporations in which to register it. We have Muslims who have repeatedly attacked our home and the police keep asking questions. Where is that gator?”

“Father, I don’t know. Ying told me it is well hidden. We were just defending ourselves. I don’t know why they were intent on attacking us in our own home….”

Just then the butler knocked on the door and identified himself. He was allowed to enter and he reported that two police officers wanted to talk to Lingbao.

“Who are they and what do they want to talk about?” Lingbao demanded.

The butler was succinct: “It is Sgt. Smith of the Palm Beach Police and a Buck Thorton of the Lee County Sheriffs Office. They want to updatc you on thc invcstigation of thc invasion of your compound and the deaths of your two guards.”

"Escort them in here." Lingbao then turned to Cartier: "We'll continue this conversation later."

"Yes father." Cartier left by another door.

As Buck entered with Sgt. Smith, Lingbao humbly presented himself. Buck looked around and whistled in admiration: "Mr. Chang, I'm in awe of your dwelling. I'm Buck Thorton. Just out of curiosity, what business are you in?"

"I own an international security company which has its largest presence in China. I also own a number of companies which produce consumer goods in China. We were a major factor at the 2008 Summer Olympics. It was very profitable….Gentlemen, please update me on the investigation into the murder of my people."

Sgt. Smith responded: "We have a large number of investigators working the case and we have some promising leads. We don't give out much information because we don't want to compromise the investigation. We have a history of solving virtually all of our murder cases. Luckily, we have few because Palm Beach is a very safe community."

Buck asked: "Do you sometimes keep a gator on the property?"

"Yes, why do you ask?"

"I heard that it's a rare yellow gator. A large one is very rare. I wondered if the reason your mansion was attacked was to steal the valuable gator."

Lingbao furled his brow. "I have many antiquities here that are much more valuable than a reptile. I have security here to protect myself and family from kidnapping and ransom. I also have security to protect my home and its contents."

"I would like to see these pieces of art. Could you give us a tour and show them to us?" Buck asked.

Lingbao tersely replied: "No. Just like your investigation, the fewer people who know what I have, the better. I value my privacy."

Buck nodded. "Have you had any other attempts to enter your property since the murders?"

"No."

Sgt. Smith quietly asked: "Do you or your staff know anyone named Haquan, Faroque or Akbar?"

"I don't know any of them. Later, I'll ask my staff."

"Can you give any reason why Muslim extremists would attack you or people in your compound?"

"No."

Buck joined in: "Your company was handling security before The Pearl was stolen. Do you have any thoughts about a connection between the theft and your home invasion?"

Lingbao replied: "No. The police in Ft. Lauderdale are handling the disappearance and my staff there has cooperated fully. Why would you think there is a connection?"

"Both incidents occurred in a short time span and involved you or your company. So what do you think Mr. Chang?"

"I already said 'no' what part of that word don't you understand?"

Buck didn't flinch. "Sometimes upon reflection people remember things or they become more insightful or honest. I'm just talking generally. No reflection on you Mr. Chang."

Fire was in Lingbao' eyes. He didn't accept insubordination and he felt that Buck had disparaged his integrity. He surmised Buck had a hidden agenda. What did Buck want to know but wasn't asking?

Buck commented: "I've lived in Florida all my life and I've never seen a yellow gator, could I see it? I assume it is inside the walled area near the gate."

"I don't know if it's around. I will inquire. I assume we are done. You will be escorted to the gate and informed if the gator is here."

Sgt. Smith decided to lessen the tension: "I hope we've been helpful and have answered all your questions. When we have more information we can release, my department will contact you."

Lingbao wasn't appeased: "I sure didn't get *any* information from your visit. I was asked questions rather than told of any significant breaks in the case. Don't bother to return. Just call and leave a message with my staff."

They were ushered out and by the time they got to the gate, were informed that the gator wasn't at the compound. Buck eyed the walled area where Frank had said the gator was kept. He wanted to scale the wall and look, but decided it wouldn't be a legal search.

As they drove away, Sgt. Smith said he was disappointed they didn't get more information from Lingbao. Buck replied: "We got plenty of information; we just didn't get any evidence." Buck intuitively surmised that Lingbao's candor was lacking. Too much action was swirling directly around Mr. Chang.

Frank was driving the Bentley back to Lovers Key with Monty Moritz busy on his cell phone talking with potential investors located in Madrid Spain. Monty was charming the man with the fact that the currency exchange rate allowed euros to buy a lot of U.S. dollars. Monty knew that Europeans were a good source of investment funds.

Frank mentally reviewed the conversation he just had with Cartier Chang. Frank surmised that Cartier was an integral part of the killing of Faroque and probably the others as well. Proving it was the challenge. Evidence had been found, but how could he tie it to Cartier and Lingbao Chang? They were careful not to be the ones doing the dirty work.

As the Bentley smoothly flowed around Lake Okeechobee, Frank envisioned the scene at Lovers Key. He could foresee tattered strips of yellow police tape snared in the bushes and TV crews pulled off the road doing follow up stories on the trio of violent deaths. He wondered about Monty's reaction that his tranquil estate was the dumping ground for dead Muslims. Would Monty be taken aback as the reality of a murder scene was vividly placed beside his estate? Frank wasn't ready to accept the proposition that the island was a magnet for violent crime. Nonetheless, while at The Breakers, he had found time to hire security to calm the neurotic Monique. Hopefully, security would be in place upon their return.

Monty ended his cell phone conversation and suggested they have lunch. They stopped in Labelle and after ordering, Frank excused himself to make a private call. Frank decided it was time to talk with Buck. Buck answered his cell phone mumbling something about not getting much sleep.

Frank cordially opened the conversation: "Well Buck, I've some very crucial information for you. I'm curious about what's happening. Why don't you update me on the investigation?"

Buck wasn't ready to do the talking: "You called me saying you had new information. I'm all ears."

Frank became more guarded; "Before leaving Palm Beach I believed that you had eliminated me as a suspect. Is that the case?"

"Yup. But you're not officially investigating this case, so I want to hear what you know before I give you information."

Frank couldn't figure out why Buck had become such a by the book investigator. "Buck, the evening before Granderson found Faroque being tortured, I was at the Lingbao Chang mansion for dinner. I can't be sure, but I think I heard the voice of Faroque inside a room in the building attached to the golden gator enclosure."

Buck became incensed: "Why the hell didn't you tell me this before?"

"Two reasons. First, I was considering it, but you hung up on me before I could tell you. Second, I wasn't going to tell you anything that connected me with evidence until you had come to the right conclusion that I was no longer a suspect." Frank paused. "I think its significant evidence. It puts Faroque inside the compound and puts him in proximity to the Chang's."

Buck's temper was still simmering. "How certain are you it was Faroque's voice?"

"I only heard him talk at the Museum of Art when he was arrested. I can't be positive. If I was positive I would've called the Palm Beach police right away."

Buck was like a bloodhound focused on a scent: "What was he saying?"

Frank said: "He wanted to be fed or be released and he said he couldn't live on just water. The response was from someone speaking Chinese in an angry tone of voice. It didn't sound like a casual conversation between two people. Even though I'm not positive it was Faroque talking, that potential plus the content of the conversation is enough to get a search warrant to search the building for evidence to show he was there and evidence of torture."

Buck grunted something about writing search warrants was a lot of work.

Frank wasn't discouraged by Buck's lack of enthusiasm: "Don't use my name as the source of the information in the search warrant. Just refer to me as a confidential reliable informant who has given information which has assisted law enforcement and has been independently verified. And be sure the warrant is sealed."

"You're sure giving me my marching orders. Do you want to draft the search warrant too?" snapped Buck.

"Informants don't draft search warrants." Frank calmly replied. "Keep me updated. You owe me. I've got to go, my boss is waiting."

Zahra, Haquan's widow, trembled as she entered the cool, confines of the morgue. Granderson was at her side for support. She shook from the apprehension of the task at hand and the chill in the air. When the Chief Medical Examiner rolled out the stainless steel gurney, only the face was uncovered. Zahra wailed and flung herself on the body of Faroque. Granderson stood back for a moment and let her release her emotions.

Just as Granderson stepped forward to console her and move her away, the sound of a gurney moving was repeated behind them. Dr. Doris Delaney had quickly revealed another corpse. As Granderson and Zahra turned in unison, her scream pierced the room. Her attempt to move towards the body was unsuccessful. Her knees buckled, she lamented "Akbar" and fainted.

Granderson's quick reaction to grab her, kept her from hitting the floor. He carried her out and Dr. Delaney soon followed. Granderson put her upright in a chair and talked to her. He was glad that her husband previously had been identified using fingerprints. He shuddered at the thought of Zahra's reaction to being confronted with his mutilated body. She remained groggy as Granderson tried to console her and Dr. Delaney looked on in obvious distain. Minutes passed and finally Zahra haltingly verbally responded to him. Between gasps, she cried out that the first body was that of Faroque and the second was Akbar.

Satisfied, Dr. Delaney walked away and considered various strategies to resolve her erroneous statement that Akbar died from a bear attack. She knew all three men were friends and she surmised they had met their demise at the hands of the same group of killers. Bite marks on all three were probably made by the same animal and most certainly were made by a big gator.

Dr. Delaney had read the report of the two wildlife officers, Cole Clancy and Billy Trickle. She knew that it would only be a matter of time before someone leaked the report to the press. She had to figure out a way to back track and report that the first body-Akbar- had been attacked by a gator. She would reveal a lot of information all at once. Then the change wouldn't be such big news. The press would concentrate on the identity of the men and seek reactions from the next of kin.

CHAPTER TWENTY THREE

Stephanie stood in awe at the entrance to the estate on Lovers Key. She was dazzled by the sapphire blue sky, the view of the sparkling, endless Gulf of Mexico and the peacefulness of the sight of two ospreys soaring overhead. She had been apart from Frank for too long and beamed with joy at the thought of his face when he encountered her.

It seemed out of context to see a security guard posted at the driveway of the estate. She approached the guard to explain she was Frank's girlfriend from Minnesota and she had arrived to surprise him. Her pretty face and fashionable attire convinced the guard that she wasn't a security threat and he let her proceed, after directing her to Frank's cottage.

In the doorway to Frank's cottage, she surveyed the modest furnishings and her elation dwindled- no Frank. She anxiously wondered how long it would take until their reunion. In her excitement to be with him, she didn't consider he might not be present for her surprise arrival. She hadn't formulated a plan to find him.

Her view from the entrance gate, of the sun dappled waters, worked as a magnet. She hoped Frank would be on the beach tanning his muscular body. At worst, she would experience embracing the seaside vista. She wandered down a footpath lined with royal palms and came upon a garden of hibiscus in full bloom. She stood there admiring the multitude of colors- red, coral, peach and pink hibiscus smiled at her. She felt a new surge of happiness. Again she looked up to admire the deep blue sky; a pleasure she rarely experienced while working long hours inside her office. She didn't see Juan Salvador, the gardener; stand up on the other side of garden. She was unsettled when his voice cracked the serenity. He asked: "Are you lost?"

"No, I'm looking for Frank."

Juan replied: "He'll be here in a few minutes. He's driving Mr. Moritz back from Palm Beach."

"May I walk out to the beach?"

"Sure, just go straight down the path."

Stephanie strolled to the beach where she was stunned at the brilliance of the white sand as it mixed with the clear turquoise water. The sand transformed the palate of water from green to deep blue as the water depth increased. Transfixed by nature's beauty, she stood there on the sand, immersed at the vastness of the Gulf of Mexico. She didn't feel a need to do anything but look. Her muscles relaxed as her senses soaked up the peacefulness. As she took off her shoes at the water's edge, she was startled by a splash just twenty feet away. As she looked at the ripples, a big fish jumped out of the water and it was immediately pursued by a large dolphin. Both disappeared below the surface, but the dolphin reappeared with the fish in its mouth. The fish flopped and escaped. She watched in wonder as the two repeatedly went under and resurfaced. They were playing a watery game of cat and mouse as they zigzagged to Stephanie's amazement.

The silent footsteps in the sand did not reveal the approach of Angeline who had been sitting in a beach chair amongst fragrant gardenias. She had been sketching a new swimsuit design when she noticed Stephanie. Previously, the two had a fleeting encounter at a pub in Steamboat. Angeline hadn't planned a surreptitious approach, but the longer she remained an unknown, the more she loved the surprise. When she spoke, Stephanie jumped.

"You must be Stephanie."

"Yes."

"I'm Angeline. What brings you to Lovers Key?" she inquired in a voice which didn't reveal her animosity.

"I came to see Frank." Stephanie replied evenly. She was disposed to make a caustic comment about the need to ask the question when the answer was so obvious.

"He's not here, maybe you could come back tomorrow; he might be here by then."

Stephanie resolved to be calm in the face of the antagonism: "The man tending the flowers said Frank would be here in a few minutes.

Is it OK if I just stay here on the beach? It's so beautiful here. It makes me feel ecstatic to be alive. I don't feel I have a mean bone in my body. How about you?"

"This setting brings out all my creativity. It lets my imagination exceed that of other designers. It's like I have an unfair advantage and I use it."

Upon hearing Angeline's egotistical self praise, Stephanie's mindset wasn't positive. Stephanie felt Angeline's comments were arrogant, sordid and selfish. She was about to let her indignation flow to the surface like lava out of a volcano. However, she quickly put her emotions into volcanic dormancy: "Angeline, did you want to join me while I wait for Frank?"

"No. I need to keep working on my new designs. Solitude is one setting which inspires my creations. Frank's the other, especially under a clear night sky with a bottle of wine."

Stephanie's emotional volcano was ever so close to letting off a plume of hot steam, but instead she released an acidic smile and "Thanks, I'll go to Frank's cottage. I know my way."

As she walked away, her vexation with Angeline simmered. When she entered Frank's cottage she calmed down when she saw the picture of her and Frank with his arm around her. They were on a picnic, on a bluff overlooking the Mississippi River, outside of Saint Paul. She remembered the tender moments they shared on Schaar's Bluff.

As she sat thinking about other romantic moments, her reminiscing turned to curiosity. She wondered if there was anything in the cottage which could show a romantic relationship between Frank and Angeline. She looked around the living room and saw nothing. A stroll through the bedroom revealed nothing.

When she returned to the living room, she smiled and then broke into a laugh. How had she missed it? There in the living room was Frank's old recliner. It was a relic when he bought it and now it looked even more tattered. Frank refused to part with it. He had it during college and it was his favorite piece of furniture.

Stephanie reminisced how Frank would sit in the beat up recliner and attempt to resolve whatever issue he was working on as a prosecutor. The recliner was a decorator's night mare- it was sorely out of date and worn. She was comforted that he hadn't changed. She sat down on the living room sofa and was now feeling better about Frank's commitment to her and them.

She was brought back to the present when she heard a car pull up and looked out to see Frank behind the wheel of a very large, expensive imported car. Soon he was in the doorway and a smile spread across his face as he saw Stephanie. She moved quickly and in two steps they were pressing against each other in a long overdue embrace. Not a word was exchanged as their lips pressed together. She wanted the moment to last as long as the sun had been warming the earth.

Frank was overjoyed and completely surprised. He wondered if he let go, whether she would disappear as if she had been an apparition. He admitted to himself that the separation had been too long and he tenderly whispered in her ear: "Stephanie, I missed you so much. I'm so surprised you could get away from work. I'm so excited you're here. You're staying a month; aren't you?"

"Just enjoy the moment." She said. Her heart was joyous and her mind was racing: "why had they let themselves be apart for so long?" She vowed to start balancing her professional life so it didn't continue to overpower her personal life.

Neither wanted the embrace to end as they again passionately kissed. They both felt the magnetism. Stephanie moved away, ever so reluctantly.

Frank was smiling like a man who just won the lottery: "I'm so thankful you're here. I watched many a gorgeous sunset thinking you should be here by my side. It would've been so much more romantic if I had shared those moments with you. I've so much to tell you since we last talked."

"You seem unusually vocal, so talk to me."

They snuggled on the sofa and Frank continued; "There were a number of nights in a row that I stood at the end of this narrow island thinking of you. I yearned for you and when I saw a dramatic sunset, I'd be mesmerized by a soulful moon rise over the bay. You know I'm not a poet but I knew in my heart that the setting was so exceptional that even I could create a poem."

Frank got up and went into his bedroom. He reappeared with a large manila envelope in his hand. "This is the poem I wrote for you, it's entitled "*Lunar Light on Lover's Key'*

Don't read it until you get back to St. Paul."

Stephanie was so touched that tears welled up in the corners of her eyes. "Frank, this is so touching. What if I promised to stay with you here on Lovers Key? Then could I open it now and read it?"

"Absolutely!" Frank said, stunned at the proposal.

Stephanie paused to consider what she had just said. She now had to back track. "I wish I could, but my career beckons me back. Let's just enjoy the time we have together."

They embraced as Frank whispered: "Enjoy the moment."

As they held each other, she remembered them being snuggled in a rugged old cabin in the woods of northern Minnesota, in the sub zero cold as they gazed into a crackling fire. Frank remembered when the two of them were on a magnificent sailboat anchored off a Caribbean island and the cascade of stars in the night sky made them feel so lucky to be together. It was a certainty that these memories had been indelibly sculpted in their love for each other. Their embrace reignited passions that had been suppressed too long.

Later, the far away sound of a phone ringing didn't stir them to answer it. The voice of Monique Moritz on the answering machine invited them to dinner on the patio. As the afternoon sun meandered over the Gulf, Frank and Stephanie listened to the message and knew that proper etiquette required attendance.

Monique was animated as she welcomed Frank and Stephanie onto the patio on a perfect evening. She offered them each a glass of Bordeaux wine. As the sun flowed to the horizon, it tried to match the deep red of the wine. The tropical waters whispered a love song as the waves inched up the sand towards the patio. Stephanie's thoughts returned to the afternoon and she squeezed Frank's hand. Their eyes met and love surrounded them. As she reluctantly turned away, her gaze did a survey of the surroundings and she was captured by the natural beauty of the island. Her eyes then came to rest on

Frank- she quickly acknowledged to herself that Lovers Key was aptly named. She lifted her glass and a prism of light moved from it towards Frank. She thought of it as a rainbow from one lover to another.

Monique usually became animated at sunset. Frank thought of it as a combination of wine and her natural joy for life. She studied Stephanie: a tall, slender, dark haired woman just slightly shorter than Frank and about the same age. As Stephanie relaxed on the patio in a casual sun dress with peach flowers on a pale yellow background, she looked as if she could be an advertisement to lure tourists to an island in paradise.

Monique absently swirled the glass of wine, her third, and remarkably asked the question: "Frank, tell me why you were so foolish to leave such a beautiful woman."

Stephanie chimed in: "Not once, but twice."

Frank decided to be brief: "I was burned out from being a prosecutor. I wanted to escape the long winters of Minnesota. But I couldn't decide if I wanted to be a beach bum or a ski bum. I elected to be a ski vagabond."

Frank continued: "I had great success with juries in persuading them to make the right decision. I thought I'd be successful using all my persuasive powers to convince Stephanie to join me. I was wrong. Not once but twice."

Stephanie followed up: "The strength of our love is shown by the fact that it has endured two long distance separations. But our love won't last forever if we're apart indefinitely."

Frank nodded. He knew he had to be with her. They needed to discuss a plan to make it happen.

Their attention moved towards the mansion as Angeline made her entrance. Greetings were exchanged and she moved up to Frank to give him a European style greeting- a light kiss on each cheek. However, Stephanie viewed Angeline's embrace of Frank as a little more intense than customary because of the prolonged embrace. When Angeline's smirking eyes met hers, Stephanie knew that Angeline was putting on a performance to get a jealous reaction. Stephanie wasn't going to let a rich harlot push her into an inappropriate response, so she ignored the challenging flirtation.

Monique was oblivious to the tension and took another sip of Bordeaux. "Angeline, what creations were you working on this afternoon?"

Angeline turned to Stephanie and replied: "Swimsuits for tall, thin women who need to have their inconsequential busts accentuated. It's not an easy accomplishment but I think I have two designs that rely on style rather than foam."

Stephanie's eyes didn't flinch from Angeline's snide smirk. She remained composed. Unknowingly, Monique ended their stare down when she exclaimed: "I'm happy that you have tackled such a significant problem. This could help women who have been afraid to wear a swim suit because they have no curves. I hope the fashion industry will acknowledge you've resolved it."

Monty Moritz could be heard talking on his cell phone as he came into view. He ended his conversation as he joined the foursome. "I hope I'm not too late. I don't want to be considered an unsocial cow."

Monique laughed and retorted: "You're my lovable old bull that remains corralled in my pasture....We've been talking fashion design and now it's time we learned more about our guest Stephanie."

Monty Moritz looked at his daughter who was silent and contemplated whether there was a conflict about the new arrival. He wondered how his daughter felt about the handsome man from Minnesota who had a beautiful girlfriend arrive unannounced. Was the girlfriend a piece of history? Angeline must have feelings for Frank; after all, she repeatedly advocated he hire Frank. The statuesque woman from Minnesota must be competition- in the eyes of his daughter. He would sit back, watch and evaluate.

Frank interrupted Monty's musings. "Stephanie is an architect who lives and works in St. Paul. I met her in college. She's been very creative and successful, especially in upper end condo design."

Monty turned towards Frank and chimed in: "Angeline didn't tell me about Stephanie when she convinced me to hire you. She raved about your legal skills and your heroism in saving her life when she was injured snowboarding at Steamboat Springs, Colorado."

Angeline shuddered. Stephanie smiled and Frank responded: "Stephanie loves Minnesota and it would be difficult to get her to move. I've tried, but to no avail."

Monty turned toward Stephanie and asked: "Are you familiar with the new designs in Vera Spain, along the Mediterranean Sea, near the Costa del Sol?"

"Yes. Those fresh looks will become the new wave in the USA. Developers need to realize that people buying upper bracket second homes will crave the look." Stephanie's gaze went from Monty to the now insecure Angeline.

Monty was charmed by her response and thought highly of her perceptions. Monique chimed in: "Monty, would it be hard to convince venture capitalists to finance a large development that is so, shall we call it 'new wave' European?"

"I've talked enough business for today. Let's have a drink and enjoy the evening. I love this place, but business doesn't let me stay here enough. I want to slow down, but there are too many projects I get caught up in. I should send Frank out on the road and I'll just stay here."

Everyone laughed but Angeline.

CHAPTER TWENTY FOUR

Buck sat in the Sheriff's Office conference room with other officers and Captain Mastif. They were meeting to plan for the execution of a search warrant at Lingbao Chang's massive compound.

Buck said: "I'm perplexed about Sgt. Smith. He's in the police department in the city where we'll be executing the search warrant. That means we have to meet with them ahead of time to coordinate it. I'm just not sure about his relationship with Lingbao Chang. He's erroneously concerned about the legality of searches involving Chang."

Captain Merrill Mastif nodded in agreement. "Information leaks-accidental and intentional are always a problem and this will be a major operation. Sgt. Smith concerns me too. I'll discreetly handle it with Palm Beach PD."

Buck replied: "Well the prospect exists that we'll encounter serious armed resistance. Chang has his own armed security forces. His security was able to repel armed intruders into the compound and Frank was met with a barrage of bullets when he peeked his head over the wall. We need to have a show of superior force so his security forces are not inclined to resist our lawful entry."

Another deputy interjected: "We need to show strength. We should use the Peacekeeper."

Buck continued: "The goal of every officer is to finish their shift alive. I should say not just alive but uninjured- no gun shot or knife wounds from criminals. Training and preparation increase the health of our cops. This is a high risk entry."

Deputies at the table agreed.

Buck went on: "I spoke with Frank Johnson and he reminded me that Akbar, the first body found at Lovers Key was never reported missing. Frank is concerned that other Muslims are being held prisoner in the compound and being subjected to torture as we speak. We need a quick entrance and ability to control those inside."

Mastif was thoughtfully silent as he considered the options. The cops in the meeting had pin pointed the issues. The Peacekeeper was an armored vehicle which had been obtained from the U.S. military and it would instantly impress an observer that it could not be stopped. It was designed for serious military combat and it held it's own against anything it ran up against on the street.

Mastif's silence concerned Buck: "If they refuse to open the gates, I'm sure the Peacekeeper would be able to penetrate the compound."

Mastif replied; "This is a quiet, wealthy neighborhood and the mere sight of the Peacekeeper is going to shock them. I have to run this by the Sheriff, but I think it's a go. What about the search warrant and getting it signed?"

Buck sighed: "It has been a major project drafting the warrant. I'll go to the judge and get it signed."

Mastif replied: "Good. Do that this afternoon. I'll be sure we have enough officers and brief the team leaders on our plan for entry, securing the premises and the search. We'll execute it right away tomorrow morning."

The meeting broke up and Buck headed to the courthouse. He patiently waited outside the chambers of Judge Melissa Grannis. A law clerk escorted Buck into the chambers and he handed the multi page document to the judge. She started reading and Buck waited. Finally, the judge looked up and commented: "You're looking for an Asian man who was shot by a law enforcement officer on open land owned by Lingbao Chang. And that man tortured a man that was murdered. You gave a general description of the man you are searching for, but you don't give his name. Is that an oversight?"

"No, your honor. We don't know his name."

Judge Grannis continued: "You don't give a home address for this man; what is it?"

Buck looked the judge in the eye and said: "We believe he frequently is at the place to be searched. He was with a man named Ying at the time of the torture of the last victim and Ying is employed by the owner of the property. Also, Ying was followed there by an undercover officer. In addition, two other men were tortured and killed by a large gator. The owner keeps a large golden gator on the premises."

As the court reporter continued to type up all of this with her little machine, Judge Grannis ruled: "I understand that you don't need clear and convincing evidence for a search warrant- you only need probable cause. That is, probable cause that the item you are searching for will be found at the location you are requesting to search. However, I find, as it relates to searching for and getting DNA from this unnamed man, you do not have probable cause. Therefore, you can't search for this man at the mansion."

Buck was poker faced and waited.

Judge Grannis continued: "You want to search for The Pearl of Tao and that is granted. So is a search for blood and other items, including firearms, to show that a man named Faroque was there after having been kidnapped, held against his will, tortured, shot and killed. I further rule that probable cause is lacking to search for stolen polo ponies or horses. Your informant saw the gator eating part of a horse, but you haven't shown that the horse was stolen. Therefore, no search for equines."

The judge resolved other items to be searched for in Buck's favor, signed the warrant and handed it back. "Officer, this is a very quiet, law abiding neighborhood. What are your plans so the neighbors aren't alarmed?"

"We'll have a Peacekeeper stationed at the front gates of the compound and we'll announce the presence of the Peacekeeper to those inside and anyone outside."

The Judge smiled and said: "Good. I really believe that by having good communication, a lot of confrontation can be avoided. These are intelligent people around Ocean Blvd., they will respond positively to well placed dialogue by a peacekeeper."

"Yes, your honor." Buck left wondering if the judge had any military training and whether they had a meeting of the minds on what a "Peacekeeper" was.

As he walked out of the courthouse, he was pleased with the result. He really hadn't lost much. The judge did not limit where they could search in the compound. So they could search anywhere the items could be found. They were searching for small amounts of blood, similar shell casings and bullets that killed Faroque. And, of course, the murder weapon. They could look high and low-in drawers, under beds, in cupboards-anywhere. If they found something that was obviously illegal, they could seize it because it was in plain view. Buck called the Captain and said everything was a go.

Frank was now sitting in his decrepit recliner, in a euphoric state, as he gazed upon Stephanie. Frank was getting up to join her on the sofa when his cell phone rang. Granderson spoke before Frank could say anything: "Buck is going to execute a search warrant tomorrow morning at the compound of Lingbao Chang."

"Did Buck tell you that?" Frank asked.

"No. Buck wouldn't tell me; even if I asked. That info is on a need to know basis and we don't need to know."

"I know you want me to ask this question, so I will. How can you be so sure?"

Granderson replied: "He called me and asked me a lot of detailed questions about my confrontation with Ying and his thugs when they were torturing Faroque. The very type of information that would go into a search warrant."

Frank interjected: "Or his report."

"If you hadn't interrupted me, you would know I called the courthouse and asked to be connected to the chambers of the judge assigned to review search warrants. After being connected, I asked if Buck Thorton was still there and they said he just left."

"Great investigation. You're right, it'll be tomorrow morning. They aren't going to sit and wait so the bad guys can eliminate evidence."

Granderson asked: "Why not watch as they assault the compound. This will not be an ordinary encounter."

"I assume you're still at The Breakers."

"Yup."

"You'll need to stay there tonight because I have a new visitor staying with me."

Granderson was curious: "Who?"

"Stephanie made a surprise arrival."

"Oh…."

Frank laughed. Granderson was familiar with the romantic relationship between Frank and Stephanie and knew he was going to have to look for new quarters. His excitement about the search didn't dwindle. "I'll be watching from the periphery as they do the warrant. Interested in joining me?"

"I already have a business meeting early tomorrow morning. It will be short. I'm sure Stephanie will be sleeping in tomorrow after today's early morning flight."

Stephanie only heard one side of the conversation and she wasn't sure she liked it. But she did fly in unannounced. She vowed that she would enjoy the evening with Frank and let tomorrow take care of itself. Frank said goodbye to Granderson and snuggled up on the couch with his love. Frank was dramatic and charming as he described the rain drenched trip to Ft. Lauderdale with Monique and the knife attack at the museum. He also told her about the missing Pearl of Tao.

Stephanie snuggled closer to Frank and again realized why she loved her colorful man. She gazed into his eyes and whispered: "I love you." Frank responded with his own proclamation of passionate affection.

CHAPTER TWENTY FIVE

The morning sun lay hidden below the Atlantic Ocean, and transformed the sky at the horizon to a peach colored glow. Dark waves, crowned with brilliant white top hats, rolled in. Neither a ship nor a person interrupted the waves to disturb the idyllic scene. It was such a memorable panorama that the viewer could summon the scene back years later and again experience the peacefulness.

Yet with many vistas and pictures, that which is just out of view can change the feeling. A look down the beach brought the viewer back to the realization that the edge of the Atlantic is inhabited by people and their civilization. Police officers dressed completely in black silently positioned themselves along the beach. They faced the wall of the compound of Lingbao Chang and their attire left no doubt that if required, they were ready to defend themselves from a violent attack. The personal armaments they strapped to their bodies and their grim demeanor oozed anticipation for battle. "POLICE" or "SHERIFF" was emblazoned on their backs and across their chests. Additional officers, less battle ready, were positioned a block north and south on the beach to stop people from walking the beach and getting too close to the action.

Chang's men monitoring the security cameras, became alarmed at the assembly, and quickly called Chang. He was startled by the ring of his bedside phone and was even more disturbed when he heard the report. The security guard believed that the men assembled on the beach were undoubtedly Muslim extremists who were ready to launch another assault on the compound. The word 'police' on their black outfits was a trick.

Chang ordered the guard to have all security forces immediately report for duty and to have the Amas women activated as well. Chang scrambled out of bed, got dressed and hurriedly left the bedroom, much to the concern of Mrs. Chang, who looked on with fearful eyes.

Buck and Captain Mastif stood behind the Peacekeeper on Ocean Blvd. The Peacekeeper was an impressive military weapon. It had portholes to shoot out of, thick bullet proof glass and formidable metal plate to encapsulate those inside. It was obviously an aberration on the posh playground of Palm Beach.

The local residents were kept a block away by means of street barricades. The nearby mansions were being evacuated. The Captain heard a lot of radio traffic from his fellow officers who reported that the ultra wealthy were calling the Mayor and Chief of Police of Palm Beach because of the outrageous intrusion on their privacy- mandated to leave their mansions before dawn. The wealthy didn't comprehend that if gun fire erupted- especially large caliber weapons, neighbors and their staff were at risk of death by a stray or ricocheted bullet.

The Captain knew it was important to find significant evidence linking the compound to the murders or there would be serious political ramifications. Palm Beach residents had their own political fire power and it extended far beyond their borders.

The law enforcement officers positioned in front of the gate stayed close to the heavily armored Peacekeeper because it gave them a sense of safety. Hopefully, Chang's forces would not have anything in their arsenal to stop the Peacekeeper. The officers were making small talk but the usual loud banter when a large group of cops assembled was glaringly absent. They knew this was dangerous business.

Buck approached the front gate and pressed the call button. In a stern voice he announced: "I'm Buck Thorton with the Lee County Sheriff's Office. I have a search warrant to search the entire compound. You must open the gate immediately and allow us to enter."

A voice on the intercom replied: "Please put the warrant in front of the video camera so I can see it. Once I know it's a valid search warrant I'll talk to Lingbao Chang about whether he'll allow me to open the gates."

Buck wasn't going to wait. Evidence could be destroyed as they stood outside. He wasn't into negotiation or compromise and his voice reflected he was in charge. "Listen closely! You have one minute to open the gates or we *will* make a forcible entry. Please take note of the Peacekeeper vehicle positioned just behind me."

The voice responded: "If you had called earlier, we could've gotten clearance ahead of time for your entry."

Captain Mastif shook his head in disbelief. No one with a search warrant is going to tell the criminals ahead of time, and give the criminals the opportunity to dump incriminating evidence.

Buck became emphatic: "FIFTY SECONDS! WE DON'T NEED ANYONE'S PERMISSION TO ENTER. YOUR CHOICE IS TO OPEN THE GATES OR WE'LL FORCIBLY COME THROUGH THE GATES."

"I'm still trying to get a hold of Mr. Chang. He's not answering his phone. Be patient. I must follow protocol."

"THIRTY SECONDS!" Buck snarled.

Mastif calmly spoke into his radio: "Thirty seconds to entry. Be sure all civilians are outside the perimeter. Front gates have not been opened voluntarily."

Buck growled into the intercom: "TWENTY SECONDS!"

Mastif was again giving direction to his forces: "Audio contact made with person inside. He refuses to open the gate. Prepare for a forced entry. Double check that civilians are outside the perimeter."

"TEN SECONDS!" Buck snapped.

"Peacekeeper prepare to move." Mastif ordered.

The voice on the intercom was now pleading: "Can't you give me another minute?"

"FOUR! THREE! TWO!"

Just then the gates started to open, but before Mastif could radio that information, a sudden engine roar came from inside the compound. A large luxury sedan was flying toward the gates. The car was about to smash into the gates, but they opened just wide enough, for the car to rocket through. Tires squealed as the car headed directly at the officers. To save their lives, the officers frantically jumped to each side of the car.

Officers opened fire. The roar of rapid bursts of automatic weapons fire changed Ocean Blvd into a war zone. Car glass shattered and bullets blasted through the metal.

Mastif screamed above the din: "CROSSFIRE! CROSSFIRE! HOLD YOUR FIRE!"

The Peacekeeper jolted forward and took aim at the car, narrowly missing officers. The metal behemoth looked like it would make a direct hit on the car, but in a split second maneuver, the car jerked to the left. The Peacekeeper was on attack and smashed into the side of the car, sending parts flying. The car bounced wildly out of control.

The luxury sedan looked like junk as it careened, but remained upright. Buck looked into the interior of the car and could only see a driver huddled just below the top of the dashboard- he was literally driving blindly.

"Officer down!" Screamed someone as all dreaded the feared words.

The focus turned from the car to the voice. Another voice angrily retorted: "I'll make it. Get the job done!"

The car banged against the curb and crazily accelerated up the street, as officers reluctantly held their fire. Two way radios directed officers at the perimeter barricades to stop the car.

Captain Mastif commanded: "Move forward. Enter the compound and secure it. Don't be distracted from our objective."

Buck had his firearm trained on the car and then swiveled toward the compound. He told himself: "be sure of your target; be sure you should fire." His eyes opened wide as he perceived a battalion of angels.

Pao and her group of 20 Amas were standing in formation in their white flowing robes and head dresses. Buck thought that Chang had somehow summoned angelic intervention to stop the cops. He kept his weapon ready to fire. He looked again, and confirmed what he had originally perceived.

Pao gave an order in Chinese and in unison the Amas pulled nun-chucks from beneath their robes. These were the same martial arts type weapons the women used to defeat the Muslims who tried to invade the compound.

Buck thought: "Angelic warriors. If I shoot an angel, my career will be over and I'll be spending eternity with the devil." Yet he kept his gun trained on their leader.

He then ordered: "Put down your weapons. We're the police. We have a valid search warrant signed by a judge. Do not interfere with us or you *will* face the consequences."

Pao gave her troops an order in Chinese. They moved apart and some moved backward- forming a semicircle. They moved forward in unison and their elliptical formation, in effect, contained the incoming officers.

"Do you understand English?" Mastif yelled

"Yes."

The Captain was getting impatient. The compound needed to be secured quickly so evidence wouldn't be compromised, but he was alarmed by the implications of divine intervention on Chang's behalf. He told Pao: "We'll immediately enter the compound. Unless you order your people to put down their weapons, ya'll face serious consequences."

Pao seemed unimpressed. "What are the consequences?" She then gave another order. The Amas snapped to attention and rapidly moved their weapons to an attack position.

Mastif knew that the tension had escalated, but his voice showed no emotion: "Arrest and prosecution are the consequences of disobeying a lawful police order. If you resist we'll use every type of force we're legally entitled to."

Pao considered her options. Mr. Chang was not around to direct her. The police had superior numbers and firepower. They also had the legal authority to enter the compound. Still she wasn't in a hurry to surrender. She stood there mute and waited.

Mastif wasn't going to be defeated by delay, so he ordered his officers to surround all the women in angelic flowing garments. The officers did so and Mastif again ordered: "Put down your weapons or face arrest."

Pao didn't respond and Mastif ordered: "Arrest her."

Her response was an order in Chinese to her angelic looking forces.

Buck worried that her command was for attack if she was manhandled. The tension enveloped all the combatants. He had his firearm trained on her, hoping he wouldn't have to fire. An officer slowly walked up to Pao, handcuffed her and she was perfunctorily lead away. The Amas showed no reaction.

Mastif ordered the angels: "Move together and drop your weapons."

In view of her warriors, the officers spun Pao around to face her companions. Buck commanded: "Order your troops to surrender or massive blood shed *will* result."

The flowing robed warriors didn't move.

Buck told the women: "Those nun-chucks are no match for automatic weapons and we have you totally outnumbered."

The angelic Amas stood their ground, but did not attack. Law enforcement officers had their fingers on the trigger of their high powered weapons.

Mastif was stunned to realize that when he ordered his men to surround the armed angels, he had ordered his men into a dangerous situation. Officers were in the line of fire of fellow officers! Quickly he ordered: "Law enforcement- back off to the gates keep your weapons on these women."

Quickly, the ranks were realigned. The tension lessened slightly, but the clock was ticking. Mastif and Buck glared at Pao.

Mastif pointed his finger at her and shouted: "Order them to surrender-NOW or we'll order them onto the ground. If they don't comply, all legal force will be used to make an arrest. This includes deadly force."

Finally, Pao gave an order. The flowing robed Amas moved together and dropped their nun-chucks. Officers marched them outside the gates and corralled them. Battle ready cops surrounded what appeared to be heavenly sent saviors.

Buck and Mastif charged towards the mansion and now had to confront a detachment of Chang's security forces- all with handguns on their duty belts.

Mastif was growing more impatient. He shouted: "Peacekeeper move forward; prepare to take aggressive action."

The Peacekeeper rumbled forward with pieces of the car dangling from it. No one doubted that this was an unstoppable weapon. Suddenly the barrels of machine guns popped out of the gun ports. The reaction of Chang's men was immediate and very visual. Their eyes widened, their chests deflated and their hands moved away from their gun belts.

Mastif ordered: "Slowly unbuckle your belts, drop them to the ground and move towards the vehicle. NOW!"

The men did as they were told and were quickly ushered to the gates.

Finally, Mastif entered the mansion as he led other officers. He was dismayed at the length of time it took to get inside. In the library, they encountered a Chinese woman and she identified herself as Mrs. Chang.

The Captain asked: "Where is Mr. Chang?"

"I don't know. He got a phone call while we were in bed. He got up, got dressed and left."

"Did he say where he was going?"

She paused, looked down and finally said: "He said he had to go talk to his lawyer."

Mastif looked around the library and was impressed with the items in it. Not just the volumes of books, but the impressive looking works of art. He noticed that one pedestal had no object on it. He walked over and looked closely at the top of the pedestal. There was a light amount of dust except on the center, which was dust free.

"What work of art was here?" Mastif asked.

After a poignant pause, she turned away and said: "I don't know. I need to go out by the pool and rest."

"You will remain right here while we execute the warrant." The Captain didn't acquire his rank by accepting everything at face value. He ordered an officer to sit with Mrs. Chang; he didn't want her to frustrate the search.

CHAPTER TWENTY SIX

"I thought you had a business meeting this morning." Granderson commented when he answered the knock on his door.

Frank smiled but said nothing as they headed out in the classic red Mustang. After a short drive, they pulled up and stopped. Their outward appearance showed a calm, patient demeanor. However, from experience, they knew how to mask their emotions in the face of a volatile situation that was about to explode.

They were parked on a side street facing Ocean Blvd, just down from the police barricades. Their eyes targeted the officers assembled a block away in front of The Temple gates. The Peacekeeper commanded respect; it evoked a perception that it swaggered in the street, anxious to launch into combat. It was an impressive armored vehicle; yet completely out of place amid the opulence of Ocean Blvd. where a mansion recently sold for eighty million dollars.

Many times Granderson had been involved in preparations to execute a search warrant; however, this was way out of the norm. In a case involving multiple murders extensive precautions must be taken because the risk to officers is high. Some murderers vow never to be taken alive. Here, the prospect for harm to law enforcement was extremely high because the suspects had their own armed and trained security force. This was entirely different from dealing with street criminals who occasionally are organized: their daily level of readiness to defend their turf goes up and down depending whether they are high on drugs. Crime knows no boundaries; yet murder certainly isn't routine on Ocean Blvd. in lavish Palm Beach.

In tune to the locale, the radio was softly playing smooth jazz as Frank and Granderson pondered the level resistance which would be encountered once the gates were opened. Promptly, the pondering ended as the quiet street was punctuated by the sound of gun fire.

They jumped and then ducked down as they held their breath. They waited until the reports of firearms ended.

The screech of tires and the roar of an engine made them look up in time to see a car blast through the barricade on Ocean Blvd. It thundered towards them. Onlookers were unnerved as the mayhem exploded upon the serenity of their neighborhood. The curious had been on the street behind the barricade and the officers containing them held their fire. The officers feared a gun battle with the fleeing car would put the bystanders at risk of getting shot by an errant bullet.

People vaulted out of the way of the staggering, fleeing car as officers tried to shield people from a terrible impact. Frank saw a head slither up from the back seat and it was Lingbao Chang! Frank cranked the Mustang to life and it responded with a growl. Tires squealed- the pursuit was on.

Granderson thought the fleeing car had been through an encounter in Palestine- bullet holes, a dangling bumper, a ripped off fender and most of the glass shattered. As they flew down the street, he tried to call Buck on his cell phone to report they were in a sizzling pursuit of Chang, but there was no answer. Apparently, Buck wasn't about to be distracted.

Chang looked out the back window as both cars blew through a red light and narrowly missed being sandwiched by a bread truck. The cars skidded around the corner onto Royal Poinciana Way and part of Chang's bumper flew off into a flower bed. Chang frantically motioned for his driver to go faster.

The cars flew over the bridge spanning the Intracoastal Waterway and made a squealing left turn onto North Olive- the wrong way! Frank was right behind. As he skidded around the corner, he gasped: Chang's car was destined for a head on collision with an armored truck coming from the Colonial Bank Building. Miraculously, the next intersection was only a few feet ahead. Chang's car banged off the armored car as it made a skidding left turn. The armored car stopped just as Frank cut in front of it. Granderson saw the armed security guard in the passenger seat had his weapon aimed at them as they just missed the front bumper. A roaring right turn onto prestigious Flagler had the duo roaring south beside the waterway. The high performance Mustang was now right on Chang.

People jogging along the Intracoastal stopped, turned and looked as the cars screamed up the street. At the last split second, Chang's driver took a quick right, skidding dangerously and was on the verge of flipping over. Frank slammed on the brakes and barely made the corner. Frank pounded the gas pedal to the floor and the tires squealed in protest.

Chang's car took two skidding right turns with Frank close behind. As they roared back onto Flagler, Chang's car narrowly missed hitting a bicyclist. Frank jumped on the brakes as the bicyclist, wearing a yellow Tour de France jersey, banged off the Mustang's fender. The Mustang skidded to a stop. Frank told Granderson to get out and tend to the fallen athlete.

Frank then roared off, but Chang's car had put distance between them. Frank thought Chang would turn off Flagler and head past the twin towers of Trump Plaza, but instead Frank was stunned as Chang's car rounded the curve, jumped the curb, and recklessly rocketed over the sidewalk. With sparks flying, it bounced up a couple of steps. It skidded to a jerky stop, just inches from an abstract art sculpture that looked like a disjointed twenty five foot tall metal beam. Pedestrians continued to scramble out of the way of the weapon on wheels. Chang struggled to get out of the car because the door was sprung. After two well placed kicks, the door shot open. Chang bolted up the steps as he carried a black lacquered box with ornate gold Chinese symbols on it.

Frank's car skidded to a stop at the curb and he gave chase. Dodging terrified pedestrians, he flew up the stairs, determined to locate Chang. He realized that this was the entrance for two separate towers- one to the left and the other to the right. He intently surveyed the area and didn't have a clue which direction Chang had taken. He sprinted to the left and looked- no Chang. He ran over to the other tower and scanned it quickly. Where had he fled? These towers must contain offices for lawyers, investment bankers, accountants- what and where was Chang's destination? He bolted back outside to corral Chang's car and driver, but it had disappeared. He stared southward and far up the street, he spotted the car as it had resumed its wild, dangerous escape.

He looked at the buildings. With "777" as the street number, Frank hoped the lucky 7's were for him and not Lingbao Chang. The building was majestic with stunning panels of rose colored glass accented by narrow structural concrete of the same color. Very impressive. The shorter tower was over ten stories tall. Frank called Granderson on his cell phone. "I lost him. When you're done with the bicyclist, get here quick! I'm directly up the street at Phillips Point. I'll stay by the tall sculpture and watch for Chang."

Frank's mind was racing as fast as a kid overcharged on sugar and caffeine. Frank told himself to slow down and mentally think through one plan at a time. Soon, Granderson arrived, ardent to apprehend the dangerous Mr. Chang. "Did you check to see if he escaped through the loading dock? Every building this size has one."

"No. I'm a one person search team. I figured his car vanished too quickly for him to go in the front, out the back, or circle around the building, back to his car. I don't think he would try to run fast for any distance carrying a black lacquered box."

"Now what?" Granderson asked.

"I think I have a scheme to find what office he is hiding in. My first priority will be lawyers. Either he wants legal advice about the warrant, or he wants to give the black lacquered box to the lawyer for safekeeping…maybe both."

"These are big buildings." Granderson lamented.

"I know. You stay around here and check the people coming out. Unfortunately, there are other exits. I'll start at the top of the taller tower and work my way down."

Buck was anxious to find some evidence. Before Faroque was murdered, Faroque had been held in a small building attached to the walled pond holding the golden gator. Buck headed there and encountered a locked door. Buck called on his radio for assistance with a locked door. A burly officer quickly appeared and with one blow from a battering ram, the door exploded open. With gun drawn,

Buck entered, but when he inhaled the air, he choked, coughed and backed out. The multiple putrid odors defied description. Buck shined his flashlight inside and on the floor in a corner, he was amazed to find a man. Buck wondered how a person could exist in such a foul environment. The man turned his face from the bright light which had invaded his windowless confinement.

Buck asked him to turn his face towards the light and Buck discovered the man appeared Middle Eastern. He was tied up and had a look of fear on his face that flowed through his being. Buck identified himself as a deputy sheriff and told the man to relax. Speaking in broken English the man said he had been kidnapped and his captors questioned him many times. Buck untied him and brought him out into the fresh air and sunlight. The man said his name was Al-Qitar.

"I must go." The man announced.

Buck wasn't sure if the man was so terrified he needed to quickly escape or if he didn't want to get involved with the police. Buck replied: "No, you must stay with me. You need medical attention, we must get a statement from you and you must help us identify the people who held you captive."

Just then Cartier Chang came out of the mansion with Captain Mastif. Cartier had taken offense to being ordered around by the no nonsense Captain.

The man now displayed angry eyes and immediately pointed at Cartier: "That man beat me." The man then pointed at red welts on his legs and bare feet.

Cartier heard the accusation, spun around, looked at the man and reported: "We arrested that man last night when he led a group of men who scaled the wall of our compound. The rest fled and we captured him. We want to know why he came into the compound armed with an assault rifle and leading what we believe are Muslim extremists, intent on taking down our government. For our own security we asked him questions. We were just going to call the police when we were overwhelmed by law enforcement. As you can see, this extremist is dressed in black just like some of your officers. Now you understand why we were so defensive."

"He lies. I in room many days, many hours. They no feed me. They show me big animal which eat me if I no talk."

Cartier was calm: "It has only been a few hours since his siege of our home. I showed him a picture of our pet alligator to explain that the smell in the room was from the gator."

Buck wasn't convinced he was getting the whole story from Cartier or the man in black. It was time to separate them and interrogate both. The Captain took Cartier back in the mansion. Buck directed the forensics team to secure the building and let it air out. It was a prime place to find microscopic evidence which would verify the murder of some or all of the victims found on Lovers Key.

Buck put Al-Qitar in his squad car and reassured him that they wanted to find out what happened to him. Buck remembered that immediately after Zahra was told by Granderson that Ying had been followed here, a gun battle had occurred. So Buck asked: "Are you related to a woman named Zahra?"

"Yes. She my sister."

"Do you know Haquan, Faroque, and Akbar?"

Al-Qitar's expression turned stern: "Yes. They friends."

"Did you live at the apartment complex in Sunrise with them?"

"I lived with Akbar and he no return."

"How did you end up here?"

"I walk down street and they point gun at me. They grab me and tie me up."

"Why were you here walking down the street?"

Al-Qitar paused before saying: "I looking for work."

"Who was with you?"

"No one."

"Why here? You are probably fifty miles from Sunrise."

"I move after Akbar go."

"So, where do you live now?"

"They tie me up; no feed me; no let go."

"Where do you live now?"

"Where you find me."

Buck felt that Al-Qitar understood what was said, but was being elusive in his answer by feigning he didn't understand. Buck wasn't buying that Al-Qitar was looking for a job by walking the streets of Palm Beach. As he contemplated a new course of questioning, he looked out the squad car window and could see Pao staring at him from the back seat of another squad car. Buck told Al-Qitar he would be right back and went to the other squad. Buck knew that Pao and Cartier had not been together since Al-Qitar was discovered; so they couldn't concoct a story.

Buck asked Pao about Al-Qitar. She said he had been with a bunch of other men dressed in black, who showed up on the beach in the middle of the night with assault rifles. They tried to scale the wall of the compound, but were repelled by her comrades. Al-Qitar was the leader and was captured a couple of nights ago. Cartier was holding him until the man would confess and give truthful information.

Buck returned to Al-Qitar and confronted him with Pao's statements. Al-Qitar now understood even less English and wasn't responsive to any of his questions. By now, a swarm of forensics techs had entered the compound and Buck had one of them obtain a DNA sample from Al-Qitar. They needed a sample to compare to any blood they found in the room. Buck was now purposefully striding into the mansion looking for Mastif.

Captain Mastif wasn't getting much out of Cartier Chang. Cartier said there were a couple of people who handled the golden gator but he, personally, had little to do with the creature. It had grown too big to be a pet and was more like an oddity that belonged in a circus. He denied knowing if horses or polo ponies were fed to the gator and didn't know where the gator was being caged. Cartier stuck to his story that the man found in the stinky building was just in there a few hours.

When Buck found Mastif, they adjourned outside the hearing of Cartier Chang and told each other what they had learned. Then they returned to him.

Buck asked: "Why don't you admit how long you have been holding the man captive? It's been a few days."

"I *have* been truthful."

"Well, I believe that the leader of the angels with nun-chucks is accurate when she says a few days. That's consistent with what the man says. It's also about the time of the gun battle here when two of your guards were killed. Give it up Cartier."

Cartier wasn't budging: "They don't understand some of the fine points of the English language. They're wrong."

"We'd hate to arrest an innocent man for kidnapping and assault, but it sure looks like you failed to turn him over to police after you arrested him. Your failure to admit you have had him for a few days casts doubt upon your contention that he was trying to enter your compound illegally. Tell us the truth."

"I am."

Mastif broke in. "Show us the assault rifle he had. We need to seize it as evidence."

Cartier hesitated. "There are a lot of firearms in the room where the assault rifle is being kept. Stay here, I'll get it." He got up to leave.

Buck and Mastif replied emphatically: "No. No. No. One of us will walk beside you and then you will direct us."

Cartier was in a no win situation. If he refused, it looked like he was hiding something. If he showed them the room, there might be a trace amount of blood from one of the murder victim's on something. Thinking quickly, he replied: "I don't have the key to the room and I don't know who does."

Buck replied: "That's Ok. We have a search warrant to search the entire mansion. We'll find the room eventually. Show us, we'll be careful in opening the locked door."

Color drained from Cartier's face and he reluctantly agreed to show the way. Once at the door Buck asked one more time if he had a key or could direct them to someone who did. Cartier replied no and Buck got on his two way radio. In a few seconds an officer arrived with a hand held battering ram and with one quick motion sent wood flying. Buck scrambled over splintered wood and was impressed at the Chang arsenal. From outside the door, Cartier directed him to the correct assault rifle.

Buck was on the radio again, this time to the forensics team. He told them he had a new room to intensively search. Wearing latex gloves, Buck picked up the assault rifle, then the door knob and commented; "We'll find the key to the door. He who has the key will be questioned about what is found inside this room; including blood, hair or saliva. Cartier didn't feel too smug about his ability to talk his way out of this. Mastif's stern, intense gaze made Cartier feel the battle was being lost and the clang of a jail cell seemed imminent.

Mastif said: "Cartier, we have to talk about what happened to three Muslim men who were here and were attacked by the golden gator. I'm sure you can explain what happened. Let's go back where we were before, so we can be comfortable."

"Captain, am I under arrest?"

"Let's just say we can't have you wandering around the estate possibly destroying evidence or impeding the search. Any problem with that?... You want to cooperate don't you?"

"Of course."

"Do you want to leave or do you want to stay so we can tell you the results of the search?"

"I want to know what you're doing. I'll stay."

Buck stayed and the other two went back to the library and sat down. Captain Mastif said: "Cartier, have you lived here the last four months?"

"Yes."

"Tell me what you know about The Pearl of Tao."

Cartier wasn't prepared for this change of subject and paused. "What do you mean?"

"I don't need to know the religious history; I just want to know what you know about it."

"It was on display at The Museum of Art in Ft. Lauderdale. It weighs fourteen pounds and was stolen."

The Captain had been thinking about the investigation as he was interrogating Cartier. He decided to test his theory: "Did your parents call this estate The Pearl?"

"Sometimes. It was more a nick name- it is The Temple."

Mastif continued: "After all, they nicknamed the mansion The Pearl after The Pearl of Tao."

"Yes."

Mastif continued: “They nicknamed their luxurious home The Pearl, and they collect expensive Chinese antiquities; it stands to reason that they would want to own The Pearl of Tao. Did they ever discuss that?”

“Yes, but it was many years ago.”

Mastif thought progress was slow. “So, did your father feel it was an honor to own the company that was selected to guard The Pearl?”

“Yes.”

“What was his reaction to Muslims repeatedly making a scene by claiming The Pearl of Tao was The Pearl of Allah?”

“He was upset because he’s a devote Taoist.”

“There is a pedestal in the library next to a red ornate chair. What was on the pedestal?”

Cartier turned ashen.

Just then Buck radioed to Mastif: “We found some important evidence. I’ll be with you in a minute.”

A sickly pallor spread over Cartier’s countenance and he trembled like a delicate pygmy date palm in a sudden breeze.

CHAPTER TWENTY SEVEN

Frank was discouraged. He wasn't sure his search plan would produce any results. He didn't seem to be getting any closer to finding Lingbao Chang and Granderson was growling at him over the cell phone. Granderson was stationed outside the building entrance and as time passed, they lost hope they would apprehend Chang and the box. Granderson's instincts told him that The Pearl was in the ornate box. The only other reason Chang would put his life at high risk was if some other stolen, precious, Chinese antiquity was in the box.

Frank entered the reception area of yet another law firm and smiled at the young, anorexic receptionist. She smiled back and in a perky voice asked: "Can I help you?"

"I'm running late. I was supposed to meet Lingbao Chang at his lawyer's office but I forgot the name of the law firm. Has he come here this morning?"

"Yes. He was here earlier, but I'm not sure if he's still here. Whom shall I say is inquiring?"

He was relieved that he had found Chang. Authoritatively he announced: "Frank Johnson, *and* I'm a lawyer with Monty Moritz III, a developer."

The receptionist called back to an office. Soon, a wrinkled man in his late sixties with a magnificent head of pure white hair appeared. "I'm Byron Manchester. Why do you want to meet with me and Lingbao Chang? I have nothing scheduled for either of you."

Frank replied: "I was aware that a search warrant was being executed on Mr. Chang's residence and he might need someone to advise him on his legal rights."

Mr. Manchester was perplexed: "If Mr. Chang needed legal advice, why would he need yours while he is at my law firm?"

Frank replied: "Some law firms only handle civil issues. I have a lot of criminal law experience. I might be helpful; especially if he brought documents or objects which were listed in the search warrant."

Manchester stood mute and stared. Frank wanted the conversation to continue in order to get information: "My boss is Monty Moritz III, he and Mr. Chang are in the early stages of a cooperative effort for a development."

Manchester responded with a stern rebuke: "I know. Thank you, Mr. Johnson. Good day." With that, the lawyer turned and started to disappear down a hallway.

Frank quickly asked: "Is Mr. Chang still here?"

Frank stood there waiting for a response, however, Byron Manchester never broke stride or replied.

Frank started in motion to follow Mr. Manchester, who quickly turned and held up his hand in a position which signaled stop. In a strict and dignified voice he said: "You should return to our reception area immediately. I am indignant about your civility. Either you are indifferent or ignorant of protocol. You don't wander into a lawyer's private domain uninvited. Cease and desist."

Frank did as instructed, but continued to walk- right out of the office and to the elevators. He knew he wouldn't get any more information.

But, the conversation wasn't devoid of value. He had learned that Chang had been there and could still be present. He also surmised that the black lacquered box was somewhere in the lawyer's office. It certainly was the size which could hold The Pearl of Tao. Chang was smart enough to conclude that his lawyer could keep it and claim it was protected from seizure by attorney client privilege.

Once outside, Frank updated Granderson on his encounter in the law office. Granderson nodded and finally said: "Should we wait, hoping Chang will appear? I doubt he will stroll past us with the box."

"Let's try calling Buck again. We'll update him." Granderson again got no answer. They surmised that Buck was focused on the search and wasn't answering his cell phone.

"Well?" Granderson asked.

"I think we need to keep an eye out for Lingbao Chang. We'll split up; I'll go to the loading dock and you stay here."

"I never had the patience to sit and wait out the bad guys." Granderson grumbled.

Frank didn't respond, but headed out to look for the loading dock. Instead he found that the towers had a parking ramp which gave an easy escape. Just as he suspected- it was the building's smokers' refuge. Just after he got there, the perky legal receptionist appeared; cigarette package in hand. As she lit up, Frank asked her: "Why all the secrecy about my friend Mr. Chang?"

"I don't know. Some lawyers in the firm love to brag up that they represent certain persons and companies. Yet today, it was a big secret that Mr. Chang was our client. I don't know the rules."

Frank decided to engage her in conversation: "How many years have you worked there?"

"Only a couple of months. I just moved here from St. Paul to escape the snow."

"Amazing. I worked in St. Paul for a number of years as a lawyer. Now I do legal work for Monty Moritz. He and I had dinner at the Chang mansion a couple of nights ago. Did you know the compound is named The Temple?"

"No."

Frank kept the conversation flowing as she continued to smoke: "I think the Chang's are devote Taoists and are very concerned with preserving ancient artifacts of their religion. Do you know about The Pearl of Tao, the biggest pearl in the world?... It's an important symbol of Taoism."

"No. I'm a Lutheran."

"Mr. Chang is agitated that criminals have tried to take some prized works of art including The Pearl and if they do, the item would be lost forever. He just doesn't have confidence the cops would recover anything."

"He sure was concerned that our law firm had a safe place to store The Pearl." She said.

"Do you know what those Chinese symbols mean that are on the outside of the box?"

"As he sat in the reception area, I asked him what they meant and he said 'The Pearl of Lao Tzu.' I didn't have the nerve to ask him who this Lao Tzu guy is. I didn't want to sound like I just got off an ice floe from Minnesota."

Frank replied: "He is the founder of Taoism and The Pearl goes all the way back to the founding of the religion, over two thousand years ago."

"Oh." She said as she took another drag off her cigarette.

"Is Mr. Chang still up there?"

"Yeah.... Well I gotta get back, my break is up." As she headed back inside, she wondered why Frank was at the unofficial smokers' lounge and wasn't smoking. Then she thought he was out of cigarettes and was waiting for some one to offer him one- he was too proud to ask.

Frank figured his luck had changed and called Granderson to report the new information. As he hung up, a white van with *Lingbao Security* on the side drove past him and up the entrance ramp. His eyes widened as he saw the driver- Ying. Quickly, Frank hustled up the ramp. Just then, Chang hurriedly appeared and Frank sprinted towards him exuding the image of a man on a mission.

"Mr. Chang. I need to talk to you."

Chang was stunned to see Frank had found him and sharply lectured: "Young man, why are you getting involved in something that doesn't concern you? Monty isn't going to look favorably upon your actions. Immediately end your meddling; otherwise, I'll be forced to report your misbehavior to Mr. Moritz."

Frank spoke harshly: "I need to have you and Ying stay here so the police can talk to both of you. The confrontations between you and the Muslim extremists must stop."

Chang was insulted at the contentiousness: "Tell that to the Muslims that keep attacking my beloved home. My people have been killed." Chang kept heading towards the van.

Tensions were high and Frank knew he had to make a quick decision. Should he try to grab Chang and subdue him? In addition to Ying, how many more men were in the van? Frank looked over at

Ying who was pensively waiting at the side door of the van. Frank pulled out his cell phone pressed "call" and put it down. As he stood up, he threw himself into Chang and bear hugged him.

Granderson answered, heard the commotion and Frank command: "Mr. Chang you must stay here and talk to the police. You know they're executing a search warrant at your residence. I know you took The Pearl of Tao from your home and brought it here."

A stunned look entered Chang's eyes, but for only a fraction of an instant. He then quit resisting and forced a momentary calm demeanor before snarling: "Let go of me!"

Frank, ever the legal whiz, declared: "I'm making a citizens arrest on you for possession of stolen property- The Pearl of Tao. Please submit to this lawful arrest and wait here until police arrive."

"YING!" Chang ordered as he broke loose of Frank's bear hug and tried to punch him in the face. Frank instinctively ducked his head and his quick reflexes resulted in Chang landing only a glancing blow. Frank jumped at Chang, again trying to neutralize him with a bear hug. Out of the corner of his eye he looked for Ying, so he wouldn't get blind sided.

Ying bolted toward them, ready to free his boss. Frank hoped that Granderson would appear to equalize the odds. Frank frantically looked to see if Ying was carrying any weapons, but didn't see any. Frank knew Ying would have something hidden. Frank's courage gave way to the realization that this was a dangerous encounter-possibly deadly –the stakes for Chang and Ying were mountainous. Ying bounded towards him as Frank reminded himself that he was no match for Ying, having seen him in action as a security guard at The Museum of Art.

Frank yelled to no one in particular: "Call 911!"

Ying was ready to pounce on him, so he spun Chang around to put him in the middle. Ying's martial arts kick connected squarely with Chang's chest. He groaned and his knees buckled.

From the corner of his eye, Frank saw Granderson coming at full speed. Ying didn't see what hit him, but the powerful Granderson was like a panther leaping on its prey. Ying went down hard beside Chang and Granderson had his muscular forearm on Ying's throat.

Granderson applied plenty of pressure and Ying futilely gasped for air.

Fearful of other attackers, Frank looked towards the van. A cargo door flew open and a man leaped out brandishing a large caliber hand gun. Frank yelled: "GRANDERSON! BEHIND YOU! A MAN WITH A GUN!"

Granderson was struggling against Ying's escape attempts and as he turned to see the gunman, Ying violently twisted free. He knocked Granderson away. Granderson jumped back on top of Ying and with his superior size and strength got his powerful hands on Ying's throat- and squeezed. Ying's strength was waning from lack of oxygen. Granderson's adrenaline was pumping and he pulled Ying up by the neck as if he was a chicken ready for slaughter.

Ying was flaying to disengage Granderson, but was ineffective, so he went limp. Granderson used him as a shield from the gunman and commanded: "Back off! If you don't, your friend will be dead meat!"

Chang scrambled on his hands and knees towards his gun toting rescuer. Frank wasn't foolish enough to try to recapture him by heading towards a gun. Chang was now behind the gunman and ordered: "Let's go. Ying can take care of himself. I'm sure the police will be here shortly and they will arrest his attackers."

Chang and his armed guard backed up towards the van. Chang's man shot off a round into the concrete and Granderson's instinctive reaction was to flinch. Abruptly, Ying slithered down like a snake and spun out of Granderson's hold. Ying scrambled away and into the driver's seat as the other two jumped in the van.

Ying slammed the van into reverse, banged into a concrete column and then roared forward down the ramp. As the van flew out on the street, impact with a new Mercedes seemed destined. The Mercedes lived up to its reputation of expert accident avoidance and narrowly avoided the collision. The van fled down the street, around the corner and submerged into the sea of day time traffic.

The sound of distant sirens made Frank and Granderson hold onto the hope that the police could apprehend Chang and his men. Two squad cars screeched to a stop-one from West Palm Beach and one from Palm Beach. Frank's hope sank like a rock in the ocean when Sgt. Mike Smith got out from behind the wheel. As their eyes met, Frank knew there would be plenty of explanation before action.

Sgt. Smith kept a poker face, but his first words, spoke volumes about his unbending attitude: "Is it mere coincidence that you two are in Palm Beach the very day a search warrant is being executed at Lingbao Chang's? The more immediate issue is your presence at the scene of a 911 call of a fight in progress. Tell me what's going down."

Frank forced himself to be even tempered: "Sgt. Smith, I thought you were a supervisor on the night shift of the Palm Beach PD. What are you doing in West Palm Beach working the street on the day shift?"

"Don't you remember, I ask the questions?"

Hodge Dobson, the West Palm Beach officer, spoke up: "I have jurisdiction on this call."

Sgt. Smith continued: "I was at the Courthouse a couple of blocks away and as I headed back I monitored the call. I'm working because the regular day shift officers are assigned as crowd control for the search warrant team."

Hodge Dobson broke in to ask: "What is going on between you two?"

Frank was succinct: "I attempted to make a citizens arrest on Lingbao Chang for possession of stolen property- The Pearl of Tao. He resisted arrest, as did his employee Ying, and another of his men pulled a gun on us."

Officer Hodge Dobson looked puzzled. Sgt. Smith was intrigued: "Where is Mr. Chang? Where's The Pearl?"

"Chang and the others fled in a white van with '*Lingbao Security*' on it. The Pearl is upstairs in Chang's lawyer's office. Radio the patrol cars to find Chang. We'll go up to the law office and recover The Pearl."

The two cops looked at each other and Smith said: "I've previously dealt with these two self proclaimed bounty hunters from St. Paul. They say there is a large reward being offered for the return of The

Pearl- valued at over sixty million dollars. I advise you to put out an attempt to locate the van, but it's your call- it's your jurisdiction."

Hodge Dobson quickly radioed an attempt to locate on the van. He paused and asked Sgt. Smith: "What about searching a lawyer's office?"

Smith slowly replied: "Searching a lawyer's office sends up all kinds of red flags. I wouldn't recommend it. Don't do anything until you get legal advice from the States Attorney."

Frank protested: "I'm a lawyer and a former prosecutor. It's OK! Trust me!"

Granderson joined in: "Chang knows that we know the location of The Pearl. We need to act swiftly or it will be hidden somewhere else. We have to move now!"

Sgt. Smith turned to Frank. "You're not the prosecutor here- you're a witness."

Officer Dobson looked at Frank: "I don't know you. I don't know how you got in the middle of all of this. I need to talk to the States Attorney."

Frank and Granderson looked at each other. Their eyes spoke: "Major Delay!"

CHAPTER TWENTY EIGHT

Buck appeared in the library with his right hand behind his back and looked directly at Cartier Chang. Cartier's eyes immediately moved down to what Buck was holding in his other hand. Arabic letters could be seen on part of a page which had been ripped out of a book. Buck held it up and said: "There's smeared blood on this page and I believe analysis will reveal two things. First, that the blood is from one of the murdered men and second, this is a page ripped from the Koran."

Characteristic library silence enveloped the room and the deputies waited. Buck then revealed his right hand which held a clear jar with liquid and a human hand.

Finally, Cartier said: "I don't know how that got into my room. Ying must have planted it there."

"Whose hand was it?" Buck asked.

"The guy Ying tortured and threw to the golden gator. I had nothing to do with it. I only found out about it after it was all done."

Mastif moved closer to Cartier and his six foot ten inch body invaded the personal space between him and Cartier. Cartier squirmed in his chair as he felt claustrophobic with Mastif towering over him.

Mastif's coffee breath overwhelmed Cartier as Mastif declared: "The problem with your claimed ignorance of the hand is that Buck never said he found the hand in your room. One victim, Haquan was missing his left hand when his body was discovered. This is a left hand. I'm sure the DNA will come back that this was Haquan's hand. Tell us the truth."

"I have.... Ok, I was keeping the hand for Ying. I had nothing to do with the torture or killing."

"What about the bloody page?"

"I don't know anything about that."

"Ever touch it?" Mastif asked.

"No."

"Are you certain?"

"Yes."

"Then if we find your fingerprints on it, you'll have lied to us. If you lied about the bloody page, then you lied to us about not being involved in the torture and murder."

"I think I better talk to my dad's lawyer."

"Do you want to keep talking with us and talk to the lawyer when we're done?" Buck asked.

"I think I'll call him now."

Buck said: "Use the phone here. The Captain and I are going to confer outside the door to determine if we are going to place you under arrest."

Cartier didn't reach for the phone. Rather, he continued to perspire and declared: "I didn't do anything wrong. You don't understand how sacrilegious it was for these Muslims to declare that it was The Pearl of Allah. Our sacred founder of Taoism, Lao- Tzu, created The Pearl and it's an important part of our religion. There're enough Muslim extremists in the world that we must be ever vigilant to protect ourselves and our religion. You must know they attacked our home and brutally killed our security guards. We're just defending ourselves. Don't you understand?'

Buck answered: "No. I don't understand why Haquan, Faroque and Akbar were killed. We're trying to solve three heartless murders."

"*THREE*? You think I'm involved in three murders?" Cartier protested.

"There's an obvious pattern to all three."

Cartier pleaded: "They wanted to steal The Pearl. Can't we exercise our Constitutional right to freedom of religion?"

Buck moved closer and smirked in Cartier's face. Sarcastically he said: "If you're looking for a Constitutional right for a defense, my legal advice is you hang your hat on the Second Amendment- the right to bear arms. If I were you, I would contend that the golden gator is the equivalent of a firearm."

Cartier silently contemplated Buck's advice until Mastif roared a mighty laugh still just inches from Cartier's face.

Mocking the Academy Awards, Buck somberly intoned: "The handcuffs please." As he pulled his out, Cartier's look went from grim to dejected.

Mastif noticed this and said: "Time to get right with Lao-Tzu and get His Divine Spirit to help you to the truth."

Cartier squirmed and announced: "I thought I demanded my lawyer."

Mastif replied: "You did and you asked us questions. We answered them. If you think of us as a couple of cops that just came out of a Florida swamp, you're wrong. We'd like cessation of your constant arrogance towards us. We seek not a confession, but information. You can lie with your eyes and you can lie with words."

Buck decided to refocus the discussion because he was afraid that the Captain's comments would be rebuked by Cartier. Buck had prepared for this interrogation by doing some research on Taoism and talking with Frank. "We understand your religious beliefs. I remember that Lao-Tzu preached: 'If one knows honor yet maintains the role of the disgraced, one will become the valley under heaven.' I believe Lao-Tzu was telling us that when a person refuses to speak the truth, they won't have a joyous after life. But getting back to my question: I need to know if you want a lawyer or you want to talk."

Cartier now started to look upon Buck in a different light: "How do you know about the teachings of Lao-Tzu?"

"I'm an educated man. Confucius and Lao-Tzu were great leaders and very inspirational.... I hope you noticed you asked me another question. Yet you need to answer mine."

Cartier still wondered if Buck understood how important The Pearl was to his religion. "Christians believe that a woman wiped the face of Christ with a cloth as he carried his cross to Calgary. That artifact is as important to Christians as The Pearl is to Taoists. Do you understand that?"

Buck replied: "Another question. The cloth you speak of is The Holy Shroud, not to be confused with The Shroud of Turin, both of which are believed to have an imprint on the cloth from Christ's blood. The woman who wiped his face was St. Veronica. The Holy Shroud scene was immortalized in classic oil paintings in the 1600's by El Greco, and others.

Buck looked closely at Cartier to determine his reaction. Cartier's facial response told Buck to keep going: "Cartier, we understand that The Pearl is a Taoist artifact and not a Muslim artifact."

"So you agree with me that it is a mere coincidence that The Pearl resembles the face of Muhammad?"

Buck wasn't going any further because he couldn't remember anything else Frank had lectured him about. "You asked me another question. You haven't answered mine."

Cartier continued: "OK. I think you know how important it is that The Pearl doesn't fall into the wrong hands. When it was on display in Ft. Lauderdale, it seemed like more and more Muslims came everyday to pay homage to The Pearl. We felt they were planning to pilfer it, probably in a violent attack. After all, a Muslim stabbed Ying. Many bystanders would be injured or killed because of their brutality. Once it was gone, it would start a religious war and would never be recovered without much blood shed and death. It had to be protected."

"All antiquities need security." Mastif offered.

Cartier continued: "I don't know. The rumor is that it's safe. But the Muslims believe it's here, so they'll continue to attack us. We need police protection."

Buck replied: "I'm making a statement, not asking a question. I was here recently with Sgt. Smith of Palm Beach PD. Your father didn't want us on the property. He sure wasn't seeking help from law enforcement."

"He's from the old school. I appreciate the police. We don't want violence."

Buck wasn't buying it. "A Muslim named Akbar disappeared before The Pearl did. Haquan and Faroque were kidnapped by Asians in a white van with the word 'security' on it. They all end up dead having been tortured using a very large gator. You have a very large golden gator. When we're done searching this place, we'll have forensic evidence and I'd be very surprised if we won't find evidence that all three were tortured here."

Mastif added: "Ying was involved, but he didn't do this alone. Maybe someone on these premises thought that the Muslims could be roughed up and released, but not killed. In other words, to send the Muslims a message. When we find Ying he will tell us what went down. We don't need your side of it."

Buck jingled the handcuffs and moved closer to Cartier.

Cartier's skin color had been changing as the dialogue had progressed. He now had a flushed face as he became more agitated: "Everything I know is hearsay and I don't know much."

Buck replied: "Let us decide what is hearsay. But first you have to decide if you want to talk to us or you want to talk to a lawyer first. If you keep talking, we'll assume you have waived your right to contact an attorney because you have a phone right next to you."

"I don't know any of the three men." Cartier declared as he refused to look away from Mastif's imposing glare; just inches from his face. Cartier made no move to use the phone.

Buck watched him squirm and waited. The silence was as painful as when a penitent waits with dread in the confessional knowing he's about to hear the priest's response to his sins. Buck wanted Cartier to admit to being part of the torture. If Cartier admitted to that, then it was just a question of what degree of homicide he committed when the victim died as a result of the torture.

Finally Buck stated: "Well, we haven't lived in a monastery all our lives. We realize people are apprehensive about saying they're part of someone's death, even if the death was accidental. I'm sure there's a reasonable explanation about how the men died. Just like the Captain said, Ying will tell. We aren't going to question you."

Mastif wanted to give Cartier a scenario which would let Cartier admit he was part of the killing, even if Cartier claimed it was accidental. "We know Ying will give his version of what happened to the men. For example, Ying could say that one of them refused to tell the truth and this agitated the questioner. Ying will say who was doing the questioning. Maybe the person being interrogated was pushed and stumbled. In an unexpected reaction to a light push, the man fell over a waist high wall, into the pit, and got killed by the gator. There are many situations that need an explanation and Ying will tell."

Cartier's body movements confirmed he was being evasive, so Buck was ready for a long session. "Ying will talk to us and hopefully he'll take complete responsibility for his actions. Unfortunately, some people like to blame others and minimize their involvement."

Mastif, still in Cartier's face, waited. Cartier was distressed at Mastif's towering presence. After a long pause in the conversation Mastif added: "We know that these three men weren't fed to a gator like the Roman's fed Christians to the lions."

"How do you know that?" Cartier asked.

"The men hadn't been devoured; they'd been attacked."

"Maybe the Muslims taunted the gator and it attacked them." Cartier offered.

"That very well could be." Buck replied.

"That's what I heard." Cartier added.

Silence again enveloped the room.

Cartier knew he had to come up with a name and he knew the cops already had their aim on someone. "Ying told me about it."

Buck was emphatic by talking slowly: "Ying didn't do this alone and the physical evidence we will find today will put you in a very bad light; unless you have an explanation. The survivor we found today points the finger at you as the interrogator. That makes me believe you're the boss. People, including Ying, work for you." Buck turned to Mastif: "Captain, what happens if Ying says Cartier ordered the deaths of the three men and he just carried out the boss' orders?"

Mastif replied: "The prosecutor will make a decision on what crimes to charge and who is charged based on the evidence at the time. Cooperation always plays a part."

Cartier wasn't sure what to say. "I just think you guys don't understand how bad these Muslims are. They attacked Ying at the museum and stabbed him right in front of the police. They're extremists."

"And they *are* criminals. They were charged with serious crimes." Buck replied.

Cartier chimed in: "But they got out on bail and were free to again terrorize everyone."

Buck wanted to get the conversation back on who was involved in the murders. "I wonder if Ying tells us Cartier interrogated each of the three dead men using the golden gator as a weapon; would it be a lie? The prosecutor has to rely on truthful evidence."

Cartier worried about Ying: "Ying didn't put much effort into controlling the gator. It got out of hand. The gator was big, but Ying showed little effort when I told him to get the gator away from these Muslims."

Buck looked at Mastif: "Makes me wonder… what Ying was trying to accomplish?"

Cartier continued: "For our own safety we needed to know how many men were in their group; who they were and what attacks they had planned. They wouldn't give up that information. We kept waiting for their cooperation. Then we got attacked by their fellow extremists. Everything was OK until that point. "

Buck commented to Mastif: "Would people think the killing of Faroque was in retaliation for the security guards being killed?"

Mastif remained silent and in Cartier's face as the tension mounted.

Cartier said: "It just happened. Our people had been killed and we needed intelligence to stop any further attacks. The men were very stubborn and refused to divulge what we needed to know to protect ourselves."

Buck commented: "Captain, I think there must have been a couple of interrogators because these Muslims are smart and tough to wear down."

"Yup someone smart like Cartier's father." Mastif opined

Cartier knew he had to protect his family. "No. He didn't even know the men were being kept here. Ying wasn't getting anywhere, so I helped him."

Buck and Mastif looked at each other and waited.

Exasperated, Cartier exclaimed: "They said they would never give up their quest for The Pearl. They're devoted to Muhammad and said they would struggle until death in order to recover The

Pearl. They planned to bring it to their holy city. I knew that it would take some terror to get them to change their minds. I didn't think the gator would be so aggressive. We couldn't pull the golden gator off."

Buck asked: "Did you personally try to get the gator off each of the three or did you just let the gator maul them?"

"Every one of them I told Ying to get the gator off."

Mastif looked him in the eye. "It's a long shot that I'd buy the story on the first death.- the bruises you and your men inflicted tell me you were ruthless. Yet, if I did believe your story, you knew after the first death that you couldn't control the gator so the second death was predictable and premeditated. The third death was an execution with a bullet to the head. Cartier, you're going to jail."

"I thought you were looking for an explanation." Cartier complained.

"A truthful one." Mastif replied.

Buck got Cartier out of his chair and said: "We are. But it must be a truthful explanation that fits with the physical evidence. Your story doesn't fly. We're arresting you for being a principal in the murders of Akbar, Faroque and Haquan."

Mastif added "and the kidnapping of Al-Qitar, the man we found tied up here today."

Buck reached in his pocket and turned off the tiny tape recorder which had been on the whole time.

Cartier looked back at the phone he never used as he was led out in handcuffs.

CHAPTER TWENTY NINE

Sgt. Smith used the speaker on his cell phone to call the States Attorneys Office as Frank, Granderson and West Palm Beach Officer Hodge Dobson listened in. The Sgt. told the receptionist that he needed legal advice about searching for The Pearl of Tao in the law office of a suspect's attorney. Smith's call was ultimately connected to a young prosecutor who had just passed the bar exam. The neophyte explained that the experienced lawyers were either in a jury trial or in court handling pretrial hearings.

The rookie explained that when a lawyer had evidence in his law office that could implicate his client in a crime, the lawyer had an obligation not to reveal the existence of the evidence. This obligation was based on the attorney client privilege. Furthermore, law enforcement was limited in the way they could obtain the evidence. The rookie's voice trembled as he admitted he wasn't sure of the correct way to get the evidence. He said he would do legal research and talk to an experienced prosecutor. He was hopeful he would have the answer to Sgt. Smith by tomorrow. The green horn prosecutor explained that the lawyer who had the evidence couldn't destroy the evidence or the lawyer would be committing a crime.

Frank laughed out loud, shook his head in disgust and dismay. "Two problems with that theory. First, it would be tough to prove the lawyer was the person who destroyed the evidence. Second, a smart criminal, like Chang, would rather be charged with a minor crime like hiding evidence rather than possessing a stolen pearl worth over sixty million dollars. Plus, he'd have evidence which linked him to far more serious crimes including murder."

Granderson was repulsed by the ineptitude of the rookie attorney and joined in the conversation: "Do you know of any reason a judge would throw out the evidence we found, if we had a search warrant signed by a judge authorizing the search? After all, a judge shouldn't sign the search warrant unless it's OK to search."

There was a prolonged silence as the young lawyer considered the question. "Judges sometimes suppress evidence based upon a search warrant and all warrants are signed by judges. I just don't know. I have to figure this out and it will take awhile. I'm pretty sure I'll have the answer by tomorrow."

Sgt. Smith thanked him and hung up. Frank and Granderson were visibly upset. They believed this major case should get higher priority in the States Attorneys Office. Before they could say anything, Officer Dobson spoke up: "We're in West Palm, so this is in my jurisdiction. Nothing is going to happen until we have the blessing of the prosecutor. They call the shots on this one. I don't want to go down in West Palm Beach PD history as the officer who screwed up a murder case by doing an illegal search on a lawyer's office."

Frank was irate. "Let's think this through. We already have clearly admissible evidence from the law office receptionist that Chang brought The Pearl to the law office. The Pearl is not a murder weapon. It is the corpus delicti of a huge theft and not of a murder. The Pearl is a motive for the murders and the motive can be established in many ways. We don't physically need The Pearl for the murder case. We need to recover The Pearl because it is worth sixty million dollars and it might just disappear from the lawyer's office. Chang could sneak back up there, reclaim it and fly it to China."

Granderson joined in on the momentum Frank had created: "Let's go! Frank's right!"

Hodge Dobson looked perplexed and then exasperated. He started to believe that Sgt. Smith had created imaginary road blocks. "I don't want stolen property worth sixty million getting away because I didn't act."

Shrewdly, Sgt. Smith quickly countered: "Let's put a cop at the doorway to the lawyer's office and if Chang comes, we'll arrest him on probable cause for having the stolen property."

Frank was concerned. "What if someone walks out with a container that has The Pearl hidden inside it?"

Officer Dobson looked more frustrated. But Smith counter punched: "Have the officer who stands guard outside the office search anything big enough to hold The Pearl. A lawyer's briefcase is too small to hold it, so don't search them. We'll keep a guard stationed there until tomorrow- after we get legal advice."

In exasperation, Officer Dobson started in motion: "Show me the lawyer's office. I'm calling *my* sergeant to get advice on what to do. I hope I'm not the one assigned to stand guard overnight."

Meanwhile, Ying was swiftly and skillfully piloting the van through traffic; he used a circuitous route to get to the outskirts of Wellington. Lingbao Chang kept telling Ying to go faster; Chang was worried that the cops would figure out where he was headed. He believed the cops would watch for him on all well traveled routes. He anxiously directed Ying to drive faster to the Far East Polo Club in Wellington. Chang was headed to his large, opulent office in the club.

Chang hurried through the back entrance of the Polo Club so no one could see him. Running into his office, he went directly to the safe. Frantically, he collected items from it and pulled items out of his desk. Hurriedly he put it all in a sturdy, silver, padded, aluminum suitcase. He scurried back to the van and as he stood there out of breath told Ying: "Disappear for awhile. The police are looking to arrest both of us."

Ying understood and sped off, still unsure where he was headed, but sure he had to distance himself from his usual hangouts. Chang calmly walked into his private garage in the building next to his office. Quickly he took the cover off his white BMW sedan, threw the cover in the trunk, and reluctantly suppressed the urge to zoom off. He didn't want anyone one at the club to be alerted to his presence. Wisely choosing to sneak away quietly, he didn't want the cops to have a trail to follow.

Once he had disappeared from The Far East Polo Club, Chang drove like a wild man. He knew there were risks, but he was fixated on his goal to escape. He tail gated other cars, pushing drivers to the verge of road rage. He shot down Southern Blvd. to the Palm Beach International Airport and roared to his private hanger.

While at the law office he had arranged to have his private Gulfstream jet prepped and ready to fly. He had directed his pilot to file a flight plan to fly to the Bahamas. As the BMW raced onto the tarmac, his jet was already there. Chang secreted the BMW in his hanger, took out his aluminum suitcase, and hurriedly threw the cover back over his car.

Lingbao Chang's flight team welcomed him aboard as he ascended the stairs and within three minutes they were moving down the taxiway to the main runway. It seemed like only a minute after takeoff that he looked north out the window and watched as they crossed over white, sandy, Palm Beach; airborne over the Atlantic Ocean. Chang loved the fact that he could quickly leave the USA and be in a foreign country in a few minutes. He didn't even bother having a cup of tea, because he knew landing was imminent.

When they landed in Freeport on Grand Bahamas Island, he directed the pilot to file whatever was necessary to fly north to Bermuda. Chang knew better than to give law enforcement an easy trail to follow using the documents his pilot filed in the USA. He regretted he didn't have the ability to get Cartier and Mrs. Chang on board. He now exuded confidence- his shrewd mind would come up with an intricate scheme to bring them to him.

The very powerful Gulfstream jet powered up to cruising altitude much faster than a commercial jet. He reminded himself that he had to use the legal advice he got from his lawyer, Byron Manchester. Now was time to formulate a master plan which would satisfy a number of objectives. He knew that part of his empire- The Temple- was under attack by the police. Momentarily, he brooded in bitterness that the police had unreasonably chosen to invade his private domain. His mood quickly changed as his vanity told him that his tenacity would again bring it all to a successful resolution. He decided he would not brood in bitterness. He knew his empire in China was secure because of his connections with influential people. With his suitcase at his side, he designed and redesigned his plan.

After his jet landed in Bermuda, he invited the flight crew to eat with him. They took a limo to a little known Chinese restaurant and once there, Chang conversed about his favorite antiquities and the history they represented. He made it appear that he was jetting around for the pure pleasure of being able to do so. As they dined, the crew wanted to know their final destination. Sternly, he said they would be informed once back at the airport; he didn't want to discuss anything in a public place with the potential of eavesdroppers.

Once inside the plane, he instructed the pilot to file a flight plan to return to the Bahamas but to a different airport- Nassau. Chang took a nap as he waited for takeoff.

Just an hour before sunset, the plane landed in the Bahamas, but not in accordance with the flight plan. The jet barely had enough runway to stop when it landed on a small island airstrip with no tower or customs office. He instructed the pilot to wait until it was completely dark then fly to Venezuela to await further instructions. The pilot was baffled, but did as he was directed.

Chang deplaned, aluminum suitcase in hand, and moved briskly to the nearby marina where he was escorted aboard his private yacht. He sipped a glass of Merlot as the yacht moved majestically from the dock and into the harbor. Once clear of the harbor the captain powered up the engines and the magnificent vessel responded quickly. The smooth dark blue water was interrupted by the classic foamy, white, "V" wake from the craft. The golden sun was just dipping behind a distant island as the palms waved at the light pink clouds the sun had painted. The setting exceeded the beauty of a cover of a travel magazine. The myriad remote islands were deftly circumnavigated by his captain as the ship headed to open waters.

Chang's eyes looked at the tranquil setting, but it didn't connect to his brain- he was too busy worrying about what the cops would find back at his compound on Ocean Blvd. Risk management gurus talk about the need to limit the extent of liability exposure. Chang knew he had a lot. Now he had to plan to end his exposure.

His yacht brought him to his private island. He disembarked, still firmly gripping the aluminum suitcase. It had not left his side since he packed it at the Far East Polo Club. He walked into the master suite of his palatial getaway and knew his travels were done- at least for today.

Frank and Granderson were sure that every proposal they made would be rebuked by Sgt. Smith. They left Sgt. Smith and Hodge Dobson at the entrance to the law offices of Byron Manchester with a promise by Dobson that The Pearl would be recovered.

They jumped in the Mustang and roared off towards Chang's estate. They took a wrong turn and their route brought them down Worth Avenue, an exclusive shopping district comparable to Rodeo Drive in greater Los Angeles. The ultra rich were going about their daily routine- shopping for clothes and accessories they really didn't need- oblivious to the fact that one of their class was having his mansion studied microscopically by the police. Granderson marveled at the dichotomy and knew that these same people would have their ignorance or indifference to a search of a local mansion ascend into indignation if their home was targeted.

As they pulled the 1965 red convertible Mustang up to the barricades on Ocean Blvd., a uniformed officer approached them and asked if this was the car that pursued Chang's bullet riddled car. Granderson said yes and showed the officer his credentials.

"So what is a deputy from St. Paul doing working undercover in Palm Beach?" the officer asked.

Granderson frowned. "I wonder about that myself. Detective Buck Thorton can tell you the whole story. Simply, the driver here is a prosecutor and two of the bodies were dumped on his doorstep. So we have an interest in this search as it is connected to the recovered bodies."

The officer joked: "Just tell whoever is in charge of the search that I've had my fill of overtime for today and they can wrap up the search." He then waved them through. At the gates, they were startled to see women who were wearing white flowing garments and head dresses seated in the shade of some royal palms. The Peacekeeper was next to them as a symbol of superiority. The women shifted around as if uncomfortable with being controlled by deputies in riot gear.

Granderson was stunned at the bizarre scene and said: "Have angels returned to earth to chastise the sinners in the Chang estate, only to be intercepted by cops in riot gear? Today, Palm Beach seems to be the city of contrasts."

Frank responded: "This is an amazing sight. These women look like the famous women pearl divers Monty told me about."

Frank looked around and saw another woman in flowing white garments and head gear as she was being put back in a squad car by Buck. Frank revved up the engine of the Mustang and the unique growl of the exhaust caught Buck's attention. Frank and Granderson got out and walked up to Buck.

Frank smirked at Buck: "This is an unusual scene. I could create a menacing metaphor about heaven, hell and these women. Or I could just say that Buck will tremble if an angel drives up in a squad car and declares she will be taking him to his eternal damnation or reward- as the case may be."

Buck wasn't humored: "I just got done talking with this young woman. Let's move away and you can update me."

After stepping over to The Peacekeeper, Frank and Granderson told Buck about The Pearl being in the lawyer's office, Chang's escape, and Sgt. Smith's road block to recovery of The Pearl. Buck updated them on Cartier's statements, Pao's refusal to give any information and the prospect that she would be jailed.

Frank asked: "What do you think will be the reaction of the women when their leader is driven off in the back of a squad?"

Buck was candid: "The Captain and I are concerned about an incident. If they resist or go after our people it could look like angels being beaten by riot police. They'd look heavenly on the news. The proverbial devil in black would be law enforcement."

Frank suggested: "Seek the leader's cooperation and if she gives it, let her and her troops go."

Buck thought about the idea and reluctantly nodded: "It's worth a try. Let's go back and talk to her."

Frank let her out of the squad and said: "I'm sorry, but I don't know your name."

In a haughty voice she responded: "Your name is Frank Johnson."

Stunned, Buck asked: "How do you know that?"

Pao's eyes met Frank's: "I saw you here having dinner with Mr. and Mrs. Lingbao Chang. Can't you help me? These officers have the wrong impression of me and my companions."

Frank replied: "Your entourage looks like the famous Amas of Pearl Island in Japan."

"Our ancestors were Amas and we continue to follow their traditions. However, we live in China. We're here at the invitation of Mr. Chang."

"I didn't see you here when I was having dinner with the Chang's."

Pao replied: "I saw you in the garden with Mrs. Chang when you got stung by something. I was out of your eyesight."

Buck was growing weary of the socializing: "She commands her nun-chuck carrying troops like General Patton. She looks like an angel, but she ain't. She's under arrest; she and her angels impeded our ability to secure the premises and refused lawful orders."

As planned, Frank acted stunned by the news: "I suppose if she cooperated now, it might make your decision easier whether to jail her or release her. I'm sure you have options regarding criminal charges."

"Well said, Frank." Buck replied as he looked to Pao. Buck knew he needed to get one of the players from within the estate to turn on the others. Buck needed someone on the inside to tell what had happened.

Pao volunteered: "The security guards here believe that the Muslims who died were negligent in getting too close to the golden gator."

The men looked at her in disbelief.

Pao continued: "The guards said the Muslims were hired to care for and feed the gator."

Buck wasn't going to reveal exactly what they knew. He sternly responded: "We know conclusively that's not true."

"That's what the guards told me." She said defiantly.

Granderson moved closer to Pao and his dark eyes magnetically met hers. His focus was resolute and she felt it. His tenacious gaze momentarily pierced her veil of independence. In an accusatory voice he said: "Tell me what part you and your companions played in all the violence that has gone on here."

Pao's face flushed, but she paused and regained her composure: "We've not been involved. The security guards defend the property. We don't."

Granderson asked: "Then why were all of you armed with nun-chucks?"

Buck added: "And you were the first line of defense when we entered the compound this morning."

Granderson continued: "Did you come into the USA legally? I'd like to know the immigration status of you and your companions."

Pao was silent as she considered her options. She needed to redirect the subject of conversation. "I'll only talk to one person. I want to deal with someone who knows about my people and my heritage." She pointed at Frank.

Buck scratched his head; he wondered what scheme she was working. He also pondered if Frank was the right person. After a pause, he emphatically responded: "I make the calls here! You don't! I need to get some info from my Captain."

Pao motioned that they move further away from her companions. She lowered her voice as she continued: "I need an agreement that my companions and I won't be deported and that we won't be charged with any crimes."

Frank put his arm around her shoulder and whispered in her ear. "They may agree not to charge you with any crime for what happened today. In other words, if you cooperate, they won't charge you with interfering with the search warrant. .At this stage, they won't agree to anything more. They won't give you a free ride for anything else because you could be involved in one or more murders."

"I'm not."

"But they don't know that for sure." Frank softly said.

Buck motioned as he said: "Go sit in that red convertible with Frank while I talk with Captain Mastif."

"What about these handcuffs?" Pao asked as she jangled them in front of her.

"They'll come off if I get the OK. Talk with Frank. I'll be back."

Frank walked her over to his car and helped her in. Frank knew he must make her feel comfortable talking with him. He got her to talk about China's explosive economic growth and its impact on their long established culture. After a few minutes, Pao began to speak freely of her native country.

Now she was ready to confide in Frank. "I feel you understand the culture I come from. Please explain why they want to persecute me when I'm only a witness. I don't understand."

"Physical evidence will tell us a lot once it's all collected and analyzed. They'll know what happened here. They have other evidence and other sources of information. Many officers have been working many days since the first body was found. They know that Chang's company, Lingbao Security employs a man named Ying who was involved in the murders because they have an undercover cop who saw it."

Frank paused as Pao's eyes opened wide, astonished at what the police knew. She tried to figure out who within the compound was a cop and had been able to penetrate the wall of security. She didn't know that Frank was referring to Granderson watching the torture of Faroque.

"I know from your reaction that you're surprised. Let me tell you one more fact. They know that until recently, The Pearl of Tao was here. They know who took it and where it is now. You will be asked where it was located in the compound. Your answer will tell them if you are willing to give accurate information."

A long silence followed. Pao pondered the implications of what she was getting into. Her palms perspired and she fidgeted with the handcuffs. Under the pressure of the moment she had lied about the Muslims being hired to care for the gator. She told herself she must not stray from her strongly held religious teachings.

Frank remained calm and silent until Pao resumed the conversation: "I follow the teachings of Lao-Tzu. He teaches that when evil people attack his followers, they must be repelled. I only attack when attacked. You must believe me."

It was hard for Frank to envision this fine featured woman being in charge of an elite group of warriors. He had to convince himself that the flowing robes belied the ferocity of the women.

"Frank, you haven't answered me." Pao said.

"I'll answer you after you have answered Buck's question."

Buck walked up and said: "I have authority to release you and your troops if you will give continuing accurate information. This means you have to talk with Frank away from your troops."

Pao asked: "What about being charged with any crimes?"

"If you cooperate and continue to give us truthful information, no charges for what you all did at the gates this AM. No immunity beyond that. If you did other crimes you will face charges. Do you understand?"

"Yes."

Buck stayed silent and intensely stared at Pao. She met his iron clad look and glared back. Tension flowed between them. Finally, with his voice overflowing with accusation: "Where was The Pearl of Tao in the compound?"

"In the library, on a pedestal, next to a red chair."

For affect, Buck let a small smile creep into the corners of his mouth before he removed the handcuffs. His newly found friendly demeanor masked his intent to turn her into a double agent.

Pao exhaled loudly and then a tremor shook her body.

CHAPTER THIRTY

Pao stretched her perfectly formed legs as she sunk into the luxurious, overstuffed chair. She surveyed the elegant surroundings of the private meeting room inside the posh hotel in upscale Boca Raton. She looked through the wall of glass which framed a sandy beach and the ever present crashing waves of the Atlantic.

Frank had driven her here to give her a fresh perspective- the feeling that she was far removed from Chang and his influence. He surmised that a non threatening atmosphere would increase her feelings towards him and would lessen Pao's need to fabricate a story to protect Chang.

Pao had delighted in the drive along the Atlantic; with mansions on one side and the majestic ocean on the other. As they drove through the city of Lake Worth, Pao felt that the city was as elegant as Palm Beach. Blue sky, azure waters, and the wind caressing her flowing hair made her forget the tension that had surrounded her. Steel drum Caribbean music from the Mustang's stereo system made her body sway to the rhythms. Her mind became mesmerized as her muscles abandoned the harshness of her day. Soothing waves of relaxation changed her. After all, this was her first ride in a convertible and she felt like she was in paradise.

As he drove her to the hotel, Frank studied her features: slender and about five feet six, fine bones in her face but long, slender, well defined muscles in her arms made him believe she had trained extensively in the martial arts. Her dark eyes and shiny long black hair accentuated her smooth skin. When Frank initially watched her at Chang's estate, her expressions showed a determination akin to a warrior in battle. Now she had the look of a person who had just arrived at a destination after a long journey- tired but mentally harmonious.

Frank pondered interview tactics as they drove. He had done plenty of them when he was a prosecutor because he routinely talked to witnesses prior to their testimony. Some witnesses were hostile and he had refined a technique that helped elicit the truth. He learned that questioning must start in a non threatening manner.

As they sat in the luxury of the hotel, Frank was ready to get Pao to open up to him: "Tell me about your group of Amas and how you ended up at the estate of Lingbao Chang."

Pao began slowly: "When we were young, we began to train and live together along the China Sea. Generations ago, our ancestors emigrated from Pearl Island. We're all Taoists and daily we studied Lao-Tzu' teachings. There's much to learn from such a great leader. I wish I lived when he did and he could have taught me. There's so much to contemplate. Lately, I've intensified my studies about The Immortals. Do you know of them?'

"Yes. I remember their diversity."

He paused as he decided to compliment her in order to accentuate her feeling of trust in him. "Watching you makes me believe you have attained one of the higher spiritual states which Taoists so revere. This is rare in a person your age." Frank knew this praise would make Pao feel exhilarated and she would open up to him.

Pao was elated over the compliment and smiled self consciously: "Why, thank you."

Frank continued: "I still don't understand all the teachings of Lao-Tzu. It takes an intense immersion into all the writings to be able to truly follow his instruction the way you do."

Pao was flattered and at the same time impressed at his willingness to start a dialogue about her beliefs. She felt Frank must be extremely knowledgeable about the teachings that were an integral part of her life. "I have studied extensively. There are experts who disagree on some points about Taoism. The important concept to remember every day is what Lao-Tzu stood for. I believe that Lao-Tzu teaches us to be humble."

He felt he was gaining her confidence. "We have much to discuss about Taoism. It's a very important way of life for many of your countrymen. I hope that through dialogues like this, you'll make me more knowledgeable. But for the moment, I'd like to get information about other things. Buck gave me a tape recorder so we have an accurate record of what you say. I'm going to start it now."

"OK."

Frank started the machine and set it between them: "How did it happen that you're in Florida?"

"A few weeks ago, Mr. Chang chartered a jet and flew us to the Bahamas. We were escorted to his huge yacht and cruised on it to his compound. He wanted us with him for two reasons. First, he had a new awakening to Lao-Tzu and desired a re- emersion into Taoism. He told me he had become too worldly with so many businesses. He wanted to surround himself with my group of devout true believers. He spoke of the need to protect the artifacts of Taoism. Just like me, he prized The Pearl and never wanted it in the hands of Muslims. Once we arrived, I began to understand he wanted other skills- our physical training. He was uneasy that he didn't have enough people to discreetly protect him."

Frank exhibited no reaction; rather he simply asked: "You must have been present when the compound was attacked and two guards were killed. What happened?"

"In the middle of the night, Muslim extremists charged the compound and scaled the front walls. My group's assignment was to guard the inside of the home and insure the personal safety of the Chang's. There was a lot of shooting. They kept asking 'where's Faroque?' Our people had already put Faroque in a white van, the golden gator in the trailer and fled. Some of the attackers were shot and the Muslims retreated taking their wounded and dying with them. The police came and we hid."

Frank asked: "What about Cartier?"

Pao remained silent and Frank decided to wait her out. She looked out at the Ocean and then her eyes went skyward. The silence continued and Frank was ready to wait for as long as it took. Finally, she said: "The Chang's have been very good to me. I need to talk with Cartier a lot more. He has fallen from the teachings of Taoism. He needs to return to the middle that's where Lao-Tzu wants Cartier. I know it."

"How has he strayed from the middle?" Frank asked.

"Cartier has a temper and when he questioned the Muslims, he would get angry when they refused to answer. He would hit them with a baseball bat or let the golden gator bite them. He promised me he would be more patient in the future. I think he will be."

"Did you know the names of the Muslim's who Cartier questioned?"

"The first one said he was Akbar and the other two were Haquan and Faroque."

Frank asked: "How did they die?"

"I don't know. None died at the Chang's home. Cartier ordered that the Muslims leave in the van with the golden gator in the trailer."

Frank asked: "I believe there is evidence that a bear was used to torture the Muslims."

Pao looked shocked: "I never saw a bear or heard anyone mention a bear. Whoever said that is trying to get Cartier in trouble. Who said that?"

"It doesn't matter." Frank casually replied. He knew the Chief Medical Examiner was wrong about one death being from a bear attack.

"Cartier only used the gator to get them to talk. He got frustrated because the men wouldn't reveal much; they were dedicated to their cause. Cartier told me the golden gator bit them a few times. One man lost a hand."

Frank felt that she was opening up to him. He decided to take a risk. "We'll need to talk again. We reserved a room for you. Rest up and we'll talk later. I trust you Pao, don't let me down."

Pao seemed relieved: "I need some sleep. It's been a day where my senses have been on high alert."

Frank stood up: "I'll talk with you after you rest. I'll call you in an hour and we'll meet."

Frank led Pao to her room and let her in. He then walked out of the hotel to the beach.

Pao lay on the bed and immediately chastised her self for revealing too much to Frank. He had been so charming and he definitely was handsome. The marvelous ride in the convertible relaxed her and his smooth demeanor made her feel comfortable with him.

She called on the teachings of Lao-Tzu, but his counsel was for truth and that would get her allies in trouble or her deported. She analyzed every angle, but the angles became a circle which led her back to the beginning- she had to remain silent because the truth would harm the Changs.

Finally, Pao resolved to escape the posh resort and somehow find her way back to the compound of Lingbao Chang. This would be very difficult. She knew her angelic robes would make her an easy target for the police. She needed to leave the hotel and hide. She told herself to stay off the street, find different clothes and travel at night.

Meanwhile, Frank needed to figure out what would be needed to keep Pao safe. Just as importantly, what technique could he employ to get her to reveal more of what happened and make her willing to testify? He was contemplating options when his cell phone rang. He looked at the display and saw it was Stephanie.

Frank's heart jumped to his throat; he knew he was much overdue. He barely was able to get out the words: "Hello Stephanie."

"Frank, where are you? Your note said you'd be back by noon."

Frank's complexion turned red as if sunburned; he needed to finesse this problem. "No 'hello.' Just, where are you? I thought you might have started with a sweet opening line."

Stephanie wasn't in the mood to be charmed. "I'd prepared an opening line and it was 'Frank, we hadn't seen each other in months, I took off work, flew down to see you and you head off. Your words and romance of yesterday are at odds with your actions today' But Frank, I didn't blast you with that as an opener. However, I *am* now."

The sternness in her voice was a sign that whatever he said, it would crumble and collapse as an excuse, weighted down by her consternation. He surmised that consequences would follow, so he decided humbleness was in order. "Stephanie, I'm sweating like an ice pitcher on an August afternoon because I made a stupid mistake. Let me explain. Granderson and I have located The Pearl of Tao and it is under police surveillance in the office of Lingbao Chang's lawyer. Soon it will be recovered."

Stephanie's tone changed: "Good, the cops have it under control; so you'll be back here in minutes."

"Well, I'm in Boca Raton."

"Boca Raton? Isn't that on the Atlantic?"

Frank's flushed feeling heightened. "Yes. Law enforcement officers are still searching the Chang estate in Palm Beach and I'll be heading back shortly."

"Shortly is a vague term. Short as compared to the amount of time the universe has existed or short meaning in a few hours?"

"A few hours. I promise. What did you do today?"

"I sat on the beach and instead of being with you, I had to talk with my clients on the cell phone. I assumed you would be here to appreciate me."

"I promise to leave here in a few minutes. We'll be together to enjoy the sunset."

They said their goodbyes and then Frank stood there thinking of things to do for Stephanie to make her feel very important to him. As he came up with a plan, Buck called.

"Frank, what new info do you have?"

"Buck, Pao says that Cartier was directly involved in the torture of the three Muslims. He used a baseball bat. You may want to check with the Chief Medical Examiner to determine if a bat was the type of object which could have caused the injuries. She also says that the golden gator was used on them. A bear wasn't involved. Ask the good doctor if she is willing to change her conclusion on the type of animal that caused Akbar's death."

"Well I'll have a conversation with her, I'm sure it won't be pleasant. What about Lingbao Chang?"

"So far no mention that he was involved in the murders. She says that she and her compatriots came into the country through the Bahamas. I need to firm up with her the legality of the entry. I think Pao and all the Amas may be in big trouble with Immigration."

Buck asked: "Where is she now?"

"She's in her room. I gave her some time alone- supposedly to rest. I think I got her in the right frame of mind and she was helpful. I'm sure she's deciding what additional information to give us. After all, she's a sophisticated warrior for her cause. I'll talk to her after we're done talking, and then I have to go back to Lover's Key. You'll need someone to protect and watch her."

Buck agreed and said he would send someone over. Frank hung up and started back towards the hotel. To his amazement, he saw Pao leaving the hotel and walking rapidly across the parking lot. She kept looking over her shoulder, but Frank was hidden by tropical landscaping.

He felt he had been duped by Pao and his antagonism towards her exploded. He started to sprint after her and he immediately had to dodge a couple of strolling tourists. Frank's adrenaline was pumping. He couldn't let her escape.

Pao turned when she heard rapidly approaching feet pounding the pavement. Her face showed that she was upset that her pursuer was Frank.

His voice was firm as he commanded: "Stop!"

She contemplated running, then considered some martial arts moves, but decided to stand her ground with every muscle taunt. Frank kept more than an arm's length away; he wasn't going to give her a chance to use her martial arts moves; whether it was with her feet or hands.

"Pao, how could you violate the agreement we had by attempting to leave? You're risking arrest. We must return to the hotel."

"I have given you all the information that I'm willing to give. I now regret telling you so much. I'm leaving." Pao said defiantly. Her head turned as she again looked in the direction she was heading.

Frank knew she was about to run. He called Buck: "Get a cop here ASAP to arrest Pao! She attempted to flee. I've got her stopped in the parking lot."

Upon hearing that, Pao turned and started to run.

Frank yelled into the phone: "Get Boca Raton cops to respond. I'm in foot pursuit." Buck said he had already sent one of his deputies, but he would call Boca Raton police to immediately respond. Frank had his phone on speaker and upon hearing that, Pao ran even faster. They jumped a hedge and were now sprinting down the sidewalk. Frank yelled out directions of flight and Buck relayed it to the police dispatcher.

A siren could be heard in the distance and then a Boca Raton squad car with lights flashing came into view. Pao frantically looked back at Frank and realized she was not out running him.

She determined that a successful escape wasn't possible, so she had a change of attitude and stopped. Panting after the long sprint, she said: "OK, OK I did agree to talk and I'll cooperate. Just don't arrest me…PLEASE!"

Frank was intense: "You're not to be trusted. That's not what Taoism is all about. Don't loose sight of your religion and become subdued by earthly devices."

"I don't want to rot in jail until I'm deported."

In a severe tone, he snapped back: "You must talk with me and express your fears before you do these rash acts. Some things can be adjusted if you cooperate. If you don't, you will suffer and possibly suffer immensely."

Just then the Boca Raton squad car roared to a stop with its emergency lights flashing. The officer jumped out of his car, quickly dropped his hand to his holstered gun and commanded: "FREEZE! Put your hands behind your heads."

They quickly complied and Frank calmly said: "I'm Frank Johnson and this is the woman that Investigator Buck Thorton wants arrested as part of the murder case on Ocean Blvd. in Palm Beach."

The officer said: "My supervisor ordered me to detain her until a Lee County deputy arrives."

A forlorn expression flashed across her face and her mouth opened to speak. Before she could, she was in handcuffs for the second time that day and in the back of the squad car. Frank was about to talk to the officer when he heard the sound of more sirens. A Lee County squad and another Boca Raton squad came into view and quickly squealed to a stop.

Frank looked at Pao and her defiance had crumbled. After some discussion between him and the cops, Pao was transferred to the back seat of the Lee County squad car.

Expressionless, Frank looked at a dejected Pao staring back at him. As the squad motored off, he wondered if Pao would give up anymore information.

Frank remembered his commitment to be with Stephanie at sunset and he jogged back to his car.

Cartier stood at the booking desk in the county jail. He wasn't aware of the indignities he would suffer in a few minutes. He was more concerned with spending the night in a jail cell with a bunch of criminals-he didn't see himself as such. He had called his father's lawyer, Byron Manchester and couldn't understand why his lawyer hadn't gotten a judge to order his release. When Cartier commented about that to the booking officer, the officer laughed in his face and commented that he was being booked as a principal for multiple murders- not for failure to pay a speeding ticket. Cartier was beginning to understand the gravity of the situation. The officer continued to laugh when he asked Cartier if he was ready for a body cavity search.

Byron Manchester was speaking with a judge, but not about Cartier Chang's release. He was indignant and dismayed that police were stationed in the hallway outside his office. He was incensed because his clients would wrongly conclude his firm had done something illegal. Of course, he called a former member of his firm who was now wearing a black judicial robe.

"Why are the police there?" Judge Grannis asked.

"I don't know." Byron Manchester deadpanned.

"Put one of the men in blue on the phone. I'll order him to reveal what they are doing."

"There's no way I'm going to let one of those cops in my office! They might draw a gun and rummage through files. They would slaughter the sacred bond of trust between myself as an attorney and all of my clients. There's so much confidential information in my files that I can't risk being revealed. I hold the attorney client privilege as sacred- *I WILL NOT COMPROMISE IT!* I doubt the cops care about it in the least."

Judge Grannis wasn't going to be sidetracked by the bluster: "Go out in the hall and have the officer call me in my judicial chambers."

Manchester complied and Hodge Dobson called.

"This is Judge Grannis. Who am I speaking with?"

"I'm Officer Hodge Dobson of the West Palm Beach Police Department."

"Why are you outside the door to the Manchester Law Firm?"

"Because a rookie States Attorney can't tell us if it is legal to get a search warrant to search for a stolen pearl in a lawyer's office."

Alarms silently sounded in the Judge's head: "A particular pearl?"

"Yeah, one worth millions of dollars that's also linked to murders. So Judge if you will answer the question about the search warrant, we'll get this problem resolved."

"I issued a search warrant for that pearl, but it was for a mansion on Ocean Blvd. I was a member of The Manchester Law Firm so I have the appearance of a conflict of interest and I'm hanging up now. I express no opinion on the legality of what you are doing now or whether a search warrant can be issued. Goodbye."

She realized she had quickly sunk into a legal quagmire that would only get worse if she said more.

Manchester was indignant. He knew swift legal action was mandated to curb such an infringement on his ability to make money and tragically, his former law partner was slamming the door on him. He told himself it wasn't fair that he wasn't getting any favored treatment for having friends in high places.

Hodge Dobson smirked: "Well. Your call to a judge got you nowhere. I didn't hear one concern from the judge that we're doing anything wrong. I'm calling my supervisor again. It's time for a search warrant. If there was a problem with us searching your office, the judge would have said. Just remember that if you do anything to hinder our ability to get the stolen property, you'll be committing a crime."

Manchester's blood was boiling: "Don't you dare tell me the law! You'll face major lawsuits if you enter this office-even if you have a search warrant. I'm telling you right now that the paper the warrant is written on is worth a dime and my recovery on a law suit will be millions."

Just then, Byron Manchester's secretary came out in the hall. "Mr. Manchester. Cartier Chang said he has been given one last phone call. He's crying. He doesn't want to spend the night in jail with rapists and he doesn't want the body cavity search which the jailer says is next."

"Tell him I'll get one of my associates to see him in the morning. I have to defend the sanctity of my law firm. The two of us will stand guard at these doors and forcefully repel any pretended authority to search this law firm. If they haul us away, it will only increase the damages we will recover in a lawsuit. "

Hodge Dobson laughed out loud as he called his supervisor.

CHAPTER THIRTY ONE

Darkness had fallen on his island utopia and Lingbao Chang was exhausted. The palms whispered a refreshing harmony with the soft breeze to welcome the weary traveler. Lingbao resisted sleep because he had much to accomplish. He didn't flinch at the thought that he was encircled by a series of major crimes. The penalties were severe and would include the death penalty. He'd been up against countless formidable adversaries in China and was able to prevail. After all, he built his empire by conquering those who opposed him.

He opened his aluminum suitcase and surveyed the contents. The world was his for the journey he told himself. He checked the multiple passports; all with his picture, but issued in different names. His connections in China allowed him to obtain passports at his whim.

The item which took up most of the suitcase was The Pearl. He looked at it, smiled and took another sip of wine. He held it and admired everything it represented. The candlelights in the room made The Pearl emit a golden glow and he marveled at its beauty. He mused how close he had been to loosing it, but he was one step ahead of his adversaries. Now he held the real Pearl of Tao, thanks to his cunning.

He wanted to be the only one to know the location of The Pearl. The one on display at his mansion was a replica he had made years ago in China. He kept it hidden until the real thing had been purloined from The Ft. Lauderdale Museum of Art. Pao was the savior who did the work for him. Her sacred devotion to Taoism made her the prime liberator of The Pearl. She could work alone and keep the theft a secret.

Covertly, she brought it to his office and locked it away. A week later, unbeknownst to Pao, he displayed the replica at his home.

He feared that at some point the police would track The Pearl to him because some one would talk. If it was discovered, they would seize the replica and he would not be guilty of anything but false bravado.

The fear he had was that Pao would at some point turn against him and reveal that she had stolen the real pearl and given it to him. Pao was committed to him, but a far greater loyalty existed in her heart to Taoism. The turmoil with the murderous Muslims made this the time to be sure that Pao's devotion to him could never falter. He needed to keep her safe and under his control.

Lingbao knew he must continue the charade so everyone would pursue the replica. He smiled at the memory of racing off with it to his lawyer's office. He must effectuate his plan, so he pulled out a satellite based cell phone and called Ying.

"Where are you?" asked Chang.

"I'm hidden away at your remote cabin near Lake Okeechobee. This cabin could use some repairs."

Chang replied: "It blends in. It's just an old ramshackle place that looks like it's still owned by a local. What have you been doing?"

"We've been catching fish and feeding them to the golden gator."

Chang wasn't amused as he ordered Ying: "Leave the gator there and go back to West Palm Beach. See if there's trouble at my lawyer's office. You know I left The Pearl in his care. I don't know if I can trust him to not open the black box and keep The Pearl. I sometimes wonder if I can rely on him. The Pearl means too much to our people. Check out the office. I'll call you in an hour."

Ying and his underlings headed back; but this time they had an old cable television truck. They stopped at a popular sports bar and found a truck in the parking lot with lettering on the side announcing that the owner was a landscaper. Ying pulled up and had his associate steal the license plate. They drove to a deserted warehouse area and put the stolen plate on. Ying figured that tonight the landscaper wouldn't notice his license plate was missing; especially if he had a few too many beers.

Ying pulled up on a side street down from Trinity Park and near

Trump Plaza. Ying could see squad cars at the majestic rose colored 777 Phillips Point Building. Ying got out of the truck and walked in a semi circle, away from the building. Finally, after coming around another corner, Chang's lawyer's office building came into view. Most of the building was dark, but as he looked higher up, he could see lights on where Chang had said the Manchester Law Firm was located. Ying also saw the squad cars parked by the building, but no officers inside the cars. He casually strolled back to the truck and waited.

Lingbao Chang called and Ying updated him. Chang was distraught: "I don't understand why the police are there. I've done much to recover The Pearl of Tao. It must not be delivered into the wrong hands. I had a divine vision and Lao-Tzu spoke to me. He said I must be the savior of The Pearl and I must not fail. Likewise, you must not fail."

Ying and his underlings listened silently as Chang told them how to bring The Pearl back to him. Chang ended the conversation: "Some have called The Pearl of Tao the 'Pearl of Death'. It's only deadly to those who aren't true believers of Lao-Tzu. Infidels must fear it, but it creates a pathway to His Holiness for those who protect it and secure it for his sake. You'll be destined for divine greatness once you accomplish this spiritual mission."

The men in the truck were charged up. Divine ecstasy is more potent than a street drug. The men went to the back of the truck and donned cable TV uniforms. Ying jumped back in the cab and drove up to the delivery entrance. He got out and easily jimmied the lock on the door at the bottom of the emergency stairwell exit. The others hopped out with an assortment of gear and started the long trek up the stairwell.

Silently they ascended and at the top floor, they looked up at the hatch cover to the roof. It was secured by a padlock. Ying looked for any sign of wires which would indicate it was connected to an alarm. He smiled as he pulled out the bolt cutters and in seconds they scrambled onto the roof. They circled the massive air conditioning equipment looking for a point of entrance. Finally, they took out their tools. Slowly, carefully and quietly, they began cutting.

Ying directed Jack Toy, a diminutive young man to climb in. Toy had a miner's headlamp attached to his head and an assortment of implements on a tool belt on his waist. With a rope attached, he disappeared into the darkness of the air shaft.

Toy had listened as Lingbao Chang described the location of Byron Manchester's office within the law firm. Ying primed Toy with more instructions based upon the point of entry they just found. Now it was time for Ying to nervously wait.

Toy used his hands and feet against the sides of the air shaft as he descended a couple of floors. Then he moved noiselessly in a horizontal air shaft, like a panther tracking its prey. He came to an area where he believed he was in the ceiling above the Manchester Law Firm so he pried away a connecting air duct and slid out. He was now above the suspended ceiling amid a jumbled network of cables and wires. In the distance he could hear the voice of an agitated man having an argument, but not giving anyone a chance to respond.

Toy decided to move at a diagonal away from the voice and then lifted a suspended ceiling tile. He looked down into an office with the door almost closed. He replaced the tile and moved over so he was directly above the desk. Silently he lowered himself onto it and disconnected himself from the rope. He peeked into the hallway and got his bearings.

Back into the ceiling he went, careful to leave no trace of his presence. Cautiously crawling, he snaked through the cables and then removed a ceiling tile. He peered down on a huge office with expensive, massive sized furnishings. Toy thought-this must be it. He kept looking, but did not see the black lacquered box with ornate gold symbols. Maybe there was more than one gargantuan office in the law firm. Toy was about to move on when he spied a gaggle of certificates on the wall including a law degree. In large letters it declared that Byron Manchester was awarded a juris doctorate.

Success would soon be his; as he carefully lowered himself into the office. Now to find the box.

Byron Manchester was livid. The Chief of Police was not available in the middle of the night to stop his minions from desecrating the sanctity of a lawyer's office. The highest ranking person who would talk to him was a lieutenant. How demeaning! Manchester let the officer know that. He also told his secretary to make a note of it.

Manchester was surly as he spoke on the phone: "Lieutenant, the Constitution of the United States and The Bill of Rights guarantee that citizens have rights including the right to a lawyer. You're trampling on the documents that all our citizens hold dear. People fear a police state and using a battering ram to get into my office will turn this city into Nazi Germany. The right to a lawyer is meaningless unless police respect it. Look at the Miranda warning card you use. The third right listed is the right to an attorney."

As Manchester was pontificating, Toy searched his office. Nothing. Disheartened, he decided to sit down in Manchester's chair and think things out. He swung his feet under the desk and hit a box. He looked under the desk-he hit the jackpot! The box with The Pearl! He grabbed it and jubilantly hoisted himself back into the maze in the ceiling. He replaced the ceiling tile and felt he had left no trace of his presence in the office. The pontificating lawyer would be baffled at the disappearance of the sacred jewel.

Toy retraced his route by following the rope he had attached to his waist. When he started from the roof, he had played it out as he descended. Now the difficult task was doing a vertical assent in the air shaft while holding the prize of his endeavor. He came out on the roof to the congratulations of his team. Elated, they silently and swiftly fled down the stairs and paused at the bottom. They put their treasure in a canvas bag and opened the door.

Trouble was straight ahead. A police officer was closely looking at the truck and he turned as he heard the door open.

"What's going on here?" the officer asked.

As prearranged, the others went to the back of the truck and Ying stepped forward. "We're with the cable company. A customer was having intermittent problems with his high speed internet service and he didn't want us trouble shooting the problem while his office was open; so we had to come tonight. Did I park in the wrong place?"

"Yes. Are you leaving now?"

"We're done." Ying replied as he jumped behind the wheel and started the engine.

The officer didn't respond, so Ying started to slowly drive off. He looked in his rear view mirror and saw the officer write down the license plate number. Ying knew the cops would be looking for the truck once they knew The Pearl was gone and the investigation started. Ying drove a couple of blocks, pulled in an alley, and reattached the original license plate. As they drove off, the stolen plate was thrown into a drainage canal. Ying was anxious to do some night fishing so the golden gator wouldn't go hungry.

The lieutenant was now outside the door of the law office, bearing the brunt of Manchester's diatribe on the disintegration of citizen's rights. The lieutenant was patient because he knew that the search warrant would arrive shortly and he would have the last word on the subject.

Finally, a West Palm Beach investigator arrived with the search warrant in hand. At his side was Buck Thorton. They could hear Manchester's voice even before the elevator doors opened. The investigator handed Manchester the warrant and he started reading it.

Buck watched and when Manchester was done reading, Buck verbally jumped into the fray. He loved to match barbs with lawyers and he put on his best legal persona: "Counselor Manchester, you can see that this is a narrowly drawn search warrant designed to acknowledge your concerns about the attorney client privilege. We're not allowed to look at any files or any paperwork. We can't look at computers or photographs. We can only search anywhere that a football sized object could be secreted."

Manchester wasn't so easily satisfied: "Any officer who enters my law firm will be subject to personal liability in a lawsuit. My secretary will be taking names and badge numbers if you dare to enter."

Buck wasn't fazed: "Your objection is duly noted. Likewise, you're advised that you may be present during the search- only to watch- you can't hinder it. If you do, you're committing a crime. We *will* arrest you and you will be jailed immediately. Then your ability to watch the search would end."

Manchester's blood pressure went off the charts. "I'm insulted that you think you can tell me what I can do in my own law office. Your department won't have enough money to satisfy the judgment I'll get."

Buck wasn't deterred as he led the parade inside: "We'll start with your office because that is the most likely place to find the object of our search. Thus, we will minimize the intrusion into the commercial premises. If you direct us to The Pearl, it will limit our movements within your firm."

Manchester was at a loss. He didn't want to do anything to acknowledge the validity of what law enforcement was doing, yet he could be accused of failing to mitigate his damages if he didn't show them the location of his office. "In no way do I want you to believe that I am relinquishing my right to sue you. You move about this law firm over my explicit objection."

Buck was not intimidated. He calmly replied: "Show me your office. Just remember, that possession of stolen property is a crime."

Manchester exploded: "Every client of mine has an absolute right to confer with me and bring to me evidence that will exonerate him! Don't be so brazen as to try to make it look like I'm holding ill gotten goods!"

Manchester led the way to his office. Buck and others followed. Officers looked behind furniture and under chairs. Buck moved Manchester's chair, yet no one observed that Manchester held his breath as Buck looked under the desk. Buck moved away and Manchester mirrored Buck's search under the desk. He looked at the empty space in disbelief.

"IT'S GONE!" Manchester screamed.

Buck knew what had disappeared, but he wanted to hear the words from the legal wizard: "What's gone counselor?"

"THE BOX WITH THE PEARL, YOU KNUCKLEHEAD!"

Buck continued to play dumb: "Where was it?"

Manchester quickly locked his emotions back inside. He felt he'd been check mated in his contest with the mouthy cop. He knew he had been out played. Another cross roads had been thrust upon him: should he ask for the cops help in finding The Pearl or should he keep quiet? What would Chang think about a lawyer who lost his client's sixty million dollar asset?

Buck intruded into Manchester's musings: "Well, it doesn't look like The Pearl is in this office; we need to move on and continue the search."

"Wait."

"What?" Buck asked

Manchester regained his regal legal demeanor: "I strenuously object to any further search. You erroneously believed The Pearl was in my office, you acknowledge it's not here, so you must immediately vacate."

"Wrong."

Manchester looked to his secretary, just outside his door, and said: "Note I again demanded that the officers leave."

Buck chirped: "And note that your boss said quote it's gone, and then said the box with the pearl, you knuckleheads, end quote."

Manchester was rattled: "She's in my employ, and she takes direction from me-exclusively."

Buck directed the officers: "Let's move on. We haven't found The Pearl yet."

The officers continued their search without success. As they left, Buck fired one last shot across the bow of Manchester's ship: "If you want to report The Pearl as stolen, contact West Palm Beach PD. They will send someone out and take a full report including when and how it came into your possession. That means who left it here and for what reason. It will take some time to get a full statement from you. You might want to hire a criminal lawyer to represent you because The Pearl was obviously stolen property…." With a smile on his face, Buck bowed at the waist and cheerily concluded: "Good night counselor."

CHAPTER THIRTY TWO

Chang nervously looked at his watch and then called Ying. He was elated once he heard the mission was accomplished. Now he was faced with the formidable task of finding a safe place for the replica Ying had taken from Manchester's office. Law enforcement would be relentless in their pursuit of it and Ying's helpers needed to be taken out of the loop regarding knowledge of its whereabouts.

Chang told Ying of the plan. One of his security guards who had been killed by the Muslims was still at the morgue. He was from China and no relatives could afford to bring him back to his homeland or even pay for internment. Chang told Ying to hire an undertaker and arrange for services. Just before the casket was closed, Ying should ask for a moment alone with the deceased. Discreetly, he would put the black lacquered box containing the replica inside the coffin by the feet. Ying liked the idea but questioned where to bury him so it could be recovered in the future.

Chang related that recently he had flown into the Daytona Beach airport and across the street from the end of the runway was a decrepit old cemetery that looked half empty and mostly untended. It was perfect because it's far from Palm Beach and when the time's right, it can be retrieved without attracting attention. Chang cautioned him not to reveal this plan to anyone. Ying swore to secrecy especially since Chang offered him a healthy sum of money for success.

Chang now turned his concern to his son, Cartier and was upset to learn he had been arrested. Ying said the security guards at the compound reported that Pao had defected to the other side. Chang was alarmed, but his voice was steady. When he asked why they believed such a devote follower would change sides. Ying said they saw the police take off the handcuffs and she rode off with a good looking man in a red convertible.

Chang was angry at this news. He never anticipated she would turn this quickly. The trail of The Pearl which led right to him was too fresh. Would she reveal information and how much? Maybe she would remain loyal and misdirect the police. Chang told Ying he would be in touch and hung up.

Lingbao Chang needed a plan. Was Pao a turn coat or a loyal person pretending to cooperate with the police? Where was she now? Chang decided he must not rush to judgment. But his plan must satisfy both prospects and it must be decisive because he was the target. He decided to get a few hours of sleep before he masterminded his new plan.

The next morning as the purple sunrise created a new hue to Chang's idyllic hideaway, he awoke with the feeling that he must talk to Pao face to face. Only then could he determine for sure if she was still to be trusted. He would see it in her eyes. A confrontation gave him the option of decisive action against her.

But first, he had to know what Manchester would say about the disappearance of The Pearl. He got out his cell phone and called directly into Byron Manchester's office. He answered on the first ring.

"Mr. Manchester, this is Lingbao Chang. I'm pleasantly surprised that you're in so early. Indeed, you *are* a hard working lawyer."

Manchester's chest fell and his mind raced. How could Chang learn so quickly that The Pearl had been stolen from him? Manchester debated what to say about it.

This pause didn't deter Chang; he was on a mission. "I heard my son is in jail. You must get him out."

"It's not that easy, he is being held for multiple murders. My associate is at the jail now, getting information as we speak. As I like to say: The Manchester firm never sleeps. In fact, the last call I got from my associate indicated that a woman named Pao had been booked into the jail late yesterday for some misdemeanor offenses related to impeding the execution of a search warrant at your estate. Do you know her?"

Chang was surprised, but his tone of voice didn't show it: "She works at the estate. She is very loyal to me. She must have gotten excited when the squadron of militia arrived."

"She'll be appearing in court this morning, do you want my firm to represent her?"

Chang saw an opening: "Of course, do whatever it takes to get her out of jail."

"That'll be easier with her than your son. His charges are much more serious and he may be held without bail. Call me back later this morning and I'll update you. Oh, one more major item. The police were here last night with a search warrant to search for your pearl. I resisted with every legal and political maneuver I could, but they got in here. Luckily, they didn't find The Pearl. So they have no physical evidence tying you to it. "

Lingbao Chang was amused at the spin his lawyer gave to losing a sixty million dollar asset. He had to play it further: "You're an exceptional lawyer to hide it so well that the cops can't find it. I don't need to know where it is now, but I hope it's in a secure place."

Manchester deadpanned: "I'm not sure it's secure, but at least neither the Muslims nor law enforcement has it. I'll keep you posted."

Chang deadpanned: "Ohh?"

Manchester needed to sidetrack the conversation about The Pearl: "Don't worry, about your son, he'll get the best legal representation in all of Florida- The Manchester Firm."

Chang hung up and smiled. Another shyster lawyer he thought. Then his thoughts turned to Pao. He now knew where she was. Once Pao was released, he would get her onto the island with him. Then he could talk to her alone. She would be out of the country- away from the authorities. Realistically, his remote island was governed by him and no one else. Things were looking up.

Chang drank his tea and organized a plan. It was almost one in the afternoon when Chang reached Manchester. "Is my son safe?'

Manchester was full of bravado: "He doesn't think so, but the jail staff does. The judge is trampling on the Constitutional right to bail! He erroneously ruled Cartier was a flight risk because of your extensive connections to China. Plus, he was swayed by the thought your son might flee because of legal proceedings which have not been filed. Completely unfair.

"What legal proceedings?"

Solemnly Manchester declared: "The States Attorney said they are considering seeking the death penalty."

"For defending ourselves from attackers within the walls of our estate? I thought you were an exceptional lawyer."

Manchester knew this would be a delicate discussion. "They contend that none of the men who died were the attackers of the compound. Two bodies were found before that happened. They contend all three were kidnapped, tortured by your son using both a baseball bat and what they describe as a rare golden gator. Who knows if they can prove it? They're mere allegations. A fearless lawyer is needed to combat the over reaching government. We need to sit down and draw up a contract for representation of your son."

"Yes, the allegations are preposterous" snapped Lingbao. "Do something-flex your political muscle, GET HIM OUT! NOW!"

"We've scheduled another bail hearing and an extensive bail evaluation has been ordered. We'll argue that bail be set at one hundred thousand dollars, he turn in his passport and he be subject to electronic monitoring."

"What's that?"

"It is an ankle bracelet that continuously tracks his location. He'll be given a limited area where he can be. For example, the county of his residence."

Chang didn't like the sound of that. It made it difficult to get Cartier out of the country. "What if he cuts it off or he leaves the county?"

"Alarms will sound at the monitoring headquarters and they'll arrest him."

Chang again became gruff: "Forget that, just agree to higher bail. He won't leave the U.S. without a passport."

Manchester replied: "That's why you need an experienced, savvy, counselor at law. It's a delicate matter. If we object to electronic monitoring too vigorously, the judge will conclude you have enough money to bail him out at any price and Cartier will flee. Then the judge will be inclined to order Cartier held without bail."

"Are they saying he committed these crimes by himself?"

"No. They name your employee Ying as a person of interest. That's double talk. He's a suspect and they're building a case against him. The prosecution isn't saying much, but my experience tells me that others are inside the web of investigation."

Chang became worried: "What has been said about me?"

Manchester paused for effect. "Mr. Chang, Your name wasn't mentioned and that worries me. The cops know you fled the site of murderous tortures with a black lacquered box. They hope to prove it contained stolen property which is integral to the motive for the murders. Prosecutors love to snare others under the guise of the legal concept entitled 'conspiracy.'"

"That's outrageous. I did nothing."

Manchester knew that the fee he could charge just increased dramatically. His tactic worked- when big money people are faced with major criminal charges, freedom knows no dollar limit. "Mr. Chang you need to come in to sign a contract of representation and pay a retainer for your son. Then we can talk about the legal travails that loom on your horizon. I suggest this afternoon."

"I…I can't make it."

"I'll be working late tonight on this case. How about this evening?"

Chang needed to know about Pao. But wasn't about to reveal to Manchester his whereabouts or that he wasn't coming back to the U.S. "Fine, I'll be there about eight. I need to have you handle Pao's case too. What happened to her?"

"We were successful in getting bail set and she is out."

"Good."

"There is a problem that looms on the horizon for Pao. The States Attorney contended that she is in the country illegally and wanted her held until Immigration put a hold on her. The judge asked why a hold hadn't already been filed. She was lucky. There was a big boatload of illegals that came ashore last night and Immigration didn't get around to dealing with Pao. So Immigration will be after her."

Chang asked: "Where is she now?"

"I don't know and I don't want to know. All I care about is that she appears on her next court date and you hire me to represent her."

"I'll take care of it when we meet." Lingbao replied.

The conversation ended and Lingbao knew he had to get Pao to come to him. She could link him to The Pearl and that meant trouble.

CHAPTER THIRTY THREE

Granderson was back at The Breakers having a well deserved massage administered by a tea pot shaped senior citizen. He wondered why he thought all masseuses were stunningly beautiful women in their thirties. Well, it was still relaxing. He could hear the waves crash ashore and the warm ocean breeze was a welcome respite from Minnesota. Yet he couldn't get the investigation out of his mind. The evidence from the mansion would be analyzed and soon they would be able to prove that the Muslims had been tortured and possibly murdered at Chang's residence.

The problem was proving who was involved besides Cartier and Ying. Granderson knew the man who he shot when Faroque was being tortured out in the field was a conspirator; at least in Faroque's murder. But where was he and who was he? Did Lingbao Chang give the orders to torture these men? Or was he oblivious to it because he was busy with his businesses? After all, the compound was so big, it was possible he didn't know the Muslims were even there.

Granderson felt Lingbao was the ringmaster in charge of the carnage; but proving it would be difficult. Lingbao was insulated just like the mafia protects the don. Frank needed to be consulted about this. Granderson tried to push these thoughts out of his mind and enjoy the luxury of the massage.

The elderly masseuse commented that his muscles were not loosing up and he had to put tension filled thoughts out of his mind. Granderson decided that a strategy to find The Pearl, the golden gator and solve the murders would have to wait for another time.

Frank sat on the white sand with Stephanie at his side. The air was still. The water was calm and it majestically reflected sumptuous shades of red and orange as the enlarged sun lazily strolled towards the water. Stephanie was happy the moment she heard Frank's car pull up. This idyllic evening made today's tensions feel like a distant memory. She snuggled even closer to him. She knew she must capture the scene in her mind to be able to replay it again and again. She loved him deeply.

"I think we should go sailing tomorrow." She suggested.

"A great idea. You're the captain, I'll be the crew."

"Of course. Just remember. You follow the captain's orders without question or comment. That rule starts even before we're on the ship. Let's say it starts at dawn."

Frank felt he wasn't in a position to argue after today's unexcused absence. "I look forward to fulfilling your wishes." Frank wondered if he sounded sincere or sarcastic.

They sat silently as the water barely made a sound as it flowed to the warm white sand. They looked up the beach to see they had a visitor. A bald eagle stood on the sand eating a small silver colored fish. The white head of the eagle repeatedly looked around as the piercing eyes were ever vigilant-the majestic bird was nervous about being on land as he zealously guarded his dinner.

Frank thought of food and they decided to go out to dinner at Flippers, a cozy beach side restaurant within walking distance. As they ambled up the beach, they commented that tonight would be a very memorable time. The weather was perfect and the love they shared continued to make them feel exhilarated.

At Flipper's, Stephanie ordered a tuna steak with a mango glaze and Frank picked coconut shrimp. As they dined overlooking the water, Stephanie wondered what the future held for their relationship. The moon was rising over the bay and a manatee's nose momentarily spouted out of the water.

She gazed at Frank and his sparkling eyes told her they must make a determined effort to live in the same community. They lived too far apart for their love to endure forever.

Frank squeezed her hand and mouthed the words "I love you."

Stephanie's eyes moistened as her mind grabbed the wondrousness of the moment. She dropped her fork and said: "Frank, we've had so many touching moments in the time we've been together. We must end our long distance relationship and be together."

"I know you're right. I go away and then I always yearn for you."

After a pause, Stephanie continued: "I have a career in St. Paul, but this place is so beautiful. I'm torn over leaving a great architectural firm, yet you're working what could be called a temporary assignment. You've been a prosecutor. Now you're dealing with all of Monty Moritz' issues- it's different."

Cautiously he whispered: "You love this place, just consider all it has to offer."

She voiced her deeply held concern: "I don't think I can abandon my firm…." She then resolved to change the subject: "Let's enjoy the evening."

They shared their entrees and their love.

Dr. Doris Delaney rewrote the press release for the third time, as she sat in her airline seat heading into the setting sun. Again she was being whisked to Las Vegas. Her third trip there in a month had been spoiled by Buck's phone call. She was incensed that Buck had forced her to take action. He didn't need to arrest the murderer right away, nor did he have to reveal that the murderer was being charged with the three murders she was doing the post mortems upon. Buck emphatically disagreed with her and she let him know her outrage.

Dr. Delaney had resolved to issue a press release while in Las Vegas so she could avoid questions by the media. She ordered a staff person to stay into the night to give the information out. She wanted her press release to come out at the same time as the information about the murder charges and thus her news would be less significant.

She knew that eyebrows of skeptics would rise if she released a new finding that the first body found wasn't killed by a bear, but a gator. She didn't want to directly state it was a gator because it would be an admission of error. She finally decided to release that Akbar was killed by a large animal and it could be an animal other than a bear. She would lead off the press release with the news that she was declaring it a homicide. Maybe the press would focus on that.

She recalled Buck told her that if reporters asked him about the conflict between her bear attack report and the admission of a gator torture, he was siding with the gator torture. She swore to herself at his lack of loyalty. He was forcing her hand.

If there was a trial, she would have to testify it was a gator and not some other animal. Buck had the two Fish and Wildlife Officers as bite mark experts and once they found the golden gator, there would be a set of jaws to compare with the bite marks on the victims. The press release would set the stage for a later outright admission it was a gator attack. The news wouldn't be as stunning if it was known it could be an animal other than a bear, especially since Cartier had admitted it was a gator. She released the names of all three men who had been murdered in order to dilute her change of course. Dr. Delaney sat back and turned her thoughts to the fun she would have in Las Vegas.

After reading the newspaper article about Cartier Chang's murder charges, Frank shook his head as he read the related article about the Chief Medical Examiner's press release. Her staff had bungled it. The newspaper reported that the press release was faxed from a casino/hotel in Las Vegas and she was not available for comment. Her staff had sent out copies of the fax which still had the imprint on the top of the hotel. The reporter made repeated calls to Dr. Delaney's hotel room, but she didn't answer or return the calls. Frank was not alone as he questioned her competence.

Frank jumped to attention and made a mock salute when Stephanie ordered all hands on deck. She laughed and then issued other nautical commands. Hand in hand they headed off to a glorious day on the waters of the Gulf of Mexico. Frank kept reminding himself which side was port and which was starboard.

The main sail was up and the salty breeze moved them quietly through the warm clear water. Frank thought that sailing had a much different feel than power boating. No engine noise, just the joyous sound of the water being divided by the bow as it rushed by, only to silently swirl beyond the transom. The brilliant white sail looked dazzling against the cloudless deep blue sky.

Frank joyously exclaimed: "Three miles off shore and nary a ship to be seen. We have the waters to ourselves."

Almost. Two dolphins emerged behind the ship and playfully swam beside them- they bumped each other and jumped completely out of the water. The sailboat was moving at five knots, but the dolphins circled it with ease.

They looked up at Frank and Stephanie. Excited Frank said: "They're inviting us into the water to play."

Quickly, he went below deck and emerged with a rope. He tied it to a cleat on the transom and told Stephanie to stay on course. He held the other end of the rope and dove in. As the rope uncoiled he prepared for a jerk. When the rope tightened, he took off to the delighted squeaks of the two dolphins. They swam around him, dove deep and jumped over the rope as Frank was pulled through the water like a slow motion water skier. The dolphins came within a few feet of Frank and smiled at his company. The trio continued to play in the warm gulf waters.

After about twenty minutes of frolicking, Frank noticed small fish swimming along. It was a school of black and silver striped sheephead. The dolphins noticed them too and decided it was lunch time. Off they went after the fish- play time was over. Stephanie let the sail luff and the boat slowed to a stop. Frank climbed aboard, smiling from ear to ear. What an escapade!

As Frank dried himself off, he could hear his cell phone ring from below deck. Stephanie looked at him and he let it ring. He turned to Stephanie and smiled. She said thanks.

Frank hoisted the sails and they again cruised northward just off Big Carlos Pass. They had a favorable breeze and she set a heading towards Sanibel Island. About an hour later as they reached the island, Frank's cell phone chirped again. They looked at each other and she said: "Ok. Answer it; but make it short."

Frank said hello and Granderson came directly to the point: "We need to find The Pearl and Lingbao Chang."

Frank agreed: "Chang's lawyer doesn't have it any longer, so they'll talk about where it is. We need to get phone records of the lawyer, so we can trace the calls of Chang and find him."

"I don't have jurisdiction to do that." Granderson protested.

"I'll call Buck and have him get the cell phone records of Chang."

"He won't like the paper work."

Frank replied: "It's not the glamorous part of being a detective, but I'll convince him." Frank looked over at Stephanie and her frown. It was time to end the conversation and he did.

Stephanie loosened the sails and they slowed to a stop. She was gracious: "Just be quick with your call to Buck."

"Buck, this is Frank."

"I know. Make it quick. I'm working on getting more evidence so Lingbao Chang can be charged with directing these murders."

"That's what I'm calling about. He'll be calling his lawyer about The Pearl and his son. Get the cell phone records and we'll track him down."

Buck grumbled: "Is it legal to intercept the conversations between a lawyer and his client? Are you doing the paper work?"

"We aren't intercepting conversations. We don't want a wire tap. We just want the phone numbers of recent calls Chang made and his location when he made them." Frank said.

"You're right. He could be anywhere. It'll take some work. I'll put a couple of detectives on it."

"Anyone talk to Pao?"

Buck said: "She's back at the mansion and she says her lawyer ordered her not to talk to us. The lawyer said she would be talking herself into murder charges. So she's told us to talk to her lawyer."

Frank asked: "What about Ying? Any charges?"

"I got a warrant for his arrest for the murder of Faroque. More charges are possible as we get more evidence together. We need to find him and the golden gator. If we get a conclusive match that the bite marks on Akbar and Haquan were made by the golden gator, Ying will be charged with those murders. "

"Call when you have news." Frank said cheerily as he hung up.

Frank's head swiveled as he heard a splash. The captain had abandoned ship. The first mate was now in charge. Stephanie yelled out: "Drop anchor and join me."

He did and they swam around the ship; all the problems in their world had gravitated beyond their horizons. For the moment, only pleasure and love existed in their watery world. Neither had a desire to abandon their amorous adventure. Floating free in the water, their embrace held them closer than ever before.

Granderson sat at the bar of an expensive restaurant in Wellington, playing the role of a Chicago real estate developer who wanted to get into polo and invest in local real estate. The polo pony cocktail hour crowd hadn't arrived and Benny the bartender was looking for conversation. Granderson sipped on a glass of ginger ale; the color of his drink made it look like he was having a mixed drink. He had read in the newspaper that a major polo tournament was starting tomorrow and he had come to this watering hole for information. Benny the bartender was happy to let him know what his customers were talking about. The old established Azure Polo Club was infuriated because the head of the Far East Polo Club had repeatedly boasted that his club would eliminate Azure in the first round.

Benny portrayed himself as an expert on the sport and his tone oozed confidence and conviction. He said that two different patrons, members of Azure, had let slip that they had very large bets on the outcome of the match. One evening, the patrons had a few too many drinks and revealed the bet was so large that each side required the money be held by a third party.

Granderson commented that he knew Lingbao Chang was the head of The Far East Polo Club. He wondered out loud if Lingbao was bankrolling the entirety of the Far East bets or if other members of his club were in on it. Benny whispered that he knew for a fact that it was all Lingbao's money.

Granderson steered the conversation to the horses involved in the match and Benny was on a roll. He described with fervor the magnificence of a couple of Azure's recently acquired prime steeds and the skills of their riders. The talk around Wellington was that Azure should win handily.

Long ago, Granderson had learned to be a good listener and Benny certainly was a verbose speaker. Granderson discovered where the horses were kept overnight and then the happy hour crowd started to arrive. Now Benny was busy and Granderson watched the gentry greet each other. Granderson's ebony skin set him apart from the others and he sat alone at the bar.

He finally resolved that he wouldn't learn anything more and was about to leave, when a tall man, with his fourth drink in hand, approached with a sincere welcome. After introductions, including backgrounds, Granderson learned that the man, named Scott, was a polo player and was willing to show Granderson the polo grounds and surrounding environs.

Granderson drove his nondescript rental car to the polo grounds as Scott's lips had loosened from the libations he consumed. He declared that this was going to be the most intensely played tournament in the annals of Wellington. When asked why, he said that some time ago, some of Azure's ponies were stolen and they suspected the Far East Club of the pilferage. Azure club members figured the reason for the thefts was to put them at a competitive disadvantage. Azure members then spent big bucks on some premier horses and now were betting huge amounts. Scott surmised the bets were both for pride and to recover the cost of their new mounts. When Granderson called the equines ponies, Scott corrected him that they were horses.

Granderson learned more about the lay out of the polo grounds as he chauffeured Scott. They agreed to meet for drinks the next afternoon as Scott was deposited back at the bar. Scott swaggered in and Granderson knew he had garnered important information.

CHAPTER THIRTY FOUR

Stephanie was in the shower and Frank was cleaning the sand out of his car when Granderson called: "Frank, I think we can find the golden gator and Ying."

"Where?"

"Wellington- tonight."

"Call Buck- I've got a date tonight."

Granderson was persistent: "Late tonight and I don't think Buck wants to do surveillance. He's already on a project at our request."

"OK. After my date. What time?"

"One AM." Granderson replied.

Frank didn't flinch at the late hour. "Tell me more."

"I recalled your rapid repel down the ladder after the sight of the golden gator dining on a horse carcass and I thought it might be time for the gator to once again dine on one."

Frank protested. "It was a life saving zoom down in response to automatic gunfire."

Granderson wasn't to be distracted: "I read in the newspaper about a major polo match starting tomorrow and I did a little background investigation in Wellington." Granderson then described what he had learned.

"What makes you think something will happen after one AM?"

"That's why I did background, so I don't have to sit and wait all night for some action. The area where the horses are stabled is busy in the evening, but after midnight it's quiet time."

Frank responded: "I'm not curious about the dining habits of the golden gator. I'm seeking The Pearl. Do you think they'll lead us to it?"

"If I didn't, I wouldn't be doing this surveillance. Think about it, Ying frantically flees with the golden gator and now its whereabouts are unknown. He appears out of nowhere and rescues Chang from Manchester's office. Currently, his location is unknown. Someone liberated The Pearl from Manchester's office. I think Ying somehow had access to it. I don't believe in coincidences like this."

"I'm in. I just need to be back by dawn."

"Any pilferage by Ying will be in the dead of night. You'll be back by sun up." Granderson guaranteed.

As arranged, Frank and Granderson met at a restaurant in Wellington and drove Granderson's rental car south, but not to the area where the polo ponies were kept. They were about a half mile away when they parked in the deep darkness, out of sight. Granderson explained that Ying and his conspirators would be watchful and cautious right at the scene of the crime.

Waiting wasn't Frank's forte. He impatiently squirmed in his seat and spoke of his theories on how to recover The Pearl. Granderson welcomed the conversation- it surely beat silence in the dead of night. However, after awhile, he tuned out his side kick. Surveillance has a lot of dead time which can be used to exercise the mind. He remembered how he often called Frank in the middle of the night when they worked in St. Paul. Frank was a human law book on the legality of police procedures. Granderson was grateful that Frank wouldn't complain about being woken up. He just wanted the facts.

Granderson recalled that Frank had taught him one of the little known rules in the often complicated law of search and seizure. The first question to ask before conducting a search is: who has "standing to object?" Not every person can challenge a police search just because the evidence obtained will be used against the person. He recalled that Frank had taught him that when he stopped a stolen car, he could search the car even if he didn't have probable cause to believe that the car contained anything illegal. If he found drugs or stolen property, the thieves couldn't object to the search of the car because it wasn't their car. They had no "standing to object". The search was perfectly legal. He smiled as he recalled how thugs would protest a search by saying he didn't have a search warrant.

Granderson would respond: "tell it to your lawyer" and kept on searching.

Granderson was pulled out of his nostalgia when a white van drove by. It was pulling a horse trailer with "Far East Polo Club" in gold letters on the side and was headed towards the stables. The van was too far away to determine who was driving.

Frank playfully punched Granderson on the shoulder. "You're a genius! But why would they advertise who they are?"

"It's less suspicious if it looks like they're hauling the cargo they would normally haul. If confronted, they'll contend the equine is a member's."

"Let's roll!" Frank shouted.

"We know where they're headed. We'll take our time. Let them get a horse loaded."

Granderson was in no hurry- he had done this a lot during his career as a cop. Traffic was as infrequent as satellites in the sky. He stayed back. He wasn't flustered by a red light; after a stop and an all clear, he was on the tail again. Frank leaned forward, anxious when the van and trailer disappeared from view for a few seconds.

Granderson pulled into the polo grounds and soon they saw two men, one of them was small. Both got out of the van and walked around the side of a building. Granderson and Frank got out of their car and cautiously moved through the shadows. Granderson pulled out his handgun, made sure there was a shell in the chamber and released the safety. They could hear the sound of horse's hooves coming from the other side of the building. They quietly moved into position to intercept the horse thieves at the corner.

Granderson cautiously moved his head around the corner and could see Ying and Jack Toy leading a well muscled, buckskin colored horse right towards them. When they got within a few feet, Granderson moved into the light and snarled: "Sheriff's Office! Put your hands where I can see them!"

Frank moved into the light as a show of force.

Ying and Jack Toy were taken by surprise. Stunned, they looked down the barrel of the gun. Instantaneously, Ying jerked down on the lead rope attached to the horse's bridle. The horse's response was to snap its head back in retaliation and then violently reared up. Ying and Toy ran back behind the horse and smacked it on the rump. It frantically bolted forward- right at Frank and Granderson. To avoid being trampled, they scrambled away. Ying and Toy ducked back around the corner as the horse galloped by like it was on the home stretch of the Kentucky Derby.

By the time Granderson could level his handgun, the men had disappeared. "They're headed back to the van." Frank shouted as they took off running.

As Ying ran towards the van, he pulled out a large caliber handgun. He told Toy to be ready for gunfire and that surrender wasn't an option. As they were within three steps of the van, Granderson and Frank appeared.

"Sheriff! Halt!" Granderson shouted as he stopped and braced to shoot. Ying got off the first shot and Frank could hear the bullet fly by his shoulder. They hit the ground as Ying jumped in the van.

Granderson propped his elbows on the ground and from the prone position, fired three rounds. All hit the trailer and one blew out the tire. He quit firing because the trailer acted as armor for the van and Ying. The type of bullet he used wouldn't do much damage after going through the trailer.

The van turned sharply and careened forward as it spit out a shower of gravel. Frank and Granderson were peppered with small stones and they quickly turned away. For a split second, Granderson now had an open shot at the front side of the van. He fired two rounds and one bullet lodged in the drivers head rest, just an inch from Ying's head. .Ying's eyes opened wide as he belatedly flinched. The engine roared as they desperately fled from gun fire.

Frank and Granderson instantly jumped up and had to sprint a distance to the car. Unfortunately, the van had a sizable head start on the relatively empty streets. Granderson surmised the van was headed towards Southern Blvd. The question was which way would they go on it?

The van and trailer took a zigzag course and Granderson was barely able to close in on them- the underpowered rental car wasn't designed for this. Frank yelled: "I'm calling 911!" as he pulled out his cell phone. He punched in the numbers, but nothing happened. In dismay, he looked at the screen- he now realized his battery was dead.

"Give me your cell. Mine's dead."

Granderson was busy trying to control the car as it skidded around a corner. The tires screamed in protest and Frank braced himself; afraid the car would roll over. Granderson wasn't talking- he was driving. As they accelerated, signs warned that they were approaching a major intersection-Southern Blvd. The van roared through just after the yellow light turned red. Now a semi was entering the intersection from Granderson's left. Frank braced for the inevitable impact and grimaced knowing the pain would be immediate.

Granderson slammed the brake pedal down and the antilock brakes gave him enough maneuverability to turn and barely miss the truck. Now they were westbound on Southern Blvd., headed for the interior of Florida and the big lake-Okeechobee.

Granderson pulled out his cell phone and pitched it to Frank. He punched in 911 and it rang twice before it quit. Frank looked at the phone- no signal- he tossed it on the seat.

They were now west of civilization and the speed of the van continued to increase. The trailer violently swerved back and forth pulling the van with it. The rig was not designed for high speed and was on the cusp of destruction. Ying was lucky to barely control it.

As they roared along the highway in the dark night, Frank kept swearing at the cell phone because he was unable to get a signal. At the last split second the van turned right and barely stayed on the road as it headed up Highway 98. The same technique was used as the van turned left onto Muck City Rd. and headed towards Pahokee. Granderson stayed back and commented: "This gets tougher. We need additional manpower. I'm betting they have a destination where they have reinforcements. I'm worried about an ambush. I'm pulling back a little."

"Don't get too far back, or we won't see them if they turn."

"Do I act like I've never done this before?" Granderson retorted.

"Sorry. I get a little excited doing this. I'm the neophyte."

They continued in a tension filled silence- ever vigilant. The taillights were like a sporadic beacon from a lighthouse- which warned the ship's captain to keep his distance from the perilous, rocky shore. They kept their distance, but yearned to see the taillights again.

Granderson looked at Frank who nodded in agreement after the red taillights had been out of sight for too long. Granderson put the gas pedal to the floor and the engine roared, but the increase in speed didn't match the roar.

Granderson groaned as he pointed to a highway sign: "There's an intersection ahead. I didn't see which way they went." He slowed and at the last moment turned left.

Frank asked: "See something?"

"No. I think Ying wouldn't lead us directly to his hideout. I'm betting he turned left and is backtracking…. I still don't see them; they accelerated to put distance between us. We only need to know their destination, yet we can't expose ourselves to getting blind sided."

They were flying. Instinctively, he felt for his forty caliber Glock in his shoulder holster. It was there and he was ready.

Still no tail lights. They passed a side road and suddenly brake lights appeared ahead of them. They were closing much too rapidly. The van and trailer were stopped in the road. Granderson slammed on the brakes and the pulsing of the antilock system told him the car was doing it's best to bleed off the excessive momentum. The seat belts locked and Frank prepared for impact. Granderson knew he couldn't stop.

At the last split second, he swerved into the other lane and flew by. They had a split second look in the van's cab. Ying's eyes had a maniacal appearance and behind him, Frank could see the shadows of two more men. Frank paid little attention to them because the closest thing to him was the barrel of a handgun. The proximity and sudden appearance of this instrument of death made the barrel look the size of a Civil War cannon. Ying's demonic snarl further enhanced the danger Frank and Granderson felt as they viewed the handgun pointed out the window right at them.

Flames shot out the barrel and lit up the night. Instinctively, yet belatedly, they ducked. The deafening sound inside the cab of the van instinctively made Toy jump and swear. The recoil of the gun banged it against the top of the window frame and Ying hoped his aim had been true because he had no hope of firing another shot.

As Granderson nervously exhaled, he declared: "He missed."

Frank was wide eyed and still stunned after being just a couple of feet from the end of the gun. He mumbled: "eighty eight."

Granderson's mind was working fast to determine his next move; he didn't have time to analyze what Frank was talking about. They had to put distance between them and Ying's firepower, but he didn't want to lose this critical opportunity. Experience told him they were close to Ying's hideout and that probably meant The Pearl was there. He kept driving up the road as he conceived a plan.

"We might be out gunned by the murderers. Possibly three in the van." Granderson then intently stared at the rear view mirror and the van wasn't moving. Granderson went around two successive curves and jammed on the brakes. "Go into town and find a phone. Call Buck and get reinforcements. I'm going to hide to see if they come by."

Frank was nervous. "It's too dangerous. You said we're out gunned."

"I'm not going to get in a shootout! I need to tail them to their hideout! They won't see me! Get going!"

Frank took off and began to wonder what Buck would think about a call at this hour of the night. Frantically, he looked for Granderson's cell phone but couldn't find it in the dark. It probably flew to the floor with the hard turns and braking. Frank kept seeing the barrel of Ying's gun and he knew his good friend was in mortal danger if he was found alone beside the road.

Frank pulled to a stop on a side street in Belle Glade and flicked on the interior lights. Distraught, he hastily searched for the cell phone and found it. He looked up and down the street to see if the van had followed him. He opened the phone and the welcome bars of a signal appeared.

He called Buck first; 911 was his back up. He loathed calling 911 and getting the dispatcher because both the dispatcher and responding officers would have many questions and be slow to help. The phone rang and rang and then switched to voice mail. Frank didn't leave a message. Impatiently he slammed the phone shut. He redialed and finally a groggy Buck answered.

"What are you doing calling me in the middle of the night?"

"We located Ying and he shot at Granderson and me- TWICE."

"Are you OK?"

Frank was animated: "Get people here! Ying will disappear! We feel he has The Pearl. I'm in Belle Glade."

"Let me talk to Granderson."

"He's not here. He's outside of town in danger as he tries to keep track of Ying."

"By himself?" Buck asked incredulously.

"Yup. That's why we need help and a lot of it. FAST!"

Anderson Granderson didn't like the feel of being alone without instant communication with other law enforcement. He recalled how he had managed to survive his encounter with Ying and his fellow criminals when they were torturing Faroque, but his luck could run out now in the predawn darkness. He stayed off the road and walked back towards the van, using the cloudy, moonless night as his friend.

Far ahead, he saw the van making a crazy maneuver- it turned around with the trailer in the middle of the road. Granderson moved quickly as the headlights no longer faced him.

The van took off and soon turned onto a side road towards the big lake. Granderson was encouraged. He surmised the van was headed towards the hideout. He had his Glock in hand and his senses on high alert.

As a precaution, Granderson stopped to listen. After a few seconds, he heard someone speaking Chinese ahead, but he couldn't see anyone. He didn't dare move. Patiently he waited until the shadow of a figure climbed over the guard rail. Just as he suspected, Toy was hiding in the weeds between the guardrail and an irrigation canal. He had been left behind by Ying as armed counter surveillance. By talking on his cell phone, Toy had made a mistake which Granderson planned to capitalize upon. Silently, he stood in the darkness, waited and watched.

CHAPTER THIRTY FIVE

As Buck put on his bullet proof vest, he contemplated how many cops were needed to apprehend the dangerous Ying and his thugs. Captain Mastif had assembled a large number to search Chang's mansion; could it be quickly accomplished again? Buck had confidence that if they found Ying they would find the golden gator. He did not have the same level of confidence they would find The Pearl. However, he felt he was due for a streak of good luck. He knew that perseverance paid off.

Buck believed that impressions from the gator's teeth would confirm that it had been used in all three murders and would strengthen the case against Cartier and Ying. It would also be significant evidence against Lingbao Chang. Lingbao would have trouble denying he knew of the torture going on at his mansion when it happened three different times and the victims were held hostage there for an extended period.

Buck rousted the Captain out of a deep sleep and after an intense discussion they decided to call out significant reinforcements including the Peacekeeper. When they executed the search warrant at Chang's mansion fortress, even with a powerful force of officers and equipment, Chang had pierced the containment and escaped. They mustn't let Ying do the same thing now. They vowed the handcuffs would go on Ying and his men.

Granderson slowly and silently moved, but only when a car went by- which was infrequently. The noise from the car muffled the sound of his movements. He used the natural cover to remain hidden. Toy kept moving around, he was impatient with the wait. Granderson watched and processed all that had happened. He kept wondering what Frank meant when he said "eighty eight" when they were shot at.

Then in the distance a car pulled out of a side road, and slowed as it approached Toy. Granderson ducked down further to be absolutely sure the headlights didn't illuminate him. After Toy was picked up, the car retraced its route. Granderson ran towards the side road just in time to see the tail lights disappear.

He sprinted down the side road and then slowed as he came to a driveway. He felt uncomfortable doing this solo and wondered if Ying had stationed another gunman near the road. He moved slowly, cautiously, and surveyed the silent rural road.

Discreetly, he was able to see that only a car was visible beside an old cabin, the van and trailer were out of sight. Then he saw a large pole barn beyond the cabin. He was in luck; there were lights on in the cabin. Slowly, as he remained hidden, he approached. The darkness was his ally as he looked inside through a small kitchen window.

Around the kitchen table were Ying, Toy and one other man. Granderson stared at the third man- he knew he had seen him before. Like the suddenness of an electric shock, it hit him. It was the man he shot and wounded as the man tortured Faroque with the golden gator. Sure enough, home made bandages on his arm covered the gunshot wound. Granderson memorized every detail and then backed off.

He dashed back to the main road and like a whirlwind he headed towards Belle Glade. He was in excellent condition, but this long distance run at a sprinters pace had him sucking a lot of air. Finally, a car headed towards him. Was this another one of Ying's men? He misjudged how quickly he would be illuminated by the headlights and the lights caught him just as he darted into the ditch. He had hoped that his dark clothing had hidden him for the second or so he was in the glare.

The car hastily slowed. The Glock was his friend and they were ready. Once he was out of the glare of the headlights, he recognized the vehicle. Thankfully, he saw it was Frank. A loud exhale by Granderson preceded Frank's calling out to him. Both were glad to be safely back together. Granderson jumped in and briefed Frank on what had happened.

After a short silence Granderson said: "As I was out on this main road watching that guy, I was puzzled why you muttered 'eighty eight.' Did you have some kind of mental collapse? It's a strange reaction to being shot at from point blank range."

Frank looked over at him: "Eighty eight feet a second is how fast a car travels at sixty miles an hour."

Granderson was even more puzzled.

Frank continued: "If we were going sixty when we passed the van, he couldn't have hit us."

"We were only a couple of feet away as we passed him! We're lucky to be alive!"

Frank paused: "But, it takes about half a second between seeing something, deciding to shoot and pulling the trigger. In half a second we traveled over forty feet. That's more than two car lengths. We were past him by the time the gun went off."

Finally, Granderson let out the emotions he had been trained to bottle up while in the midst of danger: "No question he tried to kill us! Out of the corner of my eye, I saw the flash come out the muzzle of the gun. It was damn close.... We probably weren't going sixty. It's still attempted murder in my book. I'm going to testify to that. Just because he missed, doesn't mean he wasn't trying to kill us."

Frank needed to calm Granderson down: "I agree. I was just saying 'eighty eight' at the time so my emotions wouldn't overpower me. I felt I was lucky to avoid certain death. It was my attempt to calm my very intense fears."

Granderson thought that a lawyer's brain works differently than those of normal people. They drove on in silence until they reached Belle Glade.

Just outside the Glades Correctional Institution, a large contingent of well armored law enforcement assembled. The Peacekeeper had arrived to lead the officers. Granderson rapidly delivered the intelligence he had gathered. Everyone knew they must act quickly or the murderers and the evidence would disappear.

For the first time, Frank came face to face with Captain Mastif. Frank was impressed by this formidable man. Frank looked up at him and said: "I don't want to start off on a confrontational note, so take this as a cautious thought: If you want the prosecutors to fight legal battles over whatever evidence you find in the cabin, go in without a search warrant. If you want to limit the prospect of evidence being tossed out by a judge, get a search warrant."

Mastif wasn't receptive to Frank's meddling. He was about to say so, but changed course and simply said: "Oh?"

"I can go on a long legal lecture about whether you need one, but let's talk logistics. You give me the laptop that was used to draft the search warrant on Chang's compound; I'll generate a copy and use it to create a new, revised search warrant. I should have it ready by the time you have control of the cabin."

Mastif didn't want to get delayed by a debate over legal niceties with a former prosecutor: "Start working right here, but I'm not committing to anything. We'll see what happens."

Buck and Granderson hopped in the Peacekeeper and led the entourage onto the road. Daylight was upon them as they headed down the highway. The few people driving by were impressed by the assembled law enforcement officers. They wondered what type of violent criminals had invaded their peaceful hamlet to require such a powerful response. Frank knew they would know shortly.

Ying could hear the approach of vehicles, instantly scrambled to the side of the window and intensely looked out. Moments passed and then he saw The Peacekeeper. When it had been described to him by Lingbao Chang's security men, he surmised that it's aura of invincibility was overstated. The sight of it made him immediately realize it wasn't. He decided they had no alternative but to flee. A battle couldn't be won, and surrender meant a life behind bars until he died or was put to death by lethal injection.

Toy nervously watched over his shoulder and dejectedly muttered: "We're done."

People make crazy decisions when they're trapped. They think up an absurd plan and believe it's viable. It's called delusions of the desperate.

Ying replied: "We're out of options. If we stay they could shoot tear gas in here or use that big tank to ram the cabin and then shoot us down like sitting ducks. They could just shoot us from within that tank by using the armored port holes."

"What about the gator?" Toy asked.

"We can't leave it behind. They get that gator and they'll compare its teeth to the bite marks on those Muslims. We've got to take it with and flee."

The other two echoed: "We can't leave any evidence behind."

"Stall the cops while I run to the pole barn. I'll load up the gator and when I roar up to the cabin, run out, jump in and we'll get away. Don't shoot unless you have to. We're out gunned. Just stall them."

Visible just beyond the perimeter were law enforcement in riot gear. Ying believed the cops wouldn't shoot him on sight; he figured if he was unarmed, they wouldn't fire on him.

Before The Peacekeeper could get in position, Ying was out the door and dashed less than one hundred feet to the pole barn. Officers radioed that an Asian male with a yellow and red tattoo on his neck had fled into the outbuilding. Buck radioed that the man was their main target and they had an arrest warrant for him for murder.

The Peacekeeper rumbled to a stop in front of the cabin and Buck used his bull horn: "We're law enforcement and we have a warrant for the arrest of Ying. Everyone in the house come out. Leave all weapons in the house. Walk out with your hands behind your head and lay on the ground on the road."

Buck waited. Granderson waited. The officers in riot gear waited with their armaments at the ready. Buck repeated his commands. Still no response, so Buck became more emphatic: "WE WILL USE EVERY TYPE OF FORCE ALLOWED BY LAW. WE HAVE THIS HEAVILY ARMORED VEHICLE. WE HAVE TEAR GAS. WE HAVE MANY WEAPONS. DON'T FORCE US TO USE THEM. COME OUT."

After the words had settled, a voice yelled back from the cabin: "English no good. Speak Chinese."

Buck swore and vowed he wouldn't be stalled by such a flimsy excuse. Just then some banging noises came from the pole barn and an almost simultaneous scream of horrific proportions. More screams and banging- it continued so long that it seemed like there was no conclusion.

The confrontation between cabin and cops became catatonic. The power struggle was suspended as the focus shifted to the mayhem in the pole barn. Were there two different voices? The vocal pitch varied. At times angry and at other times tearfully pained. The door flew open and a human form emerged from the dark interior.

Ying staggered out: "HELP ME! HELP MEEEE!"

He went to his knees, got up and stumbled forward a few more steps. Buck's jaw dropped and his eyes were transfixed on battered, disabled Ying as he fell to the ground a final time.

Buck radioed an order to his men to hold their positions. As the golden gator swaggered out of the pole barn, Buck was amazed at its size and ferociousness. The gator was heading towards the fallen Ying.

Granderson was stunned: "I knew the gator was hungry, I just thought he preferred horse meat." He leveled his handgun at the gator's head and then moved it slightly downward; so he wouldn't hit it. Three quick pulls of the trigger resulted in sand and rocks spraying into the gator's face as the bullets banged into the earth.

The golden gator snarled as its head jerked up. The mammoth gator swung around and grudgingly retreated into the pole barn leaving Ying crumpled in the dirt.

Buck got on the bull horn: "We aren't going to aid Ying until everyone is out of the cabin and on the ground. We won't be ambushed while giving him aid. Don't let your friend die in the dirt."

Granderson looked at Buck: "This is like the bull stomping the matador. We need to help him."

"We will. His friends will relent and give up. I'll give them ten seconds more and then we'll move the Peacekeeper to act as a shield as we rescue Ying. I want this whole ordeal to end right now. We need those criminals to surrender peaceably. "

Granderson understood the tactic and hoped it would be effective.

A voice from inside the cabin responded: "We're coming out. Don't shoot. We don't have any guns."

The men quickly came out with hands behind their heads and marched onto the road where they laid down. Officers quickly and thoroughly searched them as they clicked shiny chrome bracelets on their wrists.

The attention now turned to Ying. An ambulance made its way around squad cars and stopped beside the fallen man who had blood flowing from under him. The paramedics rolled him over and applied a tourniquet to his right arm just above the elbow because his arm was gone just below it. They said that if the arm could be found it might be able to be reattached.

Granderson and Buck looked at each other. They headed to the pole barn. Each had their firearm in one hand and a flash light in the other. Granderson flung the door open and jumped back with his gun pointed at the opening.

No sign of the gator. Buck entered the doorway and shined his light into the windowless, dark interior. He discovered the van and trailer; then two reflections under the trailer.

Buck announced: "I've hunted gators a lot at night. Those reflections are the gator's eyes and they're the biggest I've ever seen."

The flashlight beams scanned the floor, but didn't reveal the object of their search.

Buck decided: "Let's call in the licensed trappers to get this big boy before we look under or on the other side of the trailer."

Granderson agreed: "Sounds good. I'm going back to the two criminals. I need to talk to them. I have a bad feeling about them shooting at me from point blank range."

"*EASY.*" Buck cautioned.

Two experienced trappers came in and within a few minutes they had the golden gator controlled, but not subdued. The jaws were taped shut but the tail was still a weapon to be feared. Buck kept a distance from the surly reptile as he searched for Ying's hand and forearm. He found nothing and concluded it was being digested. Buck remembered a number of stories of what had been found in gator stomachs. He ran outside and told the paramedics of his conclusion. They shook their heads and said that if the arm was recovered from inside the gator, it was a long shot it would be suitable for reattachment.

Buck responded: "Well the gator is evidence and we aren't going to kill it to get the arm out."

The trappers were standing nearby and after Ying left in the ambulance, they approached Buck. They said they assumed that standard procedure would apply and they would take possession of the beast under the nuisance gator law.

Buck looked at them: "Boys, you and I know that this twelve foot yellow gator is an oddity and worth a lot of money to someone who would put it on display. You guys don't make much money trapping gators and I got no problem with you making some big bucks. The bad news is that we've a lot of legal requirements because he was the instrument used to torture and help commit three murders. We're going to have a pig's litter of criminals charged with these murders. The Sheriff's Office will pay you handsomely to transport it to a location where it will be held as evidence-alive. I'll have to talk to my legal advisor on what happens to this killer gator when the trials are done."

"You're costing us a lot of money Buck." bemoaned the trappers as they went back to subdue it.

"Think of it as an inheritance. You have to wait to receive it."

Granderson towered over the two men on the ground and glared. He said nothing and other officers backed off. Tension filled the air. The two Asian men had one side of their face in the dirt, but with one eye could view the powerful anger in Granderson's dark eyes. He was tempted to retaliate, but he grudgingly retained his composure. An eerie silence prevailed as a prolonged icy glare crumbled the mental toughness of the fallen men.

Finally Granderson quietly said: "I'm going to read you the Miranda warning so you know your rights. But I need to read it in the appropriate Chinese dialect, if you don't comprehend English. Who doesn't comprehend?"

In unison, both responded: "I don't."

The cops laughed, but Granderson wasn't amused. "You intellectuals have just admitted you know English by answering the question and doing so in English. I'm weary of this charade. Cooperation works better than confusion. Don't play the confused card; it might lead you down the wrong path. That path could be injurious to you. Cooperation is the path for smart men. You're under arrest as principals in the crime of shooting at me. We'll find the gun and get fingerprints off it. We'll talk soon."

Granderson looked at the Palm Beach deputies and his look told them a lot. He didn't need to impress upon them that a law enforcement officer had twice been fired upon at point blank range.

They moved away from Toy and his buddy to have a conversation. The deputies decided the two would be separately transported to jail and a hidden tape recorder would be running the entire time; just in case the men wanted to engage in a dialog. As Granderson walked away, he could hear Toy say that Ying shot the gun, he just handed it to him. Toy said his friend was the one that loaded it.

The search of the cabin and pole barn had been completed when Frank called Buck to announce he had the search warrant prepared and the only thing left was for a judge to review it and sign it. Buck stifled a laugh and retorted: "Search completed. We'll let the States Attorney deal with the legal niceties. Meanwhile, the golden gator is digesting Ying's arm."

Frank was tired after being up all night and barely responded.

Buck continued: "Someone has to deal with that nasty man eating gator."

Frank said: "You need someone to get impressions from his teeth."

"Yup and keep him alive."

Silence. This was a problem none of them had run across before. Frank spoke up: "I have the answer as long as the trappers will transport."

"They will." Buck assured him.

Granderson was perplexed about Frank's strategy, so he asked: "Is there going to be another victim of the golden gator?"

Frank smirked but said nothing.

CHAPTER THIRTY SIX

"We've never done this before. I'm not sure this will sit well with Dr. Delaney." Helen, the secretary at the Medial Examiners Office was timid and unsure.

Frank was aggressive. "It's imperative that this alligator be put in a cool place. As you know reptiles are cold blooded and their activity slows as their temperature drops. The morgue is a perfect place. Once this gator literally chills out, it will be easy to handle. It won't be any problem. Besides it's a rare yellow gator that looks golden at twilight. We'll take your picture with the golden gator. It'll be memorable."

"I don't know. It just doesn't feel right."

Frank put his arm around her shoulders and said: "Helen, I was a prosecutor and where I worked, the Medical Examiner was meticulous about being accurate and through. I'm sure Dr. Delaney is the same way.... Is she?"

"Yes. Certainly."

Frank felt her coming around. "Buck Thorton told me that Dr. Delaney wanted to have impressions made of the gator's teeth once it was discovered. She would then be able to determine if there was a positive match. It's important that this protocol be completed-for her sake. She wouldn't want to be questioned by those nasty defense attorneys and have to admit that impressions hadn't been done. Besides, the public would like to hear some good news from your boss. The media have been nasty to her.... So, we're ready to bring the gator in."

Helen wasn't strong enough to resist: "I guess so."

"When she gets back from Las Vegas, she'll be happy with this. We'll bring it in through the back just like the cadavers."

The fainthearted secretary haltingly added that Dr. Delaney would be landing shortly.

Frank quickly departed and instructed the trappers to bring the gator into the cool confines of the morgue. He left a note:

"Dr. Doris Delaney. We have confidence that this is the gator used to attack the three men you have in your morgue. It is important that full impressions of the teeth be taken and then compared to the bite marks on the cadavers. The gator is evidence and must be kept alive so it can be examined by defense attorneys and their experts. We don't want to be accused of destroying evidence in these high profile cases. The gator likes meat, I'm sure you have some available to keep it nourished. If you have questions call Investigator Buck Thorton."

Frank left a note on the entrance door to the morgue: "Warning: Live Gator. Don't Harm per Dr. Doris Delaney." Feeling everything was under control, Frank left with a chuckle and a belief that cool heads would prevail in the morgue.

On his short jaunt back to Lovers Key, he called Buck: "My friend, your initial skepticism of me being an inadvertent witness who found two murder victims has been proven to be unwarranted. I told you I would get the marauding, man eating gator for you and I did. I promised to deliver it so it could be used to prove it was used as an instrument of murder and I did. I delivered as promised."

"Are you saying you did this solo? A few hours ago you pleaded with me to give you help." Buck retorted.

"In a brazen way, I'm saying trust me. I'll help you. I got burned out as a prosecutor, but it's in my blood and I miss being a part of getting the bad guys."

Buck mentally conceded that Frank had been a big part of solving the case yet didn't intend to let him know. "We haven't found The Pearl. We did find some handguns and a cell phone. We lifted a partial fingerprint off one weapon and we'll check it against Ying's fingerprint card. We hope we have the gun used to murder Faroque."

"Did you check the phone for recent calls?"

"Of course. We also checked it against the call records we just got from Manchester. Both Ying and Manchester have been talking to Lingbao Chang."

Frank's interest increased: "Tell me you have the record of where Lingbao was at the time of the calls."

"The Bahamas."

"That's a lot of islands and a large area."

Buck changed the subject: "Tell me where the gator is and who is risking life and limb to get impressions."

Frank realized he was already back on Lovers Key and needed to get back to Stephanie. So he briefly answered: "The morgue.... Dr. Delaney.... I'm back home. Gotta go!"

Buck laughed long and hard. He was about to ask how that happened, but he realized Frank had hung up. Buck appreciated the humor and the break in the intensity of the murder investigation. He wondered how Frank talked the doctor into such hazardous duty. Yet the more he pondered the issue, the more convinced he became that the doctor wasn't into this type of dental work. Furthermore, Buck foresaw problems clouding the horizon. He envisioned the nasty reaction of the doctor when she was visually jolted by the huge gator in her domain. He knew this would go down in the annals of Lee County. He enjoyed the moment, knowing confrontation was inevitable.

Reluctantly, he concluded that he needed a plan to diffuse the anticipated explosion of the Chief Medical Examiner. He was now swearing at Frank for getting him into this. Before he had sorted out how to resolve the dilemma, his phone rang. Caller ID told him it was the problem doctor.

"Get that damn reptile out of my morgue! Who do you think you are leaving that creature here?" She didn't even give Buck a chance to say hello. "I'm calling the Sheriff and ordering him to discipline you! Retire now before you're fired!"

Buck wasn't ready to be stampeded. "Whoa. Dr. Delaney. I had nothing to do with this. I just found out about it myself."

"The note says to call you. I'm sure you're a part of this."

"Ask your secretary or anyone.... I wasn't there."

"Just because you weren't here doesn't mean you weren't part of it. I'm loath to admit that you may be smart enough to insulate yourself from proven culpability. Everyone knows we don't have a good working relationship."

Buck had enough. "If the only criteria for being a suspect in this is a bad working relationship with you, then the list is mighty long."

"Get that gator out of my morgue!"

"Have you done the impressions yet?"

Dr. Delaney screamed: "Helen! GET ME THE SHERIFF!"

Buck's ears were ringing as he said goodbye. The doctor had already moved on by hanging up He still had the phone in his hand as he thought how Frank's joke would have people talking at the water cooler. Buck called the dispatcher and told her that he was going off duty. Buck turned off his cell phone and headed for home.

Pao sat with Mrs. Chang in the mansion sipping some wonderful Darjeeling tea. Pao had thoroughly described her overnight stay in the jail. Mrs. Chang was impressed with the conditions at the jail compared to stories she had heard about conditions in her native China. Pao didn't feel it was something she wanted to repeat.

Pao sipped her tea and expressed to Mrs. Chang her concern about the safety of The Pearl. Mrs. Chang assured her that Lingbao had done the right thing by having his lawyer hold it. Her husband was convinced it was safe from the police and the Muslims. Both women revealed their anxiety over Cartier being in jail with hardened criminals. Pao attempted, without success, to lessen Mrs. Chang's distress over her son's confinement. Both hoped that Byron Manchester would be able to get Cartier released at his bail hearing the next day.

Frank had brunch with Stephanie and then the two headed down to the beach. Frank vowed to give her his undivided attention for the rest of the day. They sat in lounge chairs with the soothing waves daring to dart up to them. The sun warmed their bodies and a cool drink kept them in good spirits. They talked about Frank's eccentric parents who now lived in Santa Fe. They laughed about his mother's creative, although sometimes bizarre, cooking. As they laughed, a cell phone rang. The sound was coming from Stephanie's beach bag.

Stephanie answered and as he listened to her end of the conversation, he figured out it was work related. As she talked, his thoughts turned to Lingbao, the director of the murders. Frank knew justice wouldn't be done until he was captured. Extradition from a foreign country was usually tricky. Chang's wealth made it a long shot that he would ever be brought back for trial. Frank knew the best solution was to get Lingbao to return to Florida. But how?

As Stephanie continued talking architectural designs, Frank retreated to his cottage and got out his cell phone. He called Buck and left a message that he needed a tracking device to put on a car and he needed it by the next morning. He was vague about what he would do with it and ended with: "trust me."

Frank was back on the beach and she was still on her cell. She didn't even realize he had left. He watched the light puffy clouds interrupt the warm blue sky. The impatient clouds kept up their escape to the horizon.

As he absorbed the serenity of the beach, he noticed Monique in the distance. She was strolling in the whispering surf, with a glass of sauvignon blanc wine in hand. Stephanie ended her conversation as Monique came within speaking range.

'Stephanie, we *must* go shopping in Naples tomorrow." Monique declared, using her wine glass for emphasis. The wave of wine crested the rim and sprayed to the sand. She never noticed the loss.

Stephanie wasn't about to get tangled up with Angeline and Monique; she wanted beach time with Frank. "Monique, what a kind offer. But I'm sure you and Angeline are a great pair of shoppers."

"Oh, she left for New York a few minutes ago. She's trying to start her fashion design career. Heavens, I couldn't possibly shop alone."

Stephanie drew a blank for excuses that didn't sound impolite, so she looked towards Frank with a 'save me' expression. Frank didn't have a life ring to throw her.

She conceded. "Ok, but for just part of the day. I want to be on the beach with Frank."

Monique lifted her glass as her mood also lifted. "We'll leave at ten, do lunch and be back by early afternoon." She looked at her almost empty glass and continued. "My, that wine was exceptional. I *must* go back and get a refill." Cheerfully she turned and headed back.

Frank smiled. Stephanie had hoped that Frank would rescue her. She resolved in the future to be more assertive in protecting her own needs. He reached out for her hand and held it. "You did the right thing. Don't second guess yourself."

They soaked up the sun, surf and each other. Love was in the air.

CHAPTER THIRTY SEVEN

It was late afternoon and Stephanie was again on her cell phone with one of her clients. Frank decided to call Granderson and give him a major dose of artful persuasion. Frank knew he had the right theory; he just had to convince Granderson.

"I'm having a great appetizer of calamari as I sit overlooking the water. I'm enjoying a relaxing moment." Granderson calmly replied.

Frank was charming: "Great. I have two projects that won't interfere. They have to be done to have a successful prosecution of Lingbao Chang. First, we need to find someone to testify who has inside knowledge of what happened within the compound."

As Granderson chewed, he replied: "The security people and Pao are too loyal to Lingbao to turn on him. The best prospect is Al-Qitar, the kidnapped man who Buck rescued when the search warrant was executed. He might also have additional information to help recover The Pearl. So far he's refused to talk to the police."

Frank reasoned: "Well Lieutenant Anderson Granderson, you've established a good relationship with Al-Qitar's sister, Zahra, she could help get him to talk."

"I'm enjoying some great food; don't spoil it by making me work."

Frank moved on to the second project. "Tomorrow morning a tracking device should be put on the car that brings Mrs. Chang to her sons bail hearing. We need to track where they go. I'm sure they'll meet up with Lingbao."

Granderson didn't respond, so Frank kept talking: "You could do that before you stopped in to talk with Zahra. You like challenges and being creative."

Granderson kept eating as he replied: "I'm not sure these tasks are as fun as you contend."

During the discussion that followed. Frank's persuasive powers trumped Granderson's skepticism. Granderson was back in action and would call Buck.

Frank was up early and back to jogging down the road on Lovers Key. Jogging the beach was beautiful at dawn, but he had always been a road runner. Using his wireless earpiece, he called Buck.

Buck wasn't happy: "Two wake up calls in a row. This better be good. I'm not talking this early about your need for a tracking device I heard enough from Granderson yesterday. Tell me you've got Lingbao Chang cornered in downtown Miami and a pit bull is your weapon to terrorize him into giving up."

"In downtown Miami it would be a gator. Once a twelve footer was pulled out of a creek next to the courthouse downtown. Remember, this case involves gators not pit bulls."

"I'm just joking; you woke me out of a deep sleep. Well git a smaller gator and wallop Chang a few times. Use it to beat him into a confession. Awhile ago, a good ol' boy took his pet gator out of his bath tub and whopped his girl friend with it. It's damn criminal, but it's effective."

Frank got back to the point. "Pao is here illegally and I wouldn't doubt that Immigration will be after her shortly. She probably will flee the country so she doesn't have to go to jail. She expressed to me her fervor for Taoism and The Pearl. I think she will lead us to it."

"Well Frank, we know Lingbao's lawyer had it, but it disappeared. Maybe Lingbao had it on him when he fled in the van."

"No. At that time, I tried to arrest him and wrestled with him. I would've noticed if he had a fourteen pound pearl on him."

Buck continued: "Ying doesn't have it. We searched that cabin and pole barn thoroughly."

"I think Pao or Mrs. Chang will lead us to it."

"Yes, but how long will we be tracking that car before they do?"

"Not long. They know we show up at every turn. They're running out of hiding places. Another reason to use the tracking device is to find Lingbao Chang. Certainly, Mr. Chang wants to be with Mrs. Chang."

Buck relented: "All right. I'll get the equipment together. I don't have the authority to assign cops to this. Mastif won't like the overtime costs. I assume you'll spend the next few days monitoring this."

"If that's what it takes. Granderson will pick the stuff up at nine."

Buck had to give Frank some grief: "The jet set Chief Medical Examiner says you're in charge of feeding the golden gator. She said you're an expert at finding road kill."

"I've many talents but that's not one of them. I'll report back when I've recovered The Pearl. Goodbye."

Granderson anticipated interest in Cartier's bail hearing, but the intensity surprised him. As he approached the courthouse he could see people dedicated to the cause with signs parading in front of the building and camera crews dutifully recording it. They chanted slogans in unison and with the passion of true zealots. One sign implored, "No More Genocide of Muslims" and another "No Justice, No Peace"

Nearby, a number of young Asian males were steadfast in their angry gaze and took digital pictures. Uniformed deputies stood off to the side intently monitoring the simmering inferno and stood ready to keep the peace if the two sides erupted into battle. The officers knew that a minor taunt from one side would generate an over reaction from the other. Then the battle would erupt into a media epic.

Granderson waited and soon Pao and Mrs. Chang were driven up in an expensive chauffeured sedan. He looked it over and knew it wasn't the bullet riddled car used to escape during the search warrant.

Quickly the deputies moved to the car, ahead of the Muslim protesters and cameramen. The car had a swarm of people around it, like barracuda in a feeding frenzy. Tension erupted as the protesters yelled nasty things at the women and the Asian males responded by running forward yelling. Granderson braced for gunfire, but instead heard the Asian males shout that the Muslims had started the war by attacking the Changs and killing their men.

The deputies radioed for back up and helmeted police with sturdy wooden batons charged in. This power move slowed the angry factions and law enforcement prodded them back. Scuffling continued along with angry voices. The highly trained and disciplined officers kept the upper hand. The swarm of protestors frightened Mrs. Chang, but Pao's training put her on high alert. She was prepared for a physical confrontation. Mrs. Chang was shaken by the threats and the suffocating proximity of the angry Muslims. Officers opened a path and it gave the two women clear passage into the courthouse.

The combatants continued the verbal melee, but Granderson was focused on the task at hand. He followed the car around the block and watched it park. He would be back after the hearing to plant the tracking device. Emotions would be running high and in the confusion he would complete his task.

After negotiating through security at the courthouse entrance, he had to go through a second security screening to enter the courtroom. The judge presiding over the bail hearing of Cartier Chang was concerned about violence. Judge J. Davis Jefferson didn't worry about his safety- he had armed deputies at his side and his old reliable.357 Smith and Wesson was hidden under his judicial robe. He worried about the bad press if the Muslims or the Taoists erupted inside his courtroom once he made his decision.

"All rise Circuit Court is now in session The Honorable J. Davis Jefferson presiding." The bailiff intoned.

His honor was all business: "I will continence no outbursts in this courtroom. We live in a civilized society and this courtroom always has been and always will be the epitome of decorum. Anyone, and I mean anyone- including lawyers and the defendant- who doesn't respect the dignity of our legal system and this courtroom will face immediate, serious consequences."

The judge looked around his courtroom and saw heads nodding in understanding. He continued: "Mister Byron Manchester represents the defendant and is the moving party in this matter. He made a motion to change the custody conditions… You may proceed Mr. Manchester."

Byron Manchester slowly rose to his feet and even more slowly strolled to the lectern. He loved the dramatic effect that anticipation brought. He laid one large document on the lectern, took a slow drink of water and began. "Your honor, in the crush of making innumerable decisions daily, judges sometimes lose sight of the bedrock that is the foundation of the country we so dearly cherish. Thankfully, Judge J. Davis Jefferson always keeps this as his judicial bible."

Granderson rolled his eyes and thought The Bill of Rights. Sure enough, Manchester picked it up and waved it for dramatic effect- as if he needed any more drama.

Manchester proceeded: "Yes your honor, The Bill of Rights. This document isn't worth the paper it's printed upon unless men and women wearing judicial robes breathe life into it in every case that comes before them. The triumphant provision that separates us from dictatorship, oppression and savage vigilantism is that everyone from the homeless man living under a bridge to the President of the United States is presumed innocent until proven guilty. My client, Cartier Chang, is presumed to be innocent no matter what the prosecution alleges. The paper work filed by the government means nothing until proven at a jury trial.

"The method to nurture this basic right is also found in the same document- the right to reasonable bail." He paused to take a drink of water and to accentuate the drama. He was just getting warmed up.

Judge Jefferson had heard this style of argument too many times and had grown weary of it. Manchester's pause was his demise. "Thank you counselor. Unless you have a specific request for conditions of release, I assume you are finished."

Manchester realized he had been upstaged. How could he justify his huge fees if the bail hearing was too short? He literally felt he got paid by the word. "Your honor, as the bail investigation report indicates, my client is an exceptional citizen with no prior criminal record and I reluctantly would concede that some bail is warranted. Given his financial status, $100,000 should be more than sufficient."

The judge looked towards the prosecutor and nodded. The prosecutor rose but stayed at the counsel table. "Your honor is familiar with the charges against the defendant and the bail report. I just want to clarify that when Mr. Manchester calls his client an exceptional citizen, he is a citizen of China, not our country. I request the status remain unchanged- he remain in custody and not be allowed to post bail. Thank you."

Nothing new had been disclosed. Judge Jefferson decided to stick with the decision he had reached after consultation with his law clerk earlier that morning. "It is the order of this court that the defendant may be released from custody only if he satisfies each and every condition which I order. First, he post bail in the amount of three million dollars. Second, he surrenders his passport. Third, he live at his current residence on Ocean Blvd. Fourth, he use no alcohol or drugs. Fifth, because he needs to consult with his attorneys and prepare a defense, he will be allowed to move about, but only within his county of residence- Palm Beach County. Sixth, to assure his compliance with these conditions he will be subjected to electronic monitoring in any manner determined by the State and it will be paid for by the defendant.... Any questions?"

Manchester, still at the lectern, cleared his throat and the judge acknowledged him. "Bail may be posted in cash or bond?"

"Yes. We are adjourned."

The bailiff invoked the traditional "all rise", everyone did and the judge quickly flowed off the bench. Granderson took an equally hasty departure as Pao and Mrs. Chang waited to talk to Manchester. The presence of deputies forestalled pandemonium and the opposing factions squawked among themselves as to the fairness of the decision.

Granderson hurried to his car. He retrieved his gun and placed the tracking device in his pocket. The "bug" was small and was not much bigger than the magnet which would attach it to the car. A brisk two minute walk brought him to the Chang's car. He approached it from the rear on the driver side and put on an air of authority as he walked the final few steps. He looked at the outside rear view mirror and could see the driver had his chin on his upper chest-dozing.

He quickly put the bug inside the upper inside of the rear wheel well and then banged his fist on the upper fender to be sure it was securely attached. The noise and the rocking of the car startled the driver.

They exchanged stares via the mirror as Granderson gruffly began: "Don't you see the no parking sign? Do you think it applies to everyone but you? I let you sit here for far too long. I assumed you would be here for a couple of minutes. Well you've got two minutes to leave or I'll call a uniformed officer to ticket you and tow it. Got it?"

Granderson banged the fender for emphasis and the driver reluctantly nodded as Granderson stared him down. As he turned and walked away, he checked the ground. He didn't see a bug, so the banging didn't dislodge it. He knew it must be secure. Back at the car he switched on the monitoring equipment and everything was working fine. He drove off to talk to Zahra, Haquan's widow.

Luck was with him, he found her at home and she was appreciative of his presence. She was anxious to know what had happened both at the bail hearing and in the investigation. He knew that by giving her some information that the public didn't know, she would feel even more comfortable that he was her ally. Granderson was still very careful what he said because she was a pipeline to the Muslims who attacked Chang's compound.

"I was at the bail hearing for Cartier Chang and he'll bail out sometime this afternoon. We still need more information about his father to be able to bring charges against him. I hope you could lead me to your brother, Al-Qitar since he was held hostage by them."

"Al-Qitar is a very powerful man in our community and he rarely speaks with outsiders."

Granderson wasn't about to be denied: "I think Al- Qitar would like to see everyone responsible for the murders brought to justice."

"Yes. He believes that Allah's sword will bring justice and avenge the degrading way he was treated."

Granderson was puzzled: "Do you mean he would wait until they die and then Allah would act?"

"No. I think Al-Qitar and his friends are sure that Allah will see the criminals soon."

"Zahra, you must understand that they can't take the law into their own hands- punishment is for the legal system; the victim can't seek vengeance."

"What information do you want from my brother, Mr. Granderson?"

"Details of his kidnapping and I must get it directly from him. Use my cell phone and call him."

Granderson handed over his cell phone and a hesitant Zahra punched in a number. She spoke for a short time and then hung up. "He'll come here to talk to you."

A few minutes later, two men entered without knocking and looked at Granderson. He asked if one was Al-Qitar and neither said a word. They looked through the apartment and then Al-Qitar entered.

Al-Qitar looked upon Granderson with distrustful eyes. "Zahra tell you want. I don't talk to police. They bad to my people."

"You need to understand we have a different way of doing things here. I need a statement from you so those responsible can be arrested, tried and convicted."

"What happen to man who hit me?"

"He was charged with serious crimes against you and also charged with three murders, including the murder of Haquan, your sister's husband."

"Has he been put to death yet?"

"No. The system works more slowly here than in your country."

"Is he in jail?"

"Yes but he may get out until his trial."

Al-Qitar's demeanor changed as quickly as the colors of a chameleon: "That not right. Tell me where he be. Time for Allah's work!" He got up and headed towards the door.

Granderson decided confrontation was needed. He stood up, moved in Al-Qitar's path, and looked down into his face: "You must not leave. You will get into trouble. Talk to me now."

Al-Qitar tried to push him out of the way, but he was like the granite of the Rock of Gibraltar. Granderson repeated: "Talk now. It will help."

The two other men moved towards Granderson, but he wasn't in a retreat mentality. He worried about the men trying to take his handgun from him. It was imperative that the two men stay at least an arms length away. A cocoon of tension enveloped the small room. "Stop!!" he shouted.

Zahra sprang up and pulled back on her brother's shoulder. "He's here to help. Listen to him. Don't leave." This was a bold move because their culture didn't countenance a woman challenging a man.

Al-Qitar and his men hesitated. They glared at her. Granderson feared a physical confrontation. The air was hot and stagnate; the tension high. Granderson waited. So did Zahra. Ultimately, she coaxed her brother into sitting down. Gradually, the hostility lessened. After extended negotiations, Al-Qitar agreed to cooperate with Granderson and at first haltingly told what had happened to him while confined in the dungeon like room at Chang's compound.

When Granderson heard that a middle aged man came in and questioned Al-Qitar, he focused his questions on what the man looked like. The description fit Lingbao Chang. Now he concentrated on what Chang did and Granderson was stunned by the intensity of Chang's craving for detailed information. Chang repeatedly threatened Al-Qitar by saying they would use the golden gator on Al-Qitar just like he ordered that the gator be used on the other criminals.

Granderson was pointed in his questions to determine if Chang was the leader. Al-Qitar revealed that Chang was actively involved with his son and others, including Ying. Chang was the one who ordered Ying to bring Al-Qitar to view the golden gator being fed some meat. Al-Qitar was told the gator would devour him if he didn't reveal what they wanted to know. Al-Qitar was explicit in the gruesome details of his confinement and very emphatic that he told them nothing. His men were impressed by the bravery of their leader.

Granderson looked at Al-Qitar's men and realized that they nodded in agreement when Al-Qitar would say he repeatedly refused to divulge information despite solitary confinement and numerous threats. Granderson had the whole statement on tape and shut it off to talk candidly with the three men. He told them he was concerned about Al-Qitar's unyielding religious beliefs that Muslims must have The Pearl. He impressed upon them the need to be law abiding and to avoid being in a place where there would be a confrontation between Muslims and Taoists.

Al-Qitar made it clear that the mystical powers of The Pearl came from Allah. Granderson was convinced that Al-Qitar and his followers would relentlessly pursue recovery of the religious artifact. Their zealous quest had no bounds.

Granderson asked if their intensity foreclosed violence as an acceptable tool for success. He replied that Allah demanded no less. No amount of warning by Granderson would deter them from engagement in violence.

Granderson resolved that diplomacy couldn't succeed. He must be satisfied with the tape recorded statement and alert law enforcement that a new battle loomed on the near horizon.

The muscle of The Pearl still flexed itself over its divergent worshippers.

CHAPTER THIRTY EIGHT

Lingbao Chang called Byron Manchester anxious to find out the results of the bail hearing so he could set his plan in motion. The lawyer had received a retainer by courier the previous evening; Chang never left his island retreat nor talked with Manchester.

The flamboyant lawyer thanked Chang for the retainer and quickly changed the subject to self adulation. Manchester was verbose about his magnificent oratorical skills and its impact on the judge's decision. Chang listened patiently, but was more concerned whether bail was granted. He must know the timing and logistics of getting Cartier out on bail.

"Manchester, I asked you a question ten minutes ago. You know I demand results; answer my question-what's my sons bail?"

"Three million plus conditions."

When Chang heard about the electronic monitoring, it agitated him, but he said nothing. He then informed Manchester the money would be available in a few hours. They quickly resolved the procedures to get Cartier released.

Chang then turned the conversation to Ying. "I'm worried because I can't get a hold of him."

Manchester wanted to return to his account of the hearing, yet reluctantly replied: "Ying called me from the hospital. He was in pain and had lost one arm at the elbow. He had been attacked by your gator and the police had armed guards on him because he had been arrested for murder. Once he's ready to be discharged from the hospital, he'll be transported to jail and then will appear in front of a judge."

Chang didn't react to Ying's dismemberment. "What amount is his bail?"

Manchester had become ecstatic over the prospect of another large fee, but then he remembered a problem. "For my firm to represent Ying, both he and your son have to waive any potential conflict of interest. They must understand that they could have conflicting defenses and waive that."

Chang was growing impatient: "What's his bail?"

"We'll argue for low bail once he appears in front of a judge. Right now he is being held without bail."

"I need you to ask Ying if he succeeded in the project I gave him."

Manchester was intrigued: "What project are you talking about?"

Chang was irritated: "You don't need to know. Have one of your underlings go to the hospital and ask."

"He's under armed guard. They won't let anyone near him."

"Ask him once he gets to jail. I need to know." Chang believed he had to continue the hoax with The Pearl. He wanted Ying to know he was concerned whether he had secreted The Pearl in the coffin. Chang still didn't want anyone to find the imitation Ying had recovered. If no one finds it, no one can bring it to an expert to have it examined.

Manchester replied: "Fine. I assume you'll pay my legal fees for Ying."

"Yes."

"And post his bail?"

"Depends on whether he completed his assignment. The next subject is the black lacquered box. I hope and believe it is still safe." Chang wanted to hear Manchester's story and determine if he was a shyster lawyer even to his own clients.

"We need to talk about that soon and not over the phone."

Chang smirked and said: "We certainly do. Not hearing to the contrary, I have confidence in its security."

Manchester wasn't flustered and became determined to end the conversation now that Chang wasn't interested in a flattering rendition of the bail hearing: "I need to complete your projects. Goodbye."

Chang knew that his plan was predicated on precise timing and everything had to be in place before it started. He called his wife and the two spoke in Chinese because Chang feared that his home phone had been tapped. After the conversation, Mrs. Chang summoned Pao and explained Chang's orders. The two women drank tea and ate scones as they lamented that they would enjoy the opulence of the mansion for only a short time longer.

Pao worried about what would happen to her fellow angelic looking Amas. She needed to be sure there was a plan securely in place to assure their well being. So far, Mrs. Chang didn't know of any plan.

Pao told herself that she must be strong and unwavering in Lao-Tzu's teachings. He must control her actions. She would not be propelled from the middle by the Changs.

Granderson sat down on the beach with Frank, just beyond earshot of Stephanie. After they exchanged information, they resolved that Frank would monitor the tracking device. Instinctively Frank knew that Cartier would be able to post bail and something would be happening soon. Experience told them that violence at the hospital was assured. Either there would be an attempt to free Ying from the hospital by the Changs or the Muslims would seek revenge. The news coverage had let the Muslims know where to find one of their tormenters.

Frank and Granderson agreed that when he delivered the taped statement of Al-Qitar to Buck, Granderson would warn him about the high risk for violence. It wouldn't be routine hospital guard duty for law enforcement. They agreed to talk later as Granderson got up and then left.

Frank turned his gaze toward Stephanie. Just a few feet away, she was relaxing in the sun. The tropical breezes were blowing through her long hair which she had artfully done up on the back of her head with a hair clip. She laughed to herself how Monique was so persuasive in getting her to buy the yellow and bright blue swimsuit she had on.

Three pelicans soared by and then dipped one wing to make a downward right turn to the water. They made a typical uncontrolled crash with the water, big bill first. Only one gulped down a fish after shaking off the collision with the sparkling blue water.

Stephanie smiled, looked to Frank, and absorbed their serenity on the beach of Lovers Key. She didn't want her time to end with Frank. She looked over at him with a radiant glow on her tanned face. Their eyes met and he moved his towel to be next to her. Before they could start a conversation, her beach bag started to sing-it was her cell phone. They looked at each other and Frank's expression said to just let it ring. Her Minnesota bred commitment to answer it prevailed. It was a client who was severely deficient in his comprehension of architectural drawings.

Frank whispered he would get them lemonades from the cottage. Once there, he started up the monitoring equipment and determined that Chang's car was at the jail. So he called Buck and told him that Cartier was bailing out. Buck was impressed with Frank's ability to gather intelligence, but Frank said he was multi-tasking and had to go.

Lemonade in hand, he returned to his sweetheart. She finished her conversation and they strolled up the empty beach.

"Stephanie, you must stay here for awhile longer. You could do all your work by e-mail and cell phone. I bet your client didn't even know you were in Florida at the beach."

"He did comment about the sound of the waves."

"Did you tell him it was just background music- one of those recorded CDs for lessening stress?"

She smiled: "No, I just stuck to the subject of his concern."

"Well, what about the subject of *my* concern?"

"I'll be here for a couple of days. I can't design and revise things by e-mail. I have to be in the office with all the high tech equipment. My partners in the firm will grow weary of my absence."

They walked on the beach, enjoying the expanse of clear water beside them. The Gulf of Mexico was so beautiful their hearts joined in their pristine togetherness. Stephanie didn't want to delve below the surface of their idyllic moment and dive into the depths of what the future held for them. The white sand warmed their feet and being together warmed their souls.

Chang listened to the palm fronds murmur as he sat beside his swimming pool on his island retreat. He had revisited and revised his plan a number of times and was satisfied it would be successful. He climbed out of his lounge chair and strolled inside to get his prized possession out of the safe. His other belongings had been taken aboard.

He quickly boarded his yacht anxious to journey northward to Freeport, the city in the Bahamas closest to Palm Beach. The seas were calm, yet his anticipation was great. In his hand was the aluminum suitcase which he had repacked with everything it held upon his abrupt flight from Palm Beach.

The elegant ship moved away from the long dock and slowly powered up as it made its way into deeper water. He watched frigate birds soar high overhead and smoked a fine Cuban cigar as he watched the white wake jump upon the deep blue waters. They had a nautical journey ahead of them which would be done in style and comfort.

By sundown, heavy clouds had moved across Florida and over the Bahamas. The moonless night made the seas a lonely, dark desert. Chang didn't notice because his mind was dissecting all the potential glitches in the dangerous task at hand.

CHAPTER THIRTY NINE

Frank was just about to go to bed when he did one last check of the monitoring device. The Chang car had been sitting next to a swank Palm Beach restaurant for over an hour. It was about time for it to go back to the Chang's mansion. Sure enough, the car headed north and drove into the compound. Frank felt the car was home for the night and went in the bathroom to prepare for bed. He came back for one last look at the monitor when he saw that the car had left the island. He watched as it slowly took side streets and kept moving west.

Frank had a decision to make. Was this worth calling Buck or Granderson? What if the chauffeur was just giving an employee a ride home? Was Cartier even in the car? Frank watched and considered the possibilities. Cartier was only out of jail a few hours, was this too soon for a successful plan to be formulated? Yet it would be disastrous if he did nothing.

Frank took the monitoring device and headed out in his Mustang. He drove and watched as the Chang's car headed towards Wellington and stopped at a large supermarket. Maybe they dropped someone off or were doing some late night grocery shopping. Frank kept driving towards Palm Beach as the other car remained stationary. Finally, it was moving west towards the big lake and Frank increased his speed. When he got to Belle Glade, the Chang car pulled into the cabin. Frank was worried. Maybe the cops hadn't searched thoroughly. Maybe Cartier was retrieving the well hidden pearl. Frank gunned the engine as he headed out of town.

It was after midnight as Chang's yacht gently glided to the dock and tied up. At the same time, much further to the south, a small, single engine plane took off, but gained little elevation as it flew over the empty waters of Crooked Island Passage at the southern end of the Bahamas. This small plane which Chang had chartered was more than three hundred miles away. The plane continued southwestward and on course over Ragged Island. It then banked directly south, towards the eastern end of Cuba. The pilot had been paid handsomely to take this trip without passengers. Yet he was as perplexed about the route as he was about the purpose. He was flying just over the water as he headed dangerously close to Cuba. He then made an abrupt and unusual change of course to fly on a heading to Key Largo, south of Miami.

The dark night accentuated the pilots concern about the darkness of his mission. As he entered the waters of the Straights of Florida he climbed to three thousand feet and cut back on the throttle.

This unscheduled plane appeared on the radar screen and the United States air traffic controller radioed to get confirmation of its identity. Repeated efforts met with silence. The controller decided it was time to contact the Coast Guard. As he did so, the plane changed its heading to due north and increased it air speed dramatically. Quickly, the controller told the Coast Guard of the evasive action the plane had taken.

Precisely at this moment, Chang climbed aboard his jet at the airport in Freeport. Quickly, the pilot taxied down the runway to start the flight. He had just filed a flight plan to fly northward over the Atlantic Ocean to Bermuda.

The Coast Guard had only one crew and plane ready to fly and it scrambled to intercept the little single engine plane. A Coast Guard ship doing night time exercises just off of Key Biscayne was alerted and headed further out to sea at full speed.

The air traffic controller didn't like the way the small plane was flying. It reeked of drug smuggling or bringing in illegals- maybe from Haiti. Typically, Cubans came by boat; they didn't have planes to hijack. He waited to see the Coast Guard plane in the air.

Swiftly, the Coast Guard plane made radio contact with the controller. But he knew it would be a few minutes before there would be an intercept. The young, inexperienced, Coast Guard pilot's nerves were twitching as he prepared to put his training to the test.

Just a few minutes after takeoff, Chang's jet descended as it changed heading and banked to the west. It now was roaring over the waves at over four hundred miles an hour headed towards the shores of Florida. Just off shore it barely cleared the sonar tower of a luxury yacht named *SERENITY*. The huge yacht rocked in the jet wash and lights instantly appeared in the staterooms. Dolphins dove deep as the sound exploded over the water.

The jet violently jolted and came perilously close to crashing when it hit turbulence just as the water gave way to land. The pilot rescued his plane from disaster as it came over land near Hobe Sound. He flew over a darkened state park and changed his heading to the southwest.

It was less than fifty miles across the rural landscape and in moments they were over Lake Okeechobee just north of Pahokee. The pilot didn't throttle back as he made a dangerous change in heading. Lingbao fought the g-forces and the plane shuddered as it was pushed to the limit. They were so close to the water that the powerful jet engine exhaust sprayed water as they catapulted down the shoreline.

Chang had been warned it would be a rough ride, but he wasn't prepared for such violent bouncing. He felt he was in a never ending popcorn popper. He wondered if the jet would hold together and where his pilot had learned the skills to fly this way. Now the jet was a bucking bronco. He looked out the window, but the darkness was overpowering. Chang had been warned the worst was at the end and he wasn't sure he was ready for it.

Frank turned off the main road just as the Chang car pulled out of the driveway and headed away from him. Where were they going? Who was in the car? Was someone still at the cabin with The Pearl? Should he have called Granderson or Buck?

As he passed the cabin, lights were still on. He paused. Indecision could be fatal. He didn't see another car at the cabin. Hopefully, whoever was there would still be there. He looked ahead and the tail lights had vanished. He mustn't lose them. He was worried the bumpy road would dislodge the tracking devise.

He downshifted and roared down the sandy, lightly graveled road he had never traveled. Suddenly his headlights showed the road turned sharply to the left. He held his breath, slammed the brakes, banged it down a gear and skidded hard through the turn. Sand and rocks flew into the watery canal beside the road. Frank had come within inches of sliding into it. There was no time to exhale because he was fast upon a hard right turn. He held on and the Mustang again responded to his need to power around the corner. He finally dared to breathe as he frantically looked ahead for tail lights. He had no time to study the tracking monitor.

It seemed like seconds later that he saw the car turn right. After he roared around the same corner he realized he was at Glades Airport. He was closing the gap between them when the car pulled into the empty airport. It didn't look like the size of airport that would have commercial flights. He skidded to a stop beside the car. The rear window rolled down and he could see Cartier and Mrs. Chang in the car.

Mrs. Chang asked: "Why are you chasing us?"

"A better question is: why are you at this deserted, remote airport in the middle of the night?"

Neither was willing to answer the question. Frank pulled out his cell phone and called Buck. As he waited for Buck to answer, he remembered he saw a sign that announced he was at a Palm Beach County airport. Cartier had not violated the terms of his release- he hadn't left the county. Buck answered as the chauffeur got out with an assault rifle. Frank slammed the Mustang into reverse and the tires smoked. He backed off and kept his eyes trained on the high powered weapon.

“Buck, the tracking device works great. I’m at the Glades airport.”

Buck got to the point: “It must be serious. What’s up?”

“I’m joined by Cartier and Mrs. Chang. Their driver has an assault rifle and he has a mean look on his face. So far, Cartier hasn’t violated the terms of his release, but I anticipate it will happen shortly. I don’t think they came to pick someone up.”

“You got an equalizer for the assault rifle?”

“No.”

Everyone’s attention turned to the north as a formidable rumble could be heard in the distance. The noise quickly increased, but nothing could be seen in the darkness. Frank decided it was a jet plane, but no lights could be seen. The engine noise told him direction and finally, a shape peeked out of the darkness. Just then brilliant landing lights bombarded his eyes.

The Chang chauffer jumped in the car and roared directly at the chain link fence which surrounded the airport. Metal snapped, snarled and gave way as the car fought its way through the barrier. It headed to the runway as Frank told Buck what was happening.

Inside the jet, the pilot warned of impending impact. Simultaneously, the jet made a cacophony of noises- objecting to the demands placed upon it by the pilot. He came in at an unbelievable speed to a runway that was far too short for such a high speed acrobatic performance. The plane dove, but barely slowed. The flaps were set to slow the jet, yet it was coming in far too fast to land.

Frank thought it must be taking a low pass to check out if it was safe to land. Just before the end of the runway, it dropped down so quickly that he thought there was a mechanical malfunction. The wheels banged down violently on the pavement and the brakes grabbed hard at the same instant. The jet was still too fast for the amount of runway left and the pilot used the final amount of braking at his command. Chang was bucked forward in his seat and his neck hurt as if it was a whiplash. His seat belt pulled mightily against his hips.

Frank looked for the car as it drove on a collision course to the runway. Disaster was imminent.

Frank still had the cell phone on and knew Buck could hear the rebellion of the jet as it stormed by. Every muscle in Frank's body tensed as the car headed towards extinction. Just before the runway, car brake lights came on and it slid sideways. Frank hadn't seen that there was a taxiway which ran parallel to the runway. The car crazily swayed, but remained upright as it made the turn. Just then, the jet roared by, which made the car shake mightily in its aftermath.

Now there was only a hundred feet of runway before a collision with the sand and weeds. New sounds erupted and the jet rebelled as it slowed even more. Dirt flew as the plane went off the end of the runway. Finally it stopped; but only for an instant. The plane swung around and the engines roared again as it clawed its way back to the pavement. The planes landing lights were extinguished and it stopped just onto the runway.

The car roared up and stopped at the jet as its stairway came out from the fuselage.

Cartier and Mrs. Chang ran to the plane and sprinted up the stairs with luggage and a box. The driver jumped out and stood guard with his weapon. Frank knew giving chase was futile. This escape had been meticulously choreographed. For only an instant, he felt a small sense of satisfaction in the fact that his alertness had enabled him to promptly report the escape. The judge would have to answer questions about why he let Cartier out on bail.

Chang was slightly dazed from the landing and when he saw his wife and son, he screamed: "Where's Pao? She was to be part of the escape!"

Cartier was upset: "We stopped at the supermarket as planned to be sure no one was tailing us. She said she needed some feminine hygiene products and went into the store. She didn't come out. We quickly searched the store, but she had fled. We had to leave to be on time."

Quickly the engines powered up and the jet rumbled ever faster up the runway. It snarled as it passed Frank and with uncanny precision it lifted off before the runway concluded. The car roared by as Frank put the phone up to his ear.

"Buck, they took off to the north! Call the Coast Guard to do an airplane intercept. That is if they have a jet that's fast enough."

"I'm calling more than the Coast Guard. Goodbye."

Frank looked to the sound of the jet, but there wasn't anything to see. It had already flown through the curtain of darkness and disappeared. He resigned himself to the fact that the Changs had gotten The Pearl out of the country. He was dejected because he felt he had failed. He tried to rationalize that he had been a prosecutor; he wasn't a cop. He second guessed himself as to why he didn't train to handle firearms. Maybe if he had some training he could have prevented the murderers from escaping.

Frank continued to question why Cartier and Lingbao's religious fervor had blinded them to the fact that religious zeal couldn't excuse excesses. He frowned and shook his head about what he had just thought. Certainly he had just minimized the violence of murder by referring to it as religious "excess". The Muslims rationalized murder when they attacked Chang's home. The Chang dynasty excused it when they protected the beloved symbol of their religion. History is replete with men invoking belief in the spiritual to justify helping their fellow believers to attack those that don't believe.

He got into his Mustang and looked into the darkness where the plane had disappeared. He leaned his head against the steering wheel and exhaled. He could rationalize all he wanted, but the men he sought to bring to justice had escaped.

He spent his young legal career in the courtroom, successful in trials that put a stamp on the accused that he or she was guilty. They went off to prison to pay for their abhorrent behavior. Cartier and Lingbao, the ringleaders had escaped while Ying, their minion would face the death penalty.

Frank knew there were too many countries that would harbor the Changs and refuse to extradite them to the U.S. The Changs had the money and the international connections to escape punishment.

Frank banged his head against the steering wheel in disgust. For the first time, the symbol of the blindfolded woman with the scales of justice made him mad. Justice wasn't blind and it was more than imperfect. His frustration was enormous.

Slowly, reluctantly, he put his car in gear and started back to Stephanie. Hopefully, she would help him make sense of this. As he drove through the vacant unseeing night, he told himself that the love of his life would unwind the fallacies in his angry thinking. She understood him; she had stood with him. They had many late night conversations at his apartment in St. Paul about crime, punishment and the concept of justice.

He drove over the bridge to Lovers Key as the sun came up over the bay. He wondered why he had been thrown into all of this. Was it only because of the pure happenstance of what he found as he went for a sunrise jog just weeks ago? Stephanie was close at hand and would help him sort out the raw emotions that pervaded him.

CHAPTER FORTY

When Chang and his pilot planned their escape, they believed the daring plan would let them fly beneath the radar screen. Still, every possibility was explored; they didn't want to be arrogant. Military capabilities were analyzed. Homestead Air Force Base was south of Miami and Patrick Air Force Base was near Kennedy Space Center. Chang and his pilot decided to enter U.S. airspace between the two and were confident that their mission was timed perfectly. They counted on being in and out quickly. If the military jets intercepted them, they were convinced they wouldn't be shot down. After all, they would be in a private jet, not a foreign military aircraft. They'd already be some miles off shore and heading away.

Lingbao's nerves were frazzled, yet he told himself everything went like clock work. The only glitch was that Pao wasn't on board. He had to create a new plan to get her to join him. He knew the tactics must be different. She had rejected joining them and mere persuasion wouldn't work. His faithful man Ying would end up in jail and would be held there now that Cartier had escaped.

The Changs believed it was a very real possibility that Pao had turned to the other side and would tell all to Frank. She could already be in the witness protection program and on her way to a secret, remote location. Lingbao would need time and more information. He had to be successful.

The pilot's senses were as if he was on a caffeine double overload. The jet was difficult to handle so close to the ground, quick, violent, turbulence could take on fatal dimensions. His hands gripped the controls as he retraced his flight. Long before they had landed at Glades Airport, sweat had popped up on his forehead, now it streamed down his face as he repeatedly switched radio frequencies to monitor what was happening. The normal commercial airline traffic was light and he heard the air traffic controllers alert other pilots of the two rogue aircraft. His fast aircraft was the subject of frequent radio communications.

As the small plane continued on its zigzag flight many miles south of Chang's jet, the pilot knew trouble would blossom- as expected. He nervously continued to fly north, searching the short distance he could see into the dark night, for his escort. He repeatedly checked his bearings and his watch. It seemed forever that nothing changed. He searched the dark skies again, anxious because the dark night gave him no warning. He breathed a sigh of relief that it was time to bank northeast towards Nassau. Soon low flying lights rapidly approached him. As the Coast Guard jet slowed and stayed off his starboard wing, his nerves twitched as he waved and got on the radio. He tensely contended he had forgotten to change radio frequencies and just realized he was in U.S. airspace. He stayed with the script that he was just doing some night flying.

Neither the Coast Guard nor the air traffic controller was buying the story as they had tried to hail him on frequencies used by Bahamas pilots. He kept flying away from the U.S. as the Coast Guard hesitated in their decision making.

Earlier, when they heard the air traffic controller had an uncooperative pilot that was heading directly at their base, Homestead Air Force Base immediately decided to send up a tactical response. Four fighter jets were instantly scrambled. Homestead sat in line between Key Largo and Miami; they didn't want some small plane doing a suicide crash into expensive military aircraft still on the ground. They told Patrick Air Force Base what they were doing and now squadrons from both bases were airborne to join the lone Coast Guard plane.

The flight plans changed dramatically when the Air Force detected an unauthorized, fast moving, low flying jet attacking the Florida coastline. Long before September 11, 2001, the military didn't believe in random coincidences. They operated using the assumption that when two infrequent occurrences pop up, something is amiss. They already had a response plan in place. The unidentified jet upped the stakes and Patrick AFB immediately went on high alert to deal with the two intruders.

The four Patrick AFB fighter jets flew above the clouds as they headed south, just off the shoreline. The moon hadn't risen so the sky was dark. They flew in formation and had enough data to anticipate an intercept at about Jupiter.

They dove beneath the clouds and their engines rattled the windows of houses along the beach. Their electronics showed them Chang's plane and they were in visual search mode for the illegal jet. The fighter jets needed to be sure if it was friend or foe before pulling the trigger. There was no radio response to the repeated commands by air traffic controllers for Chang's jet to identify itself.

Chang's plan had a major design flaw. The little plane wasn't a diversion; it had expanded and accelerated the response. The fighter pilots weren't talking and Chang's pilot was so intense with keeping the plane aloft, that he wasn't sure if air traffic controllers had said anything about an intercept other than the Coast Guard.

Too late! Chang's pilot looked to his left as he crossed the beach. A quarter mile north and less than one hundred feet above him was the squadron of fighter jets. They roared directly over him. Frantically he ducked his head in response and instinctively he pushed the controls to make the plane dive. The massive jet wash from multiple fighter jet engines, increased the descent of Chang's jet and it banged down on the water. The plane had immense forward momentum so it bounced off the water like a flat rock skips across a smooth pond. Not once but twice before Chang's pilot jerked back on the controls to escape another water impact. The plane wouldn't be lucky enough to again bounce off the water. One more impact and the plane would dive under the surface. Their speed would make the plane into a torpedo heading to the bottom of the Atlantic. The jet rapidly gained elevation until the pilot leveled off at only five thousand feet.

The Changs were paralyzed with fear- the jet noise came so quickly and the horrendous turbulence was unannounced. They violently banged around in their seats feeling like they were on a violent amusement ride that had gone berserk. Mrs. Chang tried to pray, but neither her brain nor her mouth would function. Cartier looked at his father and hoped they had a very strategic plan so they would survive.

The Air Force commander ordered that the Chang's jet slow immediately and instantaneously make a hard turn northward. Chang and his pilot had planned to be much further out to sea before an intercept was possible. His pilot now knew that their plan was flawed.

The fighter jets were precise with their rapid ninety degree turn. The pilots were accustomed to the high G forces as the high tech jets turned to pursue their prey. As they accelerated away from the coastline, they exceeded mach 1 and a sonic boom erupted over the water. In seconds they passed over the beleaguered yacht *SERENITY* and it rocked violently. The inhabitants had just returned to their staterooms and were shocked at the second deafening interruption of their tranquility.

Chang's pilot pulled back on the throttle as ordered. Cartier felt the slowing of the jet, and shot a questioning look at his father. "We can't give up! If we surrender I'll be in prison until I die!"

Lingbo's confidence had crumbled: "Your mother must not die. We are facing long prison terms if we are convicted, but we must consider her. If they shoot us down she will not survive."

Cartier's eyes showed he rebuffed his fathers plan and he intensely repeated what he had said.

Lingbao looked at his aluminum suitcase with The Pearl carefully resting inside. "I don't want this precious piece of Taoism to be lost at sea again. It took centuries to be recovered. Who knows, some salvagers could get it and sell it to the highest bidder. Those Arabs have so much oil money, our people couldn't outbid them."

Before Cartier could respond, they felt the plane bank and turn northward towards Patrick AFB. Cartier was angry: "Father, order the pilot to turn toward the Bahamas and radio the military we will surrender there on the ground. At least there, we have a chance to fight extradition and buy off someone to remain there."

"I don't think they'll let us go there."

Cartier's temper reached a desperate crescendo as he pulled out a hand gun from his luggage. The cabin still rocked and pitched erratically. He crawled on his hands and knees up to the pilot and screamed in his ear: "RADIO THE MILITARY THAT WE WILL SURRENDER IN FREEPORT! DO IT NOW!"

"They won't let us get that far. They want us on U.S. soil."

Cartier jammed the end of the gun barrel against the pilot's skull and frantically yelled: "I'M NOT GIVING UP WITHOUT A FIGHT! RADIO THEM NOW AND CHANGE COURSE! THEY WON'T ATTACK WHILE WE TALK TO THEM!"

Fearful, the pilot did as he was ordered. When the jet banked towards the Bahamas, the immediate response from the commander was to order them to change course and fly to Patrick AFB.

Cartier kept the gun to the skull, gritted his teeth and commanded: "Don't change course, keep talking to them; we're buying time to get to freedom."

The pilot couldn't turn his head to look at Cartier. The cold steel of the barrel told him that he didn't need a visual confirmation of Cartier's intensity-the gun told him all he needed to know. He got on the radio to explain they had taken off from the Bahamas and pleaded that they be allowed to return there. He assured the commander that it would all be resolved on the ground.

The commander was having none of it as the fighter jets had caught up. The fighters closed ranks: one above, one below and two behind. The commander was explicit to turn northward without delay and without further conversation. Now, one fighter jet rapidly repositioned just off the right side of the Chang's jet. Only a few feet separated the wings of the two aircraft. The fighter jet's aura was one of invincibility. The purpose was clear: the fighter jet was nudging Chang's plane to turn away and thus towards Patrick AFB.

The helmeted fighter pilot looked fearsome as he turned his head and looked over at Cartier. The face was hidden by a mask; the image evoked a chill. The pointing of the gloved index finger gave the stern order to change direction towards Patrick AFB.

The commander knew he had little time before they were over the Bahamas. Decision making must be swift and he had been repeatedly trained for it.

Cartier wasn't giving up. He yelled at his pilot to keep talking. Terrified, the pilot did so, but the commander quickly interrupted: "Last warning. You have twenty seconds to change course or we'll shoot you down. We have abundant firepower to take you down instantly!"

The pilot pleaded with Cartier: "Spare your mother and father. They'll shoot us down. They don't want us to land in the Bahamas. Please spare us."

"Ten seconds!" announced the stern voice.

Cartier didn't respond, but the pilot radioed: "I have a gun to my head, I can't change course or he'll kill me! Please spare us!"

The jet off the starboard wing pulled back and all four jets increased their distance from their target.

Cartier exhaled loudly; "That was quick thinking. They'll let us land at Freeport."

The pilot continued to shake: "I don't think so. They've backed off because they're going to shoot. They don't want to get hit by the shrapnel from the plane and the fireball from our fuel exploding."

Doggedly, Cartier continued to hold the gun to the pilot's head, but his brain now contemplated that his time on earth had come to an end.

The radio barked: "This is your last chance to turn. Your twenty seconds are up. You're over open water and we *will* shoot. Turn now!"

Frantically, Cartier grabbed the throttles and jammed them forward. He hoped that indecision of the commander would let them get close enough to some island of the Bahamas that they couldn't risk shooting them down and killing people on the ground. Chang's jet accelerated and put distance between them and the fighter jets.

Stunned, the commander watched this act of escape and ordered his squadron: "Back off immediately."

He paused, and then fired a single heat seeking missile. It sped away from the plane and bolted towards the engine on the left rear fuselage of Chang's jet. The concussion was immediate and the result decisive. The fireball eliminated the engine and blew out a gaping hole in the rear of the fuselage. Most of the tail wings were gone. The plane corkscrewed downward, spinning out of control. The plane quickly abolished its five thousand feet of elevation and disintegrated on impact with the darkened ocean.

Overhead the jets roared by having been successful in their mission. The rolling, blackened sea tossed around the floating debris. Amid it all was the aluminum suitcase, at times camouflaged in the whitecaps. The unending five foot waves grabbed at it and battered its already misshaped body. The Atlantic finally won the battle as it descended below the surface. Slowly it found its way to the sea shell encrusted floor of the Atlantic.

CHAPTER FORTY ONE

Pao had planned for this day, but she didn't think it would be upon her this soon. She dressed in blue jeans, a plain black shirt and running shoes. Her traditional Amas garb had to be discarded. She desperately had fled out the back door of the supermarket and called a cab. She rode silently to the Palm Beach Airport and once there, quickly threw some cash at the driver as she jumped out. Long strides revealed a purposeful walk through the almost vacant airport to the car rental counter.

Lingbao Chang had unwittingly been of tremendous help to her. While she was in his compound he had used his connections to create a new identity for her. She had two credit cards, a doctored passport and a driver's license. Lingbao had told her she would need them if she had to travel overseas with him.

It wasn't long and she was driving north on Interstate 95. By daybreak she had traveled through South Carolina. She logged onto the internet as she drove, to search for the familiar discount internet sites that specialized in cheap last minute travel.

She was barely aware that nightfall had long before greeted her when she drove through Buffalo, New York. Like so many tourists, she crossed into Canada at Niagara Falls. The customs people smiled as she explained her life long desire to see the multicolored lights shine on the white waters of the Niagara River as they cascaded into the night time mist. She slowly drove by the natural spectacle and disregarded the throngs of tourists. This wasn't her destination.

She drove to Toronto and at the airport checked in for the flight she had purchased the day before. The plane landed in Vancouver and the cruise line had a taxi waiting to bring her to the ship. That night as the ship cleared Victoria and headed out into the long expanse of the Pacific, she sat out on her private balcony. The stars were glorious. She thought of the stars as so many diamonds dancing in the sky. She knew diamonds were precious, but the gem of her life was that gem which symbolized her religious faith-The Pearl.

She had stolen it from The Museum in Ft. Lauderdale at the direction of Lingbao Chang, a man whose first name meant sacred treasure. She was committed to be the eternal rescue of The Pearl-her sacred treasure. Yet she couldn't let a mere mortal trump her faith in what Lao-Tzu had destined for her. Her faith in Taoism dictated that she respond to the spiritual and not be side tracked by earthly direction.

When Lingbao Chang had started intense discussions with her about making sure The Pearl would forever be in the hands of Taoists, she became determined to do just that. It took her and Lingbao weeks to formulate a fool proof plan to steal The Pearl. During this time, she secretly contacted a Taoist artist who created a replica for her. She had time between her theft of The Pearl and turning it over to Lingbao, to make the switch. The Pearl given to Lingbao was a facsimile. She kept the real Pearl of Tao for the joy of all his followers; for the many generations yet to come. Lao-Tzu would expect no less.

She let the diamonds in the sky shine on The Pearl and marveled how the creator of it had blessed her with the skills to rescue it. All Taoists would be able to enjoy it forever. She held it high and believed the glow she saw came from within.